TRACKING BEAR

— ✶ ✶ ✶ ✶ ✶ —

AN ELLA CLAH NOVEL

AIMÉE & DAVID THURLO

FORGE®

A Tom Doherty Associates Book
New York

TRACKING BEAR

A Forge Book
Published by Tom Doherty Associates, LLC
175 Fifth Avenue
New York, NY 10010

www.tor.com

Forge® is a registered trademark of Tom Doherty Associates, LLC.

ISBN 0-765-34396-7
EAN 978-0-765-34396-3

First edition: April 2003
First mass market edition: March 2004

Printed in the United States of America

0 9 8 7 6 5 4 3 2

By Aimée and David Thurlo

ELLA CLAH NOVELS
Blackening Song
Death Walker
Bad Medicine
Enemy Way
Shooting Chant
Red Mesa
Changing Woman
Tracking Bear

Plant Them Deep

LEE NEZ NOVELS
Second Sunrise

To the 1967 graduating class of
Shiprock High School. We were all there
when the dust was flying.

AUTHOR'S NOTE
———— ✖ ✖ ✖ ————

References in this novel to the contamination of construction materials by radioactive tailings have a personal relevance to David. His childhood home in Shiprock, located across the highway from a uranium mill, was eventually demolished and buried because of unacceptable levels of radioactivity detected within the structure.

ACKNOWLEDGMENTS
———✖ ✖ ✖———

To Colleen Keane, who helped us with our research concerning radioactive spills on the Navajo Nation.

To Professor Andrew Kadak, his students at MIT, and the research engineers at ESKOM and EXELON, who developed the pebble bed nuclear power plant technology presented in this novel.

ONE

——— ✕ ✕ ✕ ———

Special Investigator Ella Clah leaned back in her office chair and rubbed her weary eyes. It was only 6 P.M., but she was tired of sitting in her office at the tribal police station in Shiprock. For the past few months things had been quiet on the Navajo Nation, at least here in the Four Corners area, but the paperwork never seemed to slow down. To make matters worse, these days almost every form she filled out was a request for additional funding.

Manpower, along with morale, was lower than she'd ever seen it at the department. According to the October staffing reports, there were fewer than 360 cops responsible for the entire Rez now—an area roughly the size of West Virginia.

To make matters even worse, their police equipment—everything from radios to the patrol units themselves—was worn or obsolete and not being properly maintained because funding cuts were already to the bone. The situation was critical, but it didn't appear to be something that would be resolved anytime soon.

It was November, and winter was still officially a month away, but already the cold evenings on the Colorado Plateau were giving the patrol officers fits when it came to starting up their vehicles in the mornings. Many of the officers, including Ella, had found it necessary to tune up their own vehicles just to keep the units in service.

Ella loosened and removed the silver barrette from her long, ebony hair and shook it loose over her neck and back, then glanced at her watch for the third time in the last half hour.

It was probably dark outside, or nearly so already, with Daylight Savings Time now in effect. It was finally time for her to call it a day. The requisition forms, the one thing they seemed to have in abundant supply, would wait until morning. Tonight, she wanted to spend some time with her three-year-old daughter, Dawn. All too often her family was forced to take a backseat to her duties as the lead investigator of the Special Investigations Unit, but there was no way Dawn was going to take second place to paperwork.

Ella turned out the light in her small office, then walked down the hall past the squad room. The place was virtually deserted, with all available officers already out on patrol. Nodding to the duty officer behind the lobby counter, she pushed open the station door and walked outside.

It was cool, and she stopped to zip up her lined leather jacket. Not being in uniform was a distinctive plus during the severe winters experienced here in northern New Mexico.

As she walked over to her unmarked blue Jeep, Ella noticed that Officer Justine Goodluck, her partner and second cousin, was heading to her own unit, a white department sedan with the gold department markings. "What are you still doing here?" Ella asked.

"I needed to finish an overdue laboratory inventory I should have completed yesterday." Justine stopped and pulled down a black stocking cap over her ears. Justine was short and slender, and looked too young to be a cop until one noticed the pistol on her belt and had a look at the hardness already appearing in her eyes.

"At least you had the chance to move around the room a little. I think I'm going to be eligible for early retirement, the way that computer keyboard is cramping up my wrists. What are the symptoms for carpal tunnel syndrome?" Ella held out her hands, then curled her fingers up. "See, just like two dead spiders."

"You think you've got it bad, cousin?" Justine smiled. "My fingers are being worn to a nub." She held up her right hand, showing her index finger, which had lost two joints courtesy of a madman over a year ago.

Ella laughed, glad that Justine had gotten over the incident well enough to kid about it now. "You win, partner."

With a wave, Ella unlocked her vehicle and climbed in, quickly starting the engine and pulling out of the parking lot onto the highway. Once she was south of the community of Shiprock, Ella pressed down on the accelerator, picking up speed until she was over the posted limit. There was no emergency, but she was feeling restless, and traffic was light. What she needed most right now was to be actively involved in a challenging case.

Ella kept an alert eye on her surroundings as she sped down the highway. This was the *Dinetah*, Navajo country. The full moon that bathed the desert revealed the scarcity of vegetation any taller than stunted grasses this time of the year. In the distance, thanks to the clean air that made everything even sharper to the eye, she could see the towering twin peaks of Ship Rock to the west, hugging the dark blue velvet sky.

Yet, despite all the beauty, the desert held its own dangers. Here, culture and beliefs all too often shaped the way a crime was dealt with and the motives behind them.

As she glanced up through the windshield at the clear sky she remembered the old police axiom that the crazies always came out during the full moon. She took a deep breath, then let it out slowly. But it was already very cold out tonight, and that would tend to keep most criminals inside—a good thing, considering the equipment problems the department was experiencing.

Ella was already slowing down as she approached the side road which would lead to her home—actually her mother's—

when her radio suddenly crackled with static. Accustomed to the sound, her mind automatically filtered out everything but the dispatcher's voice, one of three women that worked eight-hour shifts. "SI-One, this is Dispatch. We have a ten-eighty-three. What's your ten-twenty?"

Ella's heart began pumping fast and furiously. Her body's reaction to a ten-eighty-three, an officer needs help call, was always the same. She responded to Dispatch's request for her location, checking automatically for traffic as she slowed down in case she needed to reverse directions.

"Officer Franklin's exact location was garbled in transmission, and we lost contact with him after he stopped to investigate a possible twenty-seven-three," Dispatch said. "The burglary was at a gas station—actually I think he said garage—off the main highway. He was requesting backup when his radio cut out. His last reported location was west of Hogback on Highway 64. But that was ten minutes ago."

Ella felt her hands grow clammy as she brought the SUV to a stop on the shoulder of the highway. There were two stations between there and Shiprock that answered that description. "I'll try Jack Nez's station first, then if everything's okay there, I'll go on to Kieyoni Haley's place."

"Ten-four."

Ella placed the mike back on the rack, then switched on her emergency lights and siren. The sound would carry across the desert for miles like a low-flying jet.

Her hands tightened around the wheel, adrenaline surging through her as she whipped the SUV around and accelerated back north again along the blacktop. This appeared to be just the type of crisis she and nearly every other officer in the department had been warning the brass in Window Rock about for the past six months. Faulty equipment would jeopardize the lives of all the officers out in the field, and they deserved better than that.

It was bad enough that radio transmissions in some parts of the Rez were sketchy at best. But being forced to use equipment prone to malfunctions only added an unnecessary risk to their already dangerous jobs.

Once through Shiprock, Ella was able to increase her speed again as she continued east. The first gas station she needed to check was closed for the day. No vehicles were parked outside except for a derelict that had been there for years, and nothing seemed amiss. She reported in to Dispatch as she pulled back out onto the highway.

As she raced toward the Haley's self-serve, just a few miles west of the Hogback, she realized there was another old gas station in the area—one that had been closed as long as she could remember.

Ella slowed down as she approached the former business. Although the place had been closed for years, the concrete island beside the sturdy cinder-block building and the garage bay area next to it seemed in good shape. No windows were broken, and there was no graffiti on the walls.

Ella slowed further, her thoughts racing. Dispatch hadn't said that it had to be an in-service station . . .

As she aimed her spotlight toward the building and pulled off the road onto the concrete pad, she spotted Officer Franklin's tribal police unit parked near a side door. Ella swept the area with her searchlight and made a quick radio report. "I'm going to need backup here. Officer Goodluck should still be in the area somewhere, if no one else is available."

"Ten-four."

Ella crouched low as she left her unit, her nine-millimeter pistol in hand and a flashlight in her jacket pocket. Stopping by Officer Franklin's vehicle, she took a look inside. The vehicle was empty and unlocked, and Jason's uniform cap was resting on the front passenger's seat. His shotgun was still in the rack as well.

Whatever had caused Franklin to stop and look around had not given him reason to believe that he'd need extra firepower. ·

Her eyes sweeping the area, Ella tried to reach Officer Franklin using her handheld radio. There was no response, though at this distance, she was sure there were no obstacles that would prevent him from hearing her clearly.

Something was very wrong. Proceeding with caution reinforced with years of field experience, Ella used the moonlight to find her way around the front of the building, after checking the side door and finding it locked. The metal door to the small office was closed and padlocked, and from what she could see through the dirty glass, that small area was empty except for a built-in countertop and an ancient calendar still on the wall. The connecting door that led from the office into the garage bay was closed.

The bay doors were padlocked at the bottom, and when she looked through the small windows in the massive doors, there were no lights visible inside. Ella moved past the doors toward the far end of the building.

Ella continued carefully around the exterior. A window high up on the wall on the end was boarded up with plywood, and there was no sign that it had been tampered with. A rear window or back entrance had to have been the point of entry for any intruder. There was no sign of a ladder on either side when she'd pulled up, so the roof was out as a possibility, at least so far.

Listening first before she advanced, Ella crept around the corner and saw that the metal door about a third of the way down the back wall was ajar a few inches. Moving closer, she discovered a hasp on the door, and below it, on the ground, a big padlock. It had been cut off.

Two long minutes passed while she waited, looking inside through the gap, but absolute silence surrounded her. "Officer

Franklin, this is Investigator Clah." There was no response. "Jason, where are you?" she whispered.

Ella waited, crouched low, then flicked on her flashlight, holding it away from her body and directing the beam around the room.

The interior was filled with stacks of cardboard boxes and large pieces of furniture that included a bed frame, a wood cabinet, and an inexpensive metal dinette set like those that had been popular in the sixties. A few of the boxes had been torn open, probably by whoever had broken in. As the flashlight beam swept the room, something caught her eye, and she moved the light back to check again. A man's leg was visible extending out from behind some cardboard boxes. The tan trousers, complete with stripe, were part of a tribal police officer's uniform.

Bile rose to the back of her throat, but she swallowed her fear, forcing herself to remain calm. Her training told her to move cautiously in case the officer had been ambushed. The shooter could still be inside, waiting for another victim. Ella walked toward the body, hoping that her instincts would turn out to be wrong and that the officer was still alive.

As she peered around the stack of boxes, she saw Officer Franklin lying facedown in a pool of blood. A bullet had entered the back of his head, leaving a black hole soaked with blood.

Ella swallowed hard, trying to push back the horror of the scene. The officer's weapon was still in his holster, though the snap on the hold-down strap was unsnapped.

Looking cautiously around the next corner, she confirmed that the room was empty except for the cardboard boxes. Taking the first deep breath in what seemed like an hour, she tried to organize her thoughts.

A fellow officer had been killed in the line of duty, and no one in the department would rest until his killer was caught and brought to justice.

Reaching for her radio, she contacted Dispatch and made a full report.

Justine arrived first. There were only three other officers in her Special Investigations team these days. Justine, Ralph Tache, and when the need dictated it, she was allowed to pull in Sergeant Joseph Neskahi. Currently, Joseph was back on patrol duty, so it would be only the three of them here tonight.

Justine slipped on two sets of latex gloves, then along with Ella and Tache, began the task of gathering evidence from the site. None of them were traditionalists, or particularly superstitious, but some cultural taboos were too deeply ingrained. To avoid contamination by the *chindi*, the evil in every individual that remained earthbound after death, Navajos were taught from earliest childhood not to have any direct contact with the dead, and to avoid places where others had died, if possible. That second set of gloves would ensure that nothing that had come in contact with the corpse would touch them.

"The cause of death won't be difficult for Dr. Roanhorse-Lavery to figure out," Justine muttered under her breath, seeing the body clearly thanks to the floodlights hooked up to the portable generator.

"But *why* was the officer killed? And why didn't he draw his service weapon when going into an unknown situation?" Ella asked, thinking out loud. "Near as I can figure, the officer saw that the padlock had been cut and went inside for a look. He unsnapped the strap so he could draw his weapon faster, but apparently never did."

"Why would anyone bother to break into this place?" Justine asked.

"What's inside those boxes?" Ella added. "Have you had a chance to check?"

"I took a quick look inside several that had already been torn open. They contained old books, papers, clothes . . . nothing that looked particularly valuable to me," Justine said.

"Maybe the thief came in searching for something in particular, the officer surprised him, and there was a struggle," Ella suggested, but then, studying the area, added, "No, nix that. There are no signs of a fight at all." She paused, then continued. "Let's try it from another angle. The perp got behind the officer, shot him, then apparently took off before completing his search of the boxes. Or maybe he found what he wanted in one of those two boxes . . . What still doesn't fit is why an ordinary burglar would kill a cop."

"The shooting was at very close range—an execution-style murder. That's pretty drastic for a breaking and entering suspect."

Officer Tache, who was photographing the scene, joined them. "If I were a betting man, I'd say the officer didn't see a real threat, so he placed his weapon back into the holster. That's when the burglar shot him from behind. Our man may have never seen his killer."

Ella mulled it over. They were missing something. She had brought a powerful flashlight to supplement the floodlights, and squatted low, studying every detail of the floor near the victim. The room was dusty, and indistinct footprints were everywhere, but she doubted they'd be able to discern a sole pattern or narrow down the killer's shoe size.

As Ella looked below one of the boxes that had been torn open, something caught her eye. Almost simultaneously, Justine crouched and, using tweezers, pulled a medium-length black hair that had entwined itself around a torn portion of the cardboard box.

Ella looked over at the victim, then back to Justine. "Too long to belong to the officer."

Justine nodded, then placed the hair in an evidence pouch

and labeled it as Ella continued to work, scouring the floor, searching for anything else that might give them a lead.

Soon she went outside to search the perimeter. The first thing she noticed as she went outside was a partial shoe print on the pavement. She crouched low to examine the pattern up close with her flashlight.

"It looks like the killer stepped in the officer's blood and tracked it out," Justine said, coming out and looking over Ella's shoulder.

"And the perp was wearing soft-soled shoes, judging from these tracks. That might explain why the officer didn't hear anyone creeping up behind him."

Ella noticed that they were all avoiding using the officer's name out loud. They'd all been taught that to use a man's name so soon after his death was sure to call his *chindi*. But, to them, it was simply a sign of respect to the tribe and one more way to honor a fellow Navajo who'd died serving the tribe.

"It's the viciousness of the crime that throws me," Ella muttered. "Burglars run—they don't stand and fight, or wait in ambush for police officers."

"Maybe this burglar also has a grudge against cops," Justine said.

"Or maybe the officer knew his killer and didn't expect any trouble, so he let his guard down, put his weapon away, and later turned his back," Ella said.

Headlights told Ella that the ME had just driven up in her van. Ella went to meet her longtime friend, Dr. Carolyn Roanhorse-Lavery. Carolyn was the only medical examiner allowed to practice outside the network of the State Medical Examiner's Office in Albuquerque, owing to the unique cultural needs of the *Dineh*.

"I was wondering when you'd show up." Ella smiled. "Married life has been a bad influence on you."

"Life? I wasn't aware that any of us were entitled to have one." She glanced around at Ella's team. "Where's Neskahi? I'll probably need help with the body."

Ella smiled ruefully. A comment the sergeant had made once about Carolyn's weight had made him number one on her hit list.

"He's back on patrol duty. He's not part of our team for now."

"Demoted?"

"No, nothing like that. Right now the department believes that the tribe needs patrol cops more than I need another member of the crime-scene team." Ella led Carolyn inside.

The second Carolyn saw the body, she shook her head. "He's one of your own. That's very bad."

Leaving Carolyn to work, Ella joined Justine and Tache and continued examining the surrounding area.

"We'll keep working tonight for as long as possible," Justine said, "but before we leave, we'll need a uniform here to protect the scene until we return in the morning. Tache and I will go over everything once more in the light of day to make sure we didn't miss anything."

Ella nodded. "Fine. Also, as soon as possible, find out who owns this garage. Someone's still using it, obviously. Meanwhile, I'll talk to Big Ed and see about notifying the officer's next of kin."

Ella checked the interior of the officer's vehicle, searching for trace evidence. Finding nothing, she joined Carolyn and found her packing up her gear. Without waiting to be asked, Ella helped the ME place the body in a bag and transport it back to the van.

Carolyn acknowledged her help with a grateful nod. "You already know what the cause of death was, but if I find anything else on the body or in the officer's chemistry that might give you a lead, I'll let you know immediately. I'll start the autopsy tonight."

"Thanks. The chief will want fast answers, but this case is going to be a complicated one. I can feel it in my bones."

Carolyn nodded, knowing Ella's intuitions were generally

right. "I'll have preliminary findings on your desk by noon tomorrow, if not sooner. Toxicology will take longer, but I don't expect any surprises there."

Lost in thought, Ella watched Carolyn drive away. Despite her hectic schedule, there was a serenity about Carolyn these days that hadn't been there before she'd married Dr. Michael Lavery, a retired medical examiner, and an Anglo. Her friend, who'd been so ostracized because she was a Navajo woman who worked with the dead, now had a companion, and the loneliness that had punctuated her life had finally eased.

"Officer Philip Cloud is coming over to secure the scene," Justine said, interrupting her thoughts. "He's the only one available right now, and he needs the overtime. Of course once word gets around that a tribal cop has been murdered, we'll have no shortage of volunteers."

Ella nodded somberly. "The killer just made the entire department his mortal enemy."

TWO

❌ ❌ ❌

Ella had been sound asleep when the mattress jiggled suddenly, and she heard muffled giggles coming from the foot of the bed. Opening one eye, she saw a lump beneath the blankets moving upward toward the pillows.

Smiling, she allowed her daughter to get within arm's distance, then quickly reached out and began tickling her. Dawn squealed with laughter as the familiar game ensued.

After several moments and the usual untangling of covers, Dawn wriggled away. "*Shimasání* angry last night," she said, looking very serious for a three-year-old.

"Grandmother got upset? What did you do?"

Dawn's brown eyes were big and round, suiting her chubby face, and her coal black hair dropped down past her shoulders. "Lima beans are yucky. I gave them to Two."

Ella forced herself to remain stern. "You aren't supposed to give the dog your dinner. You know better than that. Two has his own food, and you have yours."

Dawn nodded slowly. "*Shimasání* got mad at you, too. You didn't come home for dinner."

"You both know I have to work late sometimes."

Dawn nodded somberly, looking away and playing with a

loose thread on the quilt. Finally, she looked up at her mother. "But we *miss* you, *Shimá*."

Something about the little round face that looked so innocent and vulnerable at the moment tugged at every motherly instinct she possessed. "Listen to me, Pumpkin. I love you and your grandmother more than I can ever put into words, but no matter what kind of work I chose, there would always be times when I wouldn't be here with you and *shimasání*."

"If I had a daddy, it wouldn't be like that," she said, suddenly looking very grown-up.

Ella suspected that Dawn had just repeated verbatim what she'd overheard Grandmother Rose say. "You *do* have one," Ella said quietly. "You know your *shizhé'é* visits you often."

Dawn shook her head. "Alice's *shimá* and her *shizhé'é* live with her."

Alice, another Navajo girl, and Dawn had become great friends at day school. "Everyone's family is different, Pumpkin. But you always have someone here who loves you, and that means you have it better than a lot of kids your age."

"But I want more better," Dawn said with a pout, looking back down at the thread on the quilt, then giving it a tug.

Ella caressed Dawn's face with her hand. Her child's simple request tore at her. She truly wished she could spend more time at home. These were special years—time she'd never be able to recapture.

Hearing Rose call her, Dawn scrambled off the bed and ran off toward the kitchen.

Dawn was growing up. Her steps were no longer halting and clumsy. She dressed herself, and ate without help, though she could still make a spectacular mess. But most telling of all, her daughter was growing independent, and Ella could see glimmers of the unique woman Dawn would someday become.

Ella's cell phone rang, interrupting her thoughts. She answered it quickly.

"I'm back at the scene," Justine said. "Unfortunately, we still haven't figured out what the burglar might have been looking for, or if he found it."

"Keep working. I'm going to the station first," Ella said. "I need to talk to Big Ed. He has probably spoken to the officer's family by now, but I'd like to make sure of that before I give the press a statement beyond what the chief has already released. After I take care of that, I'm going to track down whoever's been using the garage for storage."

Saying good-bye, Ella tossed the covers aside and hurried to shower and get dressed. One thing she intended to do this morning was file a formal report stating that faulty equipment had contributed to her delay in reaching the scene. Maybe this incident would finally force the Tribal Council to take another look at the situation.

After breakfast, Dawn ran outside in her coat and gloves to take Two for a walk. Rose sat down across from Ella at the kitchen table and glared at her. "Your daughter needs to see you more than a few hours a day. The older she gets, the more she'll need her *shimá* at home."

Ella tried to hide her impatience. "Mom, you know that's not an option. Crimes aren't committed around my schedule."

"You have a suitor now. If you paid him a little bit more attention, he would ask you to marry him. I know this."

Ella sighed. Rose was referring to Harry Ute, the former member of the SI team who had joined the U.S. Marshal's Service. Assigned now to the Albuquerque office, Harry and she saw each other as often as possible, e-mailed daily, and spoke at least once or twice a week on the phone. But as much as they cared for each other, neither one of them was ready to take their relationship to the next step, the major commitment that would radically change their lives and careers.

"Mom, some things either work out by themselves or not— they can't be forced." Ella cared a lot for Harry and he for her, but Harry didn't want to come back to the Rez and Ella couldn't see leaving her job here. And even if she'd managed to get a position in Albuquerque as a police officer or federal agent, the time they could spend together as a family wouldn't increase very much, and Dawn would still have the same situation.

Ella saw the morning paper at her mother's end of the table, and a headline caught her attention. It would be the perfect way to change the subject.

"Nuclear Casino, huh? That must be another article about NEED. You said a newspaper reporter asked you a bunch of questions about the project. Did they quote you?" Ella asked.

"Yes, but they took my comments out of context. I said that I was still studying the Navajo Electrical Energy Development project, and just because it was being pushed by a bunch of Navajos didn't automatically make it a good idea. I called it a 'nuclear casino,' and said it might present more dangers than benefits to the *Dineh*, the Navajo people. I also said that this was still the best idea the New Traditionalists have come up with yet, and if someone could prove to me it was a good thing for us, I might change my mind. But the reporter jumped on the nuclear casino comparison, knowing how I'd worked so hard against gambling on the Rez. The article came out very distorted, like I'm opposed to everything new around here." Rose handed Ella the newspaper.

Ella scanned the article. "They *are* talking about building a new kind of power plant using the latest technology, and say it will be a lot safer and cheaper than the ones in Arizona and other places around the country. I'm still trying to get all the information I can before making up my mind."

"I've been doing the same, trying to stay objective, though

you know I have a bias when it comes to digging up Mother Earth and working with radiation," Rose added.

"So it's all based on logic and common sense. You're not just naturally a little bit stubborn, are you, Mom?" Ella said, then chuckled.

"Like mother, like daughter," Rose shot back, then went to the sink and began to wash dishes. "Will you be home for lunch?"

"As usual, at this point I have no idea where I'll be around lunchtime. I started investigating a new case last night."

Rose nodded somberly. "I heard the news on the Navajo radio station this morning." She paused, then added, "Is it true that a police officer was murdered just east of Shiprock?"

"Yes."

"The man's name wasn't released. Is it someone I know?"

"I don't think so," Ella answered softly, getting her gun from the top shelf in the kitchen. She always left it there while having breakfast, knowing that Dawn would never be able to reach it.

As Ella said good-bye to Rose, she tried to block out the fear she always saw in her mother's eyes whenever the danger a cop faced struck home. Her mom had probably been thinking about it since she got up, and talking about Harry and then the NEED article had been a good way of avoiding the subject at least for a while.

Going quickly outside, Ella hugged Dawn, and sent her and Two back into the house. Mornings were usually bitterly cold, but today was worse than normal. The icy temperature seemed to cut right through her jacket. Though the sun was visible in the eastern sky, it was still below freezing. At least there was no early breeze.

As she watched the desert come alive and the long shadows begin to fade, Ella wondered what today would bring. Investigations on the Rez often took unexpected turns, because the Navajo culture was so complex—or so simple—depending on whether one asked an anthropologist or her brother Clifford, a *hataalii*, or medicine man.

But restoring order and upholding the law was her way of serving the *Dineh* and of walking in beauty. As a tribal police officer, she'd found her place within the tribe.

By the time Ella arrived at her office, she was eager to get to work. The quest for answers would become nearly all-consuming to her until everything fell into place, whether it be a day, a week, or a month or more.

Ella picked up the written transcript of the dispatcher's report. Officer Franklin's last communication was sketchy. Ella leaned back in her chair, considering the facts and trying to visualize the events as they unfolded. From what she could determine so far, Jason had seen an unidentified figure inside the building and had gone through the protocols of asking for backup. That was when his transmission had become garbled and finally cut out. Ella had heard Dispatch's tape recording of the call last night, and it was barely discernible. It was a wonder the dispatcher had been able to get as much information as she had.

Ella walked to the records room, signed the proper forms, then pulled the log of Officer Franklin's patrols for the month prior to his death, wanting to know if he'd responded to other burglary calls recently. What she found out surprised her. Although there had only been two burglaries in his entire sector, it appeared that Officer Franklin had made it a point to stop at the garage where he'd met his death at least twice a week, as if he'd expected trouble there. Unfortunately, his log entries didn't explain why he'd chosen to do that.

Often officers had a favorite locale where they preferred to stop and write their reports, usually an open restaurant where they had lighting and a cup of coffee available. Of course the local businesses loved it when an officer used their site as a regular stop, too. It offered an extra feeling of protection, at least for the duration of the visit, and it had a deterrent value even after the officer had gone. But the cold, dark parking lot of an out-of-business garage was a poor selection for all those same reasons.

Hearing someone at her office door, Ella glanced up. Big Ed Atcitty was there standing in, or rather occupying, the entire doorway. The broad-shouldered, barrel-shaped police chief had a touch of gray around his temples, but he still looked as tough as the gnarled salt cedars that survived along the San Juan River.

"Hey, Shorty," he greeted, using the nickname he'd given Ella years ago, although she was nearly a head taller than he was. "I've been trying to get hold of Jason Franklin's next of kin. His personnel file lists his father, Dr. Kee Franklin, as the relative to be notified in case of emergency, but I haven't been able to connect with him. I sent an officer over earlier, but a neighbor says he thinks the man went on some overnight fishing trip. All I know so far is that he's of the Waters Edge Clan, and is a retired professor. He's a Ph.D., not a medical doctor. One of the office staff said that he sometimes gives science demonstrations as a guest lecturer at the Shiprock Community College, but from his listed address he lives off the Rez on private land. I'm going to need you to drive to his house and see if he's returned," he said, dropping the address on her desk. "Find him ASAP."

"The officer's name hasn't been released to the press yet, has it?"

"No, we're holding it pending notification of next of kin according to procedure, but you know how the press is. They keep digging and report it anyway."

"I'll go see Dr. Franklin," Ella said. "Do you want me to work up the formal press release before I go?"

"No, I'll handle it. Have you turned up any leads yet?"

Ella gave him a brief overview. "He obviously suspected something was going on at the garage. Now I have to figure out what it was."

"Stay on it until you find the answers. If you need to pull in help from the ranks, do it. I'm not restricting you to Neskahi either. We'll tighten our patrol schedule even more if we have to."

Considering the manpower shortage, that statement alone convinced her of Big Ed's resolve to find the killer.

"Chief, there's one more thing I wanted to mention. I think this is the time to pressure the council again to get us some reliable equipment. A bad radio may have cost us an officer already."

"Every officer at this station knows I've been trying to get additional funds, but every request I've made has been turned down or placed under perpetual review," he said, expelling his breath in a hiss. "Make out a complete report, and I'll try again. Now that we've lost an officer, they may finally understand the seriousness of the situation."

"If morale keeps going down, the situation is going to reach a critical level."

"I'm aware of that, Shorty. I've already had too many resignations related to our funding problems. Our experienced officers have started joining other PDs."

"I can't say I blame them. At the very least, we deserve reliable equipment," Ella answered.

His eyes narrowed slightly. "Are you thinking of quitting, too?"

She exhaled softly. "No. There are times I've been tempted, but I belong here."

"Me too," he answered with a thin smile.

After Big Ed left her office, Ella leaned back in her chair. This case was bound to increase the tensions within the department. It wouldn't be long before everyone learned that a faulty radio had contributed to Jason Franklin's death. More resignations were sure to follow, and there could be a lot of bad press. Maybe it would take a lawsuit from Officer Franklin's family to wake the Tribal Council up.

Closing her mind to any more negative thoughts, Ella forced

herself to concentrate on the case. She picked up the report Justine had left on her desk. Martha Grayhorse was the owner of the garage where the officer had been killed. Ella scribbled down her address, stood up, and grabbed her keys. On her way back from Dr. Franklin's home she'd stop and interview her. Ella was nearly at the door when Justine came in.

"I thought you'd want to know. The officer's handgun hadn't been fired, and the only prints on it were his own. I did find some partials on the packing boxes, but my guess is that they'll belong to the person who stored them there. I found others on the furniture as well, too old to belong to the killer unless he'd been there before. I've got a computer searching for matches on the more recent ones." Justine paused, then added, "But to be honest, I don't think we'll get anything from the prints. This killer was careful, not to mention cold-blooded. Not many people would ambush a police officer at such close range."

"Do you think the officer was set up?"

"Yes I do. Think about it, Ella. From what we've seen there was nothing in the garage worth stealing, let alone killing a police officer for. And the officer didn't die after a struggle or in a fire-fight. If he drew his weapon at all, he put it back in the holster himself. Then he was shot at nearly point-blank range from behind."

"Maybe the officer knew his killer and saw no threat. That would explain him putting away his weapon. But there's one fact that still doesn't fit. I've just learned that the officer stopped by the garage several times a week, though he's never stated why in his reports. Have you heard of any crimes that could be linked somehow to that particular garage?"

Justine shook her head. "The only crimes of any consequence we've had lately are a few stolen cars, but there doesn't seem to be a connection—like a chop shop operation. Those bay doors had cobwebs on them. They haven't been opened in months." Justine paused. "From what we saw, that place has been serving as a storage place for Martha Grayhorse for a year or longer."

"The name isn't familiar to me. Do you know her?"

Justine nodded. "I've met her once or twice. She's my mom's age. She was divorced, then married an Air Force officer. She's in Germany with him now. I know because my sister Jayne is getting paid to keep her place rented while Martha's gone."

"You just saved me a trip. Thanks. See if you can track down an overseas telephone number where Martha can be reached. I'm on my way to deliver the news to the father, if he's home."

"That's one job I'm glad I've never been asked to do," Justine said softly.

Ella would have given anything to avoid the sad duty, but she had a responsibility to her fellow officer. "I'll see you later."

Ella drove toward Farmington at under fifty-five miles per hour, wanting the extra time to sort everything she'd learned. But as she reached the reservation's borders near Hogback, an uneasy feeling began to creep up her spine. The badger fetish around her neck was warm, something that always seemed to happen when danger was near. She'd never been able to explain how it worked, but she never argued with facts.

She checked her rearview mirror and took a careful look around her. There were a few cars within view behind her, and more than one had passed her recently, but none looked suspicious.

Yet, despite all logic, the nagging feeling that someone was watching her slowly grew into a certainty. She slowed quickly and turned off onto a side road that led to one of the power plants to see if any car or truck followed her, but none did.

As she turned around and pulled back onto the main highway, she caught a glimpse of something shiny behind her about a half mile, halfway around a curve, and on the shoulder of the road. But the flicker was gone so quickly, she couldn't be sure what she'd seen. It could have also been a car going the other direction, she supposed.

Ella kept a vigilant eye on the road behind and ahead of her as she drove directly to the Farmington address the chief had provided. It was located on the southwest side of the city in an old residential area among several apple orchards along the San Juan River.

Dr. Franklin's home was a well-maintained but old pitched-roof house on a half-acre lot with a few gnarled apple trees. Pulling up the gravel driveway, she parked in front of the attached garage and went to the front door.

As she reached the porch, she heard classical music coming from inside. Ella rang the doorbell, hating the news she was bringing and the pain it would cause.

A few seconds later, the door opened, revealing a Navajo man in his early sixties, with thinning gray-black hair and wearing thick wire-rimmed glasses. He was dressed casually but well, wearing a yellow shirt beneath a gray wool sweater, dress slacks, and expensive-looking loafers. The professor could have blended in any of a hundred college campuses across the country.

Ella identified herself and saw the wariness that instantly crossed Kee Franklin's features.

"Is something wrong?" he asked. "My son?"

"Can we sit down?" she asked gently.

He nodded and led her inside to a tastefully decorated living room that looked right out of Middle America rather than the Southwest. He took a seat on a worn leather chair beside a table lamp piled high with scientific magazines and journals, then waved her to a comfortable-looking sofa.

When she delivered the sad news, the man's face turned ashen and he held on to the arm of the chair so tightly, it turned his knuckles a pearly white. For several moments he sat there, shaking, unable to speak.

Ella walked quickly to the kitchen and, taking a glass from the drain rack, returned with some water for him.

He took it from her slowly, disbelief and shock etched on his face. "I just saw him . . . well, just a week ago. We had lunch and talked."

"About what?"

"The weather, ice fishing, nothing in particular," Dr. Franklin said, his voice shaky. "Jason . . . he's gone? It couldn't be a mistake? Are you sure?"

Her heart aching for him, Ella nodded and saw the last glimmer of hope fade from his eyes. Her chest tightened as she thought of Dawn and the fear that had gripped her when her daughter's safety had been in doubt. To face what Kee Franklin was experiencing now . . . she just didn't know how anyone could stand the pain. Nothing could prepare a parent for the loss of a child.

"We're going to need your help now, sir," Ella said softly. "Is there anything you can tell us? Did your son have any enemies you know about, anyone who would want to hurt him?"

His eyes filled with tears, and he watched her silently. Ella wondered if he'd even heard her words. She waited patiently.

"Where . . . and how?" he managed.

"On duty, in an old garage, late last night. He was shot, and died instantly." She'd spare him the details, except for that one important point. It was the only kindness she had to offer him. "I found the body myself not long after it happened." She gave him the address and saw him look up at her in surprise. "You know the place?"

"Yes," he said quietly. "My ex-wife uses it for storage. I keep some old books and odds and ends there myself."

"Can you think of any reason your son would have stopped

by there during his patrols? We know he was checking the place often."

Dr. Franklin thought about it for a while before speaking. "Maybe he had things of his own there . . . or more than likely, he was just keeping an eye on the place for his mother." He took an unsteady breath. "Does she know yet?"

"No, sir. We think she's in Germany with her husband. We're trying to locate her now. Do you know her address or telephone number, or the name of the base?"

Dr. Franklin shook his head. "It's been a very long time since she and I had anything to do with each other. When she remarried, that was the end of it for us. I haven't spoken directly to her in years." He took another drink of water, and as he did, Ella saw his hand was still trembling.

"She loved our son, and should be told . . ." he said. His voice broke, and he took another swallow of water.

"We'll track her down, sir. I know this is difficult, but I need you to think back. Did your son ever mention having any enemies?" she asked again.

He shook his head. "Enemies? No, it was impossible not to like that boy once you got to know him. I can't think of anyone who would have done something like this to him." He paused, and set the glass down. His hand was shaking so hard, water sloshed over the side. "But police work is a dangerous profession. Maybe a criminal, someone he had arrested . . ."

Ella watched Dr. Franklin carefully, afraid he'd have a heart attack. The man seemed to have aged ten years since she'd given him the news. "As soon as you feel you can handle it, Professor, would you look at photos of the garage, and maybe through the boxes we found in there, and tell me if anything is missing?"

"I can't help you with that. I only went there one time to drop off some extra books I needed to store away. I used to live in Los Alamos. After I retired from teaching at the branch college there,

I came back just to be closer to my son. He is, was, my only child."

The words broke Ella's heart. "Please let us know if you plan to have a funeral or a memorial service. His fellow officers will want to pay their respects."

"No funeral," he said, his words thick and heavy. "He wouldn't have wanted that. He wasn't a traditionalist, but he told me once he hated funerals. Said he wouldn't be caught dead at one. I'll hold . . . something else," he said slowly. "Where should I pick up my son?"

"The medical examiner's office is in the basement of the hospital at Shiprock," she said gently, and gave him her card. "If there's anything at all you need, or that I can help you with, give me a call—day or night. My cell phone number is on the back."

Dr. Franklin walked her to the door, but his movements were mechanical.

Ella stepped outside and, as she turned around to express her regrets one last time, she saw that he had turned around and was staring at photographs of Jason on the wall. Softly, she closed the door, returned to her car, and drove west toward the Rez and Shiprock.

Ella considered her next step. Big Ed had told her that Dr. Franklin gave guest lectures at the college. Wilson Joe, her long-time friend, might be able to give her some insight into the Franklin family—and maybe a lead.

One thing was clear. She had to find answers quickly, before the trail got cold.

THREE

---✖ ✖ ✖---

Forty minutes later, she arrived at the college, a modern facility with the core classrooms and offices constructed in an architect's interpretation of giant eight-sided hogans.

Wilson, a popular, good-looking professor about her height and a year older, sat alone in his office grading papers. Seeing her, he beamed a smile. "Hey, stranger. I haven't seen you around much lately."

"Work and family. That's my whole life in a nutshell."

"How's Dawn? I heard that she's going to day school."

Ella smiled. Everyone tended to know everyone else's business in this community, one of the largest on the Rez, but barely a "town" based upon population alone. "Yeah, and she loves it. I think it's good for her. She needed to be around kids her own age. She's learning Navajo and English and seems pretty comfortable with both—though I have to admit she makes up her own words with alarming frequency. *Shush* is bear in Navajo, but she calls her teddy bear Shooey. She's also fond of playing 'pretendly' games."

Ella stopped speaking and smiled. "Jeez, I sound like one of those mothers who's convinced *everything* her child does is adorable."

"And you're not?" Wilson laughed as he walked over to a small coffeepot on the counter, carrying his empty cup.

"Most everything she does *is* cute," she said, laughing. "And I don't have to pull out a wallet full of photos—which I have, by the way—to prove it."

"You've got your life organized the way you want it," he said, pouring her a cup of coffee without asking, then topping off his own mug. "I envy you that. I wish I could get my life more on track. Justine and I . . . well, we have things to work out."

Wilson offered her the coffee in a foam cup, and she took it silently with a nod. "But you didn't come to talk about this, Ella. What's up?"

"How well do you know Professor Kee Franklin? I understand that he guest lectures here." She glanced at a mural painted on the far wall. At one end it depicted an eighteenth-century Navajo family huddled around the fire pit inside their hogan, and at the other end was an unpainted section Ella knew Wilson was saving for a portrait of the first Native American astronaut.

Between the beginning and end, the mural featured tall vignettes in Native American history, from the prehistoric cultivation of corn to the arrival of the Spanish. It concluded with the Navajo Code Talkers of WWII and Navajos building solar collectors to provide electricity for traditionalist families on a remote mesa.

"Dr. Franklin conducts demonstrations and lectures often. And, by the way, he loves the mural as much as you and I do," he said, following her gaze. "I've had him here often, and he always comments on the space program, and his desire to see a Navajo at the International Space Station before he passes on. He's a very gifted professor, and an inspiration to my students."

"Do you know him on a personal level?"

Wilson shook his head. "We've made small talk and discussed the *Dineh*'s relationship to science and technology, but that's about it. Why do you ask? Is he in some kind of trouble?"

"Not the kind you think. Have you heard that a tribal officer was shot and killed?" Seeing him nod, she added, "It was his son."

Wilson took a deep breath. "That's going to devastate Dr. Franklin. His son was the world to him. They hadn't been close while the boy was growing up, but their relationship really improved since Kee moved back to this area. I know they went hiking and fishing together as often as possible."

"When I gave him the news he took it really hard," Ella said. Hearing someone approaching, she turned her head and was surprised to see her mother standing there. "Mom! What on earth are you doing here?"

"You're not the only one with business to attend to, daughter," Rose said, taking the chair Wilson offered, then glancing up at him and folding her hands on her lap. "I came to get your opinion on the proposed 'nuclear casino.' You explain things to people every day in words they can understand, I figured you could speak plainly to me about it."

"Would you like some coffee?" Wilson offered, waving toward the coffeepot.

"No thank you." Rose replied, then got right to the point. "What do you think are good reasons for building this nuclear power plant, Professor?"

"You have to hand it to the New Traditionalists," Wilson said. "They've come up with something original that could add a whole new dimension to the energy industry in the Four Corners. If it passes and a nuclear facility is constructed, the electricity produced could bring our tribe a great deal of revenue in the first half of the new century. Right now many outsiders operating the coal-fueled power plants, the mines, and so on, have a lot of control over what happens to our land. But with a nuclear power plant here, owned and operated by the tribe, those days would be over. We'd be calling our own shots at last."

"That must be why Permian Energy keeps talking to our council, asking for approval to run the operation," Rose asked. "If they're operating the plant, then they'll maintain control of the facility."

"Exactly." Wilson sat forward, then continued. "And if Permian calls the shots because they own and operate the facility, they'll be taking the bulk of the profits, and we won't be any better off than we are with the current coal power plants. We have to maintain controlling interest in this enterprise ourselves. There's a small core of scientists right now among the *Dineh* who have the technical expertise to get this thing started, and the uranium required to fuel such a power plant is already on Navajo land. With the need for more energy across the nation, especially the West, such a project could turn things around for us as a tribe. Marketing clean energy that we produce and control will give us economic clout in the Anglo world, and the funding we need to educate and support our own people."

"What I'm most concerned about is the safety issue." Rose crossed her hands across her chest. "It's only clean energy when everything goes as planned. The Holy People warned us that certain rocks should stay in the earth. When the *bilagáanas*, the white people, came to our land during the Cold War and council elders allowed them to take the uranium out, the mining ended up causing disease and misery. We can't afford another mistake like that. Polluting our scarce water supplies is unforgivable."

Ella glanced at Wilson. "That's been bothering me, too. Most of us who live here know that the largest radioactive spill in the history of the United States happened on the Navajo Nation, but few off the Rez had ever even heard about it. You say 'Three Mile Island' and everyone knows what you're talking about, but in 1979 millions of gallons of radioactive waste spilled down the Rio Puerco."

Rose nodded. "And when the uranium companies closed operations, we were left to clean up the mess."

Wilson spoke. "All true, but it should be different now—with scientific knowledge that simply wasn't around before. And the public is a lot better educated."

"Still, the past is hard to forget," Rose said. "For years our people lived in houses that contained uranium tailings in the concrete that made the foundations. And many of the uranium mine shafts are still uncovered, and the ground around them contaminated. Should we open up new mines? The tribe needs money, but surely not at any cost."

Wilson shrugged. "Still, operating a nuclear power plant here, even a small one, is something that could really turn our economic situation around. Do you realize that at current prices, we can make an estimated one billion dollars mining our own uranium and running the power plant—that is, if the plant is allowed to operate for twenty-five years."

"Even if we make more money, that still won't guarantee that we'll find harmony and walk in beauty," Rose said. "Even a small mistake could be a disaster."

"I understand your fears," Wilson said. "But what happened before shouldn't happen again if the plant is run properly and safe mining practices are followed. A limited, short-term partnership with the current coal power plant operators would provide enough funding so we won't be asked to empty the tribal accounts to get things set up. But control must remain with our own leaders. It's *our* land, after all, and *our* resources."

"Why would the NEED project be any better than what we

already have with the current operations?" Rose was taking notes with a small notebook.

Wilson shrugged. "The coal-powered plant we have here still puts a lot of stuff into the air we breathe, and there's the damage caused by the enormous surface-mining operations. A small modern nuclear facility, not one of the old-style monsters, is a good, clean, safe option for us."

"I'm still worried about the mines, and the miners. Before, many died, and continue to die, of what they call Red Lung—named for the blood those affected would cough up. And many are just now getting a reasonable financial settlement, decades too late for some. Certainly we know more today—but there might be something else we don't know that'll come back to haunt us in the future." Rose grew somber.

"There's an element of risk in any new undertaking," Wilson said.

"Whatever I decide, I intend to first make sure that everyone knows the potential dangers of what they're inviting onto our land before they agree to this nuclear casino. Thank you for your time and your thoughts, nephew," Rose added, using the term as a sign of affection, not kinship.

"Mom, wait, and I'll walk back to the parking area with you," Ella said.

As Rose went out to the hall, Ella glanced back at Wilson. "I need a lead that will point me to Officer Franklin's killer. If you hear anything from your students or elsewhere, give me a call."

"You've got it. I'll start by finding out if the professor's son ever attended classes here."

Ella joined her mother as they walked back to their cars. "I still can't get used to you taking such an active part in tribal issues, Mom. That newspaper interview is bound to make you enemies, especially with that nuclear casino sound bite. Sometimes I think you pick all the hot issues on purpose—payback, so

I'll have to worry about you like you have about me all these years."

Rose smiled. "We both have to accept each other's needs to be productive and useful—even if we make each other crazy, daughter."

Ella laughed. Rose was very much her own person these days. The mother-housekeeper Clifford and she had known had disappeared.

They were nearing the parking area when a young woman in her early twenties, wearing jeans and a sweatshirt, saw them and came over. Four other young women followed her.

"Aren't you Rose Destea, the traditionalist who is trying to turn everyone against a tribal nuclear power plant? I read what you said in the newspaper."

"You are right about my name. And although the newspaper gave a distorted report of my comments in that article, I do have many serious questions and concerns about the NEED project. But people are free to make up their own minds," Rose answered calmly.

"My name is Vera Jim." The woman stepped right up to within a foot of Rose, but Rose didn't flinch or give ground. "People like you are the tribe's biggest enemies. You're so used to living in poverty you can't see that the opportunity has finally come for the rest of us to break out of this cycle of misery. New Traditionalists provide leaders who can improve our standard of living, but there is always someone like you to stand in our way."

"I am *not* an enemy of the tribe," Rose said sharply. "The only ones who truly undermine who we are as the People are the ones who show no respect for our ways."

Ella was surprised by how well Rose had handled things, though she could tell her mother was furious with Vera Jim. Her gaze was on Rose when Vera suddenly pushed Rose hard.

"*Your* ways suck!" Vera snarled.

As Rose staggered back, Ella steadied her mother quickly, then in an instant stepped right up to Vera's face, pinning her against the trunk of a cottonwood tree so she couldn't move.

"You have assaulted a member of our tribe," Ella said. "I am a witness and a police officer."

"Daughter, let her go," Rose said sharply. "There's enough division among the *Dineh* as it is."

"Mom, you can press charges—"

"No. That's your way, not mine. Common sense and respect for their elders isn't something you can force into a person. If they haven't been raised properly, they have to learn it by themselves."

Still angry but unable to turn that feeling into action, Ella focused her attention back on Vera, who had wisely decided not to struggle. "If you ever pull something like that again—assaulting anyone young or old, I'll haul you in. Am I making myself very clear?"

The woman nodded but didn't speak, deciding, apparently, that it was best to become one with the tree bark for a while longer.

Ella stepped back, but Vera remained frozen in place. "Now get out of here before I change my mind and press charges myself."

It took a few seconds for Vera to get the courage to move, but when she did, she stomped away quickly without looking back, her fists tightly clenched.

One of the women who had been with her hung back. "Vera really didn't mean to be rough or anything. She's going through tough times like most of us, and sometimes she gets so frustrated she just lashes out."

"Then advise her to work off her frustrations at a job or by running cross-country. Assaulting someone will land her in the tribal courts. Guaranteed, if I ever hear about it," Ella said.

Once they were alone again, Ella gave Rose a hard look. "You should have pressed charges, or at least let me haul her in for a few hours. I've dealt with young people like that before. The kindest thing you could have done for her was show her that actions have consequences."

Rose shook her head. "She's a New Traditionalist," Rose said, referring to the growing tribal faction who professed to believe in the old ways but strongly advocated using whatever modern means were available to improve the quality of life on the Rez. "She's fighting for this tribe like I am—she just doesn't know how to do that effectively yet."

Rose paused, then continued slowly. "I have a feeling that she'll be one of my strongest adversaries someday. She's as passionate about moving the tribe forward as I am about forcing people to weigh everything before making any lasting decisions. These newly proposed tribal ventures—trial casinos and the nuclear power plant—may exact a great price from all of us in the long run."

Wilson came running up as they started walking again. "I saw what happened from my office window. Are you two okay?" He glanced toward the group of young women, now some distance away.

"Sure," Ella said quickly. "That student, Vera Jim, is a hothead, but she posed no serious threat."

He relaxed visibly. "I know who she is. Her husband works for one of the oil well service companies. He's an engineer and a financial supporter of the NEED Project. I've heard rumors that they, and others like them, overextended themselves trying to get NEED off the ground. Many have taken out second mortgages and borrowed all the money they can."

"I think I'll look into that some more," Ella said slowly. She wanted to know everything she could about her mother's enemies.

"You could talk to Samuel Nakai. He was a close friend of the Jims—that is until this issue came up. Samuel wouldn't join in with them and invest in NEED. He was in favor of upgrading the technology at the coal-generated plants. Their differences ended up destroying their friendship."

"Thanks for the tip," Ella said.

As Wilson headed back to his office, Ella fell into step beside Rose, who was walking in the direction of the parking lot. "You need to be careful, Mom. I think this issue is going to be more volatile than any of us suspected."

"I agree with you, daughter," Rose said.

Ella helped her mother into the family's pickup. She'd wanted to buy Rose a new car last year, something with power brakes and steering, but Rose had not allowed it, insisting that it was a waste of money. As long as her truck continued to start every morning, she'd use it.

Saying good-bye, Ella went to her tribal unit, which was in a special slot reserved for law enforcement vehicles. She'd speak to Samuel Nakai soon, but, right now, she needed to focus on Officer Franklin's murder investigation.

Ella checked in with Justine on the cell phone, then drove back to the station, lost in thought. Leads were few at the moment, so she'd start by trying to find any known enemies the officer might have had.

When she walked back inside the station ten minutes later, she noticed the mood in the building was subdued. By now, everyone had learned about Jason's Franklin's death. Pressure to get answers would come not only from the Tribal Council and Navajo community, but from the rank-and-file officers who'd served with Franklin.

Justine met her in the hall outside her office. "I've been waiting for you. We got Dr. Roanhorse-Lavery's report, and it was as we thought. The officer was shot at point-blank range. She's sending me a bullet she recovered, and I'll be checking it later for caliber and all the rest." She paused, then continued. "I was able to match Kee Franklin's prints to some I lifted from one of the boxes in the garage. The professor's prints are in a government database, as are Captain John Grayhorse's, Martha's husband. There's one partial I haven't been able to match up. One last thing. The black hairs we found came from a wig. They're synthetic."

"I can't imagine anyone around here, except chemo patients, buying a black hair wig. I mean, come on. Try to find a Navajo who *doesn't* have black hair. Why spend money on something so ordinary?" She shrugged. "But let's follow it up. Check and find out which stores in Farmington carry wigs, then see if you can learn the names of their customers."

"Okay."

"Have you managed to turn up anything useful on the officer's personal relationships, politics, or circle of friends?" Ella asked.

"All I know so far is that he'd taken a very strong position against NEED and other energy industry projects. I spoke to one of the uniforms who knew him for many years when he was assigned to the Keams Canyon area—Mike Kodaseet. Mike told me Jason was completely against anything that would reopen the doors to uranium mining."

"Any idea why?"

"Kodaseet said Franklin had relatives who'd died of Red Lung."

"How close were Kodaseet and Franklin?"

"They'd worked adjacent patrol areas, backed each other up, and switched schedules from time to time, but they weren't off-duty friends."

"Did Jason have a girlfriend or someone else he was especially close to?"

"Kodaseet said Jason was dating an assistant professor at the local college by the name of Belinda Johns."

"She's a Navajo?"

"Yeah. She teaches introductory physics. Apparently, she's a very bright lady."

"Let's go talk to her."

"I figured you'd say that, so I called administration on campus. Professor Johns is ill this morning, so we'll have to catch her at home. I've got her address."

Justine and Ella walked outside. Before they could head for her tribal unit, Justine stopped her. "I think we better take your vehicle, Ella. It's in better shape than mine, and it's a rough drive. I've got a bald tire that needs replacing, but you know how it is right now with the budget."

"No problem. Where does the professor live?"

"About five miles from campus, but not in a developed area. She has electricity from a generator, but not much else by way of modern conveniences. She told Mike once that she wants to live out there until she finishes her book on Navajo views of the universe. Apparently the primitive setting inspires her work."

"She sounds like a New Traditionalist."

Justine nodded. "That's what I was told."

"I wonder if she's in favor of NEED and, if so, how that impacted on her relationship with Jason, if he was really a staunch opponent." She paused, then added, "It ought to be an interesting interview."

FOUR

——✖ ✖ ✖——

I t took nearly a half hour to reach Belinda Johns's house. The road was nothing more than a long set of furrows cut into the ground by vehicles that had traveled over the hard alkaline soil.

Soon they parked beside a Ford Bronco, which was in front of a modest but well-maintained frame-and-stucco house with a pitched roof. Justine pointed to the smoke coming from the chimney. "Someone's home."

Ella walked with Justine to the front door. There was no need to wait in the car here until invited, the way things were normally done at the home of a traditionalist.

Before they reached the front door it was opened, and a slender, attractive Navajo woman appeared wearing jeans, a light blue pullover sweater, and a small strand of turquoise and heishi beads. Her eyes were red and swollen as if she'd been crying.

Ella introduced herself and showed the woman her badge. Justine followed suit.

"You're here to ask about Jason, aren't you?"

"Yes, may we come in?" Ella asked. Belinda Johns remained standing in the doorway, blocking their way.

"Oh—I'm sorry," she stepped aside, and then spoke quickly. "I should caution you that a lot of Jason's things are still here. If the thought of the *chindi* will trouble either of you . . ." She shook her head, then exhaled softly. "Never mind. Of course it won't bother you. If it did, you would have chosen another line of work."

Ella glanced around the living room. One whole wall was filled with bookshelves, and most of the titles appeared to be academic works. Not a fiction best-seller among them, it appeared.

In the center of the outside wall stood a large, heavy-looking wood-and-coal stove. It was burning now, filling the room with a pleasant warmth. A large teakettle, minus a lid, was steaming gently, adding humidity to the dry air.

Belinda gestured to a thick-cushioned sofa, then sat across the room from them in a matching love seat, spreading a wool throw over her lap. "Make yourselves comfortable, Officers. Would you like some herbal tea?" she asked, sipping a cup she'd lifted from the top of the stove as she passed by.

"No, thanks." Ella noted the photo of Belinda and Officer Franklin on an end table. "Will you tell us a little about your relationship to him?"

She nodded. "Jason and I weren't at all alike, but we had an understanding—we knew when to try and change each other's opinions and when to back off. I never liked the fact that he was a tribal policeman, for example, but that was one of those things I couldn't change." She swallowed hard. "Now I wish I had tried to get him to quit."

"For what it's worth, I don't think you can talk many police officers into quitting their jobs," Ella said softly. "All of us know the risks, but we still value the profession."

"It's the adrenaline rush, isn't it?" Belinda said with a sad sigh. "The excitement of living on the edge?"

"Partly," Ella answered, "at least for some. But it's also knowing that you're doing something that needs to be done—that you can make a difference."

Belinda dabbed her eyes with a tissue and folded her legs beneath her, curling up in the thickly cushioned love seat. "I just spoke to Jason's father. He was devastated."

"Is that how you found out what happened?" Justine asked.

"No, I knew before that. Jason was supposed to call me last night when he got off duty. When he didn't, I knew something was wrong. Keeping his word was a matter of pride to him." She took another sip of her tea. "Then early this morning I heard that a patrolman had died." Her voice broke. "They didn't give his name, but I knew."

"Did Jason ever talk to you about his work?" Ella asked.

"Sometimes. I know he was upset because of the funding problems the department has been having. He complained that he now had to buy his own rounds to practice at the police range. And he mentioned that his radio was unreliable. At least his police car started in the morning."

Ella and Justine exchanged glances, and Ella remembered the bad tire on Justine's vehicle.

"Did he talk about any of his investigations, or any specific crimes that had occurred in his patrol sector?" Ella focused back on the interview.

Belinda paused for a long time, her expression thoughtful. "I remember he said something about a few recent car thefts, and keeping his eye out. That's about it."

"Did he ever mention having problems getting along with anyone, either in the department, his neighborhood, or anywhere else?"

"The only person I know he argued with was me. I'm for NEED, but Jason and his dad were dead set against it." Belinda must have noticed her own wording, because tears began to form in her eyes.

"Do you know if Jason made any enemies because of his stand against NEED?" Justine asked.

Belinda made a feeble attempt to wipe away her tears, cleared her voice, then answered. "There were a lot of people who resented his position—some were his fellow officers. There's one cop who comes to mind right away. He supports NEED and didn't care much for Jason. His name is Joseph Neskahi. He's a sergeant, I think."

Ella felt a sinking feeling at the pit of her stomach. She'd known Joseph for many years, and he'd served in her crime scene unit several times when called upon. He was a decent, hardworking cop, not capable of killing one of his own.

"Jason just didn't have the kind of enemy that would do something like this," Belinda said. "If he had, I would have known about it." She paused for a long time. "But his father might have. He's got a lot of secrets."

"Explain," Ella said, leaning forward in her seat.

"Professor Franklin never talked about his past—with me or with his son. It was really odd, you know? I mean, I can understand why he never just chatted with me. He didn't like me much after he found out that I was pro-NEED. I think he felt that as a physicist, I should have sided with him because I could understand better than most the dangers associated with a project like this. But he was just as close-mouthed with his own son. I know that bothered Jason."

"Do you know if Jason ever talked about his work with his mother?" Ella still hadn't heard anything about the woman from the military in Europe, where her husband was stationed, though Big Ed had made a second phone call to the base in Germany in an attempt to track her down and notify her of Jason's death.

"He didn't write much, and only called on her birthday, according to him. She's been away for two years, and I've never met or spoken to the woman myself. I have no idea when he might have written her last, only she can answer those kind of questions."

A half hour later, after their interview was concluded, Ella and Justine headed out to their vehicle.

"That's some lead we just turned up," Justine said as they drove away. "I'll check it out." Justine sat back, holding on to the seat as they hit a big bump in the trail and the Jeep bounced.

"Don't forget the ballistics on the bullet that killed Jason. Also, get your tires replaced. Tell them I gave you a direct order," Ella added. "Don't take no for an answer."

Sometime later they walked back inside the station. Big Ed Atcitty intercepted them in the hall before they could reach Ella's office. "I've just posted the time and place for Officer Franklin's memorial service. It'll take place this evening after the body has been laid to rest. He'll be buried at a Farmington cemetery this afternoon. Dr. Roanhorse-Lavery has released the body. Tonight there'll be a short ceremony at Dr. Franklin's home."

"Thanks for the information, Chief. I'll be there, but a lot of our officers might not attend. I hope Dr. Franklin will understand that although Navajo cops have to deal with the dead on occasion, a lot of them still hold to our traditions. A memorial service to some is like throwing a party for the *chindi*."

"Even so, I expect we'll have a decent turnout. Dr. Franklin isn't a member of any denomination, though I gather he considers himself a Christian, so he didn't want the service held in any particular church. He wanted to have a memorial service so some of us would have the opportunity to say a few words."

As a sergeant came out of the squad room to talk to the chief, Ella and Justine continued down the hall. It was still very quiet. Ella couldn't help but notice how the tragic death had touched everyone here. When one cop died, all the brotherhood mourned.

"I'm going to start doing a background search on Professor Franklin," Ella said. "I'd like you to check with area law enforcement off the Rez. See if any trouble has been brewing that we don't know about."

"I'm on it."

Ella went to her office. Before she did anything else she needed to track down Joseph Neskahi and have him come in to talk to her. After asking Dispatch to relay a message to him, Ella began doing the background check on Kee Franklin.

An hour later, she heard someone knock on her door. Ella looked up and saw John Ray, the desk sergeant, with two Anglos. One was a tall blond woman wearing a visitor's badge. The other was Delbert Shives, a chemist at the power plant who also served as the police contact person there.

After the trouble at the power plant last year, the Tribal Council had asked plant officials to work up a plan to educate local law enforcement concerning the facility in order to help deal with any future problems more effectively. Shives had set up a visitation program and several officers from their department had already made the tour. Her SI team had been among the first, accompanied by the two local FBI agents, whom Ella knew. Ella guessed that the woman with him was connected to the program somehow, but she looked more like a security guard than office staff or a technical worker.

"Investigator Clah, how are you? I'm so sorry to hear about the loss of the police officer the other day. The whole community grieves with you." His words came across as rehearsed.

Shives, a slender, slightly balding man in his midfifties, was an outgoing, talkative man, a personality trait she had come to believe was an act required by his job as police liaison. Somehow, his attempts at sincerity always seemed forced.

Ella nodded, and noticed John Ray slipping away, rolling his eyes. The blonde with Shives noticed and smiled, but didn't say anything.

"I'd like you to meet Margaret Bruno. Ms. Bruno is a highly qualified security consultant who has been hired by your Tribal Council to conduct tactical training sessions for combined operations involving power plant security officers and your department."

"What sessions? I don't recall hearing about this project, Ms. Bruno. I'm sorry."

Margaret Bruno smiled and offered her hand. Ella took it, still wary.

"The Tribal Council authorized these workshops about a month ago," she said. "The purpose of the training is to raise efficiency levels during situations such as the power plant takeover the area experienced several months ago. Special ops training is needed here more than ever now, especially since you're all so short-staffed at the moment."

The tall blond woman, older than Ella by at least ten years and outweighing her by around twenty pounds, pointed to a green folder halfway down the stack in Ella's "In file" basket. "It's all in that folder. You probably haven't had time to get to it yet, something I understand perfectly well, believe me. It's just one example of what happens in even the best departments when you're understaffed and overworked."

"What we need are more cops, Ms. Bruno, and better equipment," Ella said, "not training sessions." She just couldn't imagine why the council was spending money on things like this. She gave Bruno a quick assessment. The blonde was attractive in a hard way, and some Navajo men had a thing for blondes. Maybe she had a friend in the council. Or two.

"No offense, but I don't know anything about your workshops," Ella added, "and I really don't have the time now."

"I've been hired to help your team develop practical strategies and skills that you could use whenever there are potential disturbances at factories, mines, and so on," she said, pressing on. "I served on a SWAT team in a Texas police department, and I've had training at the FBI Academy."

"So have I," Ella said coldly. "I was an agent with the Bureau before coming here."

"Yes, I was given that information by the tribe. But it's been a while, hasn't it?"

Ella resisted the impulse to pitch her out the window. Bruno was tough and fit-looking, and it would have been a struggle, but at the moment, Ella would have enjoyed giving it a shot anyway.

"When an officer is killed in the line of duty—it's hard for the entire department, and the staff has trouble concentrating on anything else," Bruno said. "Mr. Shives and I both agree that due to special circumstances, postponing our first session is appropriate, but I'd like to set up a firm date with you as soon as possible."

"Sure," Ella answered. In the meantime, she'd make an effort to get future sessions canceled. Funds were short—they didn't need to be squandered when the first priority was putting more officers in the field and maintaining equipment. Hopefully the contract the tribe had with Bruno allowed for cancellations, and she'd only get paid for work already done.

"I'll be in touch, Investigator Clah," Delbert Shives said, "and send you an e-mail reminder in a few days. Meanwhile, my, *our* thoughts are with the department and the family of the officer." Shives knew enough not to shake hands, so he simply nodded. Bruno smiled and turned, walking away quickly.

When the two were out of sight, Ella forced herself to forget about the misspending of scarce tribal resources. If she dwelled on that, it would just make her crazy.

Bringing her thoughts back to the case, she concentrated on

Kee Franklin. Using Professor Franklin's Social Security number, she accessed his credit report. She'd just started looking it over for unusual activity when Sergeant Neskahi knocked on her open door.

Joseph, a former wrestler in high school, had kept in shape over the years, thanks to regular workouts. He was built like a safe—all square and hard, something that seemed even more emphasized by his buzz-cut hairstyle. But there was a look about him these days that hadn't been there in years past. It was the harshness officers acquired with experience, which often came to the surface during times of stress.

"Sit down, Joseph," she said, waving him to a chair.

"What's going on, Ella? Are you going to transfer me back to the SI Unit?"

"Not right now. With the shortage of patrol cops, the department needs you out there more."

Neskahi nodded. "Things are getting pretty bad, aren't they? Half of us don't even have vehicles we can depend upon. Do you think it'll change now that an officer got killed because his radio was cutting out?"

She'd hoped that news about Franklin's faulty radio wouldn't leak out so fast, though she should have known it would spread like wildfire. A flash of anger swept through her again as she thought of Bruno's workshop and how the little funding they had was being misspent. Taking a deep breath, she focused on the sergeant. "I don't understand anything the council does these days. Their priorities are backwards."

He nodded somberly. "As always. So tell me, what I can do for you?"

"I need to know about Officer Franklin. Someone said that you two knew each other well."

"We knew each other professionally, but we weren't friends. We were on opposite sides of the NEED issue, and often debated against each other at Chapter House meetings," he said, referring to the regular community meetings on the Rez.

"You live in the same area then?"

He nodded. "But philosophically we share very little common ground. I'm a pragmatist—always have been," he said. "Refusing to go forward because of fear is a bad strategy."

"At those chapter meetings . . . how evenly divided on the NEED issue are the people who attend?"

"I get the feeling that it's almost fifty-fifty. The older ones who've seen what uranium has already done to the People are usually very close-minded about it. But those like me, who see we're running out of choices, consider it a viable option, if it's done safely."

"As far as you know, did Officer Franklin make any real enemies at these meetings?"

"Jason did make a lot of people angry when he spoke against NEED, particularly me. But I didn't have anything to do with his death, and I very much doubt he was killed because of his views on the NEED proposal. He fought hard to present his position clearly and unemotionally, and we all knew his first concern was for the tribe. Everyone respected him. The only ones I know the *Dineh* there couldn't stand were the outsiders, mostly big-company Anglos, who came with their optimistic speeches and empty promises. Experience tells most of us that the energy industry promoters can't be trusted. They don't have to live with their mistakes—we do."

"Yeah, good point."

"I've only seen one Anglo at the meetings who seems to know what he's talking about and tries to present the issue squarely, addressing both pros and cons. You know him. Delbert Shives, the guy who was just here with the leggy blonde. The Tribal Council has been sending him to Chapter meetings to give everyone an overview of how the new nuclear power plant would work. The man's quick and to the point, then leaves. He doesn't try to take part in any discussions."

"I guess I'll hear his speech sooner or later," Ella said.

"I'd say you can pretty much count on it if you go to Chapter House meetings. Is there anything else?"

"No, just keep your eyes and ears open. If Officer Franklin made enemies because of his position concerning NEED, or for any other reason, I want to know about it."

"You've got it." Neskahi stood up. "In my opinion, a good cop got killed because he interrupted a crime. I'll try to find out if any of the known perps in my area have it in for cops."

She watched him leave, lost in thought. Something told her that troubles on the Rez were only beginning.

FIVE

——— **✖ ✖ ✖** ———

The next morning, Ella joined the members of her Special Investigations Unit in Chief Big Ed Atcitty's office. Justine had spent most of the previous day following up on every crime report filed within the past six months in officer Franklin's patrol area, but had turned up nothing useful.

Justine spoke first, reporting what they'd received from the ME. "Dr. Roanhorse-Lavery recovered a .380 hollow point from the victim. It's disfigured, but obviously didn't come from the victim's own nine-millimeter, nor his backup weapon, which was a thirty-eight. Neither had been fired."

"How about rifling and ballistics characteristics?" Ella asked. "Is the slug in good enough shape to allow us to get a match if we recover a weapon?"

"I've got enough on the lands and grooves to say the weapon was probably a Colt Mustang, which has a real short barrel. It's a pocket gun, basically. I should have more later."

"Sounds like a backup weapon," Ella commented.

"That Colt is a semiauto, so unless the shell casing has been overlooked, the killer picked it up and took it with him. Pretty cool customer," Tache added.

"So until we come across the murder weapon, we're nowhere," Big Ed said, rocking back and forth in his office chair slowly.

"I'm now planning to go back three years and check any felony arrests Officer Franklin made, paying close attention to any cases where his testimony helped send someone to prison," Justine said. "But, for now, all we really have as physical evidence is that bullet, a footprint, and the hairs."

"Anyone else have something to add?"

Ella glanced at Ralph Tache, Justine, then back at Big Ed. "I think someone tailed me yesterday when I went to visit Professor Franklin to give him the news about his son."

"You *think*?" Big Ed asked. He stopped rocking and leaned forward.

"Yeah. I didn't see any vehicle I could check on, but I had a strong feeling that I was being followed. I realize that's vague, but I'm sure of it. Someone was there."

"Any theories?" Big Ed asked.

"Maybe someone wants to see what direction our investigation is taking. Or it might be an old enemy of mine working on his own agenda. There's no shortage of those."

Justine gave her a worried look. "Sometimes your enemies can devise complex conspiracies," she said, looking down at her trigger finger, which was cut off at the knuckle, and remembering. "Watch yourself."

"I want the Special Investigations team to get this cop killer ASAP. This crime goes to the top of all our lists. Am I making myself clear?" Chief Atcitty said.

"Understood," Ella answered. "I'll be doing a complete background check on Officer Franklin's family next. Maybe a motive will turn up that'll lead the case away from the apparent burglar overreaction—which I really have a hard time buying."

As Ella returned to her office, she saw Kevin Tolino, Dawn's father, waiting for her. Kevin was dressed in a dark blue silk sports jacket and turquoise-and-silver bolo tie. There was no denying that Kevin was one of the best-looking Navajo men she'd ever met. His natural charisma coupled with that tall, lanky, broad-shouldered build was a powerful combination. "This is a surprise," she said. "What brings you here today?"

"I needed to talk to you, Ella."

Ella sat down, studying Kevin's expression. He sat, too, but looked apprehensive and ill at ease. That was unusual for him. As an attorney and member of the Tribal Council, he was used to guarding his emotions and demeanor.

"What's going on, Kevin?"

"George Branch, the A.M. radio hit man, is what's going on. You know how, in the past, he's singled you and the police department out for his diatribes? Well, his last four programs have been no-holds-barred attacks on me."

"Kevin, you know that I can't do anything about that. Freedom of speech is protected, even for pompous, self-important media personalities, as long as they don't slander anyone outright. And now that you're a member of the Tribal Council, you get to climb up and serve as a shooting gallery target with the rest of the politicians and public servants."

"I'm an attorney, Ella. I know precisely what you can and can't do, but he's stepped over the line. Get a tape recorder, because I want to file a complaint. Once someone types it up, I'll sign it and make it official."

Ella placed a small tape recorder on the desk before her and waited.

"Thanks to those broadcasts by George Branch, I'm being harassed, perhaps stalked is a better description, and I've just about had it."

"Who's harassing you, and what have they done?"

"It all began four days ago when Branch came after me on his program. He referred to me as a Navajo yo-yo."

"Why?"

"Because I changed my mind about gambling on the Rez and limited the casino to one location only, on a trial basis. For that reason alone, that half-Navajo nitwit accused me of having no principles and turning my back on my political supporters and the tribe." He paused. "It's true that I altered my position on the gambling issue, but I had a very good reason to do that, and you *know* I've never turned my back on the tribe."

Ella nodded, and waited.

"After that broadcast aired the trouble began. I started getting phone calls at two or three in the morning, and when I'd pick up the phone, whoever it was hung up. The calls came from public phones all over the county, according to my caller ID system. Then I decided to leave my phone off the hook at night. The day after that, I found my new car vandalized—the windshield was broken and the headlights were busted." He paused and took a breath. "I want the police to look into this."

"The only thing we could do is contact the phone company and start monitoring your calls. But that means we'd tap your line and you'd have absolutely no privacy. Make sure you realize all the implications of what you're asking us to do."

"Tracing the calls is not going to work. He doesn't call from a private number, and your chances of catching him at whatever public phone he uses are slim." He leaned back in the chair and regarded her thoughtfully. "What I want is for the police to come and take fingerprints next time my property is vandalized. I'll make sure someone is there to meet the officer if I can't be there for some reason."

"If there's anything we can lift prints from, we'll do it. But listen, Kevin, until the person who's after you is caught, I don't want you to pick up Dawn and take her out with you. Come visit her at my mother's house, okay? I won't have her exposed to any more potentially dangerous situations. I know you haven't forgotten how close she came to being kidnapped just last year."

"How could I? Don't worry, I've already made the decision to stay away altogether for a while. Neither one of us wants a repeat of what happened before," he said. "Does she still have nightmares about the gunshots and hiding down in the cellar?"

"No, she's adjusted remarkably well."

"I'm glad. I wish mine would go away." Kevin glanced at his watch. "Since I'm not going to be seeing Dawn for a while, I bought her a present. I'd appreciate it if you could stop by the house and pick it up for her. I'll be there after three. I'm going to work mostly from home the rest of the day."

"All right. I'll come by before I go home. Just remember, Kevin, if the vandal strikes again, it may take us a while to respond. We *are* dangerously low on manpower and funds to maintain our routine patrols. That's what led to Officer Franklin's death. His radio malfunctioned. He had submitted repair orders on it before, but no money was available, and he had to use what he had. When Kee Franklin finds out, he's probably going to sue the department and the tribe, and my guess is he'll win."

"I hope the officer's father doesn't do that. We're insured, but I don't think the tribe could afford any higher liability rates," he said quietly. "I'll bring the police funding issue up again before the appropriate committees. The tribal government is doing their best with practically no funds beyond a skeleton budget."

Ella held up her hand. "Spare me." She told him about Bruno. "The tribe spent money on that, but not on manpower or equipment maintenance? Where are your priorities?"

"They have to be a little different from those of line officers, you know that. We have to look at everything at once. We also know how important training is, so at least a small amount had to be budgeted for that purpose. We certainly couldn't afford the continuing funding a new officer would require, and this was much less expensive. Besides, the way the budget is set up, we can't take training money and move it to another category." He pursed his lips. "Things are pretty crazy right now, Ella, even in Window Rock."

"Yeah, no kidding. At least give Dawn a call or two if you can."

He nodded, then stood up. "I'll miss her, you know." Without waiting for an answer, Kevin strode out of her office.

Ella sighed. She knew how hard it would be for him to stay away from his daughter. He doted on her, and in the past several months had visited Dawn regularly. But their little girl's safety came first.

Getting back to business, Ella settled down in front of her computer monitor. A lot of the initial leg work in an investigation was done this way now. Cop shows that existed primarily on a fare of car chases and shoot-outs were far removed from the reality of the job. The truth of it was that police work was hours and hours of boring, mind-numbing work, endless interviews, with minutes of sheer terror randomly applied.

Ella spent hours going over the details of the crime and double-checking everything that could possibly become a lead. She was so engrossed in what she was doing that she wasn't aware Justine had come in until her partner cleared her throat. Ella jumped.

"Sorry. I didn't mean to startle you," Justine said quickly.

"No problem. I just go into a mild semitrance whenever I'm chasing leads on the computer. Do you have something for me?"

"I've checked Officer Franklin's current finances—but he was as clean as a whistle. I've also spoken to several officers, and nobody has anything bad to say about him. Of course no one wants to say something bad about someone who just died—whether they believe in the *chindi* or not."

"Everything in life has two sides, and that includes people,"

Ella answered, echoing the Navajo beliefs Rose had taught her. "We need to find the darker side of this officer if he had one. Did he have any bad relationships? Secrets that he kept from his fellow officers and friends? Exploring things like that could lead us to his killer."

"If it wasn't just a burglar who decided to go homicidal," Justine countered.

Ella stood up and reached for her keys on top of the file cabinet. "I'm going to take off now to take care of some business."

"Should I come with you?"

"Not this time." She told her partner about Rose's encounter with Vera Jim at the college. "I want to talk to Samuel Nakai and find out more about Vera for personal reasons—but while I'm there, I'll make it a point to learn more about NEED."

"Are you thinking that someone in NEED wanted to silence Officer Franklin? He was a critic, I know."

"It's a possibility I want to check into, though I can't find any reason yet for his being singled out. There are a lot of other critics, including my mother, that have certainly gotten attention. I'll let you know if I find out anything useful." Ella waved good-bye.

As she headed out the station door to the parking lot, Ella checked the address she'd written down from police records. Four months ago, Samuel Nakai had been arrested and charged for driving while intoxicated. Although no liquor was allowed on the Rez, it always found its way within its borders.

Forty minutes later, Ella arrived at Samuel Nakai's home. He lived in a modern housing section recently built by the tribe on the west side of town, across the river and north of the high school. The single-story houses with carports looked identical to each other, and similar to another, older development on the east end of Shiprock.

As she pulled up beside the curb, a middle-aged Navajo man

in a blue flannel shirt, jeans, and cowboy boots came out and waved, inviting her to come inside. It was Samuel, apparently.

He leaned against a support beam on the porch and waited for her to approach. "*Yáat'ééh*," he greeted.

"Hello, uncle," she said, surprised that someone living in this modernist setting would greet her in Navajo.

"Do you know who I am?" she asked, suspecting that he already did, though she hadn't identified herself to him yet.

"The policewoman, sister to the *hataalii*."

Ella noted immediately that he hadn't used proper names. Maybe he was a New Traditionalist or a recent convert to traditionalist ways despite his age. "I need to ask you a few questions about a woman I met at the community college today and about the NEED project."

He nodded. "I already heard about that from my niece, who's a student at the college. I suspected you'd come." He showed her into his home.

Inside the furnishings were simple. There was a computer on a desk placed against one wall of the living room, and against the other was a well-worn fabric couch.

"Please sit," he said.

Samuel turned the wooden chair by the desk around and faced Ella as she sat down on the couch.

"I need to know about . . ." She hesitated, trying to figure out how to avoid using Vera Jim's name.

"You can use names. I have no qualms about that when it's necessary. Nothing has to be carried out to an extreme."

His answer told her he was a New Traditionalist and that her guess had been right. "Tell me about the Jims, Vera and her husband. I understand that they've invested a lot of their financial resources in the NEED project."

He nodded slowly. "If everything goes as planned, they'll be prosperous. If not . . ." He shrugged. "They funded a large part of the radio and newspaper ads NEED has taken out, and also spent their own money to hire a consultant—an Anglo expert on power plants and the sciences involved with that—to explain things to the council. That's what gave the council the idea to hire the same man to attend the Chapter House meetings and explain things to the People objectively without taking sides."

Ella realized that Samuel was referring to Delbert Shives. Neskahi had mentioned the man's participation in Chapter House business. "But you haven't chosen to get involved with NEED. Is that right?"

"I don't believe this is the right thing for us as a tribe. *'Eyónís*, outsiders, promised us much the same thing before. We were supposed to have all the money we needed. Well, we don't, and look at how things turned out. I lived my entire life on land the tribe had allotted to my family, but the sheep died, and the vegetables we grew came out tasting funny. My parents and my brother died of cancer, but the government people told us it was just a coincidence and that it had nothing to do with the uranium mines— less than five hundred yards away."

"So you moved because you were afraid of the risks," Ella said, nodding. She didn't blame him.

"I didn't feel safe living there anymore, so I gave the land back to the tribe and moved to Shiprock. Now the tribe will give that land to another family, and they'll suffer, but I can't keep it from happening." He grew quiet for a long time, then finally spoke again.

"Now, some of our own people tell us that we should build a new, even better power plant that will use uranium taken from our own ground." He shook his head slowly. "People like the Jims are convinced this will benefit the tribe. But I don't believe we can afford to take another chance. I asked one of the physicists how long it would be before the Rio Puerco was safe again. He told me that the water contained something called thorium and that had a life of eighty thousand years." He gazed at her through sad eyes. "The land is our life and our legacy. We can't afford another mistake like that one."

"How far are the ones who support NEED prepared to go to get this project approved? And how do they treat their opposition?"

"You're worried about your mother, aren't you?" he asked, then continued, not really expecting an answer. "Mrs. Destea is an opposition leader with a lot of visibility and credibility, so she's a threat to them. But although NEED will fight hard, it'll be a fair fight. They're good Navajos and businessmen, not hoods."

"Vera Jim nearly shoved my mother to the ground recently."

"She's young—much younger than her husband, and her temper gets the better of her sometimes. But I wouldn't worry about Vera. She would back down before she ever really hurt anyone."

"And there's the death of the police officer . . . he was against NEED."

Silence stretched out between them. Finally, he spoke. "I don't know any of the details, but I really doubt that had anything to do with NEED. Either way, I guess we'll both find out soon enough how they deal with those who stand in their way. I intend to make things as difficult as possible for them by reminding people of the past, and what could happen if we let the promise of wealth and easy money cloud our thinking."

Unfortunately, no matter how dangerous, Ella knew that Rose would be right there with him. And there was nothing she could do to stop her. Her mom, Dawn, Clifford and his family, and maybe even Kevin could be considered enemies of NEED, and she didn't know for sure how far these people would go when confronting those they perceived to be standing in their way.

Ella stopped by home at around two to spend a little time with her daughter, who was just home from day school. She'd have to work late tonight, so this would potentially be the only time she got to spend with Dawn today. She'd call it a late lunch if anyone asked.

Her mother wasn't in sight when Ella came in the door, but Dawn looked up from where she was playing with the toy farm.

"*Shimá!*" Dawn yelled, and ran into her arms.

Dawn gave Ella a hug and a kiss.

Seeing the tiny animals on the floor, Ella suddenly remembered that she hadn't stopped by Kevin's. She'd have to do that right after the memorial service.

Ella set her daughter down, and Dawn resumed her play. As Ella gazed at her daughter, she heard Rose in the kitchen, cooking something. Judging by the sound of pans rattling, it wasn't a soufflé.

A moment later, Rose came out, looked at Dawn then at Ella. "When she plays her 'pretendly' games, she's off in her own world. She never knew I left the room. To be honest, she reminds me of you at that age," Rose said smiling. "Your father would come home and you'd give him a kiss, then go right back to whatever you were doing."

Dawn picked up a toy horse and looked up at Ella. "I want a horse. Then I can ride like my friend."

"Her little friend's mother puts the child on the saddle in front of her and then takes her for a short ride every afternoon," Rose explained.

Ella looked at Rose, alarmed. "My daughter hasn't been out on the horse, has she?"

"No, I wouldn't allow it. She's still too young, and horses are unpredictable animals at times, even with an experienced rider. I don't care how safe her friend's mother says it is."

"Good," Ella said, relieved, then looked at Dawn. "When you get a little older, you can learn how to ride."

"You teach me?"

Rose laughed.

Ella glared at her mother, then looked back at Dawn. "I'm not very good with horses, Pumpkin." If she excelled at anything, it was at getting thrown.

"She's better with police cars, little one." Laughing, Rose returned to the kitchen.

Ella sighed. "I'll find you a good teacher. But you'll have to get bigger first."

"How big first?"

"Tall, like Big Bird," Ella said, and began to tickle her.

Dawn shrieked, but pulled away. "*Shimá*, read me story about the farmer. Please?"

It was Dawn's favorite book, and by now, they both knew the story by heart, but the request was repeated daily. "You'll hear the story at bedtime tonight, okay?"

"Okay." Dawn turned her attention back to her game, taking a small wagon out of a red-and-yellow plastic barn, and "hitching" up a horse to pull it.

Ella watched her daughter for a moment longer, then went into the kitchen.

"Are you going to that memorial service for the officer tonight?" Rose asked quietly.

Ella nodded. "I have to."

"Have you been able to find out who killed him yet? Or why he had to die?"

"Answers rarely come that fast—at least not on my cases."

Rose placed a bowl of mutton stew before her. "Here. Eat now. I have a feeling you haven't had anything since breakfast." Rose brought over a piece of warm fry bread she'd been keeping in a basket beneath a dish towel.

"You're right. I'm starving."

The wind had begun to build up outside, and Ella could hear

it rattling a loose windowpane. The temperature had gone down by ten degrees in the last hour, but inside the kitchen it was still warm and comfortable. "Mom, I don't know what I'd do without you. You've made this house a real home for all of us. It welcomes anyone who walks in, and it seems like there's always something good cooking."

She smiled. "Daughter, you can stop with the compliments. I've known you too long. What you really mean is that you wish I would go back to being the way I was . . . someone who was always here at home waiting for you, or your father, or your brother. But that can't be. That time is gone."

"But you were happy all those years, weren't you?" Seeing Rose nod, she added, "Then why change?"

"Because life did. You and your brother grew up, your father passed away, and it was a time for me to begin anew. To not grow, to not change—that is death," she said matter-of-factly.

Ella understood, but nothing would ever make her stop missing the old days. She ate quickly, knowing she had to return to work, but enjoying every bit of her food. When she swallowed the last spoonful of stew, she swabbed the bowl with a piece of fry bread to get every last drop of broth.

"*Bizaadii* is coming over tonight," Rose said, using the nickname she'd given Herman Cloud as a joke. She called him "the gabby one" though he seldom had much to say. "He and I will watch your daughter."

At least she wouldn't have to worry about her mother tonight. There was a limited amount of trouble she could get into here at home. "Mom, I'd like you to be very careful around people who are pro-NEED. I'm not sure how far they're willing to go to fight those who don't agree with them."

"I don't think they present a threat to anyone. They're hoping to sway public opinion, not turn it against themselves by using tactics and dirty tricks no Navajo would condone. That young girl was just being childish, as one might expect."

"You're probably right, but just stay alert. Okay?"

Rose nodded, then began stirring a kettle of soup cooking on the stove. "I always am, more so than you've ever realized."

Ella stood up, her mother's words troubling her. Sometimes the people you thought you knew best were the ones who surprised you the most.

SIX

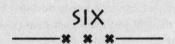

The memorial service was a simple affair, in Dr. Franklin's home. The large buffet table in the dining room was covered with all kinds of food and drink that neighbors and friends had brought with them.

Dr. Franklin greeted everyone as they entered, then moved among the gathering, giving them time to eat. After about a half hour, he stood at one end of the room and cleared his throat. The people grew silent.

His voice, weak at the beginning, grew stronger as he spoke. "I want to thank you all for coming—my son's friends and fellow officers, and those who have known our family and have come to pay their respect. My son was a man of courage who always stood up for the tribe and, in the end, he gave his life for The People. Although I will miss him every day for the rest of my life, I know he died doing exactly what he wanted to do—serve as a police officer." Professor Franklin paused and swallowed from the cup of water he held in his shaking hand.

"Today I want all of us to celebrate his life, not mourn his passing. He would have wanted it that way."

The chief stood to say a few words. Officer Mike Kodaseet

would follow and speak about what the department meant to Jason.

Ella glanced around the room, watching those who had come. She recognized all of the department staff from the station, and a few of the officers that had come a long way from their patrol areas in Arizona.

Regardless of their rank, their eyes all mirrored the same emotions. Their shared sense of loss, their shock, and their anger all drew them together, and gave them strength. What had happened to Jason could have easily happened to any of them, and they knew it. That knowledge would compel all of them to work tirelessly until Patrolman Jason Franklin's killer was brought to justice.

An hour later, Ella was walking to her unit, when Justine caught up to her.

"Most of the civilians inside who aren't with the department are anti-NEED advocates. I spoke to several of them, but there was one kid hanging around in the back of the room who particularly caught my attention. Did you see him? About seventeen or so, with a headband and wearing baggy jeans. He seemed pretty restless in a roomful of cops."

"I saw you with him after the chief finished speaking."

"His name is Albert Washburn. Officer Franklin apparently helped him out once when some gang members came after him, and the kid never forgot it. Albert's paid him back by keeping his ears to the ground and passing on any information he thought Franklin would be interested in hearing. I understand Officer Franklin made a point to meet with him every Thursday evening during his rounds."

"Where? At the garage?"

"No such luck," Justine said. "They changed the site every week because Albert didn't want to be seen with a cop. He says he's not active with the gangs anymore, but he still knows a lot of people."

"Did Albert know anything about the murder?"

"No, but he did tell me that Officer Franklin had seemed distracted lately. Last Thursday, they were supposed to meet near the hill where the high school seniors arrange whitewashed rocks to form the number of their graduation year."

Ella nodded.

"But Franklin didn't show up. Albert saw him later and went up to him. Franklin told him that he'd had to meet his dad and hadn't been able to keep his regular meeting with Albert. The kid said that it had been totally out of character for Officer Franklin to put personal matters before business."

"Was there a problem we don't know about between Kee Franklin and his son?"

"I don't know. I think we should speak to Belinda again. If she's no help, and we still haven't heard from the former Mrs. Franklin or are unable to get any help from her, then we need to come back tomorrow and talk to his father."

"I agree."

Saying good-bye to Justine, Ella drove directly to Kevin's home, which was, like her mother's home, southwest of Shiprock.

Though the drive to Kevin's was uneventful, she stayed alert for any sign that she was being tailed. As she turned down the gravel road that led to his home she noted that his porch light was on. Suddenly, out of the corner of her eye, she caught a glimpse of a shadow moving around Kevin's sporty sedan. Whoever it was had something in his hand, but she couldn't make out what it was from this distance.

Ella had just picked up her cell phone, hoping to be able to warn Kevin, when she saw the outline of a man holding what looked like a rifle come out of the house onto the porch. Ella hit her sirens at the same time, and the figure behind Kevin's car suddenly took off running up a hillside.

A second later, Ella reached the house, and seeing it was Kevin with a shotgun, ordered him to stay on the porch.

Familiar enough with the area around Kevin's home to know her vehicle couldn't cross the narrow, dry arroyo on the other side of the hill, Ella jumped out of the car with her flashlight and ran after the fleeing man, who'd disappeared over the hill. As she reached the top of the hill, she heard a thump, and aiming her light, she spotted a figure on the other side of the arroyo, running parallel to it. The arroyo's width was at least fifteen feet, and the caved-in earthen wall on the far side told her the perp had barely made the jump across the gap.

Ella followed at a jog, making sure of her footing, knowing that the arroyo narrowed even more ahead, and she'd be able to jump over a lot easier and run the perp down.

Using her ears to track the person, she listened for his footsteps, and knew from the sound that she was closing in on him. Then there was another, hollow thump, and Ella knew he'd probably jumped down into the arroyo to hide. She stopped, slipped down into the steep-sided natural ditch, which at this point was only ten feet across. It was deeper than she was tall, but she could hear the sound of the person moving ahead, and the clank of something mechanical.

Ella stopped, took out her weapon, and proceeded carefully up the narrowing, claustrophobic pathway, wary of an ambush. The arroyo was as crooked as a desert rattler here, and the perp could easily be waiting for her around the next corner.

She heard an electrical whine, then the cough of a motorcycle starting up. Ella sprinted ahead, but had barely gone twenty feet before she caught sight of a red taillight, then the single beam of a headlight as the perp roared off on a motorcycle, fishtailing slightly in the soft ground.

Ella called for backup using her handheld radio, though she knew that the chances of getting an officer in position between here and Shiprock within the next fifteen minutes was slim. And if the cyclist went south, or took a side road . . .

She had to face it. Chances were good that the perp had made a clean getaway.

Ella climbed out of the arroyo and walked quickly back to Kevin's house, about three hundred yards away. When she came down the hill, she could see Kevin, flashlight in hand, crouched by the tires.

"He got away on a motorcycle. That's the sound I heard, right?" As she nodded, he continued. "Do you see this?" he pointed to the slashed tires with the beam of his light. "Branch's talk shows are going to bury me yet. On tonight's program he kept hammering me with innuendo and, at one point, said that I was sure a well-off Tribal Council member judging by my nice home and fancy car. But, Ella, I worked my butt off for everything I've got."

His eyes narrowed as he searched her face. "Did you happen to get a good look at him, or call in for backup so someone can intercept him on the road?"

"Kevin, hasn't anyone on the Tribal Council been paying attention? I made the call, but there are probably *no* backup units within miles of this place. And manning a roadblock takes calling in cops from patrol areas, and that could take an hour or more. We can't justify it for vandalism, and it would take too long to do it anyway."

"I should have filled his pants with buckshot."

"Bad idea."

"Why? He was vandalizing my property. I'm allowed to defend myself."

"You might have killed him, then what? You're a lawyer."

"I'm not that lousy a shot." He muttered something unintelligible under his breath, then added, "I know things are tough for the police right now. I'll see if there's anything I can do to help. Maybe I can shake some money loose if I make some concessions on other issues."

"Because you need us now?" Ella asked cynically.

"No, it's more personal than that. I don't want the mother of my child killed because of the way things are."

"I don't want the mother of your child killed either," she said with a thin smile. "What really worries me is that people are soon going to be doing the same thing you just did—taking matters into their own hands because they can't count on the police." Ella took a deep breath. Almost every household on the Rez had a rifle or a shotgun.

"That bastard sliced all four of my tires. Leaving the porch light on wasn't enough. I'm going to have to get someone to guard my property while I'm sleeping. Or maybe I'll just get a big, mean dog."

"Then it'll bite you, too."

"Probably—particularly the way my luck's been going." He cocked his head toward the house. "Come on in. The damage is already done, so there's no sense hanging around out here in the cold. I've got Dawn's present inside, so I need to get that for you. Can you stay a while?"

Ella shook her head. "I really should be getting home. I just came from the memorial service, and there are a few things I need to work through in my head before tomorrow."

"Things are always complicated for you and me—both at work and in our personal lives. I wonder if that's why we stink at relationships?"

"Probably, but neither of us is going to change," Ella answered with a shrug.

"Good thing Rose isn't here to hear you say that."

Ella laughed. "Someday she's going to finally understand that being single works best for me."

He shook his head. "Just because *her* life is changing doesn't mean she's ready to let go of the hopes she's had for you," Kevin said with a smile as they stepped up onto his front porch. "She's still your mother."

"I know, and that's why it's hard for me to accept this new side of her."

He grew serious. "You really should be very proud of your mother. She's becoming a force to be reckoned with, even at council discussions."

"Yes, but she's also putting herself in a vulnerable position—being in a leadership position always carries a risk."

"That's true. She made a name for herself on the gaming issue last year, but along the way she picked up some enemies, too. But I expect what worries you the most now is that she's made her position on the NEED project very public."

"What do you mean 'very public'?" she asked, following him inside, but not sitting down.

"Haven't you heard?" Kevin shook his head. "Never mind. You should hear it from her, not me."

"Kevin, you started this. Finish it."

"George Branch interviewed her today on the air."

Ella stared at him in muted shock. She was getting to loathe surprises, particularly when it came to things involving her mother. "That weasel? Give me the highlights."

"Rose came across as very intelligent and logical, Ella. You would have been proud of her. She said that she wasn't as much against NEED as she was *for* the rights of the tribe, and that she wanted to make sure all the safety and environmental concerns were answered satisfactorily before any decisions were made on the new power plant. But Branch kept pressing her, you know how he is. Finally, she admitted based on what she knew at that moment she could not in good conscience stand in favor of a nuclear power plant on the Rez."

Kevin paused, then continued. "And that, unfortunately, is all people will remember. It was the sound bite Branch was looking for."

Ella closed her eyes, then opened them again. "So those who are against it will see my mother as their ally—and those for it will become her enemies."

"That would be my assessment."

Ella sighed. "I've got to get going. Do you have Dawn's present ready?"

"Hang on. I'll be right back." He came out a moment later with an enormous box covered with bright ribbons.

"What on earth is in there?" Ella asked.

"It's a tricycle. The plastic kind with the big wheels so she can go across soft ground. I had them find a box big enough, and then wrap it up because I thought it would be more fun for her."

Ella smiled and shook her head. "You really should stop being so extravagant with her."

"I enjoy doing things like this for her, Ella. She's my only daughter. I know you don't approve, but sometimes it's the only way I have of reminding her how special she is to me. I don't get to live with her like you do. If you were in my shoes, you'd do the same."

She couldn't even imagine not having Dawn with her. "She's crazy about you, Kevin. Even if you never give her another present, she would still think you're the best thing since Barney and Big Bird."

"Thanks . . . I think."

"In Dawn-speak, that's a big deal," she said.

"Let me help you carry it out," he said.

"Thanks," she replied, opening the front door for him. "By

the way, I intend to let the officer who's assigned to this area know about the problem here tonight. He may be able to make additional passes during his patrols," she said, as he put the tricycle in the back of her SUV.

"That would be Philip Cloud," he said with a nod. "I've seen him around."

"Is there a problem between you two?" she asked, noting his tone. Whenever Kevin's voice became too neutral, that usually meant he was trying to cover his feelings.

"The Clouds—Philip, Michael, and Herman—are all against anything that will cause the uranium mines to be opened again."

"I wasn't aware of that." She couldn't help but wonder if her mother's stand on the issue had been influenced by Herman.

"Okay, you're ready to go," Kevin said, once the box was secure.

"Dawn's going to flip when she sees this present," Ella said. "I'll put her on the phone for you tomorrow after she opens it."

"You're not going to give it to her tonight?"

"Are you out of your mind? She'll probably be asleep when I get home. And even if she's not, I'm not going to give her something that will get her so excited she won't go to sleep at all. Riding a tricycle around the house at midnight? No thanks. Tomorrow will come soon enough."

Ella drove home, troubled. Knowing that her mother had been interviewed on the air by George Branch had unsettled her. Ella knew Branch was no fan of hers, and she didn't doubt for one minute that he was capable of going after Rose as a form of payback.

As she pulled up to her house and parked, she pushed the thought from her mind. She'd take things one step at a time.

———

The next morning, Ella sat in the kitchen drinking coffee with Rose. Dawn was already outside, bundled up in warm clothes, playing with the tricycle Kevin had given her, though it would soon be time for her to go off to day school.

Dawn had been undeniably disappointed that her father hadn't come to give her the present personally, but Ella had done her best to explain that, for now, her father couldn't visit, but she could talk to him anytime on the phone. That prospect had soothed Dawn somewhat, particularly after Ella had called Kevin up so Dawn could talk to him.

Rose kept a sharp eye on Dawn as she drove the yellow-and-blue tricycle up the hard-packed gravel driveway. "She's too young for that thing."

"She's fine. She can't go very fast in the gravel anyway."

"But if it tips over—"

"Mom, she's fine. That cycle is so low to the ground her coat drags along behind her like a lizard's tail. Let's get back to what we were talking about. I want to know what happened with that self-promoting windbag—Branch."

"I had no plans to be interviewed, but that windbag, as you correctly name him, called me here at home and asked me to go on his radio program. I said no at first, but from his questions, I got the feeling he was still trying to make up his own mind on the issue, and that tempted me. I knew I could help him, and others like him, by explaining the counterarguments and the dangers. But what really got me to agree was when he asked if I was afraid to face him on the air. There was no way I'd ever allow him, or anyone else, to think that, so I consented."

She met her daughter's gaze. "You know all the pros and cons, daughter. You've heard the talk, read the papers, and listened to our professor friend. Where do you stand on this?"

"I honestly haven't decided. But I do know that the police

department needs funds badly. We can't operate safely and effectively without reliable equipment, and we can't overwork the officers we do have to the point of exhaustion because of a lack of manpower."

She nodded thoughtfully. "That's one of the reasons I've tried hard to keep an open mind about the power plant."

"I heard that your close friend and his two sons are against it."

"*Bizaadii* lost his brother to Red Lung. It was a long, difficult death. Now *Bizaadii* worries about his brother's children, and the long-term effects it would have on them. Back when the mines were open, his brother would often bring home big chunks of uranium ore into the house so his kids could see the rock glow—fluoresce—after they turned out the lights. They didn't know that he was exposing his family to radiation. No one can say what harm that has already done, or what will show up in the future. For that reason, I can assure you that he'll fight the power plant and anything that will reopen the uranium mines with his last breath."

"But you would consider it, if the tribe addressed the safety issues?" Ella asked. Seeing her mom nod, she added, "That must be creating problems between you two."

Rose nodded. "He wants me to feel the same way he does, but I don't. If I'm convinced that this new technology can be made safe, as they say, I won't fight the power plant."

"What will it take to convince you?"

"I want scientists who are not attached to this project to come and explain the things that might go wrong. I want to understand the dangers clearly, and how they are going to be prevented. More importantly, I want everyone in the tribe to understand all that, too, so no one goes into this blindly. The Gods warned us not to take certain rocks out of the earth or it would cause devastation. Before, we didn't know they meant uranium, but we do now. We have to be extremely careful."

"If you feel the Gods are against it, why are you even considering a nuclear power plant?"

"The Gods warned us of the dangers so we would be prepared. If the knowledge of the Anglo scientists can help us, and we could use uranium without harming ourselves, the Gods would know we've respected their warning and are being cautious. Then they'd work with the *Dineh* and make good things happen."

Ella nodded slowly. "I think you've got a good handle on this, Mom." She glanced at her watch and stood up. "I'll be listening to the early-morning segment of Branch's radio program as I go into work," Ella said.

"So will I."

Ella went outside to say good-bye to Dawn, and found that the air was bitterly cold. Although Dawn seemed perfectly comfortable, Ella took her back into the house, tricycle in tow. After making her daughter promise not to ride in the house, Ella gave her a kiss, then headed back out to her unit.

As she drove to work, Ella brought her thoughts back to the case. Today she'd concentrate on trying to learn more about Kee Franklin's relationship with his son. With luck, she'd be able to turn up a lead that would help her solve the patrolman's murder.

SEVEN
✖ ✖ ✖

Ella had just sat down behind her desk when Justine came to the door. "Officer Franklin's friend, Belinda Johns, is at the campus today teaching an early morning class. If we leave right now, we can catch her when the class lets out."

"Then let's go."

With Justine driving, Ella allowed her thoughts to circle around the facts she knew. "I'm still trying to come up with a motive besides an interrupted burglary. When you spoke to other officers about Jason, did you pick up any indication at all that there was a problem between him and his father?"

"No, but I did learn that his father wasn't really a part of Jason's life when he was young. His parents separated when he was ten years old, and Jason was raised from that point on by his mother.

"That's hardly unusual, particularly here on the Rez. Kids are the property of their mothers, at least from a cultural and traditional standpoint."

"Yeah, but there was more to it than that. Jason never went to visit his dad, even during summer break or holidays. From what I gathered, Jason grew up with the impression that his dad had abandoned him."

"Who gave you that information?"

"I overheard Professor Franklin talking to a woman friend of his at the memorial service. He was saying that he regretted what he called 'all those lost years.' "

"Who was the woman? Did you recognize her?"

"Sure. Officer Judy Musket."

Ella's eyebrows rose. "Did you get the impression that they're close?"

Justine paused, then answered. "He was speaking very freely to her, and most men generally don't do that with casual acquaintances. But there is a big age difference between the two of them. Judy is almost young enough to be his daughter."

"To some, that's not an issue. We'll have to make it a point to speak to her."

"Big Ed called the military again, trying to locate Officer Franklin's mother, and learned that she and her Air Force husband are on vacation 'somewhere' in Germany, or perhaps France. He has thirty days' leave, and they hadn't given their travel plans to his superiors. The military is trying not to look bad, according to Big Ed, because not only did the mother miss her son's funeral, but the military is embarrassed they can't find their officer." Justine shrugged.

"Is there any hint that something happened to them?" Ella's eyebrows furrowed.

"If there had been, I think Big Ed would have passed that information on to us. He thinks that the couple are just avoiding the big cities where the military has been checking hotels and such," Justine added. "The chief promised to keep pressuring the base commander until they find Jason's mother."

They arrived on campus twenty minutes later. Ella and Justine walked to the science building, then headed to Professor Belinda

Johns's office. To their surprise, Kevin was there talking to the professor.

As Ella knocked lightly on the open door, Kevin turned his head and, seeing her, smiled.

Belinda invited them in with a casual wave of her hand.

"I'm just finishing here, so don't let me hold you up," Kevin said, coming toward them.

As Justine went past him into Belinda's office, Ella excused herself for a moment and accompanied Kevin out into the hall. "What brings you here, Kevin?" She kept her voice low so no one in the office could hear.

"I'm trying to get more information on NEED. Dr. Johns's credentials are impressive. She attended an Ivy League college and graduated 'cum laude.' You should have heard her debating with Kee Franklin at the Chapter House meeting. Since they're on opposite sides of the issue, I thought I'd speak to each separately."

"Did she help you decide where you stand?"

"I haven't made up my mind yet. But I have to tell you, Ella, if we decide as a people not to open a power plant or a mine, I hope that it's a decision our people made based on something other than fear."

Glancing over Kevin's shoulder, Ella saw an athletic no-necked Navajo man in casual clothes standing beside the main entrance to the building. Where he was standing he could watch the halls and see anyone entering the building by simply turning his head. It was Ernest Ration, a young ex–Army Ranger she knew casually.

Following her gaze, Kevin smiled. "Ernest is my bodyguard. He stays close while I take care of business during the day."

"And at night?"

"A cousin of his who also served in the Rangers, Eugene Frazier, keeps an eye on me and the house till morning. Hopefully, this will discourage any other vandals."

"I don't know Eugene, but I think Ernest may be a bad choice," Ella said softly.

"Why? He's got excellent qualifications and special training."

"As a soldier, not a bodyguard. There's a huge difference. A soldier, especially from a special unit like the Rangers, is highly trained in active aggression. His job is more to seek out the enemy and destroy him, not defend a potential target. A bodyguard should keep you *away* from danger, not seek it out. His instincts and training make him unsuitable for the job you want done."

She remembered when Ernest had worked at a convenience store on the Rez. He'd kept a carbine with him, just hoping someone would try and rob the place while he was on the job. Ernest obviously loved a fight, and that was precisely the one quality a bodyguard didn't need.

Ella watched him approach. "Is Ernest armed?"

"Of course he is. The new state law allows anyone with training and a permit to carry a concealed weapon these days."

That was one of her least favorite laws. It was an invitation to disaster because it just begged for an armed confrontation among civilians.

"I carry a firearm now, too," Kevin said.

She hated the thought, or more precisely, she hated the need for the father of her child to be armed. But there was nothing she could do about it, and she was still grateful that Kevin had worked so hard to keep Dawn safe during the threats against her not too many months earlier. "I heard Sergeant Neskahi gave you some private instruction, and that's good. Just remember to make sure of your target, Kevin, and don't do anything that could injure innocent bystanders when a confrontation can be avoided."

"That was the topic of my first lesson. I'm always very careful."

As he strode off behind Ernest, who led the way outdoors,

Justine called to her. Ella joined her inside Belinda's office. "Sorry for the delay. I had a question for the council member."

"Would you tell her what you just told me?" Justine asked Belinda as Ella sat down.

"Investigator Clah, I was just telling your partner that although Mr. Franklin and Jason were on the same side when it came to NEED, they really weren't close as father and son. Jason never could lower his guard around his father. Jason had been hurt too much in the past, and there were still issues between them."

"Like what?" Ella asked.

"Professor Franklin left Jason's mom when Jason was ten. But he never asked for visiting rights, and he remained off the Rez for most of Jason's life. Although he provided child support, Jason never heard from him. Jason knew his dad was an important physicist, so he spent his boyhood fantasizing about him. Then, shortly after he graduated from high school, Jason found out that his dad was teaching at a branch college in Los Alamos. He saved his money and took a bus over there. When he met with his dad, the professor refused to explain why he'd never kept in touch, and he never apologized either. He simply asked that Jason let the past rest."

"And did he?"

Belinda shook her head. "Jason was very hurt. He wanted answers, but he couldn't get them from his father, so he decided to bide his time. After Jason became a cop, and he had more resources available to him, he found out everything he could about his father's life. But he never told me what he'd learned. My guess is that he was disappointed. He spent many years thinking his dad was some sort of Einstein, working on earth-shattering research. That had been his way of coping with a dad that never kept in touch. Then, when he learned the truth, he was forced to give up his idealized images. I think that probably broke his heart."

"If they weren't close, why did the professor move back here?"

She shrugged. "I'm not sure. Maybe Professor Franklin finally realized what he'd given up by forsaking his son. Or, more than likely, he heard about the NEED project and decided he should come back and speak his mind."

"So you think Dr. Franklin returned primarily to fight against NEED, and Jason was just a secondary interest?" Ella said.

"Yes, but it's all speculation on my part. Navajos are taught not to speak for others, so maybe I should just keep my mouth shut. It's possible I'm being too hard on him."

"It seems to me that being on the same side of the NEED issue would have brought father and son closer together," Justine said.

"I think it did, to some degree. Opposing the development meant that they were of one mind. But in almost every other way, they were still miles apart. Look at it objectively. The professor is a gifted physicist whose field of preference is quantum mechanics. In that area, you deal with concepts and probabilities. It's a field of science where nothing can be observed directly. By contrast, Jason's mind-set, and his profession, is one where he acts based on what he can see and therefore prove. Their ways of thinking ran along two totally different wavelengths."

Ella nodded slowly. She could sympathize with that. She'd traveled that same path with Rose. The way Rose viewed life—her adherence to the Navajo Way—had put them on a collision course many times.

Yet, despite the differences between Kee and Jason, Ella believed in the bond between father and son. Her own father and brother had held completely different religious beliefs, but Clifford had risked his own life to help find their father's killer, and Ella knew they'd loved each other in spite of everything. The importance of family, of respect for the clan, was as much a part of most Navajos as was breathing.

After taking several pamphlets Belinda had offered them that explained and described the NEED project, Justine and Ella left. "What's your take on Professor Johns?" Ella asked once they were outside the main building.

"I think Belinda's playing it straight, but I really wish I could get a better feel for Jason. I did speak to Mike Kodaseet last night, and he said that Jason had always searched for purpose in his life, but it wasn't until he became a cop that he got himself together. I gathered from our brief conversation that Jason got himself into trouble frequently as a kid," Justine said.

"So maybe that was why he helped Albert Washburn."

"I also did a quick background check on Washburn. Albert's on parole and doesn't have a job. I spoke to his parole officer, and he said that Albert spends most of his day at home. He lives with his mom, who works as a hospice care nurse in Farmington."

"Do you have his address?"

Justine read it off from the pad she kept in her jacket pocket, and they set out in that direction. A half hour later, they pulled up in front of Albert's home. The area was along the river northeast of the bridges, and was occupied mostly with worn mobile homes. The lots were small, and some were fenced off with barriers ranging from railroad ties to chicken wire. Many poor people lived in Shiprock, and this was one of the poorest neighborhoods. Trash littered many of the yards, though a few were cleaned up and weedless.

They stopped in front of one of the latter trailers. The clean white mailbox showcased the address, hand-painted in turquoise blue.

As they parked in the graveled slot wide enough for one vehicle, a young man, around seventeen, wearing jeans and a thick pullover sweater, came out and stood on the small wooden porch. Something in his gaze told Ella that he already knew who they were. Of course, that wasn't at all remarkable. Virtually every teenager in the community was aware that Investigator Ella had one of the few unmarked police units, and that it was a blue Jeep.

Ella reached the porch a step ahead of Justine and pulled out her badge. "We need to ask you a few questions."

"I don't know what more I can tell the police. I know you're after Officer Franklin's killer, and I'd sure like to help with that, but I have no idea who did it."

"Can we come inside?" Ella asked, uncomfortably aware of the brisk wind that had kicked up. Down here by the river it could really get cold. A flock of migrating ducks flew across the levee behind the trailer, and she wondered for the hundredth time how they could swim in that icy water so easily. Just the thought made her shiver.

"Sure. Come inside where it's warm."

Ella and Justine were both pleasantly surprised by how orderly and clean the interior of the mobile home was. The sofa was old and worn, but neatly arranged with two throw pillows. Facing the sofa were two folding chairs with torn cushions that had been repaired with matching vinyl tape. At the end of the living area were a simple wooden chair and an inexpensive particleboard computer desk that held a desktop computer and ink-jet printer. Several open books were arranged around the keyboard.

Following her line of vision, he added, "I'm doing some research for an assignment—a term paper. I'm trying to get my GED. Then, if I can manage it, I'm going to enroll in the local college."

"What kind of degree are you going after?"

"I'm not sure yet. Business of some kind. Maybe an MBA eventually, if I can get a scholarship." He gestured for them to take a seat on the sofa. "Now how can I help you?"

Ella got right to it. "How long had you known Officer Franklin?"

"We met two years ago last summer—July, I guess."

"How did you two meet?"

"He was on patrol, busting kids who were setting off illegal fireworks, bottle rockets and stuff. It was during that long drought. I'd wandered onto the turf of a rival gang looking for a friend of mine, and nearly got killed when they jumped me. Officer Franklin came flying out of his unit with nothing more than a nightstick and beat back about five guys. Then he loaded me up and took me to the hospital. I bled all over his car seat. If it hadn't been for him, I probably wouldn't be here today. I've got the scars to prove it."

"And you became friends after that?"

"We weren't friends, really. I just owed him big-time, so I tried to pay him back the only way I could."

"How's that?"

"If something was brewing around here, I'd let him know about it."

"Nothing more than that?"

"Not lately. I've heard about a couple of cars being stolen recently, but I have no idea who's behind that. The only thing I'm positive about is that it's not gang-related. I would have known if any of the kids were involved."

"What gang are you in?"

"The Many Devils, but I'm not active. If there was such a thing as quitting, I would have. As it is, I just see the guys every once in a while, but go my own way now."

"And they accept that?" Ella asked skeptically.

"They don't hassle me. Most of them are younger than me anyway, and I'm bigger than they are. I also know a lot people who owe me favors and would back me up."

Ella walked to an attractive watercolor painting of a stallion hung on the wall. It was done in a style especially popular in the sixties and seventies—a stylized design using bright blues and yellows and geometric shapes reminiscent of those found on Navajo rugs. "I tried doing something like this in high school, but just don't have the talent. Are you an artist?"

"No. That's the only thing my old man left behind when he walked out. He took off when I was eight or nine, and I haven't seen him since."

Ella nodded, suspecting now that one of the reasons Jason had befriended this boy was because he could easily identify with him. "Is there anything you can tell us about Officer Franklin that might help us find his killer?"

Albert paused, mulling her question over in his mind. "You probably already know this, but about two weeks ago he told me that someone had tried to break off the lock on the rear door of that old garage his mom owned. Sine he couldn't believe that anyone would want the old junk in there, he thought it might have been an initiation rite for a gang. But I set him straight."

"You don't think it was an initiation?"

"No way. For one, nobody trying to get ranked into a gang would have backed out. He would have broken in, one way or another, even if he had to break a window or ram it with a stolen car. To fail would have made him look like a wuss in front of everyone, and he'd probably have gotten the crap beat out of him. Not that he could have avoided that anyway. Most of the ranking around here involves taking on three or four of their own guys and staying on your feet."

"So what's your theory?" Ella asked.

"I've thought about that a lot because I wanted to help him. Obviously, someone wanted something that was stored in there, maybe some family heirloom, or whatever, that meant something to them, but it took time for that person to build up his courage because he wasn't really a thief. In other words, we're talking amateur night."

"That's a plausible theory." Ella stood up. "Thanks for your time."

As they went back to the car, Ella remained quiet and Justine didn't interrupt.

"So here is the way I see it," Ella said at last. "Jason saw evidence that someone was casing the place. So he started making frequent but randomly timed stops, and caught up to the perp. But it must have been someone he knew or recognized, so he lowered his guard. The perp panicked, turned the tables on Jason, and killed him."

"I get the part about Jason recognizing his killer, but if we accept the rest of your theory, that would mean that the perp wasn't out to kill Jason. Of course that would fit with what we already know—Jason wasn't *called* to the scene. That means someone was there ahead of him for a reason. It may have been because of what was stored inside that building, or what the perp believed was in there. But there was no way he could have known that Jason would show up."

"Agreed. So let's say the perp knew something of value was stored there—that's why he wanted in," Ella said. "But we saw the stuff in there—it was just old junk or used furniture, books, and magazines. So now we're looking for someone who *thought* something of value was there, someone Jason knew and caught searching through the boxes. This had to have been a person who didn't want anyone to know what he'd been doing. In other words, not a professional burglar, but rather someone with a reputation to maintain. That could explain why they were carrying a top-of-the-line firearm and not just a Saturday night special."

"We're narrowing down the field," Justine said with a nod. "Whoever did this carries a concealed handgun, and will kill anyone who threatens them in some way, even a police officer performing their duty."

"I want to interview Kee Franklin next," Ella said, "but before we do that, I want to run a complete background check on him."

"I've done a preliminary report," Justine said. "He's got an interesting background, from what I managed to find out."

"Fill me in."

"Kee Franklin was enrolled in a boarding school when he was six and spent every school year living away from his parents. Right out of high school he joined the Army. When his hitch was up he traveled to Albuquerque, took a college entrance exam, and got an incredibly high score. He received a scholarship, majored in physics, and got his doctorate in less than six years. But, after that, there's a fifteen-year gap in his work history. It's like he dropped off a cliff. Then he suddenly shows up as a professor in a Los Alamos, New Mexico, branch college."

"Maybe Blalock can help me. It sounds like he worked for the government, maybe the Department of Energy or Defense, or even the CIA. Keep digging. I have a feeling Professor Franklin is at the heart of whatever's happening."

EIGHT

--- ✖ ✖ ✖ ---

Ella dropped Justine off at the station so she could work on Professor Franklin's background check, then went to Dwayne Blalock's office. The resident FBI agent had been here for nearly a decade. Over the years he'd changed from the dogmatic Anglo she'd first met when she'd returned to the Rez to a laid-back, pragmatic man who'd learned to work effectively with the tribal police.

His office these days was on the Navajo Nation in Shiprock. Lucas Payestewa, the Hopi FBI agent who also worked the Four Corners area, had Blalock's old office in Farmington, less than a half hour away.

Ella sat down across from Blalock, and, as he looked up, she was struck again by the odd coloring of his eyes—one was brown, the other blue. That was what had earned him the name of FB-Eyes among the local *Dineh*.

Blalock had jurisdiction over homicides on the Rez, but having confidence in Ella and her Special Investigations team, he usually let the tribal cops take the lead. Ella knew Blalock better than anyone else around here, and had worked with him on many occasions. Both owed their lives to each other several times over.

Ella filled him in on the details of her case, then waited as the agent, built like a college quarterback except for a few extra pounds above his belt, stretched out languidly to his full six-foot-two length.

"Okay. It sounds like you think this was more than just a bungled burglary that went bad. Do you think Kee Franklin is implicated in his son's death?"

Ella took a deep breath then let it out again. "I think 'implicated' is too strong a word. But I'll bet there's a connection, though I'm not sure what that could be."

"And on that basis, you want me to try and get you what's probably classified background information? From what you've told me, my guess is that the guy was probably doing some kind of classified nuke work, maybe at one of the labs in Albuquerque, Los Alamos, or White Sands."

"A police officer who happens to be the professor's son has been murdered, and there may be a family connection in the motive. What I expect is for you to help us do everything possible to find the killer. You can consider that a formal request if you'd like."

"You don't have to get testy, Ella. If you had any evidence that Kee Franklin was involved, I could open some doors for you, or at least look in some of them myself and tell you if I found something. But you have nothing to go on."

"Kee Franklin's ex-wife is living with her new husband—a serviceman, in Europe. They've been there for over two years now, so I've already factored her out of the equation. Here's the family connection that piques my curiosity. I believe Jason Franklin's death may have had something to do with the controversy surrounding the nuclear power plant. Kee is a noted physicist and a qualified expert on these matters. Both stood against NEED and the proposed power plant. Kee's opinions in particular seem to carry a lot of weight, but he's against a project that could be worth many millions of dollars. Maybe a billion, in the long run."

"I see where you're going. You're thinking that the murder may have been a warning to Kee—cooperate or else. But you've got nothing solid, Ella."

"Whatever was classified twenty or more years ago can't be that earth-shattering now, but it could give me a lead. I've got to rule out motives before I can cross off any suspects."

"I'll see what I can do," Blalock grumbled.

That was the best she'd get. Ella walked out as he picked up his phone. Blalock usually managed to deliver on her requests, though he grumbled more about them now that he was getting closer to retirement age. Or maybe, when people got older, they just had less patience with the crap thrown their way. Of course maneuvering around bureaucratic red tape had never been his idea of real law enforcement work anyway.

When she returned to her office, Ella saw that Justine had left another folder labeled "Jason Franklin" on her desk, one she could put inside the other she'd already begun to fill.

She started to sort through the contents. Jason's uncle—Kee's younger brother, and at least one of his cousins, had died from cancer after working in the uranium mines. From the bits and pieces Justine had managed to gather, they'd been slow, cruel deaths.

Ella sat back and considered everything. Her next step would be finding out who the other key players were in the pro and con debate surrounding the nuclear power plant. If a killer was among them, she'd find him.

It was early by her standards when Ella left the station for home. She'd been putting in a lot of overtime lately, as had all the field officers and today she was hoping to spend some time with Dawn.

But it wasn't meant to be. When she got home, she learned from Rose and Herman that Dawn had gone over to play at her best friend's house after day school. Alice and Dawn were becoming inseparable. Both girls had working moms and grandmothers who took care of them during the day.

"You should have telephoned, daughter. Had you told me you were going to be home early, I wouldn't have let her go. But the arrangement was perfect for me. My friend and I have to go take photos to document some information we'll be presenting at a series of meetings that the traditionalists will be sponsoring at the college."

"What information do you have to document with photographs?"

"The harm the old uranium mines have done to the land. I need to show everyone what some of those places look like. I can try telling them, but as they say, a picture is worth a thousand words. Most of the traditionalists are now supporting a move to force the tribe to repair the land before we even consider opening the uranium mines again—which, of course, is what'll happen if the nuclear power plant becomes a reality."

"That doesn't sound irresponsible, but is it realistic? The tribe just doesn't have the funds for that, and the companies who caused the damage are no longer in existence."

"I know, but people have to see we can't move forward until we settle our debt to the land. Mother Earth cries out to us, and we can't ignore her. She's part of us. Changing Woman's twin sons freed the earth of monsters, but in our carelessness, we brought some back."

Ella looked at Herman Cloud and her mother. They were both in their late sixties, and their vision wasn't as good as it had been once, though neither would ever admit it. This time of year, the sun would set quickly, and the thought of them in an area that had many open mines that were nothing more than unmarked holes in the ground made her uneasy. "Let me go with you guys."

Rose's eyes narrowed. "So you can take care of the old folks? No thank you, daughter. Stay here."

"Okay, I admit I'm concerned, but I also need to be up on whatever affects the tribe. I'd like to see the damage for myself. I've never really been to one of the mines."

Rose met her daughter's gaze, then looked at Herman, who shrugged. "All right," Rose said at last.

Ella offered to drive, and was relieved when Herman accepted and tossed her the keys to a late-model SUV parked outside. "My son and I traded vehicles—my green pickup for his SUV. I've always wanted a Jeep, and he had his eye on my pickup's souped-up engine."

It took them nearly two hours to reach an area containing some of the mines in the Carrizo Mountains west of Shiprock. There were few roads—most of the routes to the mines had been recovered by time and the elements, and piñon and juniper trees dotted the rocky slopes of sedimentary rocks that contained the uranium-bearing ores.

Old drilling sites, with settling ponds now dry but still visible, showed where those searching for uranium had drilled to locate the beds of ore and determine their depths. In some places the wood and rusting metal frameworks of mining machinery stood over the vertical shafts, but in other places only graying timbers covered the pits.

Whenever they reached a mine or settling pond, or the remnants of machinery used to hoist ore and miners, they climbed out of the SUV and walked around carefully while Rose took photos.

"Here," Herman said, pointing to a mine face in the side of a sandstone cliff bearing a spray-painted number, now nearly faded away. "This was slated to be reclaimed—meaning that they were supposed to blast the entrance to the mine shaft and seal it up. But once the company shut down, the money for that ran out and the cleanup crews just drove away. I've heard that there are maybe a thousand or more holes in the earth within a twenty-mile radius of here. No one's really sure how many more there are throughout the reservation. The mining company took its records with it and, of course, many of the companies are out of business now. Who knows where their records ended up?"

"The land has to be restored—we need to find harmony again," Rose replied staunchly. They walked to the crest of a low hill, and Rose went a bit farther down the other side, watching a herd of sheep grazing on the contaminated brush growing around the perimeter of a dried-up settling pond. The ground was nearly yellow in places, and looked ill, if such a thing were possible.

Ella watched her mother. Rose wasn't afraid, but she was. She'd heard about radiation contamination, and the last thing she wanted was to linger out here. "There should be some warning signs around this area," Ella said.

"There were at one time, but vandalism and the weather have taken their toll. I recognize this place. A large uranium tailings pile was buried in the earth here. They'd left it for years out in the open beside a mill, and the winds carried it everywhere, even onto nearby school grounds. When the company was finally forced into doing something, they trucked it up here and buried it. Basically, they just poisoned the earth somewhere else."

Ella watched Rose as she sang a brief prayer and offered corn pollen to the four directions. Working together, Ella and Herman helped Rose gather and shape a mound of rocks that would serve as a shrine. Rose then placed a small piece of whiteshell on it, invoking Changing Woman.

In the Navajo Way it was said that the right prayers could

invoke and compel a deity to help overcome an evil. But in this case, not even Changing Woman, who represented the mystery of life springing up from nothing, the deity said to be the last hope of the world, would be able to bless a land so cursed.

Rose shook her head. "Indian grass used to grow here. It fed sheep and people, now there's only tumbleweeds, snakeweed, and foul earth. The land is tired. Once, our people were able to live off the land. The sheep were healthy and the grass tall. When we needed something, we would take a sheep from the corral, sell it or trade it for what we needed, or use the sheep itself for wool and meat. As long as our sheep flourished, we were never poor.

"Now, many of the Plant People are gone. The government has divided our land into parcels, and we can't even graze our livestock the way we were meant to do because the land is apportioned into grazing districts. These days, we end up fighting each other for the land. And this is what we call progress?" Rose shook her head.

"Worst of all, the *Dineh* are forced to graze sheep in areas like this—where the land is poisoned from the chemicals they brought from the earth." Herman pursed his lips, pointing Navajo style to the few head of sheep feeding on the slim pickings fifty feet away. "The animals eat contaminated plants, then the people eat the animals, and eventually we become one with the poison."

"The circle of life has become the circle of death. We poisoned our Mother Earth. We have to make things right again or we'll die along with her."

Rose took another step downhill, when suddenly the earth seemed to shift. Ella lunged forward and pulled her mother away as the earth parted, revealing an old mine shaft that had been covered by a few inches of dirt blown over the broken-down boards at the top.

Rose, still shaking from the near accident, looked at her

daughter as Herman hurried over to help her away. "Now imagine children playing here."

"I think it's time we went back," Ella said, noting that the sun was low on the horizon.

Rose nodded. "I agree. We have to go now if we're going to attend tonight's Chapter House meeting."

Ella remembered last year when her mother had started a near riot at a meeting. All the way back to Shiprock, she tried to talk her mother into calling it a day, but Rose's course was set. Once Rose made a decision, she never backed down. If anything, she picked up steam like a freight train and never deviated from the track. Herman, wisely, said nothing.

Sometime later, Ella parked among the vehicles, mostly pickups, in the gravel parking lot that surrounded a small stucco-and-wood-frame building. The Chapter House was purely functional, and no landscaping other than the surrounding desert was present, unlike most public buildings off the Rez.

People were already gathered by the doors in small groups. She could spot the traditionalist women based on appearance alone. Many of them wore long pleated skirts and velveteen blouses. Silver-and-turquoise jewelry and concha belts were common. The men, both modernists and traditionalists, tended to dress in Western-style jeans, boots, and flannel shirts. A few of the more traditionalist men wore headbands as well, though cowboy hats were most common.

As they climbed out of the SUV, Rose spoke softly to Ella. "Tonight so-called experts will be here to tell us about the different mining techniques we can use to get the uranium out of the ground. They usually end up making wonderful promises about new technology. I wish I could believe them."

"Mom, are you going to start something? Tell me now. I need to prepare myself," Ella said. "Will I need an extra clip of ammunition?"

"I'm here to listen and to share ideas. Nothing more."

For some reason those simple words filled Ella with sheer terror. Rose was on a mission. "Look out world," she said nearly aloud.

They took their turn entering and found chairs toward the back. The meeting got under way after the Pledge of Allegiance. Navajos were very patriotic, something Ella was proud to note.

As she looked around to see who was attending, Ella realized that virtually every folding chair was occupied. The meeting first took care of old business, then a committeeman from their district stood up and took the microphone.

Joe Arviso, a Navajo man in his early fifties, was wearing what was probably his best silver-and-turquoise bolo tie, and it gleamed in the light. "Thank you all for coming. I want to start by saying that no matter how much times have changed, we are all one—as a tribe and as children of the Earth Mother. From that premise we'll go on and talk of how our nation can become self-sufficient. First, I'd like to introduce the noted Anglo scientist, Dr. Shives," he said, mentioning him by name, figuring that this was one name the traditionalists would want to know. "He works as a chemist and consultant for the tribe's coal power plant over by Hogback. He has also agreed to speak at some of our chapter meetings about the newly proposed power plant."

Delbert Shives was dressed up compared to the last time Ella had seen him at the station, when he had brought that hard-nosed Bruno woman. Today he was wearing his narrow, wire-rimmed glasses and a conservative gray suit that didn't quite go with the turquoise bolo tie he'd chosen to wear. He held several pieces of paper, apparently notes, but knew his material, and rarely looked down.

Shives gave them an overview of how the nuclear power plant would work, and how it was different from older, more conventionally designed nuclear plants, like one in Arizona. He kept it simple without dumbing it down, which would have been an insult. The presentation was smooth and flawless. He'd obviously given the talk many times before. She remembered Sergeant Neskahi mentioning it.

When Shives was finished, he looked around the room. "Any questions or comments?"

Rose stood up, and Ella cringed. "You've told us how this new design will work, and why it should be better than previous nuclear power plants. But now give us examples of what could go wrong with it. We need to understand both sides."

Shives looked decidedly uncomfortable. "Quite frankly, pebble bed technology is very safe, and even in the worst-case scenario, there would be no risk of a big radiation leak, explosion, or fire. It's not possible to have a meltdown of the core, as happened in the USSR years ago. But the plant must still be run and managed by people who have experience in these matters. If that happens, the Navajo People will be safe. The tribe might even become economically self-sufficient within a decade, based upon the energy needs predicted for the Southwest and West. But it is absolutely crucial that the tribe hire properly trained people who can be trusted to do the job right."

He took two more questions about the possible financial issues, then Joe Arviso took the podium again. "For what it's worth, I'm pro-NEED. We can't live off the land anymore because there are too many of us here who need to share it. There's just not enough water or good land for all of us to raise sheep or grow corn and alfalfa. We need to find a way to bring jobs in and to pay for our police, for sewers, roads, fire protection, for scholarships, and for all the things that allow us to survive as a people. I believe the nuclear power plant will do that for us."

Rose stood up, and Ella saw everyone's gaze rest on her mother once again. Rose waited a moment before speaking, and that small pause ensured that everyone's attention was on her.

"When the coal mines were first opened here on our land, some of us thought we'd finally have enough money for all our needs. But the coal companies who leased our land gave us only a few cents for every dollar made. They were the ones who made all that money."

Rose took a breath and continued. "There were uranium companies, too. We were promised jobs at the mines in exchange for use of our land, but as it turned out, they couldn't hire everyone who applied. Then, after they poisoned Mother Earth, they left us to cope with mess they'd made. What's worse, the *Dineh* who lived around the mines discovered that their livestock and the ability to grow crops had been taken away from them because the land had become sick and the water poisoned."

She paused, exhaling softly. "I'm not saying that we don't need money, but we have to go slowly and carefully. We all have to get a lot more answers before we agree to anything."

"I can't justify what happened before, none of us can, but we've learned from the past," Arviso said. "New technology has made us wiser. The mining will be done right this time. No one has to be hurt. But let me have Dr. Shives explain."

Shives took the podium again. "There's a safer technology today that can provide most of the uranium needed for such a plant. Basically, you pump in oxygen and sodium bicarbonate in one location through a series of wells, these harmless materials combine with uranium salts deep below, and then you pump out the resulting mixture at a second location farther downslope. Uranium is removed from that mixture at a processing plant. Radioactive materials are prevented from escaping the mining area and ever getting to the surface. The aquifer remains safe as well since it's unnecessary to tap into it. There's a site already under study where very little damage will be required to extract the ore."

"But will we still need Anglo-run companies to be partners with us?" one man asked.

"Probably," Shives said. "It takes technicians and scientists with specialized training to carry out this form of extraction. Currently, the tribe doesn't have qualified workers who can handle such an operation. But increased revenue applied to education may eventually turn that around."

"I agree," Arviso said. "At the beginning there'll be jobs that none of our people are qualified for, so we'll need outside help. But someday, it'll be run solely by the tribe."

Rose took the floor again. "Then one of the things we must make sure of is that we have these training programs in place for our people. Any outside reservation partners must be in the minority and phased out as the project matures. If this project is going to benefit the tribe, *we* must maintain control."

A young woman about Justine's age stood up slowly. "I think we need someone like this woman to oversee those in government," she said, looking at Rose. "She has the courage to stand up and tell it like it is, then offer a solution to the problem."

Joe Arviso nodded somberly.

Ella tried not to cringe. As Rose took a seat, she looked at Ella calmly and smiled.

Ella went to work at seven-thirty the next morning. As she came in through the station's main entrance, Justine walked over from the front desk to meet her. "Margaret Bruno came to see me this morning and asked if we'd decided when to do the workshop. Big Ed came by a few minutes later and told me to talk to you and then schedule something ASAP. The chief remembers Bruno coming over with Delbert Shives the other day, and she's stopped by his office twice since then, reminding him that the Tribal Council has given her and the department a deadline for completing all the sessions. He wants her out of his face."

"I still haven't looked at the folder I was given with their agenda. How long is her workshop?"

"Three hours, and that includes a simulation exercise, apparently. It'll be on paper—role playing I suppose, because the tribe can't afford a training facility."

"Three hours? Is she here now?" Ella asked. "I didn't see her come in."

Justine pointed ahead. Margaret Bruno was talking to Big Ed in his doorway, a crowded place indeed with his tree-trunk torso.

Seeing Ella, Big Ed gestured with his head to get her attention. He then excused himself from the sturdy-looking Anglo woman and quickly ushered Ella into his office. "I want you to get this workshop over and done with. This woman is like a mosquito buzzing around that you can't seem to swat. I don't want nondepartmental people or outside consultants hanging around—no matter how much the council likes her."

"So that's the real problem," Ella observed with a wry smile. Big Ed hated having anything forced on him.

Big Ed shrugged. "Just set a schedule and get it over with. Her next workshop is set up for officers at Window Rock in three days. So if you and the SI team don't want to have to go all the way there, make other arrangements before that. Get her out of our hair for good."

As Ella came out she saw Bruno, wearing a tag ID that said "visitor," sitting in a chair in the waiting area at the end of the hallway. The woman was sipping from a styrofoam cup of coffee. She stood up as she saw Ella emerge and came toward her. "I've been meaning to talk to you again, Investigator Clah, but you've been out in the field every time I've stopped by. I understand how busy your team is, and I was wondering if you'd prefer scheduling three one-hour sessions that you can fit into your schedule, as opposed to trying to set aside one large block of time."

Ella nodded slowly. It would get the job done. At the moment, taking three hours for a workshop they didn't need was a luxury they could ill afford with a murder case pending.

"How about if you give us the first hour right now since you're already here?" Ella suggested. "I can round up my team. Everyone should have checked in by now."

"Sounds like a plan. I can have everything I need set up in five minutes. Where do you want to meet?" Bruno glanced around.

"What kind of facilities do you need?"

"I'm easy." Bruno smiled, obviously trying the Miss Congeniality approach after their awkward first meeting. "Just a room with a door we can close for privacy and enough chairs for your people. I have a small table, a video player, and a dry erase board. An electrical outlet would be nice. If there's an available briefing room, that would do."

"First door on your left down the hall." Ella looked at her watch. "Maybe the desk sergeant can help you bring in your gear while I notify my people."

"I can handle it. Just three trips to my unit . . . car," Bruno said, correcting herself. "I know we didn't hit it off right last time, but I'm used to a low-enthusiasm level from the line officers. I know exactly where you're all coming from. I was a cop once and remember pain-in-the-ass workshops that more than often were just a waste of time."

"Is that what it's going to be?" Ella asked with a thin smile.

"No way. I've been there, done that, and told myself I'd never waste a cop's time with doublespeak or BS games. I promise this won't put you to sleep." Bruno smiled.

Hoping the woman would be true to her word, Ella went to find the others.

———

Twenty minutes later, Ella was busy writing her responses to an imaginary scenario Bruno had given each of her team. The woman, who had a no-nonsense style that was surprisingly refreshing, was quizzing their knowledge and judgment on a hypothetical takeover of a small oil refinery.

"You have five more minutes to come up with a plan of action. And I don't want any bureaucratic communications, command-and-control theory BS. I want to know how you'd implement your plan of action under the given circumstances. Will you negotiate, sit tight and contain, or sneak in a SWAT team to take the perps down and pray you don't all end up toast? Justify your choices. We'll be going over your responses as a group, dissecting and evaluating all the specifics."

Bruno was walking slowly back and forth between Ella, Justine, Ralph Tache, and Sergeant Neskahi, who had reluctantly opted to sit in because he'd served with the unit during better-funded times and knew it was expected of him.

Everyone had come in voicing opposition to a boring, droning lecture emphasizing management theories and legal issues right out of some law enforcement journal. After about ten minutes they'd been pleasantly surprised to find the workshop was a practical one, geared to officers who'd already been on the line during a takeover. None of them would ever forget the events at the power plant last year, and this workshop recalled that crisis.

Justine was working intently, barely touching the cola Bruno had provided each officer. A nice touch, Ella had to admit.

At the end of the hour, Bruno thanked the officers, asked them to turn in a quick evaluation sheet, then sign their names and badge numbers on her attendance list. While they finished up, she started putting away her materials. Nobody was so enthused that they actually stayed around to ask questions, but as

Bruno had promised, it hadn't been boring, and Ella said as much in her evaluation of the session.

Ella said good-bye and walked back to her office, her mind back on the case. Justine joined her a moment later. "At least it wasn't a total waste," Justine said, holding up her cola and taking a sip. "What's next?"

"We're going to go talk to Kee Franklin again," Ella said, leading the way out. "Just so you know, I'm going to be pushing him harder this time. If he's holding anything back, and I think he might be, I want to know. In the past, some parents I've interviewed have tried to protect the memory of their kids by withholding information. I want to make very sure that's not the case now."

"We certainly need more to go on. By the way, I caught up with Officer Muskett in her office and spoke to her about the professor. She wasn't much help. Apparently they've been seeing each other for about three months or so, but she says he doesn't talk much at all about his past. They discuss tribal politics, and NEED, but only in general terms. She says they mostly enjoy each other's company, and have gone fishing together a few times, but mostly hang out at his house or go out for dinner and a movie."

"Did you get the impression Judy would protect him by withholding information?" Ella asked.

"No, Judy came across very professionally to me. I think it's just a case of two lonely people enjoying each other's company, despite their age differences. A low-stress relationship that both of them want to keep that way. I wonder what that's like?" Justine smiled.

"If I ever have one, I'll let you know," Ella responded.

The drive to Farmington from the station was just short of a half hour, and they arrived at Kee Franklin's home less than ten minutes later. By the time Ella and Justine reached the porch, Kee opened the door and invited them in. He was wearing a light sports jacket and dress slacks, and she suddenly wondered if the man even owned a pair of jeans.

"I saw you officers driving up from the kitchen window. I just fixed a pot of coffee. Shall I get you both a cup?"

Ella nodded. Normally she wouldn't have accepted, but right now, keeping it informal and friendly might get her better results.

They sat down in the comfortable hardwood chairs by the kitchen table. Coffee was served in white stoneware cups and saucers. Ella took a sip, noting that the coffee was excellent, and remained quiet until Kee finally sat down across from her and Justine. "This isn't a social visit, I'm certain from your expressions, so tell me how I can help you," he said.

"We're trying to get a better picture of what your son was like, which might give us some insight into what happened that night, and why. I know he was a dedicated police officer, but that's only part of the story. What was he like away from the job? Did you two share the same interests?"

He shook his head. "We really didn't think alike at all except when it came to NEED. I moved to this area about six months ago, when NEED first became an issue. All the buzz had really aroused my interest. My son, who was also against the project, found that we were on the same side of the fence and suggested we join forces. Between his practicality and people skills and my theoretical and scientific knowledge and contacts in the technical world, we were the perfect team. We might not have defeated NEED in the long run, but we would have at least slowed down the momentum long enough to give people on the reservation time to think things through."

Ella leaned forward, elbows on her knees. "Did others also see you as formidable team?"

It took him a beat, but understanding dawned in his eyes. "You mean, could that be the reason he was killed?"

Ella looked at him, but didn't confirm or deny.

Kee leaned back in his chair, apparently lost in thought. The crackling piñon wood log fire in the fireplace was the only sound in the room. It took several moments before he spoke. "I've been approached by NEED proponents on several occasions. They want me to serve as an advisor and consultant, adding credibility and approval to their venture. Although I've turned them down each time, they've never given up. But those people wouldn't have harmed my son to pressure me to change my mind. They would know that the only thing a tactic like that would have gotten them is my undying hatred."

"Did anyone ever try to pressure your son into changing his mind about NEED?" Ella asked.

He shook his head. "He's been in a lot of public debates. But trying to force my son to do anything is almost a guarantee that he'll do exactly the opposite."

Ella nodded. "Have you received any threats because of your stand on the issue?"

"No." He gave her a long, speculative look. "I must say your line of questioning surprises me. I'd understood that my son was killed during a break-in at his mother's garage. Shouldn't you be focusing on finding the thief who murdered him?"

"We're still exploring all the avenues. The truth is that we've been through everything in that warehouse and found absolutely nothing worth stealing in there, and no indication that the killer found what he was looking for and took it with him. Can you think of a reason why someone would believe there was something valuable stored there?"

Ella saw a flash of alarm in his eyes, but it was gone in an instant, making her wonder if she'd really seen it at all. The impression just added fuel to her belief that he was keeping something from them.

"My ex-wife is married to a military officer. She's traveled the world over. If she had something of value she wanted to protect, she'd stick it in a bank safety-deposit box, or a safe, not a dusty garage five miles out of town." He stood up. "Keep working to find answers, please, Investigator Clah. My son's blood was shed, and the department owes him some justice." He paused, then added, "If you don't mind some advice?"

"Go ahead."

"My job for a long time was to predict and explain the behavior of subatomic particles. To do that, I had to search for clues that would reveal the system—or, as those of our tribe would say, the pattern. To find my son's killer, you'll have to find the pattern of action, understand it, and then you'll have the upper hand." ·

Ella smiled and nodded, used to getting advice on police investigations from well-intentioned civilians whose opinions were often derived from their personal philosophies or extracted from something they'd "learned" from TV or the movies. In Dr. Franklin's case, she couldn't help but think of the old series, *Kung Fu*. Or maybe, because he was older, the Chinese detective, Charlie Chan. "My brother, who is a *hataalii*, would agree with you one hundred percent." Ella wondered as soon as she said it that Dr. Franklin might think he was being patronized, but she really didn't really care if he did at the moment. He was getting off the subject, and still wasn't being much help to the investigation.

"A medicine man's view of the world isn't at all unlike my training as a physicist. A Navajo explains the natural world by looking for the relationship between all things and finding the pattern. Physicists, too, search for explanations by identifying the forces, connections, and systems ... patterns, if you will, that weave things together." Dr. Franklin smiled.

"So your field and a traditionalist's view are similar?" Justine's eyebrows rose in surprise.

"Sure. Physics isn't much of a stretch for a Navajo. For one, we have an easier time with the required math. Our people live in eight-sided hogans and count their sheep in base eight arithmetic. That and base two are part of computer science, as opposed to base ten, which is at the heart of conventional American mathematics."

Ella followed him to the door. "Thank you for your time, Professor. If you think of anything that might help us as we investigate, call us right away."

Ella and Justine went back to the car, and as they reached the main road, Justine glanced over at Ella. "I've got an idea. A friend of my sister Jayne, Marie Betone, works at the NEED office. Jayne says Marie's been home all week with a cold. Why don't we pay her a visit?"

"All right." Ella paused. "Did you notice how easily Dr. Franklin went along with the nonburglary motive we suggested? It was as if the same thing had already occurred to him. I can't seem to lose the feeling that he knows more than he's telling us. It didn't take long for him to lead us away from our questioning with his 'advice.' "

"We can't force him to confide in us," Justine said. "So now what?"

"We dig deeper." It was more than a search for justice. This was about restoring harmony. One of their own had been taken, and now she would do whatever it took to restore the balance.

NINE

—— ✕ ✕ ✕ ——

Twenty-five minutes later they arrived at a solitary house at the end of a narrow road surrounded by dried-out alfalfa fields on the eastern outskirts of Shiprock. The fading white paint on the warped wood trim of the old farmhouse was nearly gone, and there were holes approximately waist high in the stucco where it looked like a horse had kicked the wall.

The ground around the building consisted of dead, brownish red tumbleweeds and beaten-down yellow-tipped buffalo grass in random clumps. A dog on a long chain wrapped around a basketball goalpost barked from the backyard as they parked, but didn't bother getting up.

"Marie is a modernist. We don't have to wait for an invitation before approaching the front door," Justine said, reaching for the door handle.

"Have you ever met her?" Ella asked.

"I've seen her once or twice, but like I said, she's Jayne's friend. Jayne knows a lot of people around here. That's why I asked her who might have an insider's view of NEED. She recommended Marie."

"Let's go, then."

Marie met them at the door less than fifteen seconds after Justine knocked, having obviously heard them coming up the dirt lane. She was in her midtwenties and had long black hair that swept down to her waist. She was slim, barely five feet tall, and pale. She had a wool blanket wrapped around herself and held it against her tightly. "Come in. It's cold out there."

Marie gestured for them to take a seat on the couch. "Would you like some tea?" She pointed to a small ceramic pot resting on a wooden trivet on the coffee table. "It's an herbal remedy for colds, but it's pretty good anyway, if you like mint." She sneezed, then reached for a box of tissues.

"I guess I don't have to ask why you're home, huh?" Justine teased, seeing the pile of balled-up, used tissue that filled the wicker trash container.

Marie smiled. "I get a cold once a year. This is it."

"We came to ask you a little bit about the NEED project and the people involved with it," Ella said.

Marie nodded. "Jayne said you'd probably stop by." Marie proceeded to give them a lot of information they already knew about the objectives of NEED. Finally, she added, "The people I work with really care about the tribe. They're well educated and know what they're talking about, and believe they're doing the right thing. At the moment, NEED is trying to recruit more people that the tribe respects and who have some scientific background, but it's not easy. We have scientists and experts, but each one of them has their own opinions, and they're not always pro-NEED."

"Who have they tried to recruit, do you know?" Ella asked.

"George Charley, who heads NEED, has been after Professor Kee Franklin for a long time, but Kee's not interested. Joseph Keeswood, on the other hand, did get involved. Unfortunately, his credentials aren't as impressive as Professor Franklin's."

"I don't know Joseph Keeswood. Who is he?"

"He attended that private Navajo school in Farmington, then spent most of his life off the Rez. But he lives here now. He went to one of those prestigious colleges back East—M.I.T., I think. He's a chemist, and he's well thought of by almost everyone. He works in the same department as Delbert Shives at the power plant."

"Is George Charley a physicist?"

"Technically, yes, but he's only got a bachelor's degree, which wasn't enough to get him hired anywhere doing research. In that field you need at least a master's or Ph.D. But he's always read a lot, and makes a living now by doing freelance writing for different scientific publications."

"That's got to be rough—the uncertainty of his income, I mean," Justine said.

"He has some land on the Rez, and access to water, I heard. He has a few sheep, grows some melons, corn, and alfalfa, and writes his articles. He isn't rich, but he gets by."

"How did he get involved with NEED?" Justine asked.

"He's the one who started it. During the research phase for one of his articles, he learned about some new technology that would make a nuclear power plant possible here. That led him to start the NEED project. His first step was getting investors. After that, he started contacting prominent people here on the Rez—those the *Dineh* trusted."

"Like who, besides the ones you mentioned?" Ella asked.

"People who have degrees in science, like professors at the college and teachers at the high school. He's also gotten some of our medicine men interested, but most of them are afraid of getting publicly involved in something like this."

"Has NEED made any enemies trying to pressure people to join them?" Ella asked.

Marie glared at her. "George *persuades*, he doesn't *pressure* or use strong-arm tactics." She paused for a moment then continued stiffly. "George is an honorable man who believes in what he's doing."

"Do you think he'll keep trying to persuade Kee Franklin?" Ella asked.

"Oh yeah, he never gives up. Besides, George is convinced we really need Dr. Franklin on our side. But the hitch seems to be Dr. Franklin's fear that the new technology isn't as foolproof as people think, and that what happened to our people before can happen again."

"Dr. Franklin's a highly educated man," Justine said. "Maybe his point of view is valid."

She shrugged. "I wish I could tell you more about it, but to be honest, when they argued, I couldn't understand either of them."

"Argued?" Ella asked casually.

"Wednesday Dr. Franklin came to the office, and he and George got into a huge argument."

Ella looked at Justine. That was the day *after* Jason had been murdered.

"They argued about technical stuff?" Justine asked.

"I'm not really sure what started it, or what they were really saying. I came in after lunch, and I heard the argument already going on in George's office. Then Dr. Franklin stormed out. A minute or two later, George left, too, saying he had to go cool off. I didn't see George until the next morning."

"Did you ever see Officer Jason Franklin at the NEED office?"

She shook her head. "Like his father, he was against NEED, but Jason wasn't one of the people we were trying to recruit." She looked at Justine, then back at Ella. "I'm so sorry to hear that he was killed—" She abruptly stopped speaking, her eyes suddenly growing wide. "You don't think George or NEED had anything to do with that, do you? I mean there's *no way*. We didn't even talk to Officer Franklin!"

"Calm down," Ella said. "Our questions are all routine."

"Okay. I guess you're just doing your job." Marie grabbed for a tissue just in time to cover a sneeze. "Look, if you don't have any more questions, I'd really like to excuse myself. My cold tablets are wearing off, as you can tell, and I'm really feeling lousy."

Saying good-bye, Ella walked with Justine back outside to the unit. "That went well, even if she did get a little pissed off at us toward the end."

"She's protective of George Charley," Justine said. "My guess is that she's got a thing for him."

"So let's go over to the NEED office and talk to him next," Ella said.

Rose stood in the lobby of the tribal power plant administrative center, waiting for the public affairs director, an Anglo man in his fifties, to come out and talk to her. She was wearing her turquoise and silver, her long dark velvet skirt, and her best sweater and shawl. Her hair was in a traditional bun, tied up with a silver barrette. Today, she was here to fight for the Plant People—for reclamation of the land.

"Mrs. Destea?" A very tall, balding Hispanic man with a pleasant smile and a bright yellow tie with birds on it came across the small room to greet her. "How can I help you?"

"I understand that you're the one who knows about the land reclamation efforts."

"Yes. My name's Peter Chavez. Please come in," he said, showing her into his office.

Rose sat down, noting that the red-eyed birds painted on the man's tie were Western grebes, a bird common to the nearby lake that provided cooling water for the power plant. She took a deep breath, collecting her thoughts. Chavez seemed pleasant enough, but experience told her that didn't mean he'd cooperate.

She got right to the point. "I know that the power plant and coal mines that supply it with fuel have done some land reclamation. I've seen some of the areas you've worked on."

He nodded enthusiastically. "We're very proud of the areas we've replanted. You can see long stretches of green now, and the lake is home for many species of birds."

"Yes, but I'm more concerned about the ground cover away from the lake and canals. Out of the plants you've used, which have shown the highest rate of survival?"

"Well, not all of our efforts have been equally productive, that's for sure, but we've had great luck with many varieties."

"I'm trying to put together a specific list of the plants that do well in your reclamation areas."

"Are you here, then, to gauge our success rate?" he asked warily.

"In a way. As you know, some of the plants the company planted aren't regional varieties, native to the area, and need fertilizer and lots of water. Most of them quickly dried up and died once they were left on their own. I represent people who are very worried that our native plants are quickly disappearing. We want to make sure that your reclamation efforts include native plants that will be able to survive out here—not just at this particular location, but around the other mining reclamation spots on the reservation as well."

"We strip mine, peeling back layers sometimes hundreds of feet deep, and that does take a toll on the land. But we *are* restoring the affected areas little by little, though it's a long, expensive process."

"I really need to know specifically which native plants you've reintroduced and how those plants have fared. The reason I'm asking is not just to judge the results of your reclamation efforts. The tribe is now considering resuming uranium-mining operations, but the group I represent wants to first reclaim the land past generations damaged. Knowing which plants have done well for you will help us a great deal."

"Uranium mining's impact on the earth, soil, and water table is totally different from anything we do here. You'll need information more specific to that, and I know just who you should speak to. His name is Delbert Shives. He's one of our chemists, but before he came to work for us, he was employed by one of the uranium companies that worked in this area. He stayed with them until the mines and the mills closed down. I'm sure he'll know exactly what impact uranium mining has on the soil and be able to give you accurate information about replanting."

"Then I'll talk to him. Can you set up an appointment?"

"You bet. I'll do it right now."

Rose watched him dialing and had to fight not to smile. Poor Mr. Chavez was very glad to be getting rid of her, if only for the moment. Rose knew that these days people saw her mostly as a troublemaker, but she loved the work she was doing. She was restoring balance, and harmony. She was walking in beauty.

Justine pulled up to a low cinder-block building in what was half-heartedly called downtown Shiprock, just east of the main junction and a short distance from the small Catholic church and the old high school, now a large elementary school.

Years ago the building used to house what was then called a dime store, Ella recalled. The only distinction the old building had now was a hand-lettered and painted wooden sign that read, "NEED." The display windows, never very large to begin with, were covered by blinds.

"Not exactly impressive," Ella commented.

"What did you expect? This is just a rented, temporary site, like a politician's election headquarters."

"Yeah, I know, and from what Marie said, we're dealing with

a man who feels he has a calling to do what he's doing. Those types aren't big on aesthetics generally. It's a form of tunnel vision," she joked quietly.

They walked to the aluminum-and-glass door, also equipped with blinds, and Ella pulled it open. It was pretty dark inside. The fluorescent lights overhead were turned off, and the only illumination in the room came from light leaking between the blinds. Farther in the room, the glow of a desktop computer monitor came from a unit at one of five inexpensive-looking office tables.

About twenty folding chairs were around the tables, and upon the central table rested a large architect's model of the projected facility. A big partition made of painted plywood served to divide what was formerly one big room into two. No one was visible in the room they occupied, but a light was on, visible through the makeshift passageway between rooms.

Justine and Ella exchanged a quick look, and Ella unbuckled the strap of her holster, keeping her hand near it just in case.

"Hello? Is anyone here?"

They heard a loud crash from somewhere inside the next room, and the sound of someone in pain.

Ella drew her weapon and ducked, moving swiftly to a position low to the floor, where she could peer into the next room. Justine backed her up as Ella sneaked a look.

A Navajo man in his thirties, wearing dress slacks and a white shirt but no tie, was lying on the floor rubbing his knee. Beside him was a toppled stepladder and two halves of a long board. Books were scattered all around.

Ella placed her weapon back in its holster, then turned and nodded to Justine, who was moving closer now. "Are you injured?" she asked, approaching him. "Do you need an ambulance?"

The man sat up slowly, looking at her, then Justine, who was now standing in the passageway. "No. I'm okay," he grumbled. "I just tried to put too many books on the shelf."

Ella gave him a hand up, and he gave her a wry smile. "Now that I've undoubtedly impressed both of you gun-toting hopefully police officers, tell me what I can do for you."

Ella laughed. The man had a wonderful smile. Glancing at Justine out of the corner of her eye, she saw that her partner had noticed it, too. Ella pulled out her badge and identified herself and Justine. "We're just here to find out more about NEED for background on a case we're working."

"I'm George Charley," he said, sitting down on one of the folding chairs, and motioning them to do the same. "I'm the spokesperson and founder of the NEED project. I'll help you in any way I can."

Ella sat down at a table next to his, and Justine remained standing where she could see the entrance. "Well, for starters, I understand that you're trying to gather qualified Navajo consultants and experts in related fields to support the NEED goals."

He nodded. "It'll give us even more credibility."

"Tell me how you go about presenting the nuclear power plant concept, and asking for support. I understand that you and Professor Kee Franklin have had some differences, and you haven't been able to convince him that the NEED project will be good for our tribe."

George nodded slowly. "Dr. Franklin understands our vision better than most, but the harm the tribe has been subjected to in the past broke his spirit. He's seen too many deaths to look forward to new and better lives for the Navajos still to come. But I haven't given up on him."

"And what about his son?" Ella asked.

"The police officer who was killed?" Seeing Ella nod, he continued. "I heard about that. But if you're asking me if we tried to recruit him, too, the answer is no. I'd heard that Officer Franklin stood with his father on the NEED issue, and he talked up the issue whenever he got the chance, but that's really all I know about him."

"Did you ever worry that Professor Kee would organize the opposition and defeat your plans for NEED?"

George laughed. "Not at all. But if our opponents ever joined forces, that would only make us work harder. I truly believe that we're in the right on this one. If the NEED project is realized, it'll benefit our tribe for generations."

"How much have you already invested in this?"

"Everything I have—which admittedly isn't much. But Jeffrey Jim and several of our politicians have also invested heavily in us."

"Which politicians?"

George Charley shook his head. "I'm not at liberty to say, at least not yet. But their money has helped us launch our own advertising-informational campaign. We're determined to get the word out and sway as many people as possible. In fact, I'm also scheduled to go one-on-one with George Branch on his radio program."

"Good luck there," Ella said, unable to keep the distaste from her voice.

He smiled. "I don't expect it to be easy, but without the full support of the *Dineh*, we'll never be able to get the funding necessary."

"What can you tell me about Professor Franklin's professional credentials?" Ella asked. She had a feeling that this man knew something he hadn't said, perhaps something connected to that gap in Franklin's background.

George took a deep breath, then let it out slowly. "I know he's highly qualified. He was once the best in his field—though half the stuff he did was classified."

"Then how do you know he was really that good?"

"I don't *know* anything, but it's a guess based on some papers he published. I also completed an internship at Los Alamos in one of their research labs during college, and I heard about Dr. Franklin's reputation then."

"He was also a professor at the college in Los Alamos," Justine said. "He should be very good explaining complicated technology to people who aren't on his level."

George nodded. "As I said, we want him on board, and we're not giving up."

"Do you think he'll eventually join your efforts?" Ella asked.

"He's a highly intelligent man. In comparison to him, all of us here have the IQ of carrots, at least in physics. Sooner or later, he'll see that NEED is going to give the tribe what it has never had before—self-determination."

"Thanks for your time, Mr. Charley," Ella said, then walked back outside, Justine right behind her.

"That's an interesting perspective on Professor Franklin, but it doesn't get us any closer to Jason's killer," Justine said as she climbed back into the vehicle. "In my opinion, the break-in is at the center of this. We both agree that the killer couldn't have known Jason would stop by. If Jason had been marked for murder, the hit could have taken place anywhere else and at less risk to the killer."

Ella nodded. "Jason went into that garage ready to catch a burglar. If I wanted to murder a cop, I'd catch him or her cold, not primed for trouble. I agree with you that the break-in has to be connected. Now we've got to figure out how and why," Ella said.

They were on the way back to the station, which wasn't far, when Ella's cell phone rang. She answered it on the first ring, identifying herself.

"Hey, Special Investigator."

She recognized Harry Ute's voice. They'd been dating for months now, taking things slow. He was a totally different man from the one who'd worked for her as a member of the Special Investigations Unit. "Hey, Deputy," she replied with a smile.

"Deputy Federal Marshal, please. I have an image to protect now."

Ella laughed. "What's up?"

"I'm coming to Farmington to pick up a prisoner to transport for trial in Albuquerque, but I'll be in half a day early. How about dinner?"

"Tonight? If so, it's a date. The Totah Café?"

"Yeah. Sounds good. Seven?"

"That works for me."

Justine smiled at her. "Sure looks like you and Harry have a thing going."

"You've got romance on the brain. First George and Marie, now me and Harry."

"Don't bother to deny it," Justine said nonchalantly. "I can sense things like this."

"Okay, Radar. But we're just dating. Nothing serious."

"Yeah, sure."

A comfortable silence fell between them as they drove to the station. Finally, Justine spoke. "I'm thinking that it's time I expanded my search of the database to include neighboring communities. Maybe there's a burglar prone to violence working our area."

Ella nodded.

"Your brother Clifford now goes over to the Arizona side of the Rez for Sings and to treat patients. Maybe we should ask if he's seen or heard something from other communities in the area."

"Good idea. I'll go pay him a visit while you follow up on the other things."

Once they reached the station, Justine went inside, and Ella walked over to her own vehicle. It had been a while since she'd seen her brother. She was glad for a chance to go visit him—that is, if he was at home today. His patients lived all over the reservation.

En route, she entered Clifford's number on the cell phone, but no one answered. That wasn't unusual, however, because his "practice" had expanded, and he was often gone seeing patients. There was no phone in his medicine hogan either, where he spent most of his time when at home.

Clifford's home was farther down the same road where her mother lived, and in a small canyon. As Ella pulled up, she saw smoke rising from the smoke hole in the medicine hogan's roof. Loretta's car was gone, and no vehicles or horses were around except for Clifford's pickup, but that didn't mean a patient hadn't walked here. People were still used to walking great distances on the Rez all times of the year.

She got out of the SUV, then leaned against the side of the vehicle and waited.

Soon her brother stepped out and waved at her, inviting her to come inside and join him. He was as tall as she, and two years older. As did many Navajo men, Clifford wore jeans and a long-sleeved flannel shirt. He had a simple leather belt with no fancy buckle, and wore a leather medicine pouch at his waist rather than a nine-millimeter handgun as she did. His hair was a bit shorter than hers, however, though it extended below his shoulders, and was confined somewhat by the traditional blue bandanna medicine men often wore.

"I haven't seen you for a while," Clifford said. His voice was warm, but obeying the taboo that forbade a brother and sister to touch, he made no attempt to hug her.

"I've got a crazy work schedule, and Mom's keeping me busy—almost as much as my daughter." Here, out of respect to his traditional beliefs, no names would be used. Names had power and were not to be spoken casually. "How's your wife and son?"

"They're doing fine, and have been going with me on some of

my trips across the mountains into Arizona, school permitting, of course. Very few Navajo men are learning the Sings needed for healing ceremonies in these times, and I'm being called upon more and more. It's necessary, but hard on our home life," Clifford acknowledged. "Can you stay for dinner? My wife and son went into Shiprock for groceries, but there will be plenty to go around when they return."

"Thanks, but I have plans. Maybe some other time." Ella smiled.

Clifford nodded. "So when are you going to tell me why you really stopped by?"

"Angry voices are being raised in conversation everywhere, not just at the Chapter Houses these days. I'm worried about the safety of our mother, who seems to be right in the thick of things. Of course she has a right to do as she pleases, but I sure wish she'd stay in the background more."

"Not *our* mother. There are some out there who'd like to shut her up, you know." Clifford shook his head.

Ella nodded. "I agree, but there's nothing we can do about that. You and I have spoken to her about that more than once, and our words just go in one ear and out the other."

Clifford smiled at the expression their father had used frequently when they were children, then invited her to sit on of the sheepskin rugs placed on the hogan floor. "I'm beginning to understand where you got your spirit of adventure," he said with a grin.

"It's interesting," she admitted. "Mom and I have finally found something we have in common."

He laughed and continued working, crushing some herbs inside a pottery bowl with a piece of deer antler he'd fashioned into a grinder, like a chemist with mortar and pestle. Then his expression grew serious. "I heard about the police officer. Is that another reason why you're here?"

"Mostly," she said with a nod, then told him about the theory that a violent burglar had been the killer. "Have you seen or heard anything during your travels that I can use?"

"No, but if I do, I'll tell you immediately."

"Thanks. You see so many people, so I can really use your help."

"Sure, but the nuclear power plant issue is just about the only thing people talk about these days with unemployment so high. There's a lot of opposition, but I think the ones who support the idea are slowly wearing down the others."

"We need to provide more job opportunities for our people. There's no escaping that," Ella said.

"But I have to tell you, Sister. I sure wish that we could go back to the days when people lived off the land. We would plant corn and melons, and have our sheep. These days the Rez is getting to be like the Anglo world—nothing gets done without cash."

"We can't be herders and farmers. Those days are gone. The lack of rain and the abuse of the land have made certain of that."

"These days we spend more time arguing about the land than we do working with it," he said sadly. "The ones who are really caught in a dead-end situation are the *anaashii*, squatters who live on someone else's land. They have no other place to live, or money to buy land off the Rez. They build a house wherever they can, hoping they don't get kicked off."

"The tribe builds housing, but people still have to pay rent. Our population continues to grow, and without jobs . . ."

"In my opinion, we've lost as much as we've gained the last hundred years."

"No, I don't agree," Ella said. "I like modern conveniences, like TV, electricity, and indoor plumbing with safe drinking water. I would have been miserable watching a flock of sheep, hauling in water, and staying out in the cold all night during lambing season."

"Spoken like a true modernist."

Hearing hoofbeats, she stood up. "That sounds like one of your patients."

"It probably is. I'm expecting someone."

She walked to the entrance and pushed aside the blanket that served as a door. "If you hear anything I should know about concerning NEED, call me. Something tells me I should keep an eye on them."

Seeing a young woman and another older one who looked like her mother riding up on two slender geldings, Clifford waved.

The younger woman waved back, slid off her mount, lifted away the simple bridle, and released the animal to search for grass while she continued on to the hogan. The older lady climbed down more leisurely, then began to tend her horse. Ella returned to her SUV, suspecting the mother was there for reasons of propriety.

Ella had always envied her brother. He had the respect of almost everyone in the Four Corners, and his services, unlike those of a police officer, were always valued and held in high regard. Competent traditional healers were becoming rare on the Navajo Nation, and people came from all over the Rez to see him.

As she drove away, Ella thought about the recent break in tradition she and Clifford had tacitly agreed upon. In the Navajo culture, children growing up had historically been given more attention and guidance from the mother's side of the family, usually from the aunts and uncles.

In their own situation, Clifford had found that the time he'd spent with Dawn was time denied his own son Julian because his wife Loretta's brother lived too far away to give Julian any attention, and she had no sisters. The situation was becoming a strain on their marriage, so Clifford had opted to spend less time with Dawn and more with his son. Dawn, with day school and Jennifer

Clani as a sitter when Ella was gone, hadn't suffered for lack of attention.

Ella returned to the station, hoping for positive news. As she went into her office, Justine was inside, placing a file folder on her desk.

"What's that?"

Justine jumped. "Jeez, make a little noise, will ya, Ella? You nearly gave me a heart attack sneaking up on me like that."

"Next time I'll wear a bell," Ella teased. "So what's in the folder?"

"A detailed report on all the physical evidence we've collected."

"Good." Ella leafed through the pages, then glanced up. "Save me some time. Is there anything new in here I need to know about right now?"

"I've been searching all the police data files in our area, and I've found one burglar who's shown a propensity for violence. The man broke into several homes in Farmington, all owned by single women, and then beat and robbed the residents."

"Rape?"

"No. Just generic violence."

"No commercial places, just private homes?" Ella asked.

Justine nodded. "That's the only suspect that's got an MO that's even close. But he threatens his victims with a knife, not a gun."

"And what about gang activity? Anything on burglaries?"

"There's no known activity in this area of the Rez at the moment, and this crime certainly doesn't fit the MO of any of the gangs in our area. They often wear hats or caps, yes, but not wigs. Tache and Neskahi have been talking to people, but so far, they haven't been able to turn up anything."

"That alone tends to rule out the kids," Ella commented. "They almost always brag about their activities."

"I agree. Right now, I'm following up on the wig. The dark hairs we found didn't come from a cheap model."

"Anything on that?"

"Not yet. I did go to a store in Farmington that sells wigs but they didn't have the type we're looking for—a particular blend of synthetic that's very close to human hair. They suggested I try some mail-order companies."

"Why don't we call it a night and get back to it tomorrow bright and early?"

"Sounds like a plan."

Ella stood up and grabbed her keys from the desk when her cell phone rang. "Uh-oh."

Ella identified herself, then listened to the patch from the field. "I'm on my way," she said after a moment.

Justine was looking at her expectantly. "We're not going home, are we?"

"Not by a long shot. There's been a shooting in the parking lot of the Quick Stop. We're needed over there right now. Billy Redhouse, the tribal councilman, has been shot and killed."

TEN
———✖ ✖ ✖———

Ella parked in front of the Quick Stop, a successful north side business in the Shiprock community that provided convenience store foods and gasoline and diesel fuel to those in a hurry.

Justine and Tache pulled up in the crime-scene van and parked beside her. Ella got out and glanced around. On the north side of the building, away from the lights, she could see a large cream-colored luxury sedan, the driver's side door open and the interior dome light shining. A faint mechanical purr told her that the engine was still running.

As the team got their equipment out, Ella approached carefully, searching the ground for evidence with her flashlight. There were at least three sets of footprints she avoided stepping on, and a large tooled-leather wallet lay on the ground about halfway between the open door and the left front tire. She made sure not to disturb it.

As she reached the car, a new model Lincoln with all the extras, Ella saw the body. The victim's head was resting on the steering wheel, and his arms dangled limply toward the floorboard. There was a gaping, ugly red hole about the size of a dime at the base of his head, but the flow of blood had stopped.

Ella studied the body. Most of the blood from the obviously fatal wound had flowed down the victim's neck onto his collar and beyond. Crouching low, she was able to get into a good enough position to look at the man's face, confirming it was Redhouse. A trickle of blood had flowed from his mouth, but unless that was the exit point, the bullet hadn't passed completely through the skull.

Ella stood up. Redhouse had been attacked while seated in the vehicle. He'd either just gotten in, or had been about to get out. His seat belt wasn't fastened in place, if he'd indeed been wearing it earlier. If the wallet on the ground was his, her guess was that it had been emptied.

As Justine came up Ella stepped back, pointing to the wallet on the ground and the prints. With her team at work, and Carolyn due to arrive shortly, she could do more inside the Quick Stop questioning the clerk.

"I'm going to turn off the engine, okay?" Justine said, holding up her hands, which were now covered with the Navajo standard two pairs of latex gloves.

"Go ahead. I'll check inside the store and see what those inside saw or heard."

Ella went around to the front of the store and saw the clerk, a middle-aged Navajo man with a sizable paunch, pacing back and forth in front of the counter. Philip Cloud, the patrolman who'd called in the report, was standing to one side of him.

As Ella approached, Philip took her aside. "The clerk's name is Duncan Douglas. He says that the perp, a big guy, came into the store wearing a Halloween mask, one of an ugly bald-headed man that covers the entire head. The perp waved a gun, pointing to the cash register. Douglas opened the drawer, and the perp pushed him down on the floor, never saying a word. Douglas said that he grabbed the cash with gloved hands and ran back outside. Douglas stayed down at first because he was too afraid to move, but then he heard a shot. Thinking he'd be next, he grabbed the phone and made the call from beneath the counter."

"Smart cookie."

He nodded. "He didn't come out until he heard a car racing out of the parking lot. Figuring he was safe then, he went to try and take a look at the getaway vehicle. That's when he saw that the councilman had been shot. He ran back inside immediately, called the emergency number and asked for the EMTs."

"I hope you canceled the EMTs," Ella said.

"Yeah, I did. Once I came on the scene, I could see they weren't needed."

Ella looked back at the clerk and glanced around the interior of the Quick Stop. "This place will probably go out of business now. Nobody will come near a place that has been tainted by death. People won't tempt the *chindi*, you know?"

"The owner will probably just move the Quick Stop to another location, maybe down the road. Remember the old fairgrounds? When someone died there during a ceremony they had to relocate the entire facility," Philip recalled. "Do you want me to go out there and help your team?"

"Yeah. Secure the scene and work with Justine," she told Philip. "I'll go interview the clerk and see if he can add anything new."

Duncan held a cup of coffee unsteadily in his hands as Ella drew near. She wasn't sure if it was shock or the lights, but his face looked decidedly gray.

"I'm a police detective," Ella said, holding out her ID. At a time like this, even a modernist might find offense in the use of proper names, and she needed Duncan's complete confidence.

"I know who you are. I've met many of your clan."

She nodded slowly. A long silence stretched out, and Ella leaned back against the wall and waited.

He took a sip of coffee. "I can't believe everything that's happened here tonight," he said, his words tumbling out. "When I heard that shot, I was sure he'd come back in and shoot me, too. But when I heard a car racing out I decided to take a look. That's when I saw the councilman's car. It's easy to recognize—not too many expensive cars like that around here. I ran over, but when I saw him I almost threw up. I came back inside and called for more help."

"You said you heard the robber's car racing away and went outside. Did you get a look at it?"

"I saw the back end, but only for a few seconds. It was a sedan of some kind—a light color, maybe tan because it was darker than the councilman's. It wasn't fancy, whatever it was."

"Did you notice the license plate, any distinguishing marks, like a dent, for example, or a flag fixed to the antennae?"

He considered it silently for several moments. "The license plate was missing, but it had a bumper sticker, if that helps. It was on the right hand side . . . I think."

"What kind of sticker?"

"It was one of the NEED ones that say 'We NEED Clean Air' or something like that. You've seen them. They're everywhere."

Ella nodded. "Now, I want you to remember the robber. What did he look like?"

"He had that mask on, the one I mentioned to the other officer. I never saw his face."

"What about his eyes? Get a color?"

"He had eyes," Duncan said seriously, "but I was really trying not to look directly at him. I was more worried about the gun. It was some kind of automatic, but not chrome or nickel or whatever that silver color is. I don't know pistols very well, but it was not a revolver."

"Was he tall or short?"

"Tall, maybe your height, five-ten or-eleven. And not as slender as you. He was wearing dark slacks and a red plaid flannel shirt. He also had on a pair of animal-skin Western boots, a medium brown color. I know cause I looked down a lot. I didn't want to stare at the gun and end up giving him any ideas."

"I understand. You did fine. But think. You must have seen his eyes. What color were they?" Ella pressed.

Douglas shook his head. "Dark, probably, but I honestly don't know. The only thing I remember was that mask. I would recognize it, for sure."

"The robber was working alone?"

"Only one man came in . . . but there was another person in the car—the driver," he said slowly. "I didn't even think of it until now. I barely saw him, but there *were* two shapes in the front seat."

"Okay. Thanks. You've been really helpful." Ella stepped outside and saw Carolyn, the ME, working under the glare of the crime-scene spotlights just set up.

As Ella went to join her, Carolyn looked up and turned off her tape recorder. The body was on the ground now on a stretcher, inside a body bag.

"He was shot at close range into the base of the skull. I didn't notice the exit wound until I looked inside his mouth. The bullet nicked a tooth on the way out, then entered the dashboard. From the angle, the killer must have been just a few feet away. The victim had his head turned away, maybe reaching for the car keys at the time the shot was fired."

"No struggle?"

"I don't think so. The victim was cooperating, apparently, and may not have even known it was coming."

Ella stared at the body for a second. She didn't know what caliber weapon had been used for this basically execution-style murder, but the MO was similar to the one used by Jason's killer. In her opinion, there was more to this than met the eye.

"Do you need help getting the body into the van?" Ella asked.

"Yeah. Too bad Neskahi isn't here."

Ella smiled. "You have an evil heart, Carolyn."

Carolyn smiled back. "You betcha. And a long memory."

"I'll give you a hand."

Although it was a job Ella detested, she couldn't see giving it to Justine. At the moment her partner was focusing on a footprint some distance away, where the ground was soft enough to leave a good impression. Officer Tache was photographing it while Justine prepared a plaster cast. From the looks of things, they already had more leads to follow on this case than they had on Jason's.

Once the body was put into the rear of the coroner's vehicle and secured, Carolyn climbed into the driver's seat. "I'll call you or fax you a report once I've got something."

After Carolyn left, Ella walked over to Justine. "What have you got?"

"The doc pointed out the trajectory of the bullet, and we spotted a small hole in the wood paneling around the radio. I took a closer look and found the slug resting on a bracket under the dash. It came from a .380. The slug is intact, though the nose is smashed up, but we have a little rifling to work with, like before. It might be from the same weapon that killed our officer. Didn't find a shell casing, though."

"The shooter must have picked it up. Did you check out the wallet on the ground?"

"It's the councilman's, all right. There was no cash inside, just credit cards and photos. I'll be checking it for prints later. There was blood splattered on the outside of the wallet, some of it smeared, so the victim must have brought out the wallet before being shot. He probably kept it in his inside jacket pocket rather than his hip, judging from the size of the thing," Justine said.

"Good work."

"There's also a boot print leading away from the car that showed up real good over there. It's distinctive because there's only one brand that I know of that has a small embossed circle on each heel. I also found a tiny piece of fabric caught in a tumbleweed a few feet away from the body. It's been bagged and tagged."

"Did you find any tread marks that might belong to the perp's car?"

"I know that a vehicle pulled up right behind the councilman's car. I'll be checking into the tread pattern of the tires."

Ella checked her watch, then stepping away so Justine could finish working, dialed the chief, Big Ed, at home. Ella filled him in quickly. "Thought you'd like to be apprised of the situation."

"You bet. I want you to notify the councilman's family personally. That's your next step. I don't need more political fallout than I'm already going to get."

Ella placed her cell phone back on her belt, then joined Justine again. "I'm going to go inform the family, and maybe find out where the councilman stood on the NEED question."

"Do you think there's a connection between this murder and Jason Franklin's?"

"Other than possibly the same weapon being used? Yes—NEED."

Ella headed to her car and, as she walked, called Kevin. She told him what had happened, and asked if, as a fellow tribal councilman, he'd known the victim.

"Yeah. He and his wife live in the Beclabito area. They've only been married a year. She's going to take this very hard."

"Give me a little background on her and Billy."

"Emily, Billy's wife, had been widowed for several years when they met. Billy hired her a few years ago as his assistant. She's great with people and has been a real asset to Billy." There was a pause. "I'm also their attorney. Do you mind if I meet you at their house?"

"No, that's fine. I'll drive slow and meet you there."

Ella followed the directions Kevin had given her to the Red-house home, west of Shiprock and close to the Arizona state line. It was a large stucco-and-frame house on a fenced-in area of rolling hills and piñon-juniper forest.

She parked outside on a graveled driveway leading to a two-car garage, and, as she opened the SUV's door, Kevin pulled up. She waited for him, wrapping her coat tightly around herself, trying to keep warm despite the cold wind blasting against her. It was close to the mountains here, and felt very much like winter at the moment.

"Thanks for letting me come with you," Kevin said. "I think she'll need a friend—anyone would, faced with news like this."

Ella knocked on the door, and within seconds a small, attractive Navajo woman in her forties answered. She was wearing a long, loose skirt made out of corduroy and a simple, off-white wool pullover sweater. Her only jewelry was a strand of silver beads.

Emily Redhouse's features were small and delicate, fitting her frame, and her large eyes a rich, dark brown with a charismatic sparkle that probably had an effect on men.

"Can we sit down?" Ella asked, identifying herself. Kevin just nodded reassuringly at her, having met Mrs. Redhouse before, obviously.

Emily looked at Ella, then at Kevin. Slowly, her smile faded and the light went out of her eyes. "Something's happened, hasn't it?" She led them to the couch. "Is it my husband?"

As Ella delivered the news, the color drained out of Mrs. Redhouse's face, and she seemed to age ten years in an instant. She stared at them for a moment, then sagged back against the couch. "Murdered? But how? And why?"

"We don't know yet. It appears to have started as a robbery. But there could be another reason as well. We've just begun investigating."

Emily shook her head. "I warned my husband not to carry so much money around. Someone must have seen him with his wallet out. Is that what happened?"

"How much money are you talking about?" Ella asked.

"Several hundred, at times. When I saw him pay for something the other day, I was surprised at all the cash. He gave me three hundred dollars right then, and told me that he'd left the checkbook in the car a few times and had decided that carrying cash was safer. I guess it wasn't," she whispered.

"Does anyone else besides you know about your husband's new habit?" Ella wondered.

Kevin looked at her curiously, but didn't speak.

Emily shook her head. "He always keeps his wallet low, below the counter, when taking money out, like when he's in stores. But maybe somebody else noticed. I don't understand any of this," she said, as a tear spilled down her cheek.

All Ella was able to learn from Emily after that was that Billy stopped at the Quick Stop on the way home every evening to pick up a pack of cigarettes, and sometimes a loaf of bread if she needed it. When she got to that point Emily started sobbing, and Kevin offered her his handkerchief.

Excusing herself for the moment, but promising to return later if any more news developed, Ella slipped quietly out the door, leaving Kevin to comfort the woman.

The following morning Ella and her team met in the chief's office. The murder of a councilman was now big news in the Four Corners and across the Rez, and pressure to find the killer had already started coming down on the department.

Ella made a complete report, then waited. "Since the councilman's expensive car wasn't taken, and there were no signs he tried to resist in any way—I don't think this was a simple robbery gone wrong. I think it was a hit. My guess is that the actual store robbery was strictly for show."

"But the victim's wife said he was in the habit of carrying a lot of cash, right?" Ralph Tache asked. "That's a pretty good motive. And if the councilman was used to stopping by at a particular time, well, you couldn't miss spotting that luxury sedan."

"Then the robber would have probably waited for the council-man, instead of hitting the store first, wouldn't he?" Justine said.

"Good point." Ralph nodded.

"I still want to know why the councilman had taken up the habit of carrying so much cash," Big Ed said. "To me, it suggests he'd come into a lot of money he didn't want showing up in a bank account."

Ella nodded. "I'd thought about that. Maybe Redhouse was being bribed. He certainly could afford expensive transportation."

"Or just doing something illegal that was lining his pockets with money," Big Ed added. "Government officials, money under the table . . . it all sounds too familiar. Check into it, Shorty."

Ella nodded. "Will do. What about the murder weapon, Jus-tine?"

"I did a comparison between the bullet that killed Officer Franklin and the one recovered from the councilman's Lincoln. They appear to match, though I can't be one hundred percent sure because the second bullet was really disfigured when it struck metal. But if this was the same shooter, which seems likely, does that mean the first murder was definitely not the result of a bur-glary gone bad?" Justine said.

"There's no way we can say for sure yet, especially if we take into account the amount of money the councilman was carrying. The shooter at the Quick Stop was wearing a mask, and I doubt the councilman recognized who it was. He shouldn't have been killed, unless he refused to give up the car," Ella replied.

"Why would he?" Tache added. "He gave up his wallet, we

know that, because it was already out of his pocket before he was shot. Cars can be replaced, and I'm willing to bet the councilman had insurance."

"Unless the motive is connected to something which required the theft of a particular item from the garage, then, later, the death of the tribal councilman," Ella said. "Remember, also, that two people were involved in the last crime, and there probably wasn't a driver waiting in the car at the first crime. Officer Franklin would have seen him," Ella said.

"I keep thinking of NEED. Remember the bumper sticker?" Justine added. "I've learned the councilman was against it."

The chief rocked back in his chair, as was his habit, then steepled his fingers, lost in thought. "The NEED issue has brought some very high-profile people—some who are for NEED and some against—to the foreground. But I can't really see either side resorting to this kind of violence. We're not dealing with hoods. So keep digging for a motive beyond burglary and robbery. And add the thought of under-the-table money changing hands, and all the reasons for that. Don't leave any stone unturned."

When their meeting concluded, Justine and Tache left, but Big Ed called Ella back. "These two crimes, which are almost certainly connected, are now this department's top priority. Do you need me to pull in anyone and add them to your team temporarily?" Big Ed asked.

"I'd like permission to pull Sergeant Neskahi in on a part-time basis whenever I need him."

"Done."

As Ella walked down the hall toward the station's small forensics lab, her mind was occupied with thoughts about the investigation. She couldn't shake the feeling that she was missing something.

Finding Justine, Ella motioned for her to follow. Once they

were in Ella's office, she closed the door so they could speak freely without risk of being overheard. "I don't want this to get out and damage anyone's reputation needlessly," she explained, "but I want warrants to search through Billy Redhouse's home office *and* his tribal office in Shiprock. Warrants restricted to his papers, computers, and such will do. We want to see if he has any money stashed away, maybe something Emily doesn't or wasn't supposed to know about."

"I'll get on that right now."

As Justine left, Ella sat down at her desk and mentally reviewed all that had happened since Billy Redhouse's murder. Recalling how Kevin had stayed to console Emily Redhouse last night, it occurred to her that she'd never seen him so compassionate or gentle with anyone.

She searched her feelings, trying to figure out if a part of her was jealous because he'd been giving another woman so much attention, but that wasn't it. What she felt was closer to sadness for what might have been. They just weren't right for each other. But to say that she didn't harbor any feelings for the father of her child would have been a lie. Kevin would always hold a special place in her heart.

As the phone rang, her thoughts shifted back to the business at hand.

"It's Blalock," the FBI agent said, needlessly identifying himself. "Have you made any progress on the death of the patrolman?"

"Not really, but it's possible the same shooter also offed Councilman Billy Redhouse. We're looking into that as I speak. How about the background information I asked you for? I'd still like to know more about Professor Franklin's missing years. I know now that he worked on classified projects, and I'm thinking he may have made some enemies back then. Maybe one of those had a long memory and finally got even by killing his son."

"That's thin, Clah."

"Not when you factor NEED into the equation. That's bringing in all our area's scientific talent for one big showdown."

"Okay, I get it. But I'm still working on your request. I'll shake a few more trees and see what falls out. It'll help if you can seal the tie to the Redhouse murder, so let me know, okay?"

"Will do." Ella hung up the phone and went back to see Justine in the lab. "I'm on my way to talk to George Charley again. Maybe I'll get incredibly lucky and find out that his vehicle is a match for the sedan at the crime scene, bumper sticker included. Or, if not, he may be able to tell me which of his NEED supporters has a vehicle like that."

"I think I should go with you. While he's busy answering your questions, I may be able to take a look around."

A short time later they arrived at the NEED office, which was, literally, just down the road. This time, Marie Betone was sitting behind the front desk, and the lights were on. She gave them an icy look as they walked in.

"We need to see George," Ella said.

"Is this official business? He's awfully busy today."

"It's official."

She nodded and went into the adjoining office, closing the door behind her.

Ella smiled ruefully at Justine. "I don't think we're going to win any popularity contests here."

"She's protective of George. Probably thinks we're out to get him."

Before she could reply, Marie came back out. "You may go in. He's cut his conference call short so he can speak with you."

Ella went around her and Justine followed, closing the door behind her and leaving Marie in the other room.

George stood up as they came in, then gestured toward a couple of folding chairs as he sat back behind his cluttered desk.

"We need to ask you a few questions, Mr. Charley. We'll be as brief as possible," Ella began.

"I'm having a lousy day anyway, so don't worry—you can't make it worse." Seeing the questioning looks on their faces, he added, "My car was stolen last night."

"Did you file a report?" Justine asked, "and tell your insurance company?"

He nodded. "Both—a few hours ago. I spent the night with a friend, and I didn't realize my car was missing until then."

"What make and model was it?" Justine asked.

"An '88 Ford Taurus. It's sand-colored. I figured no one would be able to tell when it got dirty that way."

"Any bumper stickers or other identifying marks on it?"

"Marks, no, but it's got a NEED sticker on the rear bumper. The one promoting clean air with nuclear energy. Why do you ask?"

"A tan sedan was used in a vicious crime last night."

He groaned. "Okay—I take it back. You've just made the bad day I was having much worse. What kind of crime?"

"The murder of Tribal Councilman Billy Redhouse."

George sat there with his mouth open for a while, then finally stood and walked to the bottle of antacids on top of the file cabinet, shaking his head.

Ella noted his Western-style boots. They were well made and a golden brown. She really couldn't tell if it was the same brand Justine had identified as having made the distinctive tracks at the crime scene. But the possibility was enough to make her want to take a closer look at George.

"Nice boots," she said.

"Yeah. They're real comfortable—" He glanced at her abruptly. "No, don't tell me. The killer was wearing boots exactly like these—and no one saw his face, but they all remember his boots?"

"Not quite," Ella said with a tiny smile.

"But close—tracks made from boots like yours were found at the crime scene," Justine said.

"Things get better and better for me today, don't they?" he said with an exaggerated sigh. "But listen, I don't want NEED to suffer from any of this, so why don't I save you some time? Take a look around here. When you finish with my office, I'll personally give you a guided tour of my home. I want to be off the suspect list as quickly as possible."

"I can't guarantee anything, but cooperating like this will help," Ella said. "By the way, do you own any firearms?"

"A twenty-two single-shot rifle my father gave me when I was twelve. It's in a closet somewhere at home, I think."

"No pistols?" Ella prodded.

"No. I hate guns, actually. Kind of makes me strange around here, huh?" George said with a shrug.

"Do you have an alibi for last night?"

Finally, he smiled a little and breathed a little sigh. "I was with Marie," he said, motioning toward the other room. "You can ask her. She'll verify it. We were at her place. Her neighbor saw us as well when we pulled in. That's the reason I didn't know my car had been stolen. We went home in her car."

"Your left yours parked here last night, and that's when it was stolen?"

He nodded. "I think someone's trying to frame me, but my guess is that NEED is the real target. They're attempting to discredit the project by discrediting its creator." He stared at the floor, his hands clenching. "You better get started. If you need help finding anything, just let me know." He sat down in a folding chair and leaned back, staring at a color sketch of the proposed nuclear plant tacked up on the wall.

Ella began searching through his file cabinet while Justine checked his computer records.

Two hours later, Ella glanced over at Justine. George was now outside waiting for them to finish. "If George had a connection to Billy Redhouse, it isn't apparent from anything I've seen," she said. "No money was being paid to George directly, and every dollar they spend here seems to be documented. Did you find anything?"

"No, and I think that between us we've looked in every computer file and record in this office. There's that list of NEED opponents and their credentials that you found in his computer, but Redhouse isn't on it—and the file hasn't been altered recently," Justine added.

Justine went to the window. "I know I protested when George asked if he could go outside for some fresh air, but it looks like your instincts were right. He hasn't run off or anything. He's still out there playing the wounded party, and Marie is still with him. They both look like they're freezing."

"It made sense to let him do whatever made him comfortable, especially because he's cooperated completely without asking for a search warrant." Ella glanced around the room lost in thought. "If he's holding back something, I don't know what it could be. Go ahead and motion for them to come back in now. We're pretty much done here."

Justine waved at them, catching their attention, and gestured for them to come inside. A moment later George stepped into the office, but Marie remained in the outer room. "Are you satisfied now that I'm playing it straight with you?"

"Your cooperation says a lot for you," Ella said. "But I have a question for you now." Ella pulled out a printout of the file that had listed all of NEED's known opponents. "How come you didn't include Redhouse in this list? I understand the councilman was against NEED."

He shook his head. "That's not entirely true. Billy was still undecided, which means we had to keep lobbying for his support.

I studied his political record personally, so I understood his tactics. Whenever he was trying to decide on an issue, he'd challenge both sides to convince him that they were right and then hammer them with questions. One weekend he debated with a pro-NEED advocate and went after him with everything he had. Then the following Saturday he did the same thing with someone who's against NEED. Putting both sides on the defensive until he made up his mind was just his way of doing things."

"Do you think Redhouse's support was for sale? Would he have been open to getting some money under the table?" Ella decided to speculate out loud and see where it led.

"No one associated with NEED would have the money to bribe an official. Even if we wanted to do that, we couldn't." George said forcefully. "Every supporter we get has to be convinced, not purchased."

Ella nodded. "Did you know the councilman personally?"

"I only met him once when I went to his office to drop off some pamphlets," George replied.

"Okay, then. We're finished here," Ella said.

"Then come on. Let's finish this. You can follow me home and have a look there, too."

Ella walked out with Justine to the parking lot. Either George Charley was a man with nothing to hide, or he was extremely clever. She toyed with the badger fetish around her neck, but it was nothing more than cool stone at the moment. Knowing that her intuition had never failed her, she searched her feelings but, this time, she found no answers there.

ELEVEN

———— ✖ ✖ ✖ ————

The drive took them east toward the edge of the reservation. North of the river on the mesa above were scattered small homes surrounded by very dry land capable of supporting only a few animals per mile. Most of the corrals they saw, constructed of split wood taken from felled cottonwoods along the bosque, contained a horse or two. Often a half dozen lean-looking goats could be seen scratching for grass along a low spot or within an arroyo.

Hogback was a few miles away when George turned off onto a narrow path to the left, north, and they continued on to a fifty-foot-long single-wide mobile home sitting beneath several elm trees. The branches were bare this time of year, and the ground hard.

Two minutes later they were at the door of the faded blue-and-white trailer, on a wooden step comprised of stacked pallets ingeniously bolted together.

"I rent the place from René Capitan," George said, opening the door after a brief struggle with an uncooperative lock, a worn key, or both. "His family was allotted this land, but they're not interested in raising livestock. He and his wife work at the coal mine that feeds the power plant over there." He pointed toward the tall smokestacks, visible for miles along the river valley and from adjacent mesas.

Ella looked around the small living-room-kitchen-dining area. The place was impeccable, and there was no clutter anywhere, even on the kitchen counter, which held a small built-in microwave and a coffeemaker, There was no sofa, just an easy chair and a long wraparound desk with three computers. Beneath and beside the central computer was a two-drawer file cabinet. A small television sat on a shelf above the window at the front end of the mobile home.

Casually Ella looked along the bookshelves, which began above the desks and continued all the way around and above the door. All the books appeared to be in alphabetical order by title.

"You'll find that I like order and neatness. My files—personal and business—are all alphabetized in that cabinet. Look through anything you want, but put things back the way you found them. I'll go outside."

"You'll freeze," Ella warned, pointing out the window. "It's starting to rain. Make that sleet."

He nodded, then sat down on the easy chair and stretched out his legs, looking down at his boots.

Justine concentrated on the file cabinet while Ella looked along the desk and associated drawers and built-in cabinets above. On the lowest shelf above the left-hand computer, beneath a black stapler, Ella saw a Farmington dry cleaner's ticket dated that day. "This says that pants and a shirt were dropped off to be dry-cleaned this morning."

George came over and stared at the ticket in surprise. "I use that dry cleaners, but I haven't dropped off anything there in a couple of weeks." He paused. "And, more to the point, I didn't put that ticket there." He pointed to a bulletin board attached to a partition serving as a divider between the living room and kitchen areas. "All pending business is tacked up so I see it every time I come in. That way I don't forget."

Ella picked up the ticket by the edges. "Do you mind if I take this? If you're sure it isn't yours, I'd like to examine it for prints. I'm also going to go to the cleaners and see what I can find."

"Knock yourself out," he said.

Ella reached for an evidence bag, placed it inside, then handed it to Justine, who labeled the bag with a permanent marker.

"I want to go with you to the cleaners," George said. "I'm getting a bad feeling about all of this. First you come and tell me that my car may have been used to commit a crime, ask me about a pistol I don't own, and now a claim check comes out of nowhere, dated today, for clothes I'm not having cleaned."

"Could someone you know have planted that ticket on your desk?" Justine asked.

"I have people over all the time, but I haven't been home since yesterday."

"Who else has a key to your place?" Justine asked.

"No one."

"Not even Marie?" Ella asked.

"She doesn't need one. I keep one at the office—" He stopped speaking and cringed. "It's on a hook, but it's not labeled," he added quickly. "And it was there this morning."

"Are you sure?" Ella asked.

He nodded. "If it hadn't been there, I would have noticed. I'm always aware of things that are out of place. It's possible someone took the key before now and made a copy, but I can't imagine that happening without either Marie or me noticing."

Justine went to the front door and checked the doorknob. "It's pretty beat-up," she told Ella. "Someone could have jimmied the lock, but I can't say for sure."

"Do you have any explanation for how the ticket got there?" Ella asked him.

"Someone obviously found a way inside while I was gone." George looked around quickly. "I wonder if anything is missing."

They searched the small mobile home, but there was no sign of a break-in anywhere else, and nothing grabbed Ella's and Justine's interest. George, following behind them, couldn't find anything missing or that didn't belong there.

At long last they left his home and headed to the dry cleaners, George following close behind them in Marie's car.

"There's something really weird going on," Justine said, watching George's car in their rearview mirror. "This guy's not stupid, nor the kind to rob the Quick Stop or kill a councilman for a roll of cash. I know you suspect that it was a hit disguised to look like a robbery, but even so . . ."

"I agree with your instincts. Too many coincidences keep popping up, and that makes me distrust what we're seeing. But we have to follow all the leads and act upon whatever we find."

"To me he seems more like a crusader than a murderer, you know? He's not rich—not by any stretch of the imagination, yet he's apparently willing to put his future on the line to get a power plant built that could really ease the tribe's burden. I think that's admirable."

Ella smiled at her. "Hey, are you getting the hots for this guy?"

"Oh, please." Justine rolled her eyes. "I'm just saying he's got a lot of courage. These days people generally aren't willing to go out on a limb for anything."

"Noted," she said with a nod. "For what it's worth, I think he's being set up. I know what it's like to be framed, so I'm going to cut him all the slack that I can."

When they arrived at Romero Cleaners in Farmington's west side mall, Ella showed the young Hispanic clerk the ticket still inside the evidence bag.

"I remember Mr. Charley's order," he said. "I was in the back, helping Shirley, when he came in. He took one of our pads and made out his own ticket for a shirt and pants. He also scribbled us a note asking that a stain be removed off the shirt. He's a regular, and I recognized his car as it was pulling away, so we took care of it right away." Glancing over Ella's shoulder and seeing George Charley come in, he smiled. "Your shirt and pants are ready. Those bloodstains on the sleeve of the shirt were difficult to get out, but they're gone now."

"Bloodstains?" Ella asked.

The clerk nodded. "We do our own cleaning on-site, and we're very good with stains," he answered. Shifting his attention away from her, he pressed a button and a carousel-type of mechanism brought the shirt and pants right to the clerk. "Oh, and we repaired a small tear on the sleeve, Mr. Charley."

George Charley stepped around Ella and looked at the clothes. "These aren't mine. I admit they look like they're my size, but I don't own dress slacks like those. Nor do I have a wool shirt. Sweaters, yes. Shirts, no."

Ella met the clerk's gaze. "Did either you or Shirley get a glimpse of the person who dropped these off?"

"I just saw Mr. Charley's car pulling out. Shirley never came out of the back at all." He looked at George. "You didn't write the note or leave these clothes?"

George shook his head. "Has anything else been dropped off in my name?"

"Just these slacks and that shirt, that I know of. You sure it wasn't you this morning?" he insisted, puzzled.

"It wasn't me," George assured.

"Do you still have the note with cleaning instructions that you said the customer left here for you?" Ella asked quickly.

The clerk looked at them and shook his head. "No. We added the instructions to our portion of the ticket, then threw the note out."

"Where's your trash?" Justine asked.

"I took it to the outside bin. But the truck has already picked up the trash for today. It's long gone."

George Charley looked at the clerk. "That figures. From now on, if I didn't drop it by personally, don't accept it."

"What would you like us to do with these clothes?"

"Give them to Goodwill, or the Salvation Army. Or throw them away, for all I care," George said.

"I'll take them," Ella corrected, handing the man a business card with her number on it. "If anyone comes in to claim them, just say they're not ready and give us a call."

After taking the pants and shirt from the clerk as evidence, Justine got a quick sample of George's fingerprints. Finally, they headed back to Shiprock.

"I don't think I'm going to be able to get any evidence out of clothing that's been dry-cleaned. But I should be able to match the fabric to what we found at the crime scene—or rule it out altogether."

"Good. I'll also want to know ASAP if there are any prints—in particular, George's—on the claim check. If it's not his ticket, and he's never handled it, then his prints shouldn't be on it. If they are . . ." She shrugged. "Well, that'll mean we're closer to solving both murders."

The remainder of the day went by slowly. Justine was working in the lab. Ralph Tache was conducting a search of the Redhouse home, with Emily looking over his shoulder, and later would be searching Billy Redhouse's office.

Unless something turned up in the lab work or from those searches, like a stash of payoff money, for instance, they still didn't have much to link a particular suspect.

Too restless to sit around catching up on the paperwork while the rest of the team was in the field, Ella decided to check with her brother, Clifford. Maybe he'd heard something that could help her.

Ella had only gone a short distance south from Shiprock when she got the distinct feeling she was being tailed. Looking back in her rearview mirror, she saw nothing suspicious, just an eighteen-wheeler coming up behind her, obviously in a hurry to get to Gallup. The company logo on the spoiler matched a big chain superstore she knew had recently opened in that near-reservation city.

The badger at her neck began to feel hot against her skin. Unwilling to disregard what had always been a reliable warning, she studied the area. There was a vehicle about a quarter mile ahead, and she remembered it having pulled out before her west of the San Juan bridge about five minutes earlier. She considered it for a moment. If someone wanted to keep an eye on her without raising her suspicions, it would have been smart to lead the way and simply keep an eye on the rearview mirror.

Ella decided to go in for a closer look, but she moved slowly so she wouldn't tip off the driver in case her suspicions were right.

Ella gained a little ground, but then lost it again as the vehicle, a light yellow sedan, matched her increased pace. It had New Mexico tags, but she was too far away to read them.

The fact that the driver was keeping his distance sent a warning bell off in her brain. There was a chance it was all coincidental, of course, but she'd acquired a suspicious mind after all her years in law enforcement.

Ella got on the radio and called Dispatch. "This is SI-One, Dispatch. Do we have any officers with a twenty south of Shiprock on 666?"

"Negative, SI One, but we can send a unit from Window Rock, if you need backup. ETA about forty–fifty minutes."

Ella had already suspected she'd be on her own for some time. Window Rock held police headquarters, but it was southwest of her location, just inside the Arizona state line. Having another unit intercept the car ahead of her would be possible, but only if she factored the delay into her plan.

She quickly weighed her choices. The car ahead was exceeding the speed limit slightly, but was the driver really a threat to her, or was she getting paranoid? Taking meager tribal resources and manpower for what could turn out to be nothing more than an eccentric motorist would be pointless. On the other hand, the payoff could be big if it led to the killer or killers.

"Dispatch, send that Window Rock unit to 666 and have the officer inform me when he's in position."

Dispatch confirmed her instructions as Ella slowed her own vehicle, allowing the eighteen-wheeler to overtake and pass her within the next three or so minutes. Once the big truck was ahead of her, she increased speed again and used it as cover to conceal her location.

Ella kept the sedan under surveillance, checking its position whenever the road curved. Within a few minutes, she realized the driver of the sedan had increased his speed to match that of the eighteen-wheeler behind him. Had the driver been keeping an eye on her, he would have let the semi go past him, too.

A little less concerned, she decided to change the rules and see what the driver would do. If it turned out to be nothing, she'd save the unit from Window Rock a wasted trip.

Placing her emergency light on the dash, she accelerated quickly and whipped out around the truck, which slowed immediately, seeing the flashing red light. Moving at pursuit speed, she narrowed the distance between her unit and the sedan.

Instead of running for it, the driver slowed and pulled off onto the shoulder. Ella pulled in behind the sedan, reading the tags. According to the small bumper sticker near the plates, the car was a rental.

She waited, watching the driver, who remained calmly seated behind the wheel while Dispatch confirmed the status of the vehicle, which belonged to a Farmington rental agency.

Ella climbed out of her unit and approached the sedan carefully, her right hand near her handgun, and her left hand holding her identification out so the driver could see her badge in the rearview mirror.

As she got within ten feet of the car, she saw the driver's face in the side mirror. It belonged to that police consultant, Margaret Bruno. Relaxing, she eased her hand away from her weapon.

Bruno stuck her head out the window and looked back at Ella. "Inspector Clah, don't tell me the department has you patrolling the highways, too. Just so you know," she added with an easy smile, "pulling me over is no way to get extra credit in my workshop."

"I saw you just ahead of me back over by Shiprock, and when you stayed on the same route I was following, I got curious," Ella said, still wondering what the woman was doing here, if not trying to keep an eye on her.

"Didn't know it was you, Inspector. Sorry if I sent up those cop antennas of yours, but I can understand why you got concerned. Cops rarely believe in coincidences."

Bruno was smiling, but Ella was still not convinced. "Headed to Gallup, or just sight-seeing?"

"Actually, I'm going to go take a look around Window Rock. I've never been there before, and I have a workshop Wednesday for some officers at the department headquarters."

Ella stepped up closer to the yellow sedan and, as she glanced toward the backseat, saw it was filled with the same boxes and papers Bruno had used at their workshop the other day. On the passenger seat cushion was a semiauto handgun in a holster, a big nine- or ten-millimeter nickel-plated model.

"Smith & Wesson accompany me on all my road trips," Bruno said, noting where Ella was looking. "A woman, alone, on the road . . . Sometimes a cell phone just doesn't provide enough backup to comfort me."

"Better make sure the officers at Window Rock don't discover that weapon by accident. Those out in the field are a bit paranoid nowadays."

"Aren't we all?" Bruno laughed, brushing her shoulder-length blond hair away from her face.

Ella smiled. She knew Bruno was referring to Ella having followed her such a distance. Had Bruno done this just to give her a hard time, or was it really just a coincidence?

"As long as I've got your attention, maybe we should try and set up the next training session?" Ella suggested, realizing that the woman was going to be roaming around the Navajo Nation until her contract was fulfilled. Bruno was dangerous, and seemed like the kind of person who felt the need to prove herself constantly. Maybe that was why she was no longer a cop.

"Well, Wednesday morning is out unless you want to join us in Window Rock?"

"It would take our officers away from the community for too long, how about Tuesday, tomorrow, midmorning or early afternoon?" Ella suggested. "Unless we're on a call, of course."

"Okay. I'll give you a call tomorrow around ten to confirm, and at the same time, let you know where I want us to meet. It'll be a surprise, but don't worry, it's not far from Shiprock."

"Woman of mystery, huh?"

"Right. Got to keep you guessing in order to make the workshops useful. Is that it, Ella? I was thinking of dropping by tribal headquarters and introducing myself to the staff. But it's getting late." Bruno looked down at her watch.

"Go ahead," Ella replied, stepping back.

Ella waited until Bruno pulled out onto the highway again before she walked back to her unit. Just as she climbed inside, she got a radio call from the Window Rock officer who was now in an intercept position farther down the highway.

Grumbling, Ella canceled the call, thanked the officer, and turned around, heading back toward Shiprock.

She arrived beside her brother's hogan thirty minutes later. Moments after she turned off the engine, Clifford stepped out from behind the heavy blanket that served as a door and waved her inside the dark, cozy structure. "If you've come to ask if I have anything for you, unfortunately the answer is no. But I'll continue to try."

"Thanks." She lapsed into a long silence that he didn't interrupt, then finally spoke.

"This case is making me crazy, brother. Usually I can rely on my intuition about people, but when I try these days, I get nothing, or a false alarm."

Clifford exhaled softly. "Maybe you're trying too hard and misinterpreting what you get. You like to analyze things, and logic and feelings are seldom compatible." He paused, weighing his words. "The children in our family have always been given a special gift by the Gods. By treating yours as just part of your training, you've dishonored our Gods and yourself. You have to learn to embrace the fact that you're a Navajo woman." He glanced down at her waist. "You still don't wear your medicine bundle, do you?"

"I've got one."

"It doesn't belong in a drawer." He took one from his belt. "This is mine. It holds a great deal of power. In it is the essence of who we are—as a clan and as a tribe. It has soil from the four sacred mountains, and other collected items. Wear it on your belt, or place it in your pocket, and remember that you are more than a cop. Then you'll walk in beauty."

Ella nodded and accepted it. "Thank you."

Clifford stood. "And keep that fetish around your neck at all times. It will always serve you well."

Ella reached up and touched the stone badger, now cool and comfortable to the touch. "I know."

"I've got to go now, sister. I've got a patient in *Tohatchi* I have to drive over and examine."

"Won't you need a medicine bundle for yourself?"

"I'll make another before I leave. I have everything I'll need already. I never go anywhere without protective charms and a blessing song."

Ella thanked Clifford for his efforts, then walked back out to her unit. Her brother was right. For years, she'd tried to ignore the fact that she was Navajo. She'd even left the reservation in an attempt to forget, wanting no part of what she'd termed superstition.

Now she was back—a little older and a lot wiser, but still trying to figure out exactly where she fit in. She'd embraced more of her culture, but the truth was that a part of her would always belong to the world outside the Rez. Maybe one day, when she found the balance point between being an Anglo-trained cop and a Navajo woman, she'd finally know peace.

As Ella drove back toward the main highway, her cell phone rang. "Hey it's me."

Ella knew Harry's voice as well as she knew her own now. "Hey, yourself, Deputy Marshal. You're in earlier than I expected. Are you in Shiprock already?"

"Close. There was a change of plans because some court

dates were moved up. I'm going to have to head back tonight with the prisoner. Any chance of us getting together for an early dinner?"

"Sure. Where and when do you want to meet?"

"I'm en route right now to the Totah Café. Are you close enough to town to meet me there within the hour?"

"I can make it there in twenty," she said. "Have you noticed that it's never candlelight and roses for us?" she added with a chuckle.

"You into that sort of thing?" There was a pause. "Or is that a stupid question? I just never saw you as the pampered sort."

"The fact that I carry a gun and handcuffs throw you off track?"

"Yes. I mean no. It's just that you've always struck me as totally practical."

"I am. But I'm also a woman—just in case you hadn't noticed."

"I've noticed, I've noticed."

"See you soon."

Ella arrived at the café near the center of Shiprock, just east of the river, a short time later. As she pulled into the parking lot, she saw Harry standing beside his white government-issue sedan.

Seeing her, he walked over, looked around quickly, then stole a kiss as soon as she'd stepped out of the SUV. "Hey, you look really good today. I've missed you."

She smiled at him. "Same here. Why don't we just get jobs with regular hours?"

"It wouldn't work for us. We've been spoiled by the wealth and high prestige that comes with law enforcement."

She laughed out loud. "Oh, yeah. And don't forget the glamour."

Laughing, they walked inside, Harry holding the door open for Ella. As they entered the lobby area, Ella saw Kevin and

Ernest Ration walking away from a table in the dining area and coming in their direction.

Kevin saw her immediately and smiled. Then he saw that Harry was right behind her. Kevin's expression darkened as he came over, Ernest staying an arm's length behind him.

"Ella, how are things with my daughter?" he asked, acknowledging Harry with only a barely perceptible nod.

She would have thought Kevin was above this kind of macho posturing. She glared at him—the kind of look meant to drill holes through a person, but Kevin didn't react. Trust a politician to be immune. "Dawn is fine. Give her a call when you find time."

"I'll call her later this evening when you're back home."

She found his presumptuousness unbelievably irritating, but she tried not to show it. The last thing she wanted to do was create a public scene. "I wouldn't wait too long. She goes to bed early. Now, if you'll excuse us, I'm really hungry tonight." As she stepped around him, a rotund Navajo man in his early fifties came rushing up.

"Hey, Councilman, I want to talk to you." The man, wearing jeans, a white Western shirt, and a black cowboy hat, pushed his way around an old Navajo couple. "You seem to change your mind on where you stand every time an important issue comes up for debate. Are you capable of making a decision and sticking to it, or are we expecting too much?" he called out.

Ella sighed. She and Harry knew Jonas Buck. He was a Tribal Council member from the White Rock area who was always confrontational. Yet, despite his in-your-face-type of attitude, he was all show and not at all violent.

As Ella glanced back at Kevin, she caught the change in Ernest Ration's expression as Buck got close. "Don't worry Ernest. He's—" Before she could warn him off, Ernest sprang forward past Kevin, and, in a lightning move, slammed poor Jonas face-first against the wall.

The embarrassed look on Kevin's face almost made Ella burst out laughing. Ernest's move had taken Kevin by complete surprise. "Let him go," Kevin blurted in a choked voice.

"Sir, he was about to get in your face." Ernest eased up a bit on Buck, and swung him back around, but didn't let go of the hold he had on him.

"It's all right. He wasn't going to do anything. Let him go— now!" Kevin said quickly. "Councilman Buck, I'm terribly sorry. My security man didn't know who you were, and you come on strong sometimes."

Jonas Buck moved away from Ernest quickly, straightening out his clothes and hiking his belt back up beneath his substantial stomach. "Is this the way you show respect to another member of the Tribal Council—hire bullies to beat the snot out of anyone who dares to disagree with you? This isn't some ditch behind the schoolhouse."

"Please accept my apologies. It was simply a mistake."

As Kevin and Jonas walked out the door, Ernest following, Ella and Harry exchanged glances. "If I were Kevin, I'd leash Ernest," Ella said, once the others were outside.

"I didn't see that coming. Man, that's one fast Navajo."

"Yeah. I'd hate to have to try and take him down," Ella answered.

"My money would still be on you," Harry replied. "He's tough, but you're meaner when it comes to a fight."

Ella elbowed him in the ribs. "Your sweet-talking needs work, Deputy."

Ella and Harry went to their favorite booth—one that gave them a view of the river valley to the west, with the mountains framing the horizon, and sat down. Both of them knew the menu by heart, and ordered as soon as the waitress came over.

"Harry, tell me something. Don't you ever find yourself missing the Rez? Family and friends, if not the place itself."

"There's always a trade-off with any job. When I was here, I worked with a good team. You know that—they were your people. But being a deputy marshal gives me the challenges I need, and I get to travel all over the Southwest. One day is always different from another, whether it's transferring a prisoner or tracking down a federal fugitive." He paused, gathering his thoughts. "But it's more than that. I wanted to live outside our borders and see what it was like. Do you realize that this is the first time I've been off the Rez for more than a few weeks at a time?"

"And you want to know if you can make it in the Anglo world, even though it means playing by someone else's rules," Ella said, understanding.

He nodded slowly. "Yeah. You had the opportunity, and proved yourself. Now it's my time."

They ate the meal in comfortable companionship, sometimes talking, often just smiling back and forth. Ella really liked being around Harry, but she was beginning to suspect that wasn't a good thing. She knew Harry liked coming and going as he pleased, with no ties or responsibilities other than to himself.

She, on the other hand, had Dawn to love, raise, and protect. Responsibilities defined her world now more than they ever had.

Harry and she were at two very different stages in their lives. The realization saddened her, because she knew there wasn't anything she could do about it. It was clear that Harry loved his life as much as she did hers.

Later, as they walked out to her SUV, Harry kept the pace deliberately slow. "I wish I could stay and we could be together until morning."

She nodded, but didn't say anything.

"Ella, am I being fair coming to see you like this, then having to leave again after such a short time? Is this enough for you—the way things are right now?"

She took a deep breath then let it out slowly. "What's the alternative?"

Harry met her gaze and shrugged, confirming what she already knew—neither of them was ready to make the compromises that a serious commitment would require.

"Let's just enjoy the time we do spend together, instead of trying to push for something that neither of us is ready for," she said.

"Yeah, I guess you're right." He gave her a quick kiss, then stepped back and smiled, squeezing her hand and looking into her eyes one more time.

As he turned and strode back to his sedan, Ella slipped behind the wheel of the SUV and took a deep breath. It was time to refocus on the job. If she wanted to get home tonight before Dawn went to bed, she'd have to get moving. She still had a lot of work to do before she could call it a day.

TWELVE
✹ ✹ ✹

Ella was nearly at the station when she got a call from Justine on the radio. They switched to a unit-to-unit frequency.

"What have you got for me?" Ella asked. "Did you get anything from the clothes left at the cleaners?"

"The shirt is the same one worn by the person who killed Redhouse. The swatch of fabric we found fit the missing section in the wool shirt perfectly."

"Did you get any DNA?"

"No, The dry cleaning pretty much ruined any chances of that. All we can prove is that it was blood."

"Keep digging." Ella dialed Wilson at home, and there was a click in the speaker that told her that his calls were being forwarded elsewhere. A few seconds later, he picked up.

"I know it's late, Wilson, but before I pack it in, I'd like to talk to you about Kee Franklin."

"I'm still on campus, in my office. I'm trying to finish grading some lab notebooks before I quit for the day. Why don't you come here?"

"I'm on my way."

Ella was halfway to the college when her cell phone rang again. It was Officer Tache.

"Hey, Ella, I just started searching the councilman's office, and guess what I found?"

"A million dollars in cash and a blackmail note?" Ella replied tongue-in-cheek.

"Actually, you're on the right track, boss." Ralph chuckled. "There were two thousand six hundred dollars in cash in a paper bag at the back of a locked file cabinet."

"Any idea what the money was doing there?"

"No. There wasn't anything like this at the Redhouse home, unless there's a stash buried in the yard somewhere. The office staff couldn't account for it, and the widow took a look at their checkbook and called the bank, but she still has no idea where the money came from."

"You've got it locked up now, right?"

"In the evidence locker for now. Justine is going to check the bills for fingerprints later, just in case we get lucky and can link it to a suspect," Tache added.

"There's always a chance. Anything else suspicious?"

"I also took possession of his appointment book, desk calendar, and the like. We can use it to backtrack where the councilman has been the past several weeks. Maybe we can find out who was gunning for him."

"Or paying him off. Good work, Ralph. Why don't you call it a day?"

"Okay, it's a day. Catch you tomorrow, boss." Ralph ended the call.

Ella set the phone down and slowed her vehicle. Ahead was the turnoff to the college. A few minutes later, she ran into Justine as she entered the science building. "Hey, partner. Are you officially off duty now?"

"Yeah." Justine yawned. "I was too tired to concentrate anymore. I figured I'd come by here and see if I could lure Wilson away from his work so we could spend some time together. But if you need to talk to him alone, I can wait out in the hall."

"No, come on in with me. I need to question him about Professor Franklin, and you'll need to hear this, too. I suppose you know about what Ralph Tache found at Redhouse's office."

"Yeah. The councilman had a cash stash his widow says she didn't know anything about. Interesting twist. I'll be checking the bills for fingerprints tomorrow."

By then they'd reached Wilson's office. Ella knocked as she opened his door, but he wasn't there. His papers were scattered all over the desk and his reading glasses were on the table, but Wilson was nowhere to be seen.

"Wilson?" Justine glanced around. "It's not like him to leave his office door unlocked when he's not here."

Justine tried the door leading to the department's storage room, which was adjacent to his office. The door opened easily, and she glanced inside. The lights were off, so she reached beside the door and turned on the switches. The large storeroom was in chaos. Some cardboard boxes had toppled to the ground, and science workbooks, texts, and papers lay scattered on the floor along two of the aisles of tall metal shelves. "What the hell?" Justine mumbled.

Before Ella could speak, they both heard a soft moan somewhere beneath the boxes, and Justine spotted a blue blazer on the floor among the chaos. It was moving slightly. "There he is!"

Ella and Justine quickly began to push the boxes aside so they could get to the figure on the floor, but by the time they reached him, Wilson was already sitting up.

"What happened? Did you climb up on a shelf and manage to

topple all this stuff?" Justine asked, placing her hand on his shoulder.

"I wish. There was an intruder in here. I came in to get some supplies, and saw someone walking around in the dark, shining a flashlight. When I reached for the light switch, I saw a flash and heard a pop. At first, the sound didn't register as anything familiar, but then there was another pop, and a sting at the back of my head, like I was being hit by a chunk of the wall. That's when I realized he was shooting at me, using some kind of silencer. I dived to the floor, using a shelf full of books and papers for cover, and that's when he pushed the textbook boxes down on me from the other side. One hit me in the head." He touched the right side of his head and winced.

"I'll call for an ambulance," Justine said.

"No, I'm fine." He reached around to the back of his head, and brought out a small piece of what looked to be concrete. "Must be a chunk of a wall pillar that the second bullet chipped off. That's what stung me, I bet." Wilson stood up, waving away their help. "I'm just lucky he ran off instead of coming around to finish me off."

"How long ago did this happen?" Justine asked.

Wilson looked at his watch. "About five minutes, give or take. I looked up at the clock in my office just before I came into the storeroom. You didn't pass anyone on the way in here, did you?"

Justine and Ella exchanged glances, and both shook their heads.

As they stepped out of the storeroom into his office, Wilson glanced around the small room. "Well, I'm not sure what else he took, but my briefcase *was* right there," he said, pointing to the empty spot on his desk next to his glasses.

"Did you ever get a look at the guy?" Ella asked.

"He had the flashlight, not me, but from the light coming in through my open door, I got the impression he was tall," he said, thinking. "And he had dark hair."

"Was it short dark hair, or long?"

"Shaggy, but not nearly as long as yours," he said, looking at Ella's cut, which swept a little past her shoulders. "And especially not yours," he smiled at Justine, who had long, straight black hair nearly to her waist.

"But you're sure it was a man?"

"Yes, a man." Wilson stopped and shook his head. "Come to think of it, I don't know why I'm saying that. I never got that close a look. I couldn't make out facial features, and the person had on a long jacket and pants. A woman's shape wouldn't have been so distinctive in those clothes. But I guess that depends on the woman." His expression was thoughtful, and Ella knew he wasn't trying to be cute or sexist.

"What could this person have wanted from the storage room?" Justine asked.

"Maybe some electronic equipment like a computer, a precise scale, or some of the chemicals we keep on hand. A person operating a clandestine meth lab might be on the prowl for things like that," he said.

"If it was a druggie, that would explain why the perp was carrying a gun. But the fact that the person took a couple of shots at you with a silencer-equipped pistol changes things. This falls under our jurisdiction now. I'm going to have my people go through the storeroom," Ella said.

"You'll have a hard time sorting out all the fingerprints and partials here. Faculty and graduate students working as aides come through there all the time," Wilson reminded her.

"We'll start with the boxes he or she buried you under. I also want to have those bullets back, wherever they ended up. We may be able to link them to a specific firearm," Ella said. "Once we're done, we'll want you to determine what, if anything, is missing," Ella added.

Justine was already on the cell phone calling Officer Tache.

From the expression on Justine's face, Ella could see that this case was now personal to her. Although Justine didn't like it when Wilson was protective of her, she was definitely protective of him.

"Tache is on his way over," Justine told Ella. "He has to pass by the station on the way, so he'll pick up the crime-scene van." She walked back into the storeroom and checked the wall Wilson had indicated earlier. A hole in the plaster wallboard showed the entry point of one bullet. The second had struck a concrete structural beam, breaking off a small chunk, then ricocheted somewhere else.

Ella looked around the storeroom, trying to determine the perp's point of entry, and found the door to the next office open a few inches. "This doorknob was twisted off with a pipe wrench or something like that. I bet the door to the hall is in the same condition."

Justine came over for a look. Ella knew bolt cutters had been used to cut the lock on the garage door where Jason Franklin had been killed, but that didn't mean this couldn't have been the same perp. Both methods of entry were common among burglars. The look on Justine's face told Ella that they were both thinking the same thing.

"Maybe we'll find a bullet, and it'll turn out to match the others," Ella said. "Look for shell casings, too."

It took two hours to go through the crowded supply room, moving papers and fallen items around to gain access, and at the same time trying to make sure they didn't miss any potential evidence. Campus security had noticed the activity and one of the guards had come to take a look. Ella learned that nobody had heard the shot, which wasn't surprising considering the storeroom was an interior room, the guard had been across campus, and, of course, a silencer had been used. No one had noticed any suspicious vehicles on campus either.

Finally, Justine came up to where Ella was seated in the storeroom at a borrowed student desk, writing her report. "I managed to locate one of the bullets, but it's mushroomed pretty bad. All I know for sure is that it's a .380 hollow point. I found both shell casings. I guess the shooter didn't want to hang around and look for them in the dark this time."

"The shell casings are a first. Is the bullet the same make as the two from the murders?" Ella asked.

"Looks like it. But we'll never be able to tie this round to a particular weapon in court." Justine shook her head.

"What about the other round, the one that ricocheted off the pillar?"

Justine rolled her eyes. "I've only found pieces of it so far. It broke up pretty bad."

"So we can probably write that one off. What else do you have?" Ella asked.

"I've got a lot of prints, and some dark hairs I recovered from the floor, but it's going to take me a while to sort it all out."

"I know. At least the storeroom had been swept earlier this evening. Hopefully the hairs belong to the perp and not staff, student, or you or me. We already know they didn't come from Wilson's head. His are much shorter." Ella glanced at her watch. "It's eleven o'clock. We have to get some sleep if we want to get a good start in the morning. Wilson looked a little unsteady to me last time I checked him in his office, so you might want to try and talk him into going to the emergency room. I'll make sure campus security keeps everyone out of this place, then I'll be heading home. Ask Ralph to start putting things away, then call it a night one more time."

Ella went to meet Wilson, who was still in his office checking inventory sheets. "Don't worry about that tonight, security is calling in another guard to remain in the building. You can get to it tomorrow, then make sure you call and tell me what was taken, okay?"

"Sure. In the morning, I can have a couple of student aides help me, and it'll go faster."

Justine came up next, and, after a brief argument about the hospital, Wilson reluctantly agreed he was still a little light-headed. He and Justine left for the hospital in her unit.

Once Ella made sure campus security knew what was necessary to protect the scene, she headed home.

Her cell phone rang at six the following morning. Ella stirred, and with a groan, reached toward her nightstand. "Ella Clah," she grumbled, pressing the answer button.

"It's Justine, cuz. I'm sorry to wake you up at this hour, but there's something I thought you should know right away. I just arrived at Wilson's home. Since the doctors insisted he spend the night at the hospital for observation, I offered to bring him a change of clothing this morning. But it looks like someone broke in sometime after he left for school yesterday. They've really trashed the place."

"Call Ralph Tache. I'll be there in fifteen. Don't bother calling Wilson yet. He probably needs his sleep. Later, we'll find out when he was home last and try to narrow the time the perp broke in."

Unwilling to leave without giving her daughter a quick kiss, Ella stepped by her child's room and peered in. Dawn's long black hair fanned out on her pillow, and she was sleeping, curled up on her side hugging a stuffed rabbit. She looked peaceful and content. Envying the dreams of a child, Ella gave Dawn a soft kiss, then grabbed her coat from the living room closet and rushed out the door.

She was nearly three-quarters of the way to Wilson's home when her cell phone, now with a fresh battery inserted, rang again. Ella identified herself.

"This is Albert Washburn, Officer Clah. You came by my mother's trailer once. Do you remember me?"

"Of course I do. What's going on?"

"I have something that might help you catch the guy who capped Officer Franklin."

"I'm listening." The teenager had her complete attention now.

"A friend of mine told me that on his way to and from work, he drives past the garage where Officer Franklin was killed. He's a janitor at the medical center in Farmington. He was on his way home a few days before the officer was killed, around ten-thirty at night, when he saw someone with a flashlight going around the corner of the building. He didn't know if it was Officer Franklin or not, though."

"Did your friend mention seeing a vehicle?"

"I asked him that. He said no. It could have been around back, I guess."

"Thanks, Albert."

"If I hear anything else, I'll let you know." He hung up before she could get the name of the witness.

Jason Franklin had helped Albert, and it was possible Albert simply wanted to help her find the killer as a way of repaying his debt. Or he might have been trying to divert her attention from his own possible involvement. Informants had been known to set up an officer when they started getting heat from their criminal associates. She just didn't know enough about Albert's character to decide one way or another.

Looking back at her cell phone, she saw that the caller ID listed "caller unknown." Albert hadn't phoned from home, obviously, so trying to return the call would be a waste of time. She made a note to call the Washburn home later. Stopping by to see Albert might get him in trouble with his contacts, if he was legit.

Moments later, Ella parked in front of Wilson's new three-bedroom home in a rapidly expanding neighborhood. The small residential area had a waiting list of professors and staff, and Wilson had said that he'd been really lucky to get one of the homes.

Justine, who had been holding back on a permanent commitment with Wilson, had mentioned her concern that he was sounding more "domestic" all the time. The fact that he'd settled into a home large enough for a family had made her even more uneasy.

Ella walked up the small path leading to the door. Lights were on in several rooms, and over the front porch. Before she got to the steps Justine opened the door. "Wait till you see this place."

As Ella stepped through the doorway she was amazed at how thorough the burglar had been. The closets had been emptied and every drawer had been pulled out, their contents dumped in a pile in the middle of the floor. The bookshelves in the den were bare. About three hundred books were scattered randomly around the tiled floor as if someone had picked each one up and searched through the pages.

"The back rooms are in much the same shape. Even the laundry basket was dumped out, and the kitchen cupboards are open. Whoever did this took their time."

Ella put on a pair of plastic gloves and followed Justine into the kitchen, noting that items from the refrigerator freezer were sitting on the counter, forming pools of water as they melted. "This wasn't a burglary. Someone came in looking for something specifically."

"I haven't started to process the scene yet, but lifting prints here might actually do some good as opposed to the large number we've found in the college storeroom and have yet to sort out."

"We have to check for prints just in case, but my guess is that the intruder wore gloves. This was a professional search," Ella commented thoughtfully. "It was almost certainly the same person that hit the storeroom, or someone working with him. And the use of a silencer in the storeroom means we're dealing with a pro who's willing to kill anyone who threatens him or gets in his way."

"But what could they be searching for?" Justine asked.

"We'll have to ask Wilson later and see if he has any ideas. Meanwhile, we can check for the obvious, like missing guns or electronic gear."

Officer Ralph Tache arrived several minutes later looking a bit bleary-eyed, but awake. "I need coffee . . . and a raise. Okay, raised doughnuts, if the tribe is really as broke as they say. But they have to be the apple cinnamon kind. I'd forgive a lot for those."

"I'll keep that in mind," Ella said, chuckling. "Doughnuts we can spring for, but as for money—well, I wouldn't count on it unless the tribe starts printing twenties and fifties. Or they start giving finder's fees for money found in paper bags in the back of file cabinets."

Time passed quickly as they worked, though processing of the interior was painstaking work. Sometime later, Justine emerged from the den and met Ella, who was dusting for prints around the back door.

"Wilson's hunting rifle, ammo, and his computer are gone. I know where they're supposed to be."

"Have you found anything that links the break-in at the storeroom to what happened here?"

"There would be work-related files in his home computer and papers in his stolen briefcase. That could suggest the thief was looking for records or documents. We can check with Wilson on that angle. As far as physical evidence, the front lock was twisted off in much the same way the storeroom door was, except that Wilson had a dead bolt so it needed to be kicked in as well. I've also found some black hairs, but they're my length, so my guess is that they're mine. I'll let you know more later."

"Okay. While you process the evidence, I'm going to go speak to Wilson. Everyone starts early in the hospital, so they've probably woken him up by now. If you find out anything we can use, call me right away."

"There's one thing . . ." Justine said slowly. "I've been talking to people about the dead councilman, I didn't get the impression that anyone thought he was dirty, though with the discovery of that hidden cash, maybe he was just good at keeping a secret. On the other hand, there's a lot of gossip about Emily, his wife."

"What kind of gossip?"

"I'm told she has a way with men—the ability to wrap them around her little finger is the cliché I'm thinking of, I guess. She's good-looking, charming, and can apparently make men act real stupid around her. Nobody has ever suggested she's been unfaithful, but she certainly gets a lot of attention."

"I could see circumstances where she could be a real guy charmer, all right."

"I met her once," Justine said. "It was at a barbecue the councilman sponsored before the last election. You know Wilson can't pass up free food."

Ella laughed. On the Rez, few ever people did. That was why it was such an effective way to reach the voters.

"Maybe someone wanted to make sure Mrs. Redhouse was a widow again," Justine speculated. "Someone waiting to step in and comfort the grieving woman. Men have killed for love before, and there could be a disturbed guy out there who may have mistaken a wink and a smile from Emily for a lot more than a casual gesture. But I realize that doesn't have anything to do with NEED, the break-ins, or the unexplained cash he had around."

"Jealously and obsession are very good motives for murder. Let's keep digging. While you're working up the evidence, I'll pay my brother a visit. Clifford may know if there was another suitor or two before or after Emily married the councilman."

"Could this person with the three-eighty who killed Officer Franklin have decided to kill Redhouse for an unrelated reason since he'd already committed one murder?" Justine asked.

"Sounds unlikely, especially when we consider that break-ins or robberies are associated with all the recent shootings. And then there's the unexplained cash." Ella took a deep breath. "But there has got to be a common link somewhere between all the crimes. The use of the same weapon makes that clear. Let's see if we can find out what it is."

"Better get back to work, then. Oh geez, I almost forgot. The reason I came here in the first place was to get Wilson some clean clothes. If you're going to the hospital, will you take some to him?"

"Sure."

Ella headed back into Wilson's bedroom with Justine and waited while she picked out a sweater, jeans, and clean underwear from the piles of clothes that had been dumped on the floor. As Ella reached for an athletic bag to carry them in, she saw a photo of Wilson, Clifford, and her taken back when they'd been in high school more than a decade ago. The boys were wearing letterman jackets, and she was wearing a red-and-silver Lady Chieftains sweatshirt.

Memories poured into her mind unbidden. It had been so long ago . . . Back then she'd wanted nothing more than to just leave the reservation and never come back. Now her life, and the things that gave her the most comfort, were all here. It had taken a long time for her to find home again.

Ella placed the photo on the dresser. Wilson held on to his memories just as she did. To know yourself in the present, you had to know who you'd been in the past.

Five minutes later, after telling Justine that they might be taking Bruno's training workshop later in the morning if there were no new complications, Ella was on her way to the hospital. She intended to press Wilson for answers. He had to know something that could bring all these crimes into focus.

Ella arrived a short while later, parked, and went inside. She stopped at the front desk, intending to get Wilson's room number, when she saw him walking in her direction from the main hall. "Where the heck's Justine? I've been ready to leave since sunup."

Ella quickly filled him on everything that had happened and saw the shock register on his face.

"You should have called and had somebody wake me up, Ella." Ella started to argue, but he held up a hand. "Let's just get out of here. You owe me a ride home."

"Fine. We'll talk on the way." Ella allowed the silence to stretch out as they walked to her Jeep, giving Wilson a chance to collect his thoughts. Finally, once they were well under way, she asked, "What do you have in your possession that would compel someone to search the storeroom where you work, steal your briefcase from your office, then ransack your home looking for it?"

Wilson said nothing, his eyebrows knitting together as he considered it. "I have no idea. That's the truth. And I can tell you this—if I had something of value, I certainly wouldn't put it in the storeroom. Too many people have access to it."

"This person seems to be searching for something that's work-related—papers or documents or files on your computer. But wait. Maybe I'm off base on that. There's the loss of your hunting rifle to consider."

"My rifle?" He groaned. "Don't you get it? That rifle is an almost irresistible temptation! Had I broken into a home and had seen that gun, I would have taken it, no matter what I'd originally gone in there to steal. It's a Savage Model 99 lever action in .243 caliber. It's smooth and sweet, right on the money at two hundred yards over open sights, and fits great on my pickup gun rack. That's one rifle I'm really gonna miss," he said with a sigh.

"Okay, I'll get the serial number from you later. But let's get back to what I was asking. What do you have that someone might want bad enough to risk killing somebody over? Something that is written down—like a document or something, I'd guess. We're dealing with a professional thief, or somebody into something even badder than that because it probably includes killing Officer Franklin and the councilman. And while you're thinking, add this to the equation. What books, documents, or whatever do you own that might have somehow ended up being stored in the garage where the patrolman was killed?"

"Nothing that I put there, that's for sure," he answered quickly. "I know Professor Franklin, but have never met his ex-wife, who, if I'm correct, owns the garage. I've never had any dealings with anybody connected with that family other than the professor."

"But Professor Franklin stored some of his boxes of stuff there . . ." she said thoughtfully. "Did he also store anything in your storeroom, or give you anything to keep for him?"

"He doesn't use the storeroom. You've seen that place. It's barely large enough for the staff. And as far as him giving me anything—I think he handed me the notes to his lecture once, but I filed them away somewhere. It wasn't a big deal, you know? He's not exactly an integral part of my curriculum except as a role model for my students. What makes you ask? And what's the tie-in to the garage where the professor's son was killed?"

"Nothing I can think of, except it seems like the same person has been responsible for all this. I'm just trying to find connections and a motive."

The rest of the trip Wilson quizzed her on the condition of his home, and she did her best to describe what he'd soon be viewing.

When they arrived Ella walked with him to the door. Then, as they stepped inside, she heard Wilson expel his breath loudly.

"Why the hell would anyone do this to me? This is nuts." He stopped and looked at her. "That's your answer. You're dealing with a crazy," he said.

Ella waited until Wilson had checked for missing items, but it had been as Justine had reported. Cautioning him not to overdo it, Ella recommended that he stay elsewhere for a few days. Wilson refused the suggestion, but at least agreed to pay one of his student aides to come over and help him restore order to his home.

Ella and Justine returned to the station, and Ella had just sat down on her office chair when Sergeant Neskahi appeared at the door. "Ella, that training woman, Bruno, called about a half hour ago, and left this number for you to call back. She said it was about today's workshop session."

"Thanks, Joseph." Ella took the note with the number he handed her. "Hang around a second, and I'll be able to let you know if the session is on for today."

Ella punched in the cell phone number, one she recognized already, and the ex-policewoman answered by the second ring. "Bruno," the woman answered cryptically.

Ella listened to the instructions Bruno gave her, then disconnected the call and looked up at the sergeant. "The training exercise is on for ten-thirty this morning. She wants us to pick up a note that she's leaving for us at the security office in the Navajo power plant, and asked us to come together, and not be late. But she wouldn't say what the training topic was."

"Any ideas?" Neskahi asked.

"No, but obviously it must have something to do with the power plant itself. My guess is that it's some sort of a combined forces drill, our team and plant security." She looked at her watch. "It's less than a fifteen-minute trip if we make good time, so maybe we should get the team together now, spend a few minutes trying to figure out what she may be planning, then ride over in the crime-scene van."

Neskahi nodded. "A good officer goes over the possibilities and knows his options ahead of time. I'll go find Tache. Is Justine back in the lab?"

186 ✻ AIMÉE & DAVID THURLO

Ella nodded. "I'll tell the chief where we'll be, then go by the lab and get her. We'll meet at the van in five."

In four minutes Ella and Justine arrived in the small fenced-in area where the crime-scene van, a small RV with special facilities, was parked. She and Justine climbed into the vehicle to join the two men, already seated up front.

"What is *yálti'í nééz* cooking up for us today, Ella?" Officer Tache asked as he started the engine. "The sergeant said it might be some kind of combined drill, maybe like a takeover or hostage situation."

Ella laughed, noting the Navajo term, a kind of nickname, really, that meant "tall talker." It certainly applied to Margaret Bruno.

"Anybody read through their green training folders yet?" Justine asked, looking at their blank faces. "That's what I thought. Well, I did, and one of the sessions she suggested was meant to evaluate our response to a simulated act of sabotage or violence from an individual who goes postal. My guess is that Bruno is going to set up some sort of imaginary threat that we'll have to counter."

"Sounds reasonable to me." Ella looked around at their faces from her small jump seat in the back beside Justine. "Any more thoughts?"

"I think she'll manipulate events to make sure we lose," Ralph said. "Bruno struck me as an ex-cop with an ego, maybe a little excess self-esteem. We did pretty well last time on the paper exercises, and already knew the answers to most of her questions. She'll want to remind us this time that she's the 'expert,' if only to justify her training sessions," he said, then after a brief pause, added, "I think she's competing with you, Ella. She wants us to see her as the authority figure, but you have a hell of a lot more experience than she does and already know the jargon."

"I agree with Ralph," Neskahi said. "No offense, but I find women associated with law enforcement are extremely competitive, for a lot of reasons we already know. But how can we make sure we beat Bruno at her own game?"

Ella glanced over at Justine to see if she agreed with the men's assessment. Her assistant nodded, adding, "I think there's a lot of truth in what the boys are saying, boss. How are we going to make sure we win? Cheat?"

"No," she said, chuckling. "Let's play this out by Bruno's rules, at least this time. My ego is secure. Besides, we're a great team, and if anyone can pull off an impossible training exercise, we can."

They all exited the van immediately, gathering around Ella outside the security office. "Okay, boss. What now?" Justine asked.

"We're guessing that Bruno is almost certainly around here somewhere, in disguise because otherwise that Amazon would really stand out. If she is, that means she's either going to play the bad guy, or try to observe us without us knowing it's her. I'm betting she's the bad guy in this upcoming drill. It's in keeping with everyone's estimate of her personality. Now let's go pick up that note."

Ella led the way into the security office, a small room attached to the main plant facility, a massive structure several stories high and covering several acres adjacent to the large lake that provided coolant water.

Ella looked up from the note. "Okay, team, here it is. Without clearing the facility, which can't be done except in a real emergency, we're supposed to find Bruno, who's playing the role of a disturbed former employee planning on setting off a bomb. There'll be a major explosion unless we 'kill' her with a paintball hit before she sets it off, which will be at 11 A.M., less than fourteen minutes from now." Ella took another look at the paintball gun she had picked up from the security desk, along with Bruno's note, which had, according to the security man at the desk, been left there by Shives earlier. The three other members of the team had similar weapons, each capable of only one shot.

"How will we know when this 'bomb' goes off—if we lose?" Neskahi asked.

"We won't lose. It says to avoid scaring the employees, instead of a loud bang we'll hear a well-known Doors tune from her location. 'Light My Fire' would be my guess. But enough of that, we need to track Bruno down before the time runs out. We'll make good use of the cell phones the community-policing program has provided."

She pointed to a sign on the wall listing power plant offices and their phone numbers. "Justine, call the guardhouse at the gate and see if Bruno or any visitors came into the plant this morning, when they arrived, and where they were headed or might be right now. Ralph, call the administrative offices, and see if anyone saw Bruno or Shives this morning. Joseph, you call the control room and do the same. Make it quick, people."

Ella made a fast call to Delbert Shives's office, hoping to find out something from his secretary. Shives knew Bruno, and the chemist had probably helped her facilitate the exercise through his superiors. Shives's secretary might have seen them today and still not have been cautioned to keep their location a secret from the SI team.

Ella punched out the number, and was still trying to get a connection when Justine turned toward her again, putting away her own phone.

"I've got something, boss. Bruno must have arrived with Delbert Shives disguised as a male school teacher, unless we're being victimized by a terrible coincidence. The person with Shives was a tall blonde wearing sunglasses, a cowboy hat, denim jacket, and brown Western-cut jeans," Justine added.

Joseph Neskahi turned to listen, already having disconnected his call. "Nobody saw anyone but regular staff in the control room, which is off-limits normally anyway."

Ralph was still on the phone, but had tuned in on their conversation and nodded to show he'd heard.

Ella looked at her watch, then finally ended the call attempt. "I couldn't get anyone to pick up the phone at Shives's office, so that wasn't much help. Bruno's probably already made herself scarce, hiding out somewhere until eleven o'clock, when she says she'll be setting off the 'bomb.' Even if she took off her disguise, she'd stand out around here among all the nonblondes. We couldn't hear any music from most of the power plant area and farther south where the coal is brought in, and I think she'd want us to know we'd failed just to make a dramatic point. I think the administrative and support areas are our best bet." Ella took off down the hall, and the others followed.

Ralph finally ended his call. "The secretary at Administration said that Shives and the teacher with him went into his office as soon as he arrived, and nobody saw the teacher come out again, though Shives left about twenty minutes ago."

"Shives's office is our best bet, then. I'll go there, and you three check out all the employee rest rooms you can find. Facilities like that are good places for bombers to hide when they need some privacy."

The rest of the team hurried away, and Ella followed the signs on the wall to the area where Delbert Shives had his office. She'd just entered the lobby when Shives's door slammed shut and the booming sound of a fast-moving Doors tune, "L.A. Woman," came from within. Ella had come to hate that song after she'd first returned to the Rez. Navajos here, looking at her as an outsider, had given her the nickname L.A. Woman because she's served at the FBI office in Los Angeles. Ella knew it was no coincidence that Bruno had selected it. The woman had really done her homework.

Bruno appeared at the door, open now, wearing slacks and a colorful blouse, her long blond hair combed out and gleaming. She was holding a big portable CD player with powerful speakers. Ella couldn't hear anything but Jim Morrison, but was able to read Bruno's lips. "You lose," Bruno mouthed. Then she smiled.

Ella nodded coldly, wondering if the tribe would make her repeat the training if she gave Bruno a black eye.

Still unable to believe that they'd failed the exercise, Ella looked at her watch, her heart still beating fast with excitement and anger. Her mouth fell open. Then she looked at a clock on the wall. Both timepieces showed that it was only 10:55. Bruno had cheated, and set the "bomb" off five minutes early.

An hour and a half later, Ella was back at her office. She'd managed to remain civil through the briefing and evaluation conducted by Bruno in Shives's office, and something in her expression during the quiet trip back had kept her team from ever mentioning the particular tune Bruno had chosen. Ella could sense, however, that they were all in agreement about two things—Margaret Bruno's training sessions weren't boring, and two, the woman was a devious bitch.

Ella glanced at her watch, something she'd been doing more than usual today. She'd missed breakfast, but maybe she could still find time for a late lunch. She picked up the phone and dialed Carolyn Roanhorse. The ME picked it up on the first ring.

"I already sent the Redhouse autopsy report to your office, Ella. There was not much more to find, really. Massive trauma from the bullet Justine recovered was the cause of death, all right, and she's probably already given you the criminalistics analysis on it."

"I wasn't calling about work, Carolyn. In case you hadn't noticed, it's past lunchtime," Ella teased. "I haven't eaten since yesterday, and have had one hell of a morning. How about getting away for a while? If you've already had lunch, at least come with me and I'll buy you dessert."

"Hey, that's a terrific idea. I'm running late myself, and still haven't eaten." She paused, then added, "But it'll have to be off the Rez. I'm not that welcome at restaurants or coffee shops here."

"You've got it. Shall I pick you up, or do we meet somewhere?"

"I'll meet you over at Con Chile on West Main in Farmington. Know the place?"

"I've been by there. Sounds good to me."

About forty-five minutes later they sat at one of the corner tables inside the small diner. Carolyn's large proportions made it nearly impossible for her to be comfortable in a booth, but Ella preferred tables anyway. As a cop, she'd learned to keep an unobstructed view of her surroundings while in public, and booths always had two blind spots.

After ordering, Carolyn sat back and regarded Ella thoughtfully. "Okay, give. What's this all about? Do you need a special favor? If so, you may have to pay for my entire lunch, and I brought a big appetite."

Ella laughed. "No, that's not it. Believe it or not, I suddenly realized that all I ever do is work, and that I'd forgotten what it's like to get together with someone other than family."

Carolyn's gaze softened. "It was worse for me, until I got married and at least had someone to come home to. But to tell you the truth, most days I'm too drained to do much else except go home and try to forget about work."

"I hear you," Ella said with a nod. "It's not supposed to be like this, you know."

"Says who?" Carolyn smiled. "I knew what I was getting into when I agreed to become an ME for the tribe. And you must have known what being a cop entailed."

Ella nodded slowly. "Sure, and when I was younger I loved all the demands work made, but now it can get pretty overwhelming at times. I still love being a detective. Don't get me wrong. It's what I was meant to do. Sometimes I hear people talking about their jobs, saying things like 'work isn't who you are—it's what you do.' But, to me, it's all wrapped up together—inseparable. The problem is that I have Dawn to think about now, and I'm always worrying that I'm not doing enough for her."

"Dawn adores you, and she's a great kid. What are you talking about?"

"I don't spend enough time with her, and she's growing up so fast."

"That doesn't make you a bad mother—it makes you a modern one who has to juggle many things in her life."

"I wonder if it isn't time for me to find another line of work. Maybe it's a sacrifice I should make for her."

"You wouldn't be happy anywhere else, Ella, and being miserable isn't going to make you a better mom. What we've always had in common is that work is the fabric of our world—it defines and fulfills us. In that way, I'd say you and I are luckier than the majority of the population. We both have an incredible sense of purpose. And that's exactly what makes you a great mom."

"When I'm working a case, putting in long overtime hours, I sure don't feel that way."

"There are plenty of times I don't feel like I'm a great wife to Mike. For what it's worth, I can't tell you how many times I've thought about moving away from the Rez and taking a permanent vacation."

"What keeps you here?"

Carolyn smiled. "The same thing that keeps you from moving away and taking another job. I *belong* here, though that might sound strange coming from someone who isn't welcome in most homes on the Rez. Although my job requires me to be in close contact with the dead, and that makes me a pariah of sorts, I do have my place. I'm doing something that's both needed and essential."

"Yeah, that's the way I feel, too." As they looked at each other, Ella realized how comforting it was to be with Carolyn. They understood each other so well. "It's not always easy, is it?"

"No, but it's right—for both of us."

"You know that no matter how busy I get, you can always count on me if you need a friend."

"And vice versa. But I've got to tell you, I really worry about you now. The police department's in trouble, isn't it?"

Ella nodded. "Yeah. Too much work, not enough funds, and not enough support from the tribe. We're really out there on our own, even more so than usual."

Carolyn grew somber. "I hear you. I desperately need some new equipment in the lab. I keep hounding administration and the tribe, but you know how that goes."

She nodded. "Right now, we're short of officers and reliable equipment, but money that should have been used to repair or replace radios and vehicles was spent on a series of training exercises we've been going through. We have one more session to go, but I swear I'm going to kill our instructor before it's through." Ella shook her head.

"You looked really whipped when I first saw you today. Was this what that 'hell of a morning' was all about?" Carolyn asked.

Ella explained what had happened at the power plant, and when she got to the part about "L.A. Woman," Carolyn cringed.

"How did this Bruno woman find out about that?"

"She knows one of the chemists from the power plant, Delbert Shives. He's worked there for several years, and must have heard it from a Navajo employee. Bruno's really competitive, an ex-cop, and obviously did it just to bug me."

Carolyn nodded. "But you've heard that before, and nowadays even your enemies call you 'that woman detective' or 'Investigator Clah.' Your actions have earned you the respect of the People. But I have a feeling an old nickname isn't what bugged you the most today."

Ella thought about it for a moment, then sighed. "I failed the team today, Carolyn. I made some mistakes, and we were beaten because of that. I hate to lose, even during training."

"Come on, Ella. The woman cheated. She said you had fifteen minutes, then set off the imaginary bomb five minutes early when she saw you enter the lobby. She was watching for you. There was no way you could win. It was an exercise in character—or humility." Carolyn smiled. "You're the best cop around, nobody could have done better."

Ella shook her head. "I know. And Bruno was a hundred percent correct to point out in that way that bad guys, terrorists, or mentally disturbed people make their own rules. I should have known that from the very beginning and come up with another strategy where she couldn't see any of us coming in time to set off the 'bomb.' In a real situation, I'd have gotten us all killed, and the knowledge that I could screw up again scares the hell out of me. From now on, in a situation like that, I'll do whatever it takes to win."

"Ella, if you're half as hard on the bad guys as you are on yourself, the rest of us can continue to sleep comfortably at night. Learn from this, certainly, but don't go beating yourself up just because something went wrong during a drill. You're supposed to make mistakes in training so you can identify pitfalls and avoid them on the job."

Ella nodded, then switched the conversation back to the case they were working at the moment. As they talked shop, the connection between them strengthened. Finally, Carolyn looked at the clock on the wall. "I better be getting back. At least I'm not keeping a patient waiting."

Laughing, Ella paid the bill for both of them, despite Carolyn's protests, then walked outside with her. "Let's try to do this more often—despite our schedules."

"Deal. You going to be okay?"

Ella nodded. "Life always seems easier on a full stomach."

"Words to live by."

As Carolyn pulled out of the parking lot, Ella started the engine. She'd just started to back up when she heard the sudden blast of a siren somewhere close, followed by the squeal of tires. A heartbeat later, a vehicle pulled up right behind hers. It was Sheriff Taylor.

THIRTEEN
——— ✕ ✕ ✕ ———

Ella pulled back into the parking slot and waited. Sheriff Taylor, a rugged cowboy in his late fifties with pale blue eyes, came over from his unit to meet her.

"Hey, Ella," he said, leaning in her driver's side window. "I thought I recognized your Jeep. How about having some coffee with me. There's something I really need to discuss with you."

"Sure."

Ella went back inside the diner and joined him at a center table against the back wall. From where they were seated they both had a clear view of the room and the only entrance.

The waitress smiled, recognizing Taylor, who was in uniform, and immediately brought over two cups of coffee without being asked.

"I was planning on calling you at the station, but they gave me your twenty, and I decided to stop by. I wanted to talk to you about one of your officers, the one that was killed the other day. I didn't really make the connection until I started catching up on some crime reports the Farmington Police Department sent us as a courtesy since our jurisdictions overlap. Did you know that the officer's father had his home broken into just two weeks ago?"

"Kee Franklin?" she asked, needing to make sure.

"Yeah, that's him. He's a physics professor."

"I've spoken to Professor Franklin about his son, of course, but he never mentioned any break-in. I wonder why," Ella said.

"He probably never connected the two events. We've had a rash of residential burglaries in that neighborhood, and the city cops are working on some leads in conjunction with my department. Their jurisdiction ends just west of that area. But I thought I should pass this information along to you, especially when it looks like Officer Franklin was killed when he walked in on a burglary."

"Have the burglars off the Rez been targeting anything specific?"

"Mostly cash, jewelry, and consumer electronics—stuff that they can stuff into a pillowcase and carry away, you know? But the break-in at Franklin's place didn't exactly fit that profile. That's what bothered me about it and why I thought I'd let you know. They took a laptop computer and some backup CDs, and went through his files. But they left a three-hundred-dollar game system that's the hottest thing around on the black market. Apparently Professor Franklin is addicted to leading-edge arcade-style games."

"Burglars *never* leave those expensive gaming systems behind. They're too easy to sell at flea markets and such."

"No kidding. Truth is, I've never heard of a burglar passing one up. Sometimes, it's the only thing missing after a break-in."

"Was the game well hidden?"

"Yes and no. It was out of sight, but because the burglar had broken into the cabinet where it was kept, he knew it was there. Of course it's possible something spooked him, and he left in a hurry."

"Thanks for the tip, I appreciate it." Ella said, standing up. "I better get back to work now." She reached into her wallet for money, and the sheriff held up his hand.

"It's on me. You can buy the coffee next time, Ella."

"I'll hold you to it, Sheriff. Thanks."

"If you uncover anything on the robberies that I can use, pass it along, okay, Ella?"

"Of course."

Ella left Taylor at the table and walked out. Right now, she wanted to talk to Kee Franklin. She was already in Farmington and knew his address, so she went directly there from the diner. When she arrived Professor Franklin was outside raking up leaves. Officer Judy Musket, a tribal cop Ella recognized, was sitting on the porch step wearing her street clothes and sipping something from a cup.

Seeing Ella, Judy stood and walked over to her immediately.

"I'm on leave this week, in case you're wondering why I'm visiting Kee during my regular duty hours," she said.

"I wasn't," Ella said. "I'm just here to ask the professor a few questions."

"Mind if I stick around?"

"No, just don't interfere."

Franklin came up then, greeted Ella, and invited her into the comfortable living room. "What brings you back here, Investigator Clah? Do you have a suspect yet?"

"We're still working on the case, and that's why I'm here. I understand that someone burglarized your house about two weeks prior to your son's death."

"Yeah, that's right. Other families in this neighborhood have also had break-ins, if I recall correctly. Why do you ask?"

"Do you see any connection whatsoever between the break-in at your house and your son's murder?"

"No. Is there one?" He gave her a puzzled look.

Ella noted that his response was almost immediate. She'd expected him to think about it first, and his rapid answer made her wary. "Your son was killed during the course of a break-in."

"Well, yes, but the gangs that run around on the reservation don't come into the city, and vice versa."

"What makes you think the break-in at the garage in Shiprock was gang-related?" Ella pressed.

"I've been checking around on my own, and I've learned that my son befriended a young man, a gang member by the name of Albert Washburn. My son had asked him to keep an eye on things in that neighborhood. If gang activity hadn't been a factor in the area he patrolled, my son wouldn't have recruited Washburn."

Ella remained quiet. She wouldn't argue police business with him, nor explain that Albert hadn't just been keeping an eye on gang activity. He'd been watching for any signs of criminal activity. Instead, she allowed the silence to stretch.

Finally, Dr. Franklin stood and walked to the window. "I don't really know what to believe anymore. But I still don't think there was anything of any real value in that garage. My ex-wife liked holding on to things, except me, but she wasn't a fool. She wouldn't have kept anything worth more than a few dollars in that old building." He turned around and faced her. "But if you're following up on something like the burglary of my home, that must mean you have no solid leads on the murder of my son."

"I wouldn't say that, sir. We do have leads. I just don't like to leave loose ends."

"Just find my son's killer."

"We *will* do that. But perhaps you can help me a bit more. I understand you worked for the government before you taught in Los Alamos. Could you have made any enemies who have followed you here?"

An emotion she couldn't quite identify flashed in his eyes, but it was gone in a second. As she gazed at him speculatively, his expression became guarded. "You've seen too many spy movies, Investigator Clah. My work at the labs may still be labeled classified, but these days it's mostly out of habit than the need for secrecy. I don't rate the kind of enemies you speak of." He stopped, met her gaze, and held it. "If that weren't true, I wouldn't say so. There's no way I'll ever find peace and harmony again in my life until my son's killer is behind prison walls."

His words rang with conviction, but she couldn't shake the feeling that Professor Franklin knew more than he was admitting. The professor was a highly intelligent man—but not one practiced at deception. She was sure Franklin had an idea about what had happened to his son, but for whatever the reason, had decided not to share it with her.

"Thank you for your cooperation, sir," Ella said, standing.

"Can I walk out with you?" Judy asked her.

"Sure."

Judy remained silent until they had reached Ella's unit. "I know what you're looking for, but believe me, whatever happened to Jason isn't connected to his father. Kee's been looking into his own past, too, wondering the same thing you have, but he hasn't found any links." She paused then added, "By the way, I wouldn't take everything Albert Washburn tells you at face value."

"I haven't caught him at a lie—yet."

Judy shrugged. "I've lived on the Rez almost all of my life, and I've been a tribal cop for the past fifteen years. I know a lot of people around Shiprock, and Albert in particular. When I patrolled that area a year or so ago, Albert often talked to me about local crimes. He liked being involved, you know? But I never could shake the feeling that *he* was the one behind the petty crimes I was looking into and that he liked trying to lead me around in circles."

"Did you ever get any evidence to back that up?"

"No, and I tried very hard. There was something about that kid that always bugged me. I did arrest his cousin, Oliver Washburn, once, for slashing somebody's tires, and the boy told me that Albert had a finger in every pie. Rumor has it that he's made a bundle fencing stolen property. But I couldn't follow the trail, so I had to let it drop."

"Do you think Albert Washburn may be involved in what happened to Jason, then?"

"If he is, you're going to have a really hard time proving it. That boy is *very* street-smart and a skilled liar."

Ella drove away with Judy's words still echoing in her mind, recalling Albert's last phone call and his failure to identify his source. Had he made up the whole thing? This case was filled with leads that detoured, and half-truths. But somewhere within that maze lay the answers she needed to find. Ella had intended on calling Albert back, but hadn't done so yet because she'd been so preoccupied with other matters. She made a note either to call or stop by his home soon.

It was seven in the morning before Ella was able to contact her brother. When she arrived at Clifford's medicine hogan, he was speaking to one of his patients in the doorway. Ella waited in the SUV until the elderly woman turned and walked off, heading into the desert.

As Ella went toward the hogan, her gaze stayed on Clifford's patient. The elderly woman had chosen a path that Ella had gone down many times when jogging. That section of desert was rugged, and even at a walk, could become strenuous exercise after a mile or two.

"Maybe she shouldn't be going in that direction," Ella said, pointing by pursing her lips, Navajo style.

"She'll be fine. She's tougher than you and me put together. She's going to go tend her sheep. They graze on whatever they can find this time of year. Toward evening her daughter meets her in their pickup and they haul the animals back to their pen."

Ella smiled. "Old meets new. It's that way everywhere these days."

"Including in this hogan, sister," he said, glancing down at the shield on her belt. "So what brings you here this early in the morning?"

"I need to ask what you know about the wife of the councilman who was killed."

"I've never met her, but I've heard from my wife that other woman have already begun gossiping about the widow. My wife says the others are just jealous."

"Tell me what you've heard?"

"That the councilman's wife won't have to look far for another husband," Clifford said as he began making preparations for his next patient.

"Her husband just died. Who's giving her attention already, according to the gossip?"

"I'm not sure I want to discuss that with you."

Her brother was stubborn, and Ella knew she'd have to word what she said carefully or she'd never get an answer. "Do you think our tribe will be better served if you withhold information when I'm trying to catch someone who's killing Navajos?"

Clifford pursed his lips. She had him now. Whenever he got that expression on his face, it usually meant that he didn't like what he was going to do, but he'd do it anyway.

"Your child's father has been over to her house at least twice already," he said at last.

Ella stared at him. "Then it's just since her husband's death. It's probably just lawyer business. No way he would have done anything out of place with a married woman. He's better than that."

"No one has suggested that she was unfaithful to either of her late husbands. But that doesn't mean other men weren't pursuing her, or harboring desires that aren't always hidden."

She remembered how Kevin had been so attentive to Emily. But Kevin was no murderer. She was as certain of that as she was of tomorrow's sunrise.

Clifford studied Ella's expression. "Does this gossip bother you?"

Ella considered it. "It's never easy to acknowledge the ending of a familiar situation . . . particularly one that left me with a wonderful daughter," she said slowly. "Do you understand?"

He nodded. "Our mother has a new life, and your child's father is finding a new path. But what about you? How will you move on, sister? Is your future with the Deputy Marshal?"

She shrugged. "Are there any others you've heard of that have shown a romantic interest in the widow, either now, or before the death of her husband?"

"Yes." He wrote a name down on a piece of paper and handed it to her.

Ella read it. She knew Larry Tso—a married man, at least the last time she'd heard. Tso owned a restaurant in Farmington—the Fair Winds. It was said to be an expensive, classy place, catering to businessmen. "Thanks."

"You should listen more to the spirit of the Navajo Nation. Wind carries messages. Tune in to the People, and you'll have all the answers you need without ever asking a question."

"That works for you—but I'm a cop. Asking questions is the only way for me to ferret out secrets people choose to keep."

When Ella returned to the station she tried to call Albert, but either nobody was at home, or he didn't want to answer. She'd try again later. She got to work, trying to catch up on all the pending reports. She'd just started with one due on the chief's desk at the end of the day when Big Ed walked into her office.

"Are you any closer to finding the killer or killers?" he asked, taking a seat.

"I don't know," she answered honestly, and filled him in on the physical evidence, the money Redhouse had hidden, and her impressions of those they'd interviewed, including the gossip about possible men in Emily's life.

"I don't think Councilman Tolino is our killer," Big Ed said. "He's got too much character to kill except in self-defense, or to save the life of another. And if the same person killed both our officer and the councilman, what motives are we talking about? If Tolino killed Redhouse, what would be his motive for killing our officer first?"

"I agree that Kevin doesn't fit the profile, so I'm currently checking on the other name mentioned in connection with Mrs. Redhouse."

"Let me know what you find out."

"Of course."

"How did the training session go yesterday at the power plant?" Big Ed asked.

"Bruno caught us off guard, and we failed to stop the simulated bomber. It was a humbling experience, but I think we all learned something from the session. I won't be caught like that again."

"Pissed you off, huh? I know what a perfectionist you are, Ella." Big Ed leaned back in his chair.

"You've got that right."

"Just remember that you're the team leader, and the others respect your training, ability, and self-confidence, Shorty. Don't let a little training setback become a big thing. You're the best cop around, but you're not perfect. Learn, adjust, and move on." Big Ed stood, and smiled. "Okay?"

Ella nodded. "Carolyn told me the same thing."

"Good advice from two very smart people."

As soon as Big Ed walked out of her office, Justine walked in.

"The only fingerprints I was able to find on the bills from Redhouse's hidden money stash are his," Justine announced.

"Were the bills new?"

"No, so I expected to find partials on whoever else had them before Redhouse, maybe even a bank clerk. But they'd been wiped clean, which makes them even more likely to be dirty."

"I agree," Ella said. "What else have you been able to find out since yesterday?"

"Well, I've done some testing on the hairs we found at Wilson's home. Some came from a wig, and seem to be a match to the ones we found in the garage where Jason Franklin was killed."

"Any theories?" Ella asked.

"I can't even begin to imagine what this person is looking for, but we can at least find a roundabout connection between Wilson and the Franklin family. Professor Franklin has been to the garage and to Wilson's office. Do you suppose the burglar-killer was looking for something he thinks Franklin left at the garage, or in Wilson's storeroom? Of course when he didn't find it in either place, his next move was to check and see if Wilson had taken it home. I'm sure he figured that the missing briefcase and computer were possible hiding places, which tends to support the notion that he's searching for a document of some sort. But that still doesn't tell us why Redhouse was killed."

"I know, and I was thinking along those lines myself."

"Maybe the thefts took place simply to mislead us, and the rifle was taken to provide extra firepower for the next crime." Justine suddenly cringed. "Our vests won't stop a rifle bullet like that."

"You're right," Ella said with a shudder, then filled Justine in on the theft at Kee Franklin's place and everything else she'd learned so far.

"I know you want to tie all the break-ins and thefts together, but the evidence just doesn't support that yet," Justine said. "We didn't find any matching wig hairs in the storeroom, and the bullets recovered, though they are of the same caliber, are too deformed to make a positive match. Ejection markings on the shell casings might have helped, but these are the first the shooter has left behind. We need more."

"True, but the absence of hair may be because the perp's wig didn't shed at the college. It's a good bet that the same person broke into the storeroom and Wilson's home. He or she apparently spent a lot more time at Wilson's home and did a lot of hard work going through everything so thoroughly. But you're right. We need more to go on, like a motive," Ella said. "I'm going to pay Oliver Washburn a visit. Why don't you come with me?"

"He's a tough cookie, Ella. He's not going to give you much. I met him here at the station once when he was brought in for trying to shake down a neighbor by threatening to vandalize his car. I'll be surprised if he even talks to you."

"He talked to Judy Muskett on at least one occasion. Let's give it a try and see how far we get."

They drove to a small residential area on the eastern edge of Shiprock occupied mainly by employees of the local power plant and local mines. The houses were small, eight to a block, generally. A few had carports, but most of those only served to shelter discarded household items, old stoves, bald tires, and piles of trash.

"I used to look at places like this and wonder why people lived this way," Justine said softly. "Then I grew up and learned that when circumstances defeat you, externals don't matter much,"

Ella nodded slowly, thinking much the same thing. The despair and loss of hope that went hand in hand with poverty often manifested itself in this way.

"There he is," Justine said, pointing to the house just ahead. A young man about nineteen was sitting in an old folding chair under the carport, smoking a cigarette.

As soon as they pulled up, Washburn recognized Justine and bolted. Throwing the car door open, Ella raced after him and caught him before he could get around the house, where he had a motorcycle parked. "If you gave up smoking," she said, twisting his arm and pinning him to the wall, "you'd be in better shape when you need to make a run for it."

"Tell it to someone who gives a damn."

Ella held him against the wall. "I'm not here to arrest you, so try and keep your cool, and I won't have to change my mind."

"Yeah, right. Let me guess. I just won free tickets to the pig ball, and you're my escort."

"Cut the crap. I don't have the patience today," Ella said, twisting his arm a little farther up until she heard him gasp. "Let's make this easy on each other. Talk to me, and I'll be on my way. If you'd rather not be seen talking to a cop, we can do it in my unit, where we'll have some privacy. I'll even be glad to handcuff you to keep up appearances."

"Why should I talk to you about anything?"

"Because otherwise I'll escort you back into your house and my partner and I will stay and visit you for an hour or longer. I'll also make it a point to stand in front of the window long enough for people to see me writing things down—like maybe all the names and addresses you're giving me. It'll be a great visit."

"Your patrol car," he muttered.

Ella loosened her hold and cuffed his wrists behind his back. "Let's go," she said, just as Justine came over.

Ella rode in the front with Justine, who drove, while their

prisoner remained in the back behind the wire screen. Oliver didn't say a word until they were out on the highway.

"Where are we going?" he asked.

"For a drive. You probably don't want to be seen or overheard as you tell us all about Albert."

His eyes widened slightly. "What about him? Concerned that he's smarter than you?"

"I'll ask the questions, okay? Any idea where he's getting his extra money?"

Oliver shook his head. "Even if I knew, I wouldn't tell a cop. I don't want to end up with a knife in my gut."

"He'd do that to you? His own cousin?"

"No. One day when everyone else has forgotten all about it some guy I've never seen before, from someplace on the Rez no one's ever heard of, will come up and stick me. And my cousin won't be anywhere around. In fact, he'll probably be in church beside a priest and three nuns."

"Oh, come on. You make him sound like a crime lord," Ella said.

"Well, whenever something big goes down around here, he seems to know all about it."

"It's probably just talk."

"No way. He always knows exactly what's going down."

"Okay, so his sources are good. That doesn't mean he's behind the crimes," Ella responded. "Let's move on now. Did Albert ever mention Officer Franklin?"

Oliver nodded. "I think he really respected that cop. But he also told me that Franklin's days were numbered—that he'd end up dead."

"Do you think his remark was meant as a threat against the officer?"

Oliver shook his head. "No. I told you. He liked him. Besides, he *never* threatens. When Al has an enemy, that person ends up getting hurt somehow. There's never a warning." He saw they were near the reservation line now. Beyond was Waterflow, a farming community on that side of the San Juan River. To the south a few miles was the coal power plant, on reservation land.

"Okay, Oliver. Thanks."

"If you're finished, then drop me off here."

"Are you sure? It's a long walk."

"I'll be okay. Just don't come back to me with any more questions. I've told you all I'm ever going to tell you."

Justine pulled over to the side of the road, and Ella stepped out to open the door for Oliver. He scrambled out of the SUV quickly, then after she'd removed his handcuffs, he hurried away from them, walking south toward the old highway without looking back.

"That was an interesting meeting," Justine said softly, when Ella returned to her seat. "What do you think? Is Albert trying to run a crime ring here on the Rez, or is Oliver just trying to give his cousin a reputation? It sounds like mostly BS to me."

Ella considered it. "I wish I knew. What bothers me most is that comment about Officer Franklin's days being numbered." Ella thought about that a moment longer, then glanced at Justine. "Let's go see what Albert has to say about that."

They arrived at Albert Washburn's trailer twenty minutes later. He answered their knock and invited them inside almost immediately.

Ella could see his computer was on and that he'd been working on something. As she got closer to the screen, he turned off the monitor casually and invited them to sit down. "So what brings you two here?"

"We need to ask you a few questions, Albert," Ella said.

"Go ahead," he said with an almost regal nod as he sat on the easy chair across from them.

"You told me that one of your friends saw someone hanging

around the garage a few days before Officer Franklin was killed there. Who is this friend?" Ella asked.

"He made me promise not to say. Trust me that he didn't know any more than I told you." Albert crossed his arms across his chest.

"Trust isn't at the top of my list right now. I've been hearing some very disturbing things about you, Albert," Ella said.

"Disturbing things about me? Don't you know gossip on the Rez can't be trusted?"

"Yet it's interesting how often your name comes up in relation to the crimes being committed here. Let me give you an example. You were one of Officer Franklin's snitches. Now he's dead, and one of your friends may have seen the killer," Ella said.

"What's your point?"

Ella sat back and regarded him thoughtfully. He didn't rattle easily. Even worse, he seemed to be enjoying their cat-and-mouse game.

"What brought us here was a comment you made about Officer Franklin. I'm told you said that his days on the force were numbered."

"Was I wrong? At the time, it seemed a reasonable assumption."

"Why is that?" Justine jumped in.

"I don't know how well either of you knew the officer, but he sure didn't seem like a team player to me. He was trying to save the world all by himself. He tried to investigate every crime in his area, even if it meant working on his own time. He took too many risks. That's why I figured he'd end up dead sooner or later."

Ella met his gaze, but said nothing. Washburn allowed the silence to stretch out with a serene expression. Ella was patient, but so was Albert. Justine also remained silent, looking around the room casually as if sight-seeing. If Albert really knew more, Ella was sure he'd tell her. He'd want her to know, because he'd want her to owe him something in return. Albert was a user and manipulator, that was clear.

"Well, if you've run out of questions," he said at long last, "I have work to do."

"Did you ever tell Officer Franklin you thought he was in danger?"

Albert shook his head. "He knew that already. He liked taking risks and getting his adrenaline going. That was all a part of who he was."

As much as she wanted to believe that Albert was all hot air, Ella couldn't quite convince herself of that, at least not completely.

"If you ever find out that *my* days are 'numbered,'" Ella said, "let me know right away."

"If that's what you want. But you've also chosen your own path—what you encounter in that journey is all part of your destiny."

"Is that traditionalist or New Age?" Ella asked him with a hard smile that never touched her eyes.

"I follow no predetermined path or philosophy. I carve out my own way."

Ella stood up. "Just try to keep your nose out of trouble."

"Always, it's one of my 'gifts,'" he said, his tone faintly mocking.

Once they were under way, Ella glanced at Justine. "You were too quiet in there. What's on your mind?"

"I wanted to study him while his attention was focused on you. I was trying to decide if he's the mastermind Oliver said, or just a kid who wants to feel important and is a damn good actor."

"And what did you decide?"

"Truthfully, I don't know. He's smooth, and plays a good

game, I'll give him that. I think he was lying about his anonymous friend, though. He avoided looking at either of us directly, though I doubt he realized it. Other than that, he was hard to read."

Ella nodded. "He may have made that up to add to his own importance, or maybe he saw someone there himself and wants to avoid anything that could get him called to a witness stand. But there's one thing we have to admit—he's got a pretty good information network."

"Maybe that's why Jason Franklin used him."

"Yes, and that brings up another interesting question. If Albert had known a hit was going down, don't you think he would have told Jason? He strikes me as the kind who takes pride in repaying a debt. Not because he's honorable, mind you, but because it's part of that reputation he's building—friends get treated well, enemies get squashed."

"Yeah, that sounds about right to me, too." Justine reached the stop sign at the highway and glanced at Ella. "Where to now?"

"Let's return to the station. I'll make some calls and get some background on Larry Tso before we go out to talk to him."

As they headed back, Ella shifted in her seat and her gaze dropped to the side mirror. "Don't look now, but we're being tailed."

FOURTEEN

✖ ✖ ✖

Justine kept her speed even so she wouldn't tip off the person following them. "How do you want to handle this?"

Ella studied the tan SUV a quarter mile behind them. It remained back far enough so she couldn't make out the driver's face.

"If we go to the station, he'll spook. So let's head on out of town, east again, then drive down to the dirt road that parallels the river on the south side of the farms and orchards between here and Waterflow. With all the trees between us, he'll have to follow closer just to keep us in sight. Start varying your speed, like we're looking for the right farm road," Ella said. "Whoever that is doesn't know where we're going. That's probably one reason for the tail."

Once they reached the area Ella had in mind, Justine left the highway and drove down one of the larger dirt roads that led perpendicular to the highway between fields. They continued down the road that paralleled the main irrigation ditch on their side of the river, passing fields on their left. To their right lay what remained of the bosque, the natural forested area that lined both banks of the river.

"Is he still there?" Justine asked, slowing as they intersected another road leading back to the highway between fields.

"I can't see him back there, or spot a dust trail, so he didn't follow us closer to the river. But I don't see him giving up this easily." Ella turned in her seat, and watched for a few minutes. "I was right. He didn't. He's following, creeping along the highway and staying on the shoulder. I can see him from time to time between the trees."

Justine squinted. "I'm not so sure about this, Ella. How do you know that's the same vehicle we saw a while ago?"

"It's the same color and model. Besides, there's not much traffic on the highway at the moment." She watched for a moment longer. "He's a smart one. He stayed where he is so he can speed up and pull back onto the highway if he sees us crossing over to try and get behind him."

"Can we find a spot where he can't see us, then get far enough ahead to cut him off? Or get another unit out here to catch him if he makes a run for it?"

Ella picked up the mike, but soon learned that the closest patrol unit was at least a half hour away, far to the west of them. It was no surprise. "It's up to us." She mulled it over for a second. "There's only one way to get close to him. Stop the unit at one of the road intersections where we'll be visible to him, but with cover close by that leads all the way to the highway. We'll fake car trouble, lifting the hood and all that. Then I'll duck down and use the cover of an orchard to cross over to the highway where he is. Of course, this is all assuming he stops to wait for us."

"Ella, that's risky. If he's armed, and he sees you when you get close, he could pick you off. The last dozen or so feet of your approach will be completely in the open. If this is the perp we've been looking for, we already know he'll kill a cop."

"I still want to know who's tailing me. I'll try to find a place to cross where there's a ditch I can use for cover."

"All right. Let's pick the spot carefully for our phony car trouble."

"Go to the end of the next alfalfa field, pump the brakes to simulate a dying engine, then stop where the dirt track leads past the green farmhouse. I'll use the cover of the car to duck down, then cut through the trees."

Justine slowed and looked toward the highway. "Where's he now?"

"Still moving, but slowly, and a faster vehicle is passing him now. My guess is he's keeping tabs on everything we do. Maybe he has a pair of binoculars."

"I advise against doing this, Ella."

"Noted. Now pump the brakes a few times and let's get this show on the road."

Justine did as Ella had asked, making the car lurch. She then pulled to a complete stop and got out. Ella joined her, walked around, and threw the hood open. While Justine stood by the driver's side fender, looking into the engine compartment, Ella made a great show of crawling beneath the vehicle. Once there, she slipped out beneath the passenger's side.

"I'm off."

"You said it, not me." Justine laughed.

Ella moved as silently as Wind through the mature apple orchard. The branches were barren but low to the ground, so she had plenty of cover as long as she moved from tree to tree rather than in the open.

When she reached the end of the orchard, there was an irrigation ditch, running perpendicular to the highway, which led underneath a culvert. The irrigation water wasn't flowing this time of year, so she was able to slide easily into the four-foot-deep ditch and walk along its sandy bottom. Saplings and tall grass along the edges helped hide her, though the cover wasn't as complete as she'd have liked.

She was less than twenty-five yards away when she heard the SUV start up. She knew the driver couldn't have heard her, but his instincts had been right on target. She scrambled out of the ditch, but by the time she got onto the shoulder of the highway, he was gone.

Ella informed Justine on her handheld radio. "I didn't even get close enough to read the vehicle tags, though they were in-state based on the color." She paused for a moment, then added, "This person is like the old trickster, Coyote, and I hate these mind games. I prefer an adversary who stands and fights."

"Don't we all?"

By the time they reached the station, the tension was giving Ella an industrial-strength headache. "I need you to do a background check on Larry Tso. Try to find out where he stands on NEED."

"I'll get on that right now," Justine said.

Ella went to her office and sat down. Her head was pounding. Reaching into her bottom drawer, she brought out a bottle of aspirins. She'd just flipped two tabs into her palm when Officer Tache came into her office.

"I need to talk to you. Do you have a moment?"

"Sure, Ralph. Have a seat. What's going on?"

Worry lines crisscrossed Tache's round face. "I've been thinking of applying for a job with the Albuquerque Police Department. I've already told Big Ed."

Ella stared at him, shocked. Ralph had been with the department practically forever. "I wish you'd reconsider this, Ralph. Our PD is undergoing hard times right now, I know, and things are always at their worst before they get fixed. Can't you stick it out a while longer?"

He shook his head. "My wife heard how Jason Franklin died, and she wants us to move. APD has a lot more officers who can back you up when it's needed, and their equipment is reliable."

"Ralph, haven't you lived on the Rez all your life?"

"Yeah. And so has my wife. But she has a sister in Albuquerque who has a real good job and a nice house in the Northeast Heights, and she wants to move there. She says she deserves nice things, too."

Ralph shrugged. "Anyway, I just wanted to give you a heads-up. I haven't actually applied to the APD yet, but I will soon, and I need to start training someone who can take my place here. If you come across someone who's interested in criminalistics, let me know. I'll teach him the basics he needs to know, and he can take the rest of the courses at the college. I won't leave you in the lurch."

"Your experience is invaluable to us. Think about this some more. We really need you here, Ralph."

"I know. That's what makes it so difficult to leave. But I have a family to think about, Ella."

She nodded. "If you need a good reference . . ."

"I'd appreciate it. I'll let you know when my application goes through."

When he left, Ella leaned back in her chair and rubbed her temples. She had to get some paperwork done today.

At that moment, Margaret Bruno showed up at her door, wearing a visitor's badge on a lanyard around her neck. Ella looked at her speculatively, noticing that the tall blonde wore a gold choker and hoop earrings but no rings. Her makeup was limited to lipstick. She was appealing and tough-looking at the same time, and might have attracted a police officer who liked the kind of woman who could match him drink for drink, and even arm wrestle him to see who paid the tab.

"Hi, Ella. I just had a word with Chief Atcitty, and he suggested we finish the last session of the training program today."

Ella sighed. This was the last thing she needed, but she knew that Big Ed was just trying to get the training over with so they wouldn't have to worry about it anymore.

Margaret sat across from her. "I know it's a pain, and I understand your still being ticked off after the curveball I threw you at the power plant. But today will be different. We'll go over some of the latest techniques in pursuit driving, focusing on operations in built-up areas such as neighborhoods and industrial areas. I promise you'll see the benefits of what you learn out on the streets."

Ella looked at Margaret and nodded. "I'll get the others."

Nearly two hours later, Ella returned to her desk. The training session had run long, but the exercises, centering on pursuit driving, had been informative and practical.

First, they'd had some hands-on work at the vacant fairgrounds, where they'd had room to maneuver without interference from traffic. Then they'd moved to an old neighborhood across the highway from where the uranium mill had once stood. The streets were still intact, but virtually all the houses had been torn down and replaced because their foundations had contained uranium tailings.

Bruno had demonstrated real driving skills, teaching them some fast turns and techniques that her team had been eager to learn, though Ella had been through equivalent sessions years ago while in the FBI. Encouraged by their interest, Bruno had spent the extra time they'd needed so each could practice the maneuvers, and seeing that Ella already had the skills, had shown a little humility herself and asked Ella to help her train the others so they could all get more practice.

The best part, however, had come when they'd all seen Margaret Bruno finally drive away. She was now out of her team's hair for good, and they could concentrate completely on the pending cases.

Ella spent the next few hours catching up on reports using her computer terminal. Midway through a manpower utilization update, the computer screen froze, and she was unable to go on.

Big Ed came into her office. "You might as well shut down your workstation. There's something wrong with the system server, and it won't reboot properly. We're having people look into it now."

Ella looked at the monitor and scowled. "This is not my day for good news," she said, and discussed the situation concerning Ralph Tache's planned departure. "I really don't want him to leave."

"I hate to lose him, too, but Tache has to make his own decision," Big Ed said, then walked to the door. "Go home, Shorty. It's almost quitting time, and you did a good job today helping train the others on the SI team with the pursuit driving exercises. Officer Tache mentioned it to me when he returned. You'll probably be coming in early tomorrow, as usual, so that'll be a good time to catch up on the paperwork."

"But I have a truckload of work to finish."

"Write down whatever notes you need in longhand, then enter them tomorrow. The work will still be there. Spend a few hours with your family. Remind them what you look like," he added with a ghost of a smile, "before you change."

She sighed. "Yeah, right." Ella reached for her keys and stood up. The truth was that she was still angry and frustrated, not only with herself and the poor performance they'd shown at the power plant scenario a few days ago, but also with the department and tribe for failing to provide for their officers when it came to adequate field support. She needed to get away for a while, and spending time with her daughter was the perfect way to soothe her spirit.

————

Rose arrived at the community college lecture hall several minutes late. Lena Clani, her best friend and fellow member of the Plant Watchers, had called just a half hour ago and asked for her to participate in a college-sponsored lecture on Navajo herbs. Rose had been scheduled to take part in next month's lecture, but one of the Plant Watchers had become ill at the last minute, and Lena, coordinator for the events, had begged, cajoled, and insisted. A bribe of prickly pear jelly had finally convinced Rose to take over.

From where she stood at the main door, Rose could see that the lecture hall was about half-full, with maybe forty people attending. It was a good-sized gathering for midday, when most of the regular students were having lunch.

Lena was introducing her, obviously killing time, and when she saw Rose, she waved enthusiastically. "And there she is now!"

Rose walked up the center aisle, embarrassed to see everyone watching her come in, but she tried to put the awkwardness aside, knowing that she'd be speaking about something really important—the damage to native vegetation by human activity, primarily mining and other industries.

Rose, her back to the audience, made a face at Lena, who whispered, "Thank you, I was beginning to repeat myself." Rose smiled at her friend, steeled herself to the prospect of public speaking, then turned toward their guests.

"I'm glad you all came to listen and share your thoughts today, and I assume that our host has already given you the topic I'll be presenting, so let's get right down to the issue—the decline in native plant species caused by industry—specifically mining—and what actions we can take to reverse the current situation. If you have a question, please don't hesitate to raise your hand so I'll know I should stop and give you the opportunity to speak."

Rose began by describing in detail what she'd observed around the abandoned uranium mines and waste ponds, apologizing for not having time to convert the photographs taken recently into slides or computer images that could be displayed on a screen. Instead, she'd brought the prints themselves, labeled on the back with date and location. She invited those interested in seeing what she was describing to come up at the end of her talk to look at the photos.

Rose explained what she'd seen and responded to a few questions from the audience. Afterward, she began to discuss the decline of herbs especially important to Navajo traditions, including the plants used in Sings and for healing.

A question came up almost immediately from a voice that sounded familiar. "What do you think is more important to the *Dineh*, the health and welfare of a few varieties of plants, or the health and welfare of our children—which are in jeopardy if we insist on living as herbalists or sheepherders while the rest of the Southwest moves into the next century."

Rose searched with her eyes for the speaker and recognized Vera Jim immediately.

There was a brief murmur of whispered comments and disapproval among the gathering, then the room grew silent, all eyes on Rose.

Rose refused to look back at the woman as she tried to gather her thoughts and decide exactly how to answer her without making things worse. Vera wanted to make trouble, and Rose was determined not to give her the satisfaction.

Vera stood up again. "Do you suppose you could come up with an answer *before* my lunch hour is over?"

Lena came forward and stood beside Rose. "Please sit down, young lady, and give our speaker time to respond to your question. There's no need to be rude."

Several others echoed Lena's words, but Vera remained standing in spite of the fact that the young woman next to her kept pulling at her sleeve.

"I'm glad that you realize that there might be a connection between mining operations and the health and welfare of our children," Rose began. "If you're interested, I can tell you briefly about some children I remember, some of them not yet born at the time, who became permanently ill as a result of the biggest spill of radioactive waste in the country. Did you know it took place on our land? Those who survived are about your age now." Rose shook her head slowly, and started walking away from the podium, a move calculated to keep everyone's eyes upon her. "Are you able to guarantee, and wager the lives of your children, that it won't happen again?" Rose stopped and looked directly at Vera.

The young woman squirmed as the focus turned back to her. Vera muttered something that sounded like "bitch" as she noisily stepped out into the aisle and fled the room. The woman who'd been next to her started to get up, then, deciding not to follow, sat back down instead.

"We obviously have to reach some sort of middle ground—a settlement that will allow us to keep what is important to our culture and still provide for the economic future of the *Dineh*. Unfortunately, our impatient friend didn't wait around to learn how we all can have some of what we want, and what we need, if we plan carefully and do the right thing." Rose smiled, and walked back to the podium.

"First of all, if we are going to have various industries on our land, we are going to have to protect the Plant People and Mother Earth. That requires all of us to get better educated on the issues facing us. That's the real reason I came here today—to contribute, to listen, and continue to learn."

Rose knew she was about to take an important step, and that some of the traditionalists would think she was compromising too much, but it was a step that needed to be taken. Vera Jim, in spite of her rash and rude behavior, had made her realize how important it was to walk in another woman's moccasins for a while.

The following morning, Ella arrived early for work, ready to tackle a mountain of paperwork. For the first time in days, she actually felt rested. Last night she'd played with Dawn, helped her telephone her father, and heard a million stories about her friend's new pony. Dawn was determined to find a way to get them to buy her a horse of her own.

In desperation, Ella had offered to buy Dawn a lamb or a goat, but that was as far as she was willing to go. She just didn't have it in the budget to cover feed, vet bills, riding lessons, saddles and tack, and the rest of the expenses a pony would bring.

Yet, although it was out of the question now, Ella knew she'd have to cave in and buy Dawn a horse someday. Owning a horse was practically a rite of passage here on the Rez, and it didn't seem right to deny that to Dawn when she was older. Both Clifford and she had grown up with a few goats and a horse to take care of, to teach them responsibility. In fact, the corral that they'd so painstakingly built was still intact. It had been one of the tasks their father had assigned to them and then had supervised. Her father, who'd been a preacher, had referred to the animals as his "other flock."

Dawn was still very young, however. She wouldn't be getting a horse for several more years, so there was no sense in worrying about that now.

Ella sat down at her desk, and turned on her computer. It took a while to come on-line, but at least the system appeared to be working today. She'd complete her manpower report first, then take another stab at finding out more about Professor Kee Franklin.

Ella had been at it for fifteen minutes when Justine walked in.

"I've got the information you asked me to get. Larry Tso is pro-NEED and considered a very influential modernist."

"Any record?"

"Larry has a few parking tickets in Farmington, but that's it."

"You have his address?" Ella asked.

"You bet."

"Then let's go to work, partner." Although she'd told Justine about Larry Tso yesterday, they'd had no time to follow up the possible lead until now, and Ella was eager to get going.

Moments later they were on their way. It was early, barely seven-thirty.

"You know, almost everything that's going on around here of a criminal nature—well except for a few petty thefts—seems to involve NEED to some degree. Have you noticed that?" Justine asked.

Ella nodded slowly. "And Professor Franklin plays a major role in NEED, so he's definitely a player in all this. But we still don't have anything solid. Until we do, we have to pursue aggressively anything that turns up."

"So it's on to see Larry Tso. Where you do you want to try first—his house or his restaurant?"

"I don't think the restaurant has a breakfast business. Let's go to his home. The earlier it is, the more off guard he should be to our questions."

They were nearly at the Tso residence when Ella's cell phone rang. She was surprised to hear Sheriff Taylor's voice.

"I'd like you to come out to the Angel Peak turnoff south of Bloomfield. A Navajo man's been murdered—he was shot to death. We're still working the crime scene, but we found a matchbook nearby. It's from the Fair Winds Restaurant. I believe a Navajo man owns that place as well."

"Talk about coincidences. Yes, his name is Larry Tso. I was on my way to question him at his home on an unrelated matter. But we'll come see you first. Be there in forty-five minutes, less if the traffic is good." Ella hung up and glanced at Justine. "Turn around. We're going to Angel Peak, south of Bloomfield. Homicide scene." Ella placed her cell phone back in its case while Justine found a place to make a three-point turn.

"A pattern's emerging, though right now it's more like separate pieces of yarn that have only just begun to be woven together."

"Searching for the pattern," Justine mused. "You're getting to sound more like a traditionalist every day," she said, teasing.

"Navajo teachings are useful to everyone, including cops—we just view them from a different angle," Ella said with a ghost of a smile. "Now hit the emergency lights."

FIFTEEN

———— ✖ ✖ ✖ ————

A deputy met them at the junction of the main highway and the Angel Peak turnoff, and led them to the crime scene in an arroyo a few miles east down one of the gas well service roads.

The entire area was dotted with natural gas wells, which fed their production to a plant just outside Bloomfield, north of Angel Peak, and other sites. The victim was in a car down in an arroyo just off one of the dirt service roads. The immediate area around the vehicle had been cordoned off with crime-scene tape, and several county crime-scene investigators were working the scene.

Ella couldn't decide if it was a sin or a blessing to have died near such a breathtaking place. A quarter mile farther east, the vast mesa they were standing upon gave way to beautiful sandstone spires and sculptures reminiscent of Bryce Canyon in Utah, but less colorful and on a much smaller scale.

Sheriff Taylor, seeing them pull up, went over to their car. "It's messy," he warned. "He was shot to death in his car. One bullet to the head."

"Close up, from behind?" Ella asked.

"Yeah, the victim has what looks like powder burns."

"What else have you got besides the matchbook?"

"According to the driver's license photo, which matches enough of his face to make the ID, we know that the victim is Robert Whitesheep."

"I know him," Justine said. "He supports the idea of a nuclear power plant, but is against the NEED proposal. He wants outsiders who have experience with that sort of thing handling the critical stuff for the tribe."

"Are you sure?" Ella asked surprised.

"Yeah, he dated my sister, Jayne."

"You think all the murders here and the ones on the Rez are related to that nuclear power plant proposal?" Taylor looked at Ella, then Justine.

"We're certainly looking at the possibility at the moment," Ella said. "Mix money, politics, and high emotion, and trouble's bound to follow."

Justine caught Sheriff Taylor's attention. "Would you mind if I take a look around? I won't disturb the scene or touch anything."

"Go ahead, Officer Goodluck." Taylor glanced back at Ella. "I wanted you to be in on this because I suspected it was linked to the murders over on the reservation," Taylor said, showing Ella the matchbook they'd found, now in a signed and numbered plastic bag, as Justine slipped under the yellow tape to move in closer. "Since you seem to have guessed the killer's execution-style methods, I guess I was on the right track. Tell me more."

Briefly, she told him what she had on Officer Franklin and Councilman Redhouse's deaths so far, and the various leads she was investigating. "Yet, no matter how I turn it around, the fact is that people who are or seem to be against the NEED project are the ones who turn up dead."

"Since this murder happened on my turf, I'm going to want everything you can give me on Whitesheep and the owner of the restaurant."

"You'll have it, but let's keep communication open both ways.

I'd like your findings as well. Especially any info about the bullet used to kill Whitesheep, if you manage to recover it."

"Not a problem," Taylor responded.

Justine returned, and nodded to Taylor. "Thanks for the opportunity to look around. Your team seems to have it all together. Will we get a chance to look at the report?"

"Investigator Clah and I have already agreed to share information on the recent murders," Sheriff Taylor replied, "and any new discoveries that may point in their direction."

"By the way, I have to go talk to Larry Tso on another matter. Do you want me to question him about his connection to the murder victim here?" Ella asked.

"Yeah. I'd appreciate it. I'm going to have my hands full for a while here. Call me later and fill me in," Taylor said. Nodding to both officers, he added. "I'm sure our paths will be crossing again on these cases. We're dealing with a cold-blooded killer here. Watch your backs."

"You too, Sheriff," Ella replied.

As Taylor walked back to join his crime-scene unit, Ella and Justine returned to their vehicle.

"You said you knew the victim?" Ella asked Justine as soon as they were under way.

"Yeah. He and his father were really on the outs. His dad is a traditionalist, dead set against bringing *leetso*, the yellow monster, back among the People."

Ella remembered the traditionalist beliefs her mother had taught her. One way to defeat an enemy was to name it. That's how the uranium had been named—*leetso* meant "yellow dirt." But, unfortunately, naming it hadn't helped defeat the damage that had already been done.

Justine pursed her lips for a moment. "I can't swear to this, but I think the dead man was in the same clan as Councilman Redhouse."

Ella looked at her partner. "Verify that as soon as you can. This could add a brand-new spin to the councilman's death."

Justine nodded. "I also remember Jayne telling my mother that Robert Whitesheep had been talking about moving off the Rez. He'd been involved in some business that had gone sour."

"Did Jayne mention anything more, like who Whitesheep had been dealing with and exactly what had happened?"

"Not that I recall, but I'll ask her. She probably knows. Jayne's as nosy as I am."

"This case is really bugging me, Justine. We're getting led around in circles. It reminds me of one of the creation stories my mother loved to tell us." Ella's expression grew distant as she remembered. "One day Sun decided he wanted the People's riches, so he taught his son, Gambler, how to acquire things for him," Ella began. "Gambler thought he was invincible, and assured of his own power, he defied his father: Sun got angry and created another who could defeat him. One of the ways Gambler's adversary got the better of him was by creating doubt in his mind. Once Gambler was no longer sure of himself and his capabilities, that led to his downfall."

"Do you think someone's trying to throw a bunch of false leads at us, hoping to confuse us and make us doubt our ability to solve the crimes?"

Ella nodded. "I think we're up against a very smart opponent. He uses what's there already to muddy up the trail."

Once back in Farmington, they stopped by Tso's restaurant, which only contained the cleanup crew. There they were told Larry was at home today with the flu, and wouldn't be coming in. They set out again, continuing on west toward the Rez.

"My gut feeling is that if we can find out what the perp was searching for when he broke into the garage, Wilson's storeroom, and his home, we'll have all the answers we need," Justine said. "The killing of Redhouse has got to be related to that. We know the shooter was the same." She paused, lost in thought, then added, "You don't think these could be contract jobs, with different clients but the same perp?"

"If that's true, we'll almost have to stumble across the killer, because none of the motives would fit. But I don't think that's the case. We'll just keep following the trail and see where it takes us."

"Next stop, Larry Tso's."

"We need to push Tso hard," Ella said. "Watch him carefully for body language."

Justine nodded, her eyes on the road, but her thoughts obviously on the case, judging from her expression.

Despite his rumored success in the restaurant business, Larry Tso's home was a simple pitched-roof stucco-and-wood-frame house in a large area of land just east of Shiprock along the river valley. This meant he or his wife's family were allottees—one of the many families that had managed to hold on to their land for generations. About a dozen head of sheep could be seen in a corral about fifty yards from the main house.

Ella knocked hard on the front door, then stepped back, looking around casually. The porch was a painted concrete step, and a metal plate was imbedded into a spot toward the edge to function as a scraper. "Make sure to wipe the mud off your shoes before going in," she joked, indicating the scraper. Ella couldn't remember the last time it had rained.

"Of course, Emily Post," Justine said with mock seriousness.

Within thirty seconds, a pretty young Navajo woman in her late teens answered the door. She was wearing jeans and a pale oatmeal-colored turtleneck sweater. A heavy-looking turquoise-and-silver squash blossom hung from around her neck.

Ella introduced herself, taking out her badge, and Justine remained silent, just producing her own identification.

"My dad's sick today. Can you come back tomorrow?"

"Sorry, no. This may be very important. Can you get him for us?"

She nodded. "Sure, but he's going to be in a real bad mood," the young woman warned.

The first thing that caught Ella's eye was that despite the modern setting, the house reflected traditionalists' tastes. The simplicity of it soothed her. There were sheepskins on the living room floor, a wood-and-coal stove, and meticulously made Navajo rugs hung on the walls. There was no television or radio within sight. The room reminded her of her brother's medicine hogan, except here there was electricity and the walls were textured and painted drywall instead of fitted pine logs.

A heavyset man wearing a terry-cloth bathrobe came out from the hall moments later. "My daughter said you just had to talk to me?" he grumbled.

Ella had to admit that Larry Tso looked ill. His face was flushed, his nose was red, and, as he lowered himself onto one of the sheepskins, his movements were unsteady.

"I feel awful, so unless you want my flu, I suggest you get on with it," he snapped.

"I'm sorry to come at such a time, but there's been a murder, and we need to ask you some questions." Ella hesitated, uncertain whether to mention Whitesheep by name or not. Tso's house was modern, but the style in here spelled traditionalist.

He wrapped the thick bathrobe even more tightly around himself, revealing sheepskin-lined moccasins on his feet. "Is it cold in here?"

Ella shook her head, looking toward the woodstove, which was radiating heat even from ten feet away. "It's a little warm, if you want to know the truth."

He shrugged. "It's this blasted flu then. Okay, speak to me. Who's turned up dead now, and what does it have to do with me?" Meeting Ella's gaze, he added, "Don't let the sheepskins throw you. The things in here are a concession to my wife. I don't believe in nonsense like the *chindi*."

"Robert Whitesheep," Ella said softly in deference to Tso's wife, in case she was within hearing distance.

He nodded thoughtfully. "I know the man. Knew him, rather. Robert came by my restaurant once in a while. Sometimes, when I was free, we talked."

"About what?"

"Local matters. He knew I was a successful businessman, and he wanted my support. He thought a small nuclear power plant was a good idea, but he was totally against the tribe running it, like NEED is pushing for. Robert felt we needed people with more expertise, even though it would mean bringing in a bunch of Anglos."

"Did he have any particular company in mind to run it? Arizona Public Service? PNM?"

"I know he wanted to license the operation, but I don't think he had any particular company in mind. He just wanted to make sure that we gave it to a company with a lot of experience." He shrugged. "I didn't go for that. I'm pro-NEED. We've had enough outsiders running things here, and look where that's gotten us."

"Who else was Whitesheep working with on this?"

"I know there were others—Billy Redhouse might have been in league with him, but I'm just not sure. I never liked for Robert to bring up the topic, since I knew we'd argue. NEED is the only way to go, as far as I'm concerned. It'll bring jobs and give us the ability and funds to buy more land, so we can expand our borders."

"Can you think of any reason why someone would want to kill Robert Whitesheep?"

Larry considered it for a long moment. "Robert was on a mission, and was really hardheaded about this project. A lot of what he said came across to me as lack of faith in our own people—that we were just too ignorant or stupid to run this on our own. Men like that are bound to make enemies." He coughed, then took a breath that ended with a wheeze. "But why did you come to talk to me about him?"

Ella paused for effect, then looking him directly in the eyes answered. "A matchbook from the Fair Winds was found near the body."

He shrugged. "So? The restaurant has hundreds of regular patrons, and the matchbooks are theirs to take. If there are fingerprints on it, I doubt they'll be mine."

"We're involved in several other investigations as well," Ella answered. "As a NEED proponent, I understand you've had dealings with Councilman Redhouse as well."

"Nobody could ever pin Billy down. To this day, I'm still not certain how he would have voted." Tso cleared his throat. "But my own gut feeling is that he would have ultimately come out in support of NEED."

"Were either the pro-NEED factions or those who oppose a nuclear power plant afraid of what would happen if he didn't side with them?" Justine asked.

"I wouldn't say 'afraid,' but he was certainly a potential prize, politically speaking. He'd pushed things through before just on the strength of his personality. NEED wanted him on our side, but people like Professor Franklin were also trying to recruit him for the opposition."

"What about Redhouse's widow, Emily?" Ella asked carefully. "Was she for or against NEED? Her opinion must have carried some weight with her husband."

"Emily was there at the meetings and always had intelligent comments. She never spoke for or against NEED, but she seemed the type that would support her husband and stand by him no matter what." Larry lowered his voice. "She sure is . . . was an asset to his career. Always made her guests feel special."

"That's what I've been told. But I heard he had a roving eye," Ella said, hoping Tso would volunteer more information.

"I really wouldn't know, but he never gave her much attention, at least when I was there."

"What else can you tell me about Emily?"

His expression grew guarded. "Oh, come on. You can't believe she'd kill her own husband."

"I wasn't suggesting she's involved in any way," Ella said with a shrug. "But to solve a murder, I have to get into the life and the head of the person who was killed. That means delving into every facet of his life."

Larry nodded, then glanced toward the kitchen, as if making sure no one was listening. "Emily was a real asset to Billy. She could bring in votes from the traditionalists *and* the modernists. As long as he was married to her, reelection would have never been a problem. Charming woman."

"Was Emily happy being his wife?"

"You'd have to ask her. In a lot of ways I think Billy was a bit jealous of his wife. She'd always been well-off, so she'd never had to struggle like he had. That touch of class—the very thing that probably attracted him to her—was something he never had." He paused. "But that's just my opinion." Larry stood up. "I've told you all I know. Now I'm going back to bed. If there's any justice at all in this world, both of you will catch the flu."

As Tso wandered back down the hall, his daughter came out of the kitchen and offered to show them to the door. "He's usually not so crabby. Really."

Saying good-bye, Justine and Ella returned to the car. "Let's go pay Professor Franklin a visit," Ella said. "I'm going to take him to where his son was killed—if he'll go. I'd like to have him look at all the papers and books there and tell me anything that comes to his mind."

"And we can study his reactions, and see what he doesn't choose to discuss. Even the most brilliant of thinkers can't always hide their emotions," Justine added.

"Exactly."

SIXTEEN
————— ✖ ✖ ✖ —————

As Justine headed back to Farmington, silence stretched out between them. Finally, Ella glanced over at her partner.

"You seem distant, and haven't had much to say at our interviews, cuz. Is there something on your mind?"

Justine sighed. "I've got something going on in my personal life that's really been bugging me. But don't worry. I'll get a handle on it soon enough."

"If you want to talk about it, I'll be happy to listen."

"I've got a problem with Wilson," Justine said, her words followed with a long sigh. "We've been dating exclusively for several months, but I know he's not happy leaving things between us where they are. He wants to get married, Ella, and I'm just not ready for that. I've taken a close look at the other officers who are married and the struggle they have finding time to spend with their families. I've seen that same thing with you, too, of course."

Ella nodded, but said nothing.

"Police work can take everything out of you, physically and emotionally. Then there's not much else left for anyone else at the end of the day. That's why so many of us end up divorced. I just don't want to put myself in a position where I'll always be torn between my job and my family."

"There's a lot of truth in what you're saying. I never feel I have enough quality time to spend with Dawn. I rush home at the end of the day, but I'm lucky if I make it there before it's time for her to go to sleep. It's a constant tug of war that can tear you into pieces if you're not careful."

"I don't want to live that way," Justine said flatly.

"Don't misunderstand me. Despite everything I just said," Ella added, "Dawn is the best thing that's ever happened to me. She's made me a better cop, too, in a lot of ways. I see my job differently now. What I do is so she and all the other daughters and sons inherit a Rez that's worth having."

"But Dawn doesn't have all the expectations Wilson does. As far as Wilson's concerned, a working wife should always put her job in second place. He'll provide for his family. But that's not me, and that's not police work."

"I hear you."

"If Wilson really understood how I feel about police work, we might have had a chance, but as it is . . ." She shook her head.

"If you really love him, you owe it to yourself to try and work things out. Don't walk away unless you're absolutely certain it's not something you'll end up regretting for the rest of your life. Avoiding marriage won't release you from the conflicts and potential problems in your life when a man is involved. Do you want to cut yourself off from any kind of long-term relationship?"

"I see what you mean. But tell me something. You're dragging your feet with Harry Ute. He's crazy about you, and I can see you really like him. Your mother would dearly love to have him as a son-in-law, and I think he'd be a good father for Dawn. So why hasn't your relationship gone any further?"

Ella took a deep breath, then let it out again. "I think both he and I are gun-shy. We both know that our marriage would be tested from the very beginning if we continued our present jobs. He'd be gone all the time, and my life is here in Shiprock."

"But it's no different now, and you're making it work."

"But the way it is, he's not a part of Dawn's world, nor she of his. To change would mean risking a lot—including hurting my own child, if things don't go right."

"And deep down you don't think things will work?" Justine asked, zeroing in on what Ella had left unspoken.

"I don't have the greatest track record with men," Ella admitted. "I married once when I was still a teenager, and it didn't end well." Ella remembered the day she'd learned that her husband had been killed by skinwalkers. In a roundabout way, that one event had led her to becoming a cop.

"Then, after a lifetime of dates that went nowhere, I met Kevin and, before I really understood he and I weren't right for each other, Dawn was already on her way. I could have accepted his proposal for Dawn's sake, but his love for politics would have eventually destroyed everything—including our friendship. I'm just not cut out to be a politician's wife."

"Wilson and I are suited to each other in most ways. That's why it's so hard to walk away." Justine took a deep breath, then let it out slowly. "In all fairness to Wilson, I can understand why he wouldn't want the mother of his kids working for our department. After Jason Franklin died, a lot of us have had to take a really close look at our jobs. Dedication is one thing—suicide is another."

"I know," Ella answered softly. "This was the first officer we've lost here since you joined the force, isn't it, Justine?"

"Yes, and it's forced me to reevaluate my priorities in life all over again. I haven't sat down and thought about what I'm doing with my life this seriously since my own brush with death, what was it, two years ago now. But like I decided then, I'm staying. I'm not just a cop—I'm a tribal police officer. I've lived within the Sacred Mountains all my life. Although I'm not a traditionalist, I always carry an earth bundle with soil from the Sacred Mountains in my pocket. It reminds me of who and what I am. Does that sound crazy coming from a modernist?"

"No, not at all." Ella reached for the badger fetish around her neck, then opened her jacket, revealing the medicine bundle her brother had given her. They were both part of the People. At the center of every modernist or traditionalist, beat the heart of the *Dineh.* "My brother says that the Sacred Mountains are alive and that they're our guardians. They provide structure and protection. This is our home—and what we fight to protect."

As they pulled into Kee Franklin's home, they saw that his SUV wasn't parked in the driveway.

"Maybe his vehicle is in the garage," Justine said, looking around.

"Could be. Let's go take a look around anyway," Ella said.

They walked to the porch, but when no one responded to their knock, Justine went to look through the garage window while Ella peered inside between the parted curtains. There was a torn duffel bag discarded on the sofa, and she could see through the open door that the closet was empty.

"The car is gone," Justine reported, returning to where Ella was standing.

"I hope he didn't decide to go out of town," Ella said.

"I would think he'd want to stick around and see what we turn up on his son's murder." She followed Ella's line of vision. "I suppose a man could have an empty closet. That's a very big house for just one person."

Ella studied the room. On the table beneath the window was a medicine bundle and a small bag of herbs like the ones she'd seen her brother give to his patients. "Well, it's clear nobody's home right now."

"You want to wait?"

Ella considered it. "We have no idea when he'll return, so let's go talk to Clifford," she said, pointing the medicine bag out to Justine.

"You think the professor's been to see your brother—that he's now a patient?"

"If he has, it's probably a recent development. But he's lost his son, and that will profoundly affect any parent. Franklin is going through a lot of pain and stress right now. Maybe Clifford can tell me something without compromising his confidentiality."

They arrived at Clifford's medicine hogan shortly after noon. Ella's stomach felt empty. She couldn't remember the last time she'd eaten.

"After this, we stop and get something to eat. I'm famished," she told Justine.

"You won't get an argument from me."

Ella climbed out of the SUV, then leaned against the side of the vehicle, waiting for her brother to come to the door of the medicine hogan and wave her inside. His wife's car was gone.

It took several minutes, but when Clifford came outside, he nearly stumbled, then stopped to lean against the doorway for support. "Wait for me, Justine," she said, then went to meet him. "Are you okay, brother?"

"I did a Sing for a patient that took all night. I'm tired and sleepy, that's all." He sat down in one of the sheepskins on the ground, then motioned for her to join him and share some herbal tea.

Ella took the warm cup he offered. "Where are your wife and son?" she asked, suspecting Loretta had gone to see her family. When she was at home Loretta always insisted on Clifford getting enough rest.

"She went to her mother's for a week. Her cousin's coming down from Utah." He took a deep breath. "She's lonely here, you know. She really wants to live close to her family, not mine. But my patients are mostly from around here. I've lived in this area all my life, and people depend on me. I know where the Plant People live, and when they move away. I'm always guided to the right places at the right times when I need to gather herbs. If we left . . ." He shrugged.

Seeing the pain in her brother's eyes touched her deeply. If it hadn't been a taboo to touch a close member of the same clan, she would have hugged him. "Is there anything I can do?"

Clifford shook his head. "It's my problem. I'll take care of it." He paused and met her gaze. "But that's not why you're here."

"I'd like to talk to you about a man I believe may be your patient—the anti-NEED scientist who recently lost his son."

He nodded. "I know who you mean. He's not a regular patient of mine, but he did come by to talk to me about the possibility of having a Sing done for his nightmares. I gave him some herbs to help him sleep and offered to arrange a time with him, but I don't think he'll come back. He was uncomfortable here."

"I needed to speak to him, so my partner and I went by his house. He wasn't there either. Do you have any idea where I might find him?"

"No. He didn't say anything about going away, if that's what you're wondering about."

"Can you tell me what kind of nightmares he was having?" Ella asked.

"He told me he was having bad dreams about a bear chasing him. He could never get away, no matter how hard he tried. He'd spoken to friends of his about it, and they'd recommended he come see me." Clifford took a sip of tea, then continued. "I told him that it sounded like Tracking Bear. In our stories of creation, he was an evil from which there was no escape."

"What did he say about that?"

"He told me that the only evils he would never be able to escape were the results of his research in Los Alamos. I tried to warn him that nightmares have power and have to be dealt with, but I got the feeling that he didn't really believe I could help him." Clifford looked down at his boots, then shook his head.

Ella considered what Clifford had told her. "The effects of uranium could be likened to Tracking Bear. You can't escape it. It finds you. Uranium causes illnesses that no doctor—Anglo or Navajo—can really stop. All they can do is hold it off as long as possible."

"A Sing would have helped him find peace," Clifford said. "But you mentioned that you were trying to find him?" Seeing her nod, he added, "Then why don't you go speak to his aunt? The scientist's mother and father have long since passed away, but his aunt will probably speak to you if you approach her with respect. She's a traditionalist and lives just past Hogback, across the old road from the Trading Post over there. She has a small orchard, and sometimes sells fruits and vegetables from a stand just off the main highway."

"Thanks, brother, I appreciate your help." She started toward the door of the hogan, then stopped. "I know you hate to ask anyone for help, but if there's ever anything I can do for you, all you have to do is let me know."

He smiled and nodded. "I know that, little sister."

Ella joined Justine outside a moment later, and they set out to see Kee's aunt, who lived at the eastern edge of the Rez a short distance from Highway 64. "Do you know her?" Ella asked.

Justine shrugged. "Not personally, but from the background check I did on him, I know that Thelma Jacks is Kee's closest living relative. I understand that they don't really get along."

"Let's see what we can find out."

On the way through Shiprock they stopped long enough to

pick up a bucket of fried chicken. Ella was famished, and ate greedily. Justine mostly picked at her food as she continued to drive.

"Do you want me to take the wheel for a while so you can have a chance to eat?" Ella asked after she'd finished her second piece and was wiping her hands with a napkin.

"No, it's okay." Justine had a half-eaten drumstick in her hand.

They arrived in late afternoon, and the tall shadow of Hogback already shaded the entire area. Hogback, an enormous outcropping that ran for miles, was so close they could make out individual boulders on the steepest side, which faced east. As they drove down the narrow lane leading to the house, Ella saw the outline of an elderly woman ahead pulling a large red wagon filled with boxes of apples. The small cart, normally a child's toy, was widely used in the area by nurseries as well.

"That must be her," Ella said.

"Should I pull up beside and offer her a ride?"

"No, stop when we're almost even, then let me get out and help her. Maybe if I buy some apples, it'll show her I respect her as a farmer and a businesswoman. It may also make her more receptive to my questions. We'll both get something out of this that way."

"Great idea. I'll drive to her house and wait for both of you there."

"No, don't do that. Remain here until we get to the house, then come get me. That way she won't feel that we're trying to hurry her up or double-team her. Traditionalists tend to distrust people who are too direct or come on strong."

"You're right." Justine slowed to a stop behind Thelma, and Ella climbed out.

Thelma glanced back at Ella as she came up. "If you've come for some of my apples, I've already closed the stand for the day, but I could sell you some if you don't need me to make change."

Ella asked for a grocery bag of apples, seeing several small sacks folded and stuck between the boxes. The woman stopped and filled a bag, two apples at a time.

"Do you need anything else? Business was slow today, so I decided to quit an hour early and go home. The price for the apples is five dollars a bag."

"I'll walk along with you, if you don't mind." Ella handed her the money. "May I pull the wagon for you?"

The old woman nodded, placing the money in the pocket of her thin cardigan sweater, and they started walking toward the old cinder-block home a hundred yards farther down the lane.

"Do you know who I am?" Ella asked.

"Yes. You ran those troublemaking Navajos out of the power plant across the river. I think you were once called L.A. Woman."

It had been many years since anyone had used that nickname, and nowadays, if she had a new one, she didn't know what it was. For a moment, Ella's mind went back to the days when she'd just resigned from the FBI and had joined ranks with the tribal police. She'd tried very hard at first to get accepted by the tribe, but to them, she'd become an outsider.

"You proved them all wrong, including me, you know," Thelma said softly. "I thought you would be just like my nephew. He left, then forgot who he was. But you remembered after you came back, and many respect that now."

"Would you be willing to talk to me about your nephew and his family?"

She nodded and smiled. "You did the right thing, buying some of my apples, even if you don't need them."

Ella laughed. "I'm glad you approve."

"I knew you'd come, you know," Thelma said. "The death of my nephew's son has touched us all. Now I'm the only one my nephew has left. We've even started speaking again, and I've been to his home off the Navajo Nation." She paused, then added in a somber voice, "Tracking Bear has found all the members of my family now—except me."

Ella glanced at Thelma. "I know the story of Tracking Bear. But what does that have to do with your nephew?"

"My nephew has had many nightmares about that Navajo monster. It haunts his dreams. I told him to go see a *hataalii*, and he did, but I don't think he's going to have a Sing done over him. Even with his son dead, he still won't listen. Before long, Tracking Bear will claim him, too. When we allowed that uranium to be taken from the earth, we dishonored Earth Woman, and she cursed us."

"Has he ever spoken to you about what he's trying to do now for the tribe?"

Thelma nodded slowly. "He wants to stop the uranium mines from ever being opened again. He's afraid things will go wrong again and the *Dineh* will pay dearly, as they have in the past." Thelma paused. "He's also trying to get better medical treatment and benefits for those already injured. But something goes wrong for him at every turn."

"We went to his home and couldn't find him. Do you know where he might have gone?" Ella asked.

"When his heart aches, he likes to go off by himself. He's always been that way. But, no, I don't know where you can find him, except to say that he'll be camping someplace on the reservation."

Ella bit back her frustration. That didn't narrow the field much. The Rez was a large place.

As they reached the house, Thelma took the handle of the red wagon. "Do you have all you want now?"

"Yes, even the apples. Thank you."

As the elderly woman went inside, Ella walked over to the SUV where Justine was waiting. Once they got under way, Ella told her what she'd learned.

"We still can't explain the reason for all the break-ins, or the murders, and now we can't even locate Franklin. We're not making headway—we're losing ground," Justine said.

"No, I don't agree. We just haven't pieced together what we know in the right way. Father and son were staunchly opposed to NEED, but deep down, they must have realized that it was a fight they wouldn't win—not without more leverage than they had. I'm wondering if either of the Franklins somehow managed to get some kind of documentation that would discredit NEED."

"You're talking blackmail material, right?"

"Yeah, exactly. It's possible that the common denominator is blackmail material that the professor hid somewhere. What we have to do now is stop guessing and lean hard on Kee Franklin— but first, we'll have to find him again."

"We can put out an APB . . ."

Ella considered it then shook her head. "No, let's not resort to that yet. The bottom line is that we have to persuade Franklin to cooperate with us. Strong-arm tactics won't get us what we want." Exasperated, Ella ran a hand through her hair. "We're still missing an important piece of the puzzle. I can feel it in my gut. But unless Blalock can get the government to open a few files for me, we're never going to see how it all fits together."

"Ask FB-Eyes again. Sometimes it pays to bug people."

"Yeah, I think you're right. But to be fair, I know he's as frustrated as I am with this. He doesn't like to get bureaucratic doors slammed in his face."

"At least he has the connections. We don't."

"True," Ella admitted.

"What do you want to do now?" Justine asked.

Ella said nothing for a long moment. "It's close to quitting time, and we both started early today. I think we both should go home and then start where we left off tomorrow morning."

"I thought you'd never say that," Justine said with a relieved sigh. "Why don't I drop you off at home? I can pick you up tomorrow and you can retrieve your own unit at the station then."

"Sounds good to me."

SEVENTEEN
— ✷ ✷ ✷ —

By the time Ella got home, Dawn had already had supper, so she sat down on the floor in the living room to play with her daughter and her toy farm. The set of animals, stables, and barns had taken on a new significance to Dawn since she'd acquired an interest in horses.

After a few minutes Rose brought a sandwich out from the kitchen and placed the plate on the coffee table next to Ella.

"Are you any closer to solving any of the cases you're working on?" Rose asked, not being more specific in deference to Dawn.

"Not as close as I'd like to be." Ella shrugged, reaching for the sandwich. "Thanks for the dinner."

Dawn reached for the remote and switched on the TV. The Cartoon Channel appeared, and Dawn began to giggle at the antics of a cartoon mouse. With her child distracted for the moment, Ella nibbled on the sandwich and turned to talk to Rose.

"What about your reclamation work?" Ella asked.

"I had an interesting morning, daughter." Rose smiled, then proceeded to tell her about the college lecture and its outcome.

"This Vera Jim. She didn't threaten you, did she?"

"No, she was just very rude. But in spite of everything, I learned one thing from her. It's important to see every viewpoint, no matter how convinced you are that you're in the right," Rose said.

"Does that mean you've changed your mind on NEED and the proposed new mining operations?" Ella asked.

"I'm still concerned about safety, and what the project might do to Mother Earth, and our air and water. But I've realized that there may be ways to address all that. So now I'm going to try and educate myself on the subject. I've gotten photos that show what has worked and what hasn't when it comes restoring the land. But it's really hard to get hold of some of the people I need to talk to, like Delbert Shives. I've left messages on his answering machine, but he hasn't returned any of my calls. That Anglo knows a lot about the impact uranium mining has on the plants and ground cover, so I'm hoping he can suggest ways to help us. No matter what, I'm not giving up. Sooner or later I'll catch up to him. I'm very persistent."

Ella smiled. "Gee, you think?"

Rose gave her a stern look. "I do my best, and that's pretty darned good, if I say so myself."

"Which you do, and with such modesty!" Ella teased.

Rose's eyes flashed with annoyance, then she smiled. "You've always been a difficult child."

"Blame heredity." Ella chuckled softly. Still sitting on the floor, she leaned back against the side of the easy chair. As she did, she saw a medicine pouch near the table lamp. The leather had been sewn with care, and there was a bit of embroidering at the top. "Is that yours? I've never seen it before."

"Yes, it's for good luck. I made the pouch, and your brother collected the contents himself. I'm going to need all the help I can get to complete what I've started."

"So he came to visit today?" Seeing her mom nod, Ella added, "I wish his wife would spend more time at home. He seems really lonely over there with his family gone so frequently."

"She shouldn't leave her husband, if you ask me," Rose said angrily, then shook her head. "Well, maybe it's best that she's away. Right now your brother has his hands full with his patients. Being a *hataalii* demands much, you know. He can't be blamed if he doesn't have time, like we do, for all the little things family life requires."

Ella found her mother's words unbelievably irritating. Rose considered whatever Clifford was doing—no matter what it was—of prime importance. Everything and everyone else had always taken second place to Clifford.

"Don't look at me like that," Rose snapped. "Police work is important, but your brother's work is crucial to our culture."

Ella would have argued, but she knew it would get her nowhere.

"Right now, between his work and the research he's doing with me, he has very little time for anything else."

"What research?"

"Your brother and I have been looking into NEED beyond what we've already learned from our college professor friend. It's such a complex issue, we got together so we could discuss every side of the problem."

"I wish I'd been in on that."

Rose shrugged. "We never know when you're going to be home."

Ella just stared at her mother, but she'd never gotten Rose to back down before, and this time was no different.

As her favorite cartoon came on, Dawn began to sing the opening lyrics. She was never on key, but she always tried to make up for that with volume. That broke the tension between Ella and Rose, and both laughed before retreating into the kitchen.

"So tell me, how do you both feel about the issue?" Ella asked once she was seated at the dining table.

"Your brother and I understand the necessity of bringing jobs to the reservation, but there's one more problem with NEED no one's really answered to our satisfaction. Something will have to be done with all the radioactive waste produced by the power plant. My guess is that it would probably end up buried here on our land. Then, eventually, it could end up bringing more sickness and death to the People. We need to know how the waste can be stored safely, and what checks will be in place to ensure it doesn't become a threat."

Ella nodded slowly, thinking of the others Tracking Bear already followed. She was pretty sure that no containment facility or burial site could ever be considered one hundred percent safe.

"We've read about that waste storage site down near Carlsbad for storing materials less radioactive than the spent fuel itself. It's supposed to be secure. Many of the people in that area welcome the money the place brings in, setting aside the long-term risks. Maybe a similar one could be built here, but for higher-level material."

"That's an idea," Ella said. "There's talk of a nationwide storage area in Nevada for the most dangerous material, but many of the people in that state are opposed to it. Meanwhile, most spent radioactive fuel rods are stored around the power plants that used them, which seems fair. That probably won't change anytime soon."

"The safety of the *Dineh* is our first priority, and the only way we can ensure it is to have a supervising committee of experts paid by the tribe to oversee everything NEED does. In other words, NEED will have to be subject to us—and if they didn't immediately fix things we felt were not right, they would have to shut down." She took a deep breath, then let it out again. "But those running the facility aren't going to like putting their operations under our control, so that's another roadblock to approving the project."

Ella nodded slowly. She suddenly had a vision of her mother and other Plant Watchers like Lena Clani forcing the experts to account for everything they did. "I like your ideas, Mom. They wouldn't impede progress, just ensure that things stay on the right course."

"Exactly. I'm glad you agree, because I intend to speak on this issue soon, then start working to get even more support."

Ella was about to say more when her cell phone rang.

"It's Kevin," the familiar voice said.

It surprised her. Normally, he called on the house phone so he could speak to his daughter. That let her know, even before he said anything, that this wasn't a social call. "I thought I'd better give you a heads-up. You're going to get a phone call from George Branch tomorrow morning."

She tried not to cringe. "That weasel, why?"

"You remember the trouble I've been having with vandalism and harassing phone calls?"

"Sure. That's why you've got round-the-clock protection."

"My problems stopped after I did that, but now, Branch is being subjected to a different kind of harassment. It's not my fault—but *he* thinks I'm responsible. I suspect he's going to file a complaint and give me a lot of bad publicity."

"Kevin, tell me straight. You haven't lowered yourself to his level by using his own tactics against him, have you?"

"I swear that I'm not behind *any* of the trouble he's been having."

"Okay, then I'll do what I can."

"Thanks," he said, sounding very relieved. "Is it too late for me to talk to my daughter?"

"I don't know. Let me see if she's still awake." Aware that Dawn was no longer singing, she went into the living room and found her child asleep with her head on Two. The old mutt looked up at Ella when she walked in, then closed his eyes again. Dawn never moved.

"I'm afraid she's conked out for the night," Ella said, turning off the Cartoon Channel.

"All right. Maybe tomorrow."

"Remember, until we're sure no one's still targeting you, I'd like you to visit our daughter here at my mother's house," Ella said.

"That's really not necessary anymore. I've got a bodyguard. Dawn will be safe."

"His responsibility is you, not her. She's safer here, and I'd rather keep it that way."

Kevin paused, then answered, "Yeah, I see your point. I just hate thinking that my job is keeping me from seeing my own kid. Think of it—you wouldn't react any better than me to that if the conditions were reversed."

"I know." She would have been bouncing off the walls. But she knew Dawn would be safe as long as she was under Rose's roof. Anywhere else would be a gamble. "For now we'll just have to play it this way."

The next morning, Ella gave Dawn breakfast and got her ready for day school. She didn't always have the luxury of spending the morning with her child, but today she wanted to make time.

Dawn insisted on holding her stuffed pony as Ella dressed her. Maneuvering around the stuffed toy, especially when putting arms in sleeves, made things difficult, but somehow they managed.

"I want a pony," Dawn said, for the umpteenth time.

"You have a pony. Right there in your hands."

"No, I want a real one, like my friend's."

"Someday, when you get a little older." Ella sighed. When her daughter got something in her head, it was nearly impossible to dissuade her.

Ella hurried Dawn to the breakfast table and ate a buttered hot tortilla as her daughter finished her oatmeal.

"I'll take over," Rose offered. "You need more than that for breakfast. It's cold outside this morning."

Ella saw the frost on the windows and brought two eggs out of the refrigerator to scramble, when her cell phone rang. It was Justine.

"I'm on my way to pick you up."

"Great. I'll be ready."

As soon as she hung up the phone, it rang again. This time it was Big Ed. Ella could tell simply by the way he'd said "good morning" that it was anything but that.

"I got a call from that radio show guy, George Branch, a few minutes after seven this morning. I don't like early morning calls at my home—on my home number—particularly from the public. He's complaining about Councilman Tolino. He wants you to arrest him. Do you know anything about this?"

"Kevin told me last night that there might be a problem."

"See what's going on and handle it. Then find out how he got my home number. That bugs the hell out of me. It's unlisted and supposed to be private."

"I'll do my best."

As Ella hung up, Justine walked in the door, and Dawn ran over and threw her arms around her.

Justine picked her up, laughing. "Hey, cousin!"

Dawn shoved the pony between them. "See? I've got a pretty pony! And I'm going to have a real one, too, someday."

"Really?" Justine glanced over at Ella, who rolled her eyes and shook her head.

Justine put Dawn down as Ella reached for her jacket. "Let's go, partner," Ella said.

Giving her daughter one last hug and kiss, Ella left with Justine.

"Our first stop has to be George Branch," Ella said, giving her the highlights. "The chief is really ticked off this time. He wants us to find out how a talk radio moron like Branch got his number."

"And since George is so cooperative, I'm sure he'll tell us right away," Justine said sarcastically.

"Branch wants something from us, so we may—with luck—actually get a straight answer from him."

They arrived at the radio station right after George Branch finished his two-hour early-morning program. Today's entire program had been centered on dirty politics and tactics, as they learned by listening to the last half hour of the show on the way over. Although he'd alluded to Kevin as being one of the ones who'd adopted this practice to coerce his political enemies, Branch was careful never to mention Kevin by name. That was different from what he'd done before—when he'd taken every opportunity available to name him and put him in as bad a light as possible. Ella wondered about the sudden change of tactics.

George Branch, the overweight, boisterous, and thoroughly annoying half-Navajo gadfly, came out to meet them in the lobby as soon as their arrival was announced.

"Finally—a response! I guess that the chief of police doesn't like to get early morning complaints at home. But that seems to be the only way to arouse anyone at the department these days." He waved them to his office down the hall, then invited them to take a seat.

Moments later a young Anglo woman brought him a cup of

coffee and offered Justine and Ella the same, or a cup of tea. They declined.

"Okay, let's get down to it then. Kevin Tolino is harassing me, and I want it stopped." Branch was using his radio voice now, the one he referred to so often on the radio as the voice of reason.

"How, exactly, has he been harassing you?" Ella asked.

"Lately, every time I've said anything negative against Tolino on the air, something bad has happened to me. And I'm talking *every single time*."

"Specifics, please." Justine reminded him. "For example . . ."

"I'm getting to that." Branch glared at Ella. "I know you and your cousin are going to side with him—he *is* your kid's father. That's why I called your chief first. I don't want this swept under the rug." Branch paused, just like he did on his program, for dramatic effect. "Last week I pointed out how Tolino excels at straddling the fence instead of actually taking a stand on *any* issue. After that broadcast aired, my garbage pickup service was canceled. Then after my next show, a follow-up, my phone was disconnected."

"How do you know Kevin Tolino's to blame?" Ella asked.

"He's the most likely suspect. I take a jab at him on my program, and he gets back at me. What in the hell has happened to my freedom of speech?"

"Mr. Branch, you're a public figure who makes a great deal of money taking shots at others without any thought of fair play," Justine said. "It's no secret that you have a political agenda. I'd be willing to bet that there's a long list of people who'd love to make *your* life as difficult as you've made theirs."

Ella almost burst out laughing, but somehow, she managed to keep a straight face. "There's no evidence, then, only coincidences?"

"Look, I tried getting proof that could be used in court, but all

I can tell you is that some guy called up the phone company and the waste management office, saying he was me."

"And on the basis of that, you're accusing Councilman Tolino?" Ella asked.

"Tolino called me not long ago complaining that he had become the target of vandalism and harassment. He blamed it all on my broadcasts, saying I was rabble-rousing. Then, all of a sudden, the same things started happening to me. Can't you see it? Tolino's trying to even the score."

"So what you're saying is that the person who was harassing Tolino changed his mind and started harassing you?" Justine asked.

"I think Tolino caught the vandal in the act and cut a deal with him. Now *I've* got the problem. Ever since Tolino called to complain that my programs were creating trouble for him, my life's been screwed up. About two nights ago someone got into my SUV. They must have used a Slim Jim or had a key, because the door was locked when I got in to drive to work the next morning."

"What did they do, trash the interior?" Justine asked.

"No."

"Then how do you know anyone broke into it?" Ella pressed.

"Because all the radio station buttons were set to that annoying evangelical station," he said sourly.

Ella laughed out loud, and Justine joined her.

"Yeah, now it seems harmless, but it could escalate. I don't like this, and I shouldn't have to put up with it."

"Hey, you dish it out all the time to anyone and everyone who doesn't happen to share your views," Ella countered. "I wonder how your listeners would feel if they knew that you can't take the heat when the tables are turned?"

"But I shouldn't *have* to take it. That's my point, Clah. I'm exercising my constitutional rights on my radio program. There are laws protecting me and my property, and the harassment has to stop."

"Yes, and speaking of property, you live off the Rez. What makes you think I can help you out when it's happening out of my jurisdiction? Have you spoken to Sheriff Taylor?" Ella asked.

"Yeah, but he gave me the same song and dance you're giving me now. He said I've got to have proof, evidence, or an eyewitness." He met her gaze with a stony glare. "I figure you can watch the station in case the vandal hits here. I also want *you* to tell Tolino that I won't let up on him. If he thinks this will make me back off, he's crazy. I'll just push harder."

"Why don't you tell him that yourself?" Ella asked.

"Because if I see him, I'm almost certain I'll slug him, and then he'll have me arrested for assault."

"Nah, you won't even get close. His bodyguard is very capable. Feel free to tell Kevin yourself, it's not my job."

"Bodyguard? That pantywaist got himself a bodyguard? It figures. He doesn't have the balls to stand up under the pressure, does he?"

"Are you forgetting why *you* called us here?" Justine smiled sweetly. "Sounds like two peas in a pod, if you'll forgive the comparison."

"What I really don't get is *why* you're fighting with him. You're both pro-NEED," Ella said, trying not to laugh again.

"*I'm* pro-NEED, but he's still tap dancing with a lot of rhetoric. That's what he does best. Until he gets the . . . guts to speak plainly and say what he means, I'm going to stay on his case."

"There may be a way for me to help you . . ." she said slowly. "I can go see Councilman Tolino and ask him if he has any idea who has been harassing you. If he's responsible, knowing we're involved now might deter him. But I want something in return," Ella said.

Branch's eyes narrowed. "Such as?"

"I'd like to know how you got the chief's home number."

He smiled slowly. "That bugged him, did it?"

Ella said nothing.

"Just tell your chief that I can get any telephone number I need in this area. If he changes it, I'll just get it again. Having friends everywhere is one of the perks of being a radio legend in this community."

Ella gave him an incredulous look.

"Okay, okay," he said relenting. "My second cousin is a friend of his wife's. It was a fluke. That's all. Tell the chief not to get himself in an uproar."

Ella nodded. "Thanks. And, for what it's worth, I don't think Kevin's responsible for what's happening to you. That's just not his style."

"Yeah, yeah. He's above reproach."

"No, he's a politician and deal-maker. But he doesn't break the law."

"That would be refreshing if I believed it."

Ella shrugged. "My advice is stay sharp. It could be anyone you ticked off, and that doesn't narrow the field much."

As they walked out, Ella glanced at Justine, and they both started laughing hard. "*A legend?* In his own mind maybe," Ella said. "It's rich, isn't it? I'm just sorry I never thought of a little harmless retaliation like that myself when I was the target of nearly every broadcast."

Justine shook her head, still chuckling. "You'd have never stooped to that—as tempting as it might have been. In that respect, you're just like Kevin—you may hate what he says, but you'll defend his right to say it with your life."

"Sad, but true." Ella sighed. "Rats."

EIGHTEEN
—— ✖ ✖ ✖ ——

As they drove west toward the reservation, Dispatch patched through a call from the county sheriff. Justine was driving, and Ella picked up the mike.

"I thought you'd like to know that my deputies found five hundred dollars in cash hidden in the spare tire well of Whitesheep's car. Any idea where that might have come from?" Taylor said.

Justine and Ella exchanged glances. "Sheriff, would you have your lab check the bills for fingerprints?" Ella said.

"Sure, looking for anyone in particular?"

"Besides Whitesheep's prints, see if you can find any latents belonging to his clansman, the late Billy Redhouse," Ella added, glancing at Justine, who nodded. "Also, would you share your ballistic report from the Whitesheep murder."

A few seconds went by, punctuated by static, then Taylor responded. "Will do. I've been reading the reports your office has been faxing me. If there's evidence of a link between the two men, I'll let you know pronto."

"Thanks. We'll keep in touch." Ella hung up the mike just as her cell phone began to ring.

It was Big Ed. "I want you back here. I'm talking to Emily

Redhouse," he said. "She's learned that you've been asking a lot of questions about her, and came in to talk to you. She feels she's being unjustly singled out. And Kevin Tolino is with her."

"Chief, I'm conducting an investigation into her husband's death. I have to ask questions about relatives and acquaintances."

"I'm aware of that, Shorty. What I need you to do now is get back here as soon as you can and smooth some feathers. I realize that diplomacy has never been your strong suit, but I don't need a councilman and a widow with as much influence as Emily Redhouse has on my case."

"I'll be there within the hour," she said. Ella filled her partner in on her conversation while on the way. "I have a feeling that this wasn't Emily's idea—it was Kevin's. It sounds like a lawyer thing."

Justine glanced over at Ella, but she didn't speak.

When they arrived, Ella met Emily and Kevin in the chief's office, where they were discussing the weather and sipping coffee.

Kevin had on his lawyer face, and wore a nice sports jacket that made his broad chest and wide shoulders look even more appealing, if she hadn't already gone past that. Ella remembered him mentioning, back when they'd been dating years ago, that he wasn't above influencing a woman juror with his "masculine side."

"I'm here representing Mrs. Redhouse," Kevin began immediately. "She's making herself available to answer any questions you might have concerning the loss of her husband. My client has nothing to hide and is anxious to help in any way she can."

Ella nodded.

"I understand you've been asking questions about Mrs. Redhouse's relationship to her late husband. Instead of soliciting gossip and hearsay, my client prefers you ask her directly," Kevin said.

"Then we can get down to business, Councilman Tolino," Ella answered, then glanced at Emily.

"Others have mentioned to me that they've observed situations where your husband treated you very coolly, maybe even ignoring you in public," Ella said. "How would you like to respond to those reports?"

"Billy was a good husband, but his manner with me when he was conducting the business of the tribe always tended to be brusque. People didn't understand that it was simply his way of catering to those he represented politically. He could also be a very kind and generous man."

Ella held her gaze and decided to push. "Forgive me for being blunt—but you're an attractive, financially secure, well-known woman in this area. Is it possible that you may have attracted another man, someone who has a romantic interest in you and who may be willing to do almost anything to advance that potential relationship with you?"

Kevin's face began to redden, and he started to object, but Emily placed a hand on his arm and shook her head. "So you're thinking that someone attracted to me, a potential suitor, as you seem to be implying, killed my husband so I would be available again?" Emily shook her head. "First of all, anyone who knows me more than casually will tell you that I don't fool around. I was married to the man I wanted, and I was happy. During my marriage I was an important part of both his home and professional life. My husband needed me, and I needed him. Things were balanced."

"Then you don't consider it even a remote possibility that someone, a suitor wanna-be, may have killed your husband?"

Emily shook her head. "I come from a clan that's well-off. And, I may have a small amount of charisma, I suppose you can call it, that gets me extra attention. But the reason my husband was killed has nothing to do with me. My guess is that it's the result of the way he manipulated people—both in politics and outside of it."

"Can you be more specific?" Ella asked.

"He was quite involved with the NEED people and with others who wanted a nuclear power plant, but privately he rejected the strategy of having the tribe run it. He met with an Anglo man, someone connected to the energy industry, several times to discuss other options for the tribe."

Emily paused, measuring her words carefully as she added, "I know he was using the likelihood that he'd support the nuclear power plant as a way to do a little fund-raising for his next campaign. But he never made any firm commitment to anyone in exchange for money—he never would have sold his vote. He just loved playing political games and manipulating others."

Ella instantly clicked on the idea of fund-raising, especially after finding the cash Redhouse had hidden. And now there was the money that Whitesheep, a member of Billy's clan, had hidden in his car before his death. "Do you know the identity of the Anglo man?"

"I never saw him, or heard his name mentioned that I'm aware of. I usually attended most of my husband's meetings, but he never wanted me around when he met this man. I think he knew I'd disapprove of his tactics and didn't want me exposed to the less flattering aspects of politics."

"Do you know Robert Whitesheep?" Ella asked.

"Of course. Whitesheep and Billy grew up together, they're in the same clan. Whitesheep knew the Anglo man from work, and introduced the two of them, as a matter of fact. How did you know that?" Emily looked at Ella, then Kevin.

Ella ignored her question. "Why didn't you tell me about this Anglo man before, especially after knowing your husband was searching for financial supporters? Determining the motive for a crime helps us narrow down the suspects."

"My husband is dead, so it doesn't matter now how he might have voted on the issue. I just didn't want either side to use his name to strengthen their own position, especially since he's not around to confirm or refute their statements. And that cash you found could have come from legitimate political supporters. I'm sure my husband would have reported it sooner or later."

Ella shrugged. "Is there anyone else he may have told about these meetings with the Anglo man? A secretary, aide, or another colleague on the Tribal Council? Robert Whitesheep knew about them, apparently."

"I have no idea. All I can tell you is that when it came to political issues, he liked to play things close to his chest. That way he didn't make himself a target for either pro or con factions. People never knew how he'd vote, so they not only had to court him, they had to play it straight, or he'd have ammunition against them later on. He was well-known for that kind of political maneuvering."

"But this time you knew how he was going to vote. Do you think someone else might have also guessed what he'd decided and disapproved strongly?" Ella pressed.

She thought about it for several long moments. "It's possible that some of the NEED people might have picked up on it from something my husband said, or maybe didn't say."

"Thanks for your candor. I appreciate you coming in to tell me this," Ella said.

Emily stood, nodded to Big Ed, who'd merely listened the entire time, then looked back at Ella. "Find my husband's killer. I've told you all I know, and you now have a new trail to follow."

Better than Emily realized, Ella added silently. As Emily walked out she followed, then grabbed Kevin's arm and took him aside for a moment in the hall.

"I realize it's none of my business, but I'd like to know. Is something going on with you two, or do you think it's a possibility in the future?" she asked softly. "I noticed your face turning red, and you certainly gave her a lot of attention the night I visited her with you there."

Kevin met her gaze, then shook his head. "My life is complicated, you know that better than most. I've made enemies, professionally and privately. I'm not even free to see my daughter as often as I'd like because of that. I have no plans to get involved with anyone."

"You have your bodyguards. A wife could also be protected like that."

He exhaled softly. "I don't think I'm meant to have a wife, Ella. I've lived by my own rules for too long. I don't want to compromise or adapt to someone else. I like the way things are. If you're honest, you'll admit that you and I are alike in that way."

Ella was about to argue the point when Justine came up to her. "I've got an overseas call from Martha Grayhorse. The military finally tracked her down for us. Apparently she and her husband have been traveling around Europe on vacation, and the base personnel didn't have the itinerary."

"Thanks. I'll take it in my office."

Ella excused herself, hurried to her desk, then sat down and picked up the receiver. Someone had already given Martha the news, and the sorrow in the woman's voice touched her deeply.

"There's something I really need to know, Officer Clah. Did my son suffer before he died?"

"I believe his death was instantaneous," she said, recalling the execution-style murder.

"The information I received is that someone was trying to burgle that old garage where I keep some of my junk, and when my son walked in on them, he was killed. Is that true?"

"We believe there was more to it than that, but I can't disclose the direction our investigation is taking at the moment. Can you tell me if there was anything of substantial value stored in that garage, or a reason why anyone would think there was?"

There was no answer for such a long time, Ella wondered if Mrs. Grayhorse was still on the line. All she heard was electronic noise caused by the distant connection.

Finally, the woman cleared her throat. "My son had been storing some things that belonged to his father there. I'm not sure what they were, but the rest is just old furniture, books, and junk."

Ella remembered her feeling that Professor Franklin had been holding out on her. Kee's house was large—particularly for one person, and was not in the least bit cluttered. There was no reason, as far as she could see, why he couldn't have kept his own belongings at his home—unless he'd wanted to keep someone else, like whoever had broken into his house, from finding them.

"Have you heard of NEED, Mrs. Grayhorse?"

"Oh, of course. I spoke to my sister a few months ago, and it was all she talked about." She paused. "Imagine, a nuclear power plant on the reservation. But if you have questions about that, I think you should talk to my ex-husband. He was approached to join them because of his particular expertise in physics. He's ideally qualified to direct such a project, but I'm certain he'll never join them."

"Why do you say that?" She wanted to keep Martha Grayhorse talking. If anyone knew the answers she'd been searching for, Martha might.

"Kee always felt personally responsible for the plight of the Navajo miners who'd destroyed their health working in the uranium mines in the seventies. That's because his work at the labs contributed so much to the demand for uranium."

"Can you tell me a little more about his work?" Ella said, forcing her tone to stay casual.

She hesitated. "I don't think it's a secret anymore. That was so many years ago," she said, thinking out loud, then continued. "I don't understand all the details, but Kee specialized in photochemistry. He applied new laser technology—well, new at the time—to purify and enrich uranium, which was then used to power nuclear reactors and make nuclear weapons. Then Kee learned how uranium was being mined on the reservation and realized the danger those miners were in. Without adequate protection, they were risking their lives, and their employers were just letting it happen."

"Did Professor Franklin protest what was going on?" Ella asked.

"Of course. He went back to the Rez and met with several miners' groups and tribal officials. He explained what radiation could do, but back then, no one took him very seriously because there were a lot of jobs in mining. He spoke to the companies and insisted that the miners be given respirators, and that attention be paid to adequate ventilation, but the companies said they couldn't afford to spend the extra money. They wouldn't even issue the miners special clothing."

"It must have been very difficult to get people to listen."

"You have no idea. Kee tried, he really did. His own family worked the mines. But the miners needed the jobs badly, and they were making more money than they'd ever made in their lives. The risks of something they couldn't see didn't seem so great. The politicians listened quietly, but did nothing. They were more afraid of the Russians."

"So he was forced to accept the way things were?"

"Yes, but he had a lot of difficulty continuing his work at the labs after that. He couldn't reconcile with it because he knew what was happening back home. I saw him become very withdrawn, so much so that he even pushed his son and me away. Eventually, he quit his job at the labs and started working as a teacher, making a fourth of what he'd made before. He was never quite the same after that. It was like all his dreams had been shattered. In the years that followed, Kee changed even more. I think what hit him the hardest was the death of his brother from Red Lung."

"Do you think your ex-husband's ever made peace with his past?"

There was a pause. Finally, Mrs. Grayhorse answered. "I don't think Kee will ever find peace. He left the work he loved—his work with lasers—because he knew that the research he was being paid to do would never help people—that it would only lead to more deaths. His dreams turned into nightmares."

After Ella hung up, she tried to take in what she'd learned. Kee Franklin was a complex man, but somehow she had to earn his trust, and get him to tell her what he knew. The solution to his son's murder most likely depended on it.

As Ella leaned back in her chair, she saw that someone had left a copy of the evening paper on her desk. That usually meant there was something there pertaining to one of her cases. As she opened the paper, she saw that the lead story was about infighting among the Tribal Council members.

Kevin, now a committee leader, was speaking openly about NEED and how the nuclear power plant was quickly becoming a financial necessity for the tribe. Others, just as outspoken, were voicing their own concerns, quoting Rose's research on the failed land reclamation efforts and the fate of many Navajo miners.

A note from Big Ed was stuck on the center of the article. "Stay on top of this. If this is going to turn into a war as it did with gaming, we all better be prepared."

Ella sat back, wondering if her mother knew she was now being quoted on page one, when Justine came in.

"We've got more trouble. No one was hurt, but someone in a pickup drove by Councilman Jonas Buck's house and fired off several rounds through the windows."

"Let's go," Ella said, heading for the door.

NINETEEN
✖ ✖ ✖

They arrived at a large residence west of Shiprock a few miles off Highway 64 near Shiprock Wash, the main channel of a long branching network of arroyos that ran for miles before entering the San Juan River. The area was relatively flat here, part of the old river's floodplain, and was dotted with low alkali flats, dried-up marshes, and salt cedar—a non-native species that tapped into the precious water table.

No other houses were within view, and had other buildings or vehicles been there, they would have certainly seen them. The dirt road passing by the Buck residence led all the way to the river. As Justine parked in the narrow lane leading a hundred feet to the house, Jonas Buck strode out toward them.

"It took you all a heck of a long time to get here. Where have you been? I called over a half hour ago! This is an emergency! That truck is probably halfway across the county now."

"Tell us what happened," Ella asked quickly, looking toward the stucco, wood-framed house. A picture window was shattered, and the stucco in several spots had been broken loose from the impact of gunfire. From where she stood, the spacing and marks looked like those made by a shotgun blast, unless the shooter fired more than a dozen small-caliber rounds.

"I got off lucky. My wife's already at work, and my kids are at the college for morning classes. I was alone inside, and out of their range because they fired from the road." Jonas shook his head. "For the first time in my life I wish I lived in one of those residential areas closer to town. Then maybe someone might have seen something."

"When you called Dispatch, did you give them a description of the pickup?"

"Well, as much as I could. I was having breakfast in the kitchen and ran to the window as soon as I thought it was safe. All I saw was the tailgate of a light blue Ford pickup headed for the highway. But I can't say for sure if it was the shooter's vehicle or someone else passing by."

"Did you check to see if any other vehicles were around, maybe headed toward the river, or see anyone on foot?" Justine asked.

"There was nobody walking around outside that I could see, and there were no other vehicles in sight by the time I went out to look."

"Does anyone in this area have a light blue truck?" Ella added.

"Not that I've seen before."

"About the truck. Did you see anything that could help identify that particular truck from any other Ford models of the same color?" Ella asked.

"Well, there was a pro-NEED sticker on the back window—you know, those that practically glow in the dark. And they wonder why I'm against the entire project! Their people have fancy college degrees but not one lick of common sense."

While Justine collected the rounds that were still imbedded in the stucco and in the sheetrock wall at the back of the living room, Ella took a look around outside. Once again, events tended to indicate a campaign of terrorism and harassment against NEED project opponents. But it was too neat. Someone sure was going to a lot of trouble to make NEED advocates look like prime suspects and loonies.

"They used a shotgun," Justine told Ella, showing her the buckshot. "It's going to be practically impossible to track this down. If we'd have found some of those damn .380 pistol slugs, we'd have something. The way it stands, we sure don't have much to go on except that sticker and the fact that it was a light blue Ford pickup."

Ella nodded. "It's either someone pro-NEED but not too bright, or someone who is out to bury them with innuendo and circumstantial evidence. There are a lot of NEED stickers around these days, though."

"When I think of the ear-shattering blast of that shotgun going off inside a pickup, I vote for the not-too-bright analysis," Justine said with a shrug.

After they'd taken Buck's statement and photographed what tire imprints they could find where the pickup had apparently turned around in the road, Ella and Justine got ready to leave. "Where to now, boss?" Justine asked.

Ella looked at her. "According to Buck, his closest neighbor lives at the house we passed, out by the highway. There's always a chance of him having seen something pertinent since the pickup must have passed by twice. We can check on that when we go by. Then I want to go to Jason Franklin's duplex."

"I checked it out myself the day after his death. I couldn't find anything to connect to the crime."

"I still would like to take a look. Now that we have some direction to a motive, maybe something will connect this time. Do you know if it's been rented out yet?"

"Dr. Franklin paid the next month's rent, I heard. I don't think he wants to go through his son's things yet. But I doubt many Navajos will even go look at the place while Jason's possessions are still there. His things would be associated with the *chindi*."

"That's good luck for us. We need to refocus our thinking and start at the beginning—with Jason."

No one was at home at the house closer to the highway, so Ella left a card with a note asking the resident to call her, then they drove to Officer Franklin's apartment. The small rental unit was just below the bluff in the older, central section of the town of Shiprock. Ella remembered the drive-in theater that had been close to that spot once.

The apartments were nothing more than a hastily built duplex on land that belonged to an allottee. Instead of trying to graze livestock on the small parcels of land, some families had decided renting was more profitable.

"I wonder where the Rez will be fifteen, twenty years from now?" Justine said as she pulled up and parked. "It sure is a mess these days—we're not industrial, but we're not rural anymore either. We're stuck in the middle in a limbo of sorts."

"Yeah." Ella nodded in agreement. "But we've survived worse as a people."

"The way things are going, do you think there'll be anything left of the way things were when our mothers grew up in another, say, twenty years?"

"I don't know. But we're at a crossroads as a tribe. The decisions we make now will affect what kids like Dawn inherit."

As they reached the building, Ella glanced around. "Does the neighbor have the key?"

"He did before," Justine answered.

They knocked on the adjacent door and soon a young man wearing jeans and a sweatshirt with the Washington Redskins logo and colors appeared.

Ella flashed her badge, and he nodded wearily.

"Here's the key," he said, reaching for a hook on the wall behind the door. "When you're through, bring it back. We had a break-in while my neighbor was still alive, so the owners asked me to keep a special eye on the place now that nobody's there. Of course only kids would go in there now. The *chindi* and all that."

"Wait. There was a break-in?" Ella asked, then glanced at Justine, who shook her head, letting her know this was the first she'd heard of it. "When?"

"It wasn't a big deal or anything, but someone broke into both my place and Jason's about a week before he was killed. Nothing much was taken, so we decided not to bother reporting it. It wouldn't have done any good anyway, not the way the police are running around like crazy these days."

"What was taken?"

"Jason lost his VCR, but they left his TV, so he didn't really care. He was going to get a DVD player anyway. I lost twenty bucks from a drawer and a boom box with a bad speaker, so they won't get anything for it. They took my tapes, too. All in all, not exactly a haul. Jason bought better locks for both of us after that. We needed new ones anyway, because they twisted off the old doorknobs with a pipe wrench, probably."

"Did they trash the place as they searched?" Ella asked.

He shrugged. "Not really, but there wasn't much to trash. Neither Jason nor I have a lot of stuff."

"Okay, thanks. If you think of anything else . . ."

"I'll give one of you a call. I still have Officer Goodluck's number." He smiled at Justine, and she grinned.

As they walked next door, Justine glanced at Ella. "In my experience, bachelors never spend much money on their places except for electronic stuff—boys' toys. But Jason's apartment didn't even have much of that."

They stopped at the window, and Ella peered in. "I can see an old-looking computer with floppy drives and a TV. Is that pretty much it?"

"If I remember correctly."

A moment later they walked inside and looked around. The desktop computer was bulky, and probably too old for anything except word processing and simple games, which she confirmed after locating a few floppy disks. The color TV had rabbit ears instead of an antenna or cable. Ella turned it on just to check it out. The picture was snowy, but at least you could hear well enough. "Lousy reception, maybe he only watched rental movies. Did he have a radio?"

"I don't remember seeing one. There's nothing much of value here. And no reason to believe there would be, judging from the duplex itself," Justine said. "Do you think this was associated with the breaking and entering at Dr. Franklin's place? That occurred at around the same time."

"Then there's the B and E at the garage where Jason was killed," Ella said. "That's three burglaries, all connected to two men—Jason and his father, if you dismiss the neighbor's burglary as a cover-up."

"So we go back to the theory that gains more credibility by the second—that someone's searching for something that belongs to Professor Franklin. That tends to indicate that Jason's murder was not premeditated but something that happened because of the circumstances, just as we first thought," Justine said.

Ella sat on the sofa and looked around. "If you were Jason, and you were trying to hide something here, where would you have put it?"

"Behind the bookcase or between the pages of a book, if we're dealing with papers. But just in case we're wrong about that, I think I should go through his computer files and take a closer look at everything here."

"Okay—let's search for a printout or maybe a disk stashed someplace," Ella said. "Come to think of it, if he were trying to hide a disk, the very best place would be in plain sight, mixed in with those old games."

"I checked through all those when I was here last, but I'll give it another go."

As Ella walked around the rooms, searching in drawers, inside books, and behind furniture, Justine turned on the computer and went through every floppy disk she could find. Then she searched all the files on his hard drive.

After an hour, they'd still found nothing to justify their efforts. Ella met Justine back in the living room. "I came out empty-handed."

"Me too. At least the computer hard drive was small, and it didn't take long to open every file."

Ella rubbed her shoulder with one hand, trying to ease the tension she felt. "I've been thinking . . . if what we're searching for belongs to the professor, it could be anything from a research paper to mathematical equations he jotted down on a napkin."

"I thought of that. Believe me, I went through everything. There was zip. Even the computer coding on the nontext files looked authentic."

"We've got to talk to Professor Franklin and make him see that he has to confide in us. No more dancing around."

"Do you want to check again to see if he's home?"

"Yeah. Let's call first." Thirty seconds later, Ella canceled the call. "No answer, but maybe he's just not picking up."

"Last time we called ahead, too, and nobody answered, so we didn't stop by," Justine said. "Shall we check anyway?"

"Yeah, let's go."

Ella remained quiet as they drove to Farmington, where Kee Franklin lived. A peculiar restlessness gnawed at her. She had a feeling that she was overlooking something.

When they arrived at Franklin's home they saw that his SUV

still wasn't in the driveway, and there were no fresh tracks leading to the garage. "It looks like he isn't ducking our calls," Justine said.

Ella nodded. "I'm going to take a look around." As they climbed out of the unit, they saw a woman walking a small brown-and-white dog.

The lady came closer. "If you're trying to find Professor Franklin, he's gone. I think he was going camping. I saw him packing his supplies early this morning."

"Any idea when he was coming back?" Ella asked. As she flashed her badge, she noticed that the dog was staring at the Franklin house, growling softly.

"Quit that, Hannibal!" She looked back at Ella. "I'm afraid I can't help you there, Officer. He never said. My name is Elsie Springer, and I live two houses down. I'm retired, so I try to keep an eye on things for my neighbors."

As Mrs. Springer walked away with her dog, Ella took a deep breath and let it out again. "Let's take a close look around the property before we go. I have a bad feeling about this."

"You think he left town so he wouldn't have to answer questions?"

"The thought occurred to me, but what worries me most is that I think he had an idea all along about who killed his son. If my gut instinct is right, he withheld information from us because he wanted to deal with the killer himself."

"He's an incredibly intelligent man. He wouldn't go off half-cocked that way," Justine said.

"No, he'd plan things well, but as bright as Professor Franklin is, I don't think he's factoring in how ruthless this killer is prepared to be. The criminal mind has a different type of intelligence—the feral kind that's programmed to survive. I have a feeling that Franklin's going to find himself hopelessly outmatched."

As they walked around the side of the house, Ella studied the windows, and even tried to open two of them. They were firmly locked. But when they reached the back, they discovered the door was wide-open.

Recalling the dog growling at the house earlier, Ella undid the strap of her holster but didn't draw her weapon. Justine did the same. As they drew closer, they both saw an indentation in the middle of the door and realized that the doorjamb had been splintered around the locking mechanism. With their backs pressed to the wall, they remained perfectly still and listened. Silence enveloped them, interrupted only by the sporadic cry of a bird somewhere outside.

Holding one finger up, Ella signaled Justine that she'd go in first. Pistol drawn and crouching low, Ella slipped inside.

As she entered the kitchen, she heard the sound of someone opening drawers in the next room over—the living room. Ella moved forward silently, then, crouching behind a sofa, spotted a tall figure wearing dark glasses, a baseball cap, and what looked like a jogging suit bent over a desk. "Police! Don't move!"

The thief spun around and fired two quick shots, forcing Ella to flatten. Justine, who was coming through the doorway, fired back, then ducked and rolled behind an easy chair.

As Ella brought her pistol around the side of the sofa to take aim, she could hear the intruder already on the move. An instant later, he hit the front door and raced outside. Ella followed, but another bullet struck the doorjamb, forcing her down again.

When Ella looked up, the shooter was on the run again, racing full speed down the sidewalk. She was after him in a heartbeat, racing out the gate and parallel to the fleeing figure. She was gaining ground by the time they passed a second house, but then he veered to the right at the intersection and jumped a three-foot-high cinder-block wall. Turning, now behind cover, the intruder fired another shot, forcing Ella to stop and crouch low, hugging the wooden fence beside her.

Another bullet whined by her ear, and she heard a dull smack she recognized as the sound of a windshield breaking. Turning her head, she saw an oncoming sedan swerve abruptly, heading right toward her.

"Oh crap!" Ella dived over the fence, landed hard beside the base of a tree, then rolled behind the trunk. The car struck the curb and leaped up onto the sidewalk, coming to a halt halfway through the fence, less than four feet from her.

Ella looked over for the shooter, but the person was gone. With barely enough time to take a breath, she stepped back over the fence and ran to the driver, who was screaming hysterically.

It took a few seconds to calm the middle-aged Anglo woman enough for her to see she was now safe. Despite the fact that the bullet had struck the windshield, the woman's only visible injuries were a few facial cuts from the glass that had sprayed into the vehicle. The bullet had ricocheted off the windshield, and would probably never be found.

Justine arrived then and called for paramedics, while Ella ran on to pick up the thief's trail. A hurried look around the block made it clear that he was long gone.

Justine caught up to her a few minutes later. "The driver is all right, apparently, but she's pretty upset. She's sitting on the porch of that house with the neighbor. I spoke to the woman when she came out, but she didn't see or hear anyone breaking into the professor's home. She heard the first shots, saw the intruder run past her house, then heard the car crashing over the curb."

"Let's go talk to the other neighbors and see if anyone saw anything useful," Ella said. "You've called the Farmington PD, right?

"Yeah, and Sheriff Taylor will be coming on behalf of the county. We've been asked to secure the scene until the crime unit people get here, then begin canvassing the neighborhood for witnesses."

Justine remained outside Professor Franklin's home, and Ella began checking with the neighbors. Neither one of Franklin's immediate neighbors was home, and no one down the street had seen anything except for the lady who was with the accident victim, and the retired woman they'd spoken to earlier. She'd greeted them clutching her small dog, but although she'd heard the shots from down the block, she hadn't seen anyone.

When the first officer arrived, a Farmington Police Department patrolman, Ella gave him a description of the suspect she'd seen. Unfortunately, she'd never been close enough to get a good look at his face.

Taylor arrived just after the EMTs, surprisingly quickly, and met Ella and Justine on the front lawn of Franklin's home. Ella recounted to Sheriff Taylor what had happened while Justine helped the FPD officer string up the crime-scene tape.

"What made you take a look around?" Taylor pressed, already familiar with her investigation into Jason Franklin's murder. "Were you expecting trouble?"

"Not really. But we haven't been able to find the professor, and I need to question him."

"You're still looking for a break in his son's case?"

"Yeah, and the other deaths as well. I'm not sure what part Professor Franklin has played in everything, but I'm virtually sure that he's been holding back on me." She gave him a quick update on NEED and everything she'd learned.

"Farmington PD will be responsible for handling this break-in and the shooting, but why don't we go into the house and have a look around?"

"Yeah. The possible connection between what happened today and my murder investigation gives us the perfect excuse."

Before going inside, Ella checked with the Farmington cop

and got his okay. Then, wearing latex gloves, she went inside with Taylor. Ella stopped by the open hall closet. Franklin's coat was gone. Justine checked the bedroom and came out a moment later. "His drawers are almost empty, so he either doesn't have much, or he's taken most of his winter stuff with him."

Ella checked in the den. The rifle rack hung on the wall was empty, and a small shelf underneath had the clear outline in the faint dust of where a cartridge box had probably been.

"Did the thief have the rifle when he left?" Justine asked.

"Not with him. Only a small pistol, a semiauto. He wasn't carrying anything else either that I could see. I figure that he'd just begun his search when we surprised him."

"There should be shell casings around, Ella. The shooter didn't have time to pick them up," Justine pointed out.

A quick search located one casing beside the desk where the perp had been searching. "It's a .380," Ella pointed out after taking a close look. "Why isn't that a surprise?"

"Same caliber was used to kill Robert Whitesheep, though we didn't find a casing there. Did I tell you that already?" Taylor asked.

"No. When can Justine have a look at the bullet?" Ella asked.

"It'll be another day, maybe two. The body was sent to Albuquerque for the autopsy, and we haven't heard back yet, except for a few details. There was a preliminary examination by the Office of the Medical Investigator," Taylor said, "and we got a fax this morning."

Leaving the discovered shell casing in position for the Farmington crime lab team, they continued to look around, splitting up. They met again in a few minutes.

"Franklin's refrigerator is nearly empty, and the only food I found in the cupboard are cans of lima beans and sauerkraut," Justine said. "He must have taken the nonyucky stuff with him. My guess is that he has gone camping, just as his neighbor said."

"Or into hiding." Ella stood by Franklin's desk, looking at an empty spot beside a relatively new desktop computer, monitor, and combination scanner/printer. "Something was kept here," she said, looking down at a dust-free area on the desk. "From the size and shape, my guess is that it was a laptop computer."

"Strange camping trip . . ." Justine said.

"Maybe the thief took the laptop and left the heavy stuff?" Taylor suggested, coming up behind her.

"No way. I would have noticed, even if he'd stuck it beneath his jacket," Ella said.

Justine studied the equipment. "His scanner and desktop are expensive models. If I'd been the thief, I would have taken them, even if it meant parking a vehicle in the drive."

"I don't think this was an ordinary thief," Ella said as she wandered around the room. "I think this crime is linked to the burglaries on the Rez and Jason Franklin's death. The same caliber gun keeps popping up everywhere. I can't wait to get a look at one of the bullets, and the one from the Whitesheep shooting."

By then, the FPD crime-scene unit had arrived, and one of the officers was taking photographs while another tech was surveying the scene.

Ella saw the tech examining the holes in the wall where both of the shooter's bullets had apparently lodged. "Since you'll probably have more than one round for immediate examination, will you sign one of the rounds over to me for twenty-four hours? I'd like to compare it to other rounds we recovered at a crime scene. One of the professors at our college had a burglar take a shot at him, and I'd like to see if both came from the same gun. The caliber is the same, we know that already."

"All right, if my supervisor says okay. But he'll want the evidence back promptly and a full report on whatever you find."

He checked with his superior, then recovered the round for Justine, who completed the proper paperwork before returning to

Ella. "If Kee Franklin has gone into hiding, do you think it's possible that instead of planning to go after the killer, he's actually afraid he'll be next?"

"He may be afraid, Justine, but he's not running, or he would have just gone off without all the supplies. My guess is that he went away to some favorite spot of his to plan out strategy so he can play things his way."

"Three deaths and so many break-ins, shootings, and burglaries ... Who is behind this, and what the heck are we up against?"

"I don't know yet, but this is all connected to NEED and Kee Franklin. Our job now is to make sure that no one else ends up dead."

TWENTY

——✕ ✕ ✕——

While Justine went to work in the lab to check out the bullet and do a comparison, Ella tracked down Officer Judy Musket, Kee Franklin's friend. Ella found her at a desk compiling quarterly crime records for a required report.

Judy greeted her with a smile and swiveled around in her chair to face Ella. "What can I help you with today, Ella?"

"Judy, I've been trying to find Kee Franklin, and he doesn't seem to be at home. Do you have any idea where he might be?"

Judy nodded. "He told me he was going camping for a week or two. He needed some time alone after the loss of Jason. He'll be back once he gets his head clear."

"Do you know where he goes camping?" Ella asked.

Her affable expression changed into one of concern. "What's going on?"

"We just need to talk to him," Ella said, deciding to keep the news of the break-in and shooting incident at Franklin's home from Officer Musket until Justine got the results of the ballistics comparison.

"I really wish I could help you, Ella, but he's done it before, and all he's ever told me is that he doesn't go very far. The only clue I can give you is that he won't be in any camping grounds. It's mostly likely a place where he won't come in contact with anyone else. Check isolated areas still accessible to SUVs like his."

"Thanks. If you hear from him, please have him contact me immediately."

"Sure, but I doubt that'll happen until he gets back."

With a nod, Ella left Judy at her work and walked out. As she went down the hall, she noticed that Justine's lab door was closed, indicating she was still working on the evidence.

Mentally trying to find a connecting thread between all the crimes lately, Ella headed out the side door to her unit. She was hoping that the bullet recovered at Kee's house would match the one used to kill Jason, and maybe the ones used to kill Billy Red-house, Robert Whitesheep, and shoot up the college storeroom. It would be one piece of solid evidence connecting the burglaries and the robbery of the Quick Stop.

That's why she needed to talk to Wilson, who'd also had dealings with Kee Franklin. Maybe together they'd be able to figure out what the killer was looking for.

Ella pulled into the visitor's parking area, then headed directly to Wilson's office inside one of the large hogan-styled college buildings. Wilson's door was locked, and he wasn't there, but she could hear him lecturing in the classroom next door.

She listened for a while, standing just outside the open door. Wilson was a charismatic professor, and didn't lecture his students as much as he presented, questioned, and discussed a topic, getting them involved in the process of learning. She knew he also placed a lot of emphasis on student activities and laboratory work, what he called "hands-on" learning, which made his courses especially popular and valuable to the college as well.

Class was over ten minutes before the hour. Wilson answered a few more questions for students who had come to his podium, actually a large table with visual aids. Then, seeing Ella, he came over to meet her as the last student walked away.

"Hey, it's good to see you, Special Investigator Clah. What brings you here in the middle of the day?"

"Same old—business," Ella answered with a smile.

"What's going on?"

"I need to know if you've spoken to Professor Franklin recently."

Wilson shook his head. "No, as a matter of fact, I called him the other day and left a message, but he hasn't gotten back to me. I was going to invite him to make a presentation. I'm teaching a section on molecular biology and its relationships to chemistry and physics, and I wanted him to give the students his views."

"If Kee gets in touch with you, ask him to call me immediately. I need to ask him several questions. It's very important."

"Sure," Wilson said, placing his materials in a box he had under the table, then carrying it with him as he led the way into the storeroom via a back door.

"Wilson, think back to all the lectures Kee gave here. He used the classroom we just left, correct?"

"Yes." They continued through the storeroom until Wilson found a particular spot on the shelves to place his materials.

"And you said he brought in his own materials, too. Did he bring them in a briefcase?"

"No, he'd bring two or three boxes, which had everything he'd need. He'd unpack them after he got here, set them up on the demonstration table in the classroom, make his presentation, then take his stuff away with him afterward."

"Think hard. Are you *sure* he didn't leave anything behind?"

"He'd bring a couple of boxes and leave with a couple of boxes. I only paid attention during his lectures."

"Did he unpack his materials in this storeroom?"

"Yeah, I suppose." He paused, his expression one of concentration as he tried to remember. "I know he didn't have the boxes with him in the classroom, so he must have set them somewhere. He went back and forth from classroom to storeroom several times during each visit."

"Have you taken a real hard look around here to verify that there's nothing belonging to Professor Franklin?"

"Ella, look around. There are, what, ten rows with metal shelf units on each side, and there are five shelves per unit. There are hundreds of boxes in here of different sizes, plus rows of books, workbooks, and papers, some in boxes, most not. It would take me months, and annoy nearly everyone when they found I was looking through their materials. A lot of professors keep their stuff there, and others outside the department often borrow space. I must have fifty boxes here myself just along the aisle closest to the door to my office. I store grade books, copies of notes, and student projects I wanted to keep for one reason or another in this area." He paused, taking a breath. "The chances of Dr. Franklin leaving some valuable materials behind in here are pretty slim. Everything about the man is organized, Ella. It's the way his brain is wired."

"I'm not talking about an oversight or accident. He might have hidden something in here purposely. I really need you to look through the storeroom and see if you can find something that belongs to him, or that doesn't belong here at all."

"All right," he answered with a beleaguered sigh as he opened the storeroom and waved her inside.

"Do you, by any chance, have any idea where the professor would go camping?"

Wilson thought about it for a few minutes, then shook his head. "We never spoke about hobbies or personal stuff like that. He came to do a job, and he did it very well, but he wasn't chatty."

"Was he talkative with anyone else that you know of?"

Wilson shook his head. "Sorry. We never spoke about topics outside my work or his planned lectures. He was very professional, but not personable. He came to do a job, and he did it very well, but except for answering student questions, he didn't get involved in anything outside the lessons. He always seemed moody and detached when he wasn't actually teaching."

Ella checked her watch. "Okay, thanks for your time. I better get going."

Wilson insisted on walking Ella to her tribal police unit, claiming he needed fresh air, but she could sense that he had something else on his mind.

Halfway there, he finally broke the silence between them. "You know, I'm beginning to have doubts that Justine and I are going to be able to make things work between us. What she needs and what I need are just too different."

"I'd hate to see you break each other's hearts," Ella said honestly. "If you're asking what I think, I'd have to suggest that no matter what, don't give up. Some things are worth fighting for."

Wilson took a deep breath, then let it out again, leaning against the side of her car and looking down at the pavement. "There's a difference between fighting for something you really want and trying to force something that wasn't meant to be."

Ella nodded, thinking about Harry and herself. "You have to decide what you want, and what you're willing to give up to get it, but it's something both of you have to work out on your own. Just keep the lines of communication open. That's all I have to add."

"I'll try," Wilson said, then, with a weak smile, walked away.

Ella left the campus quickly, her thoughts focused on the case. She tried Kee's home number again and got his voice mail. Leaving yet another message, she continued to the station, hoping to see if Justine had been able to complete her forensic work. But before she could get there, her cell phone rang.

Rose's voice was taut. "Can you come home soon, daughter?"

Something in her tone made a shiver race up her spine. "What's wrong, Mom?"

"Can you come home soon, daughter? Your daughter is fine, and everyone's safe, but there's a small matter—actually a large one, you'll need to handle. Get home before nightfall if you can."

Ella tried to get more information from her mother, but Rose refused to talk about it on the phone.

By the time she arrived at the station ten minutes later, Ella's insides were turning into knots. She decided to check in with Justine, then go home and see what was happening. Knowing that it was precisely what her mother had hoped she'd do irritated Ella even more.

Ella stopped by Justine's office and found her working on a report.

"Anything I can use?" Ella asked.

"Yeah." Justine never looked up from the computer screen. "The pistol round the Farmington lab tech extracted from the wall in Kee's house was fired from the same weapon used to kill Officer Franklin and Councilman Redhouse. It's also a match for the ones we dug out of the wall in Wilson's storeroom. And, based upon a comparison already done with the Whitesheep bullet by the county, which managed to get the bullet back early, it's a hundred percent. The same gun, and shooter, is responsible for nearly all of the crimes we've been investigating lately."

Ella leaned against the wall, lost in thought. "I've been wondering what direction to take if it turned out this way. Okay, now that we know it's the same guy, all we have to figure out is what he's looking for, and why. We have to find the common thread."

"I don't suppose different people have been getting the same person to commit all these crimes, but for their own reasons. Maybe there is a hired gun out there?" Justine shrugged. "I know it seems far-fetched."

"Too far-fetched."

"One more bit of news, or maybe not, at this particular moment," Justine added. "I got a fax from Sheriff Taylor. Guess whose fingerprints were on that stash of cash Whitesheep had hidden in his car—besides his own," Justine said.

"Billy Redhouse's?"

"Exactly. So we might be able to connect the Anglo man, Whitesheep, and Redhouse—*if* the Anglo man was paying Billy to vote a particular way on the NEED issue. The problem now is to determine the Anglo man's identity," Justine said.

"I have a feeling he'll turn up soon." Ella shrugged. "But I have this little matter that's been bugging me."

"What's that?" Justine asked.

Ella took a deep breath. "I'm going to go over to the garage where Jason was killed. Mrs. Grayhorse said Kee kept something there, though he all but denied it. I want to find out the truth."

"Ella, do you think Jason knew exactly what his father was storing in there?" Justine asked.

"I'm beginning to think so now—and that would explain why he was keeping an eye on the place."

"Give me a few minutes to finish this report for FPD, then I'll drive you to the garage."

Ella shook her head. "It'll be better if I just meet you there. I have to stop by home first."

"Is everything okay?"

"Yes and no. There's some sort of crisis brewing that Mom insists I come and take a look at myself. She wouldn't say anything over the phone, and you know how mothers are when they want you to do something. Rather than speculate all afternoon on what's happening, I'm going over right now."

"Okay—we'll meet at the garage. I'll get the key from the case file."

As Ella drove home tension began to build inside her. She hated to take off in the middle of the day for a personal matter, but there was no way she was going to be able to concentrate on anything until this was all settled.

The one thing she knew about her mother was that she wouldn't have made the call if she hadn't thought it was necessary. Her mother was only manipulative when she felt it was important. Fortunately, it had been less than forty-five minutes since her mother had called, so she'd be able to deal with it relatively soon.

When Ella came up the driveway, she discovered a large pickup with a horse trailer hitched behind it parked in the spot she normally used for her own vehicle. Ella parked beside her mother's truck and walked around to the side of the house to see what was going on. As she approached, she saw Rose inside the old corral speaking to a Navajo man Ella had never seen before. He was holding a lead rope attached to the halter of a beautiful deep chestnut Shetland pony with a long, flaxen mane. Dawn was standing beside it, petting the animal.

Seeing Ella opening the corral gate, Dawn ran over and launched herself into her arms. "Please, Mommy, please, can I keep it? Can I?"

No other words could have made Ella's stomach plummet as fast. "Just whose pony is it?"

"Surprise! Your child's father sent it to her," Rose said, with a look that spoke volumes.

For a brief moment all Ella could think of was of finding Kevin and throttling him until his head squeezed right off his neck.

"*Shimá*, he's so pretty! Can we take him in the house? He can stay in my room."

Ella managed to find her voice. "Sweetheart, I'm sorry. We can't possibly keep him."

Dawn's lip came out in a pout, and tears began flowing. "Please?"

"I was told to assure you that the councilman would pay all the bills for the animal's upkeep," the elderly Navajo man said, "including cleaning out the corral and hauling away the manure."

"See? Daddy will help!"

Rose hadn't said a word. She stared at Ella and shrugged.

"Sweetie, we don't even have a stall or a shed big enough for the little guy when the weather is bad," Ella said.

"He can sleep with me! Two's in the house!"

"It's not the same thing." Ella thought about their already strained budget. She'd have to go to Kevin each time the animal needed a vet visit, or horseshoes, or any of the myriad things that an animal that size was bound to need.

"It's traditional for our children to know how to ride and handle horses," the elderly Navajo man said, looking at Rose, then at Ella. "This pony is full-grown, has a very stable temperament, and is small enough for a preschooler to ride as long as an adult is there to supervise."

"This is '*Atsidii*,'" Rose introduced using the man's nickname.

Ella searched her memory for the word. "Smithy, right?"

Rose sighed. "The young ones don't always know our language."

Ella stared at the look on her daughter's face as she petted the pony and considered her options. Unfortunately, hog-tying Kevin and dragging him across the mesa behind a galloping pony wasn't an option.

"Your father and I will have to talk about this," Ella said, crouching to look her daughter in the eyes. "But I don't think we can keep him."

Dawn's eyes filled with tears. "But it's *my* present!"

"I'm not the previous owner, and wasn't paid to take the pony back. My job was to bring it here, along with ten bales of alfalfa hay, saddle and tack, a water trough, and a trace mineral

292 ✖ AIMÉE & DAVID THURLO

block. I've done that. If you decide not to keep the pony, you'll have to make arrangements for someone to pick it up," Smithy said, then handed her a business card. "If you want me to do that, I will be available tomorrow afternoon, maybe. I wrote the name of the person who sold the horse to the councilman on the back of my business card. Now I have to go pick up some calves in Cortez to deliver to a man in Waterflow."

Without another word Smithy turned and walked out through the small gate, fastening it with three small sections of rope, then continued back to his pickup. Ella stood helpless as the man drove away with the horse trailer.

"Mom, could you watch Dawn around the pony for a few moments? Don't let her get behind it where she could get kicked, and warn her about getting stepped on or doing something that scares the animal. I'm going to go inside the house and make a personal call."

As soon as she was inside, Ella flipped open her cell phone and dialed Kevin's private line. He answered on the first ring.

Ella didn't bother to introduce herself. "Have you lost your mind? She's three years old. She can get *hurt*."

"I trust you and Rose to watch her, and I'll pay for riding lessons. Tell me, did she like the pony?"

"She *loved* it, you moron. What little girl wouldn't? But what am I going to do with an animal that size?"

"Didn't Smithy tell you? I've already provided saddle, tack, and a water trough. There should be some hay and one of those salt blocks, too. I'll pay for the upkeep *and* the riding lessons."

"But she's a *baby*! She can't ride that thing. She wants to keep it *in her room*! How dare you get her something like this without asking me first!"

"She can sit on a horse already, I'm sure. She'll just need some guidance. You *are* going to let her keep it, aren't you, Ella? She'll be heartbroken if you don't."

"I'd like to break you—into tiny pieces. You've created a disaster here, and set me up as the bad guy if I say no."

"But she's wanted a pony so badly. This little Shetland is a charmer. And you used to ride—it's not like you've never been around horses. Most Navajo kids grow up around horses, often riding with an adult before they can even walk. They're as much a part of our culture as dolls, footballs, and bicycles are to Anglo youngsters."

"I'll grant you that. And I rode back in my teens, but I haven't been on a horse in ages. But in our case it's just not a good idea right now? I barely have enough time to spend with her, and now I'm going to have to share her with that pony."

"If you're worried about her being around the horse all the time, set some ground rules."

Dawn came in, tears streaming down her face. "*Shimasání* says we don't have enough money for a pony."

"That's because it costs a lot of money to feed the pony, and if it gets sick, he has to go to a horse doctor."

"You don't have to buy me toys anymore. Not ever."

"Ella, I really meant it. You don't have to worry. I'll cover all the bills," Kevin, who'd heard Dawn, said. "I remember that the gate in the corral is just hanging there by some rope, and I've already hired someone to repair it, build a stall or loafing shed for the little guy, and arranged for someone to come by regularly and muck out the stall and corral. Rose can use the manure for her herb garden, too." When Ella didn't answer, he added, "Do you remember how badly you wanted a horse as a kid? Are you really ready to take that away from her?"

Ella sighed, looking at her child's rosy face, now streaked with tears. She would have had to have a heart made of pure steel to say no. "Kevin, I want you to get a written agreement with whoever you talked to about cleaning out the corral and building a stall. We'll take care of feeding, watering, and grooming the pony, but I won't have me or my mother cleaning out the manure."

"Hey, I'm a lawyer. I've already got it in writing, and you'll be getting a copy in the mail. So is it a deal?"

Dawn was looking right at her, her mouth open expectantly. "All right, Pumpkin, you can keep the pony, but only *if* you promise to follow all the rules of safety around him. We'll go over those a little later."

Dawn, nodding already, launched herself into Ella's arms, then demanded to speak to her daddy.

Ella gave Dawn the phone, then went back outside to talk to Rose, who was checking the ropes holding the gate upright and in place. "I'm going to find my child's father, then I'm going to kill him. I'll go to prison for the rest of my life, but it'll be worth it."

Rose gave her a wry smile. "He's trying to buy her love, but he doesn't realize that he has it already."

"I know. Do you think our sitter will be upset with this new development?"

Rose shook her head. "No, not at all. She's been riding horses since she could walk. 'Atsidii was right. Riding is traditional for us, you know, even in this age where pickups are more plentiful than horses. It's not a bad gift, it's just that the timing is wrong. Your daughter will want to invite her little friends over, and they'll have to be watched as well. Our sitter may need a raise."

"Fine. I'll make sure the councilman understands and is willing to help out. He started this, and he's going to see it through."

Dawn came running back, handed Ella the phone, then slipped under the fence and went to the pony's side with an apple she'd taken from the refrigerator.

In all fairness, Ella had to admit that the little animal seemed extremely gentle. And she'd never seen Dawn look happier. She put the phone back up to her ear. "I'm here."

"Girls and horses ... there's always been a special bond

there," Kevin said, though he couldn't see Dawn. "Thank you for saying yes, Ella."

"I'll talk to you later," Ella said, then hung up.

"She's happy," Rose said. "Console yourself with that."

Ella sighed. "Okay, I won't kill him. I'll just beat him unconscious."

Rose smiled as Dawn began speaking to the pony softly. She seemed a natural around the animal.

"What else do we need for tonight?" Ella asked. "Smithy mentioned hay and other things."

"Smithy brought everything," Rose said. "The water trough is over there, just inside the corral, and he'd just filled it from the garden hose when you arrived. He carried in ten bales of hay, too, and for now they're in my gardening shed."

"I'm going to stay out here with him tonight, okay?" Dawn said.

"No, not okay. But you can watch him through your window."

"The corral, overall, is big enough to serve as a riding arena, and is still in good shape," Rose said, as Dawn shifted her attention back to the pony again. "It'll hold him. Tomorrow we can get that gate fixed so we we'll be able to open and close it a lot easier. In the meantime, the pony will settle in just fine as soon as we give him a flake of hay."

"It's going to be a long night, Mom," she said, looking at Dawn, who continued to pet the pony.

"Yes, I think it will be."

"I better get back to work," Ella said at last. She was glad she'd come. Knowing what was going on at home—even if it had the makings of a disaster—was preferable to not knowing. Now she could concentrate on her job.

Ella managed to tear Dawn away from the pony long enough to get a hug, then walked back over to where she'd parked her tribal unit. Her daughter had a new best friend. That was all there was to it. And if they were all lucky, she wouldn't do the same thing Ella had done at the age of six, bring the pony into the house during the first snowstorm.

Justine was already at the garage, checking through boxes, when Ella finally arrived. "Sorry, Justine. That took a little longer than I expected," she said, filling her partner in on the complications at home.

Justine laughed out loud. "Oh, boy! That's some present. I guess he's trying to make up for the fact that he isn't with her every day like you are."

"Frankly, I don't think he could cope with that every morning and evening," Ella said honestly. "Dawn can be very difficult at times." She looked at all the boxes Justine had searched. "Any progress?"

"No, not really. There's nothing here that could be categorized as a physicist's old equipment, research papers, or books. The closest to research papers I found were some essays Jason wrote when he took a course in criminalistics at the college."

"Maybe it's time I called Belinda Johns."

Five minutes later, after Justine had returned to her own office, Ella managed to reach Belinda at her college office.

"What's going on, Investigator Clah?"

"We need to track down Professor Franklin and ask him some questions related to our investigation. Do you have any idea where he goes camping or when he just wants to be by himself?"

There was a pause on the line. "Jason once told me that he and his dad had found a great place. I remember he said that it was very quiet because no one went there anymore." Belinda paused again, then sighed. "I don't remember the location, though. I'm sorry."

"Think about that conversation and see if you can remember.

It's very important. We believe that Kee may be in danger, which is why we need to speak with him."

"What kind of danger?" Belinda's voice grew louder and more focused.

"I can't discuss any specifics right now, but we'd like to help him. If you remember anything at all, please give us a call."

"I will, and I'll try asking around. Maybe father or son told someone else about the place."

"Do that. Just call me if you get the slightest hint of where to look," Ella said good-bye and ended the call.

Leaning back in her chair, Ella opened the case folder, looking through it for clues, but didn't see anything that triggered a possible location to look. Somehow she had to find Kee and get some answers from him. Nothing was more pressing than that, but she wasn't even sure where to start.

She considered making a request for officers to stop and detain Franklin if anyone spotted him, then decided that was a bad idea. She wanted—needed his cooperation. Finally, she walked down the hall and into the communications center, where the dispatcher was at her radio console. Ella instructed the young woman to put out a call for a Code Five—instructions for officers spotting Kee's vehicle to keep it under surveillance but not attempt to make contact with the occupant. If any of the units saw him, she'd be notified immediately, hopefully without him knowing.

When she entered her office again Ella had a visitor waiting. Dwayne Blalock, the resident FBI agent, had made himself comfortable in one of the chairs and was leafing through an FBI Law Enforcement Bulletin.

"I just stepped out a few minutes ago. What brings you here?" Ella asked.

FB-Eyes sat the magazine aside. "I heard that you're searching for Professor Kee Franklin."

It shouldn't have surprised her that Blalock knew. Blalock had his own way of working things, but he always knew what was going on around him and had worked with Sheriff Taylor frequently. He also monitored police calls.

"I've been told he's somewhere camping, and the evidence from his home supports that, but I can't pin down his location."

"I want in on this case."

"What's your interest in this all of a sudden?"

Blalock hesitated, then sighed. "What I'm about to tell you goes under the category of 'professional courtesy,' so keep it to yourself. Professor—Doctor Franklin—is a very important scientist despite his modest lifestyle and the fact that he quit his work at Los Alamos. His work with lasers at the labs, apparently, was ground-breaking. Dr. Franklin was a man ahead of his time. He came up with concepts and processes that are just now being used industrywide. Near as I can tell, he's the only one who understood certain key aspects of some highly technical and classified research that goes way beyond today's technology. The Bureau's kept an eye on him since he left Los Alamos, on behalf of the DOE and the DOD. Our government has always hoped he'd return to work at the labs."

"Now that his son has been murdered, and shots were fired at a break-in at his residence—not to mention the fact that the man can't be found—the Bureau is officially worried?"

"That's about it."

"Finally. I can use your help. I want to go to Los Alamos, and you're going to get me in."

"Pushy, aren't you?" He smiled.

"Yeah. It's one of my most endearing qualities."

TWENTY-ONE
———— ✖ ✖ ✖ ————

Ella set out with Blalock the following morning after picking him up in her tribal unit. The trip to Los Alamos, going southeast through Bloomfield and Cuba all the way to the village of San Ysidro, then northeast through Jemez Springs on State Road 4, would take them around three and a half hours. The last section was on mountain roads, which would require them to reduce speed.

"This case is turning out to have a lot more ramifications than either of us suspected at first," Blalock commented once they were under way.

Ella nodded. "Yeah, but the bottom line for me is that a tribal cop was killed, then a councilman, and finally another member of the tribe, all by the same shooter using a .380 semiauto. One way or another, I'm catching the person who did all this. Kee Franklin has been holding back on me from the very beginning, and that's going to stop."

"If Professor Franklin's the type of scientist I've been told he is, keeping secrets may come as naturally to him as breathing. He never violated any security procedures in his years at the labs."

"But he's vulnerable now. We need to find out once and for all if his work can provide us with a motive for all the crimes that have been committed within the past several days. The more time passes, the farther away the killer gets from my grasp. I can't let that continue."

"You could also use a win on this for practical reasons. Closing the case will prove to the tribe that your PD is top-notch, and deserves better funding. Right?"

"Yeah, but it goes beyond that." She was quiet for a long time, but he never interrupted her, having learned a lot about dealing with Navajos the past few years. "It's the reason Jason died that bothers me most, you know? His equipment *failed* him, and he couldn't get the help he needed. Now the department *has* to come through for him. It won't even begin to balance the scales, but it's the only thing we can give him."

Blalock shook his head. "You're too personally involved in your job, Ella, and you worry about the tribe like it's your family. You'd make your own life easier if you would ease up a bit."

"I know, but I'm not programmed that way. My clan, and the tribe, is my family."

"I hear you. Dedication is what keeps most good officers going at times like this. I coasted for a while after I got the post I have now. Then people like you reminded me of a part of myself I'd all but forgotten. I can tell you this much from experience, Ella. The day you stop doing what's right and giving one hundred percent, you will lose the part of yourself you respect the most."

"Yeah," Ella said quietly. "I guess I better enroll in over-achievers anonymous."

"I can see it now. A twelve-step program."

"Nah. Overachievers can do it in six."

When they finally arrived at the labs in Los Alamos, which was still recovering from the devastating forest fire a few years earlier, they reported to the Public Information Office. They were given visitors' badges on lanyards to be worn around their necks, then led through a breezeway to a section of an administration building filled with offices. The brick-and-metal buildings could have been found anywhere in the country, but the clear, crisp air of the high mesa was refreshing and invigorating this time of year.

They were asked to wait in a small lobby, but they were there only a few minutes before a door opened leading to an inner office. "I'm Jonathan Frawley," the public information officer introduced himself, ushering them inside the first doorway to their left. "Sit down, please," he said, waving them to the chairs. "How can we help you?"

"We need to know about former employee Dr. Kee Franklin's work," Blalock said, "and about any problems he may have had with contacts and associates while he worked here at the labs."

As FB-Eyes made their request, Ella watched Frawley. He was in his late fifties, with gray-green eyes that seemed as focused as the lasers associated with high-tech research.

"I'm sorry. Unless you can produce evidence that proves his work here at the labs has something to do with his son's murder, his recent absence, or any crimes committed, no one here can help you."

So he knew about Kee's disappearance. Ella wasn't surprised. "We can't make those connections until we have more information about his work and associations," Ella said.

The man leaned back in his chair and gave her a slow, penetrating look. "I can give you a general overview of the work he did for our country here, but my guess is that you know that already."

She nodded. "Answer this for me," she pressed, leaning forward in her chair. "Who would want the results of that research now, and be willing to pressure Dr. Franklin for his skills or expertise?"

Frawley considered the question for a long time, drumming his fingers absently on the desk. "I can't answer that," he said at last. "Even if I knew, all it would be is speculation, and you need more than that. The best I can do is share generalities with you dealing with uranium research and the enrichment process. I have several press releases we've worked up in the past that you're welcome to have."

Ella was sensing a snow job, and could see Blalock's frustration as well. When someone was lying to FB-Eyes or trying to con him, he usually crossed his arms or put his hands in his pockets. She wondered if, not too many years ago, he'd grabbed a suspect and tried to shake the truth out of him, then later regretted it.

"Could we at least talk to some of his former colleagues?" Ella asked, hoping to salvage their journey. "Our questions will focus on Dr. Franklin's behavior and attitude while he was working here."

Frawley considered it for a moment, then finally nodded. "I can introduce you to one person he worked with who's still here, but I'll have to be present, and if the conversation strays to anything even remotely classified, that'll be the end of the interview. Are we clear on this?"

"Perfectly."

Their host led them down the hall and out the side door, then down a sidewalk to another, smaller building. Finally, they were ushered into a large office. The sign on the door read, "Dr. Fred Ellison."

Ellison was in his midsixties and seemed to have his mind on several things at once. He nodded absently as they came in, but his light blue eyes kept darting to a computer screen filled with symbols and numbers and the dry erase board against the wall that held more of the same in black marker.

Frawley introduced them, then turned things over to Ella while he sat to one side.

"How closely did you work with Dr. Franklin?" she asked.

"We were colleagues, and worked together often because our

work converged or overlapped at certain points. But we each handled our own projects with our respective teams."

"How well did you get to know Dr. Franklin?"

"I held him in high regard, and he made strong contributions to our project missions, but we weren't friends on a personal level. Neither one of us had a lot of time to socialize back in those days. There was a lot of competition between the research teams, and we were all trying to build our reputations and make the breakthroughs that led to special project funding. But I think the games we all have to play in order to get what we need to complete our research was really a thorn in Kee's side. He was totally immersed in his work and didn't like to get sidetracked. I think the idea of competition for resources went against his Navajo cultural beliefs."

"I've heard that he lost heart in his work after he realized the plight of the uranium miners, especially those on the Navajo Nation."

"We all were shocked when we learned how deplorable the working conditions were for those people, but it affected Kee much more," he said, meeting her gaze for the first time. "Kee loved his work, but he wanted to maintain control of what happened to his research, and how it was used. That, unfortunately, is a luxury none of us have. We're just links in a long chain, and policy decisions belong to the bureaucrats and politicians."

"Did Dr. Franklin become a close friend to anyone here in particular? Maybe someone on his team?"

Ellison thought about it a moment, then spoke. "The only person he ever worked closely with was a young chemist named Delbert Shives, who was a subcontractor employee and more or less Kee's assistant. Shives's former employer is no longer connected with the research here, and I believe the man now works at the tribal power plant near Shiprock."

"Can you tell me a little about Shives?" Ella asked, wishing she'd learned more about this relationship long ago. If she'd only known enough to ask the right question!

"Shives was Dr. Franklin's right-hand man, and did a lot of the hands-on work. He was really enthusiastic, annoyingly so, and wanted the doctor to continue his work here. Shives felt that the dead end Dr. Franklin had reached in his research could be surmounted. But by then, Kee had already made up his mind to quit."

"Before you ask," Frawley said, "the nature of the research, and of the 'dead end,' is classified."

Ellison spoke again. "We might have been able to hold on to Dr. Franklin longer if he'd worked with someone other than Shives. That man was an opportunist, and not to be trusted. He tried to appropriate one of my processes at one time and get it patented, claiming he'd developed it independently. But his notes paraphrased my own."

"So was Shives fired?"

Frawley interrupted. "His security clearance was down-graded, but we didn't have strong enough evidence to make sure he got fired. The company he worked for just reassigned him to a coal-gassification project in another area of our facility."

"But no one trusted him after that, not even in his own company," Ellison said, "and Shives knew he'd blown his credibility. Eventually, he resigned and moved out of state for a while. Texas, I think."

Blalock and Ella left the lab a short time later after getting everything the lab could provide them on laser research and uranium processing and refinement.

"That wasn't as big a waste of time as I thought it might be," Blalock muttered, once they were under way. Ella didn't look over, keeping her eyes on the twisting forest highway.

"That's interesting news about Shives. He never mentioned that he worked with Kee. He and I are going to have a long talk real soon," Ella said.

Instead of eating in Los Alamos, they drove about a third of the way back to the Rez, then stopped in the small community of Cuba, located in a mountain valley surrounded by pines and junipers. While Blalock went inside and ordered for them, Ella stepped out of the car into the parking lot beside the highway and called Justine.

"There's a connection between the work Franklin did and Delbert Shives. See what you can get me on him," she said, and told her what she'd learned. "I want to know what else is in Shives's background that we don't know about."

"I'll get on it right away."

Ella dialed home next, and Dawn picked up the phone. For some reason she always whispered a tiny "hello." "Hi, short stuff," Ella said.

"*Shimá!*" Dawn's voice rose slightly as she recognized Ella's voice. "I helped fill up the pony's water tank with the hose. And I gave him a carrot after he ate his hay. But when I gave him a cookie, *shimasání* got angry."

"Your grandmother made those especially for you, not for the pony. Have you decided what to name him?"

"Uh-uh."

"Okay. You think about it. Now let me talk to your grandmother."

Ella heard the phone thunk as Dawn set it down.

Rose got on the phone a moment later. "That horse is all she thinks about. I had to make her come inside before she froze out there. But you don't need to hear this now. Tell me why you called. Is something wrong?"

"Mom, I need to ask you about Delbert Shives. I've met him at the station, and he's taken officers for tours of the power plant and mines. But I don't know much about him. Didn't you tell me you'd contacted him about uranium mining?"

"Yes and no. It took me forever to get in touch with him and then, after all that, he wasn't much help. Mr. Chavez at the power plant had told me Mr. Shives would be very knowledgeable about the impact uranium mining had on the land. But when I spoke to the man, he was very rude."

"What happened, exactly." Ella had always known Shives to be outgoing and friendly to the department.

"I waited for over an hour for him to come out of his office. Then, when I told him who I was and what I wanted, he said that everything I wanted to know was a matter of public record, and I'd have to do my own homework. Without even so much as saying good-bye, he turned around and went right back into his office. His secretary tried to apologize for him, saying he'd had a very hard day, and maybe he had. Even though his door was shut, I'd heard him arguing with some woman in his office, both before and after I spoke with him. But I don't know what that was all about."

"Okay, Mom, thanks."

Ella went inside and joined Blalock for dinner. He'd ordered stuffed chicken sopaipillas. The fare wasn't fancy, but it was surprisingly good, and the green chile was just the right temperature.

Blalock didn't seem in a mood to talk much, so she allowed the silence to stretch.

Finally, he met her gaze. "I gather you think Kee Franklin is in some kind of trouble?"

"Yeah," she said. "But I don't think he really understands what he's gotten himself into. He's smart, academically, but he's out of his league on this. When it comes to street smarts, his opponent is holding all the cards."

When they started out again, silence fell between them. About ten miles from Shiprock and just inside the Rez by Hogback, Ella began to feel uneasy. The badger fetish began to feel warm against her throat.

"Something's wrong," she said, glancing back in the rearview mirror.

Blalock who'd been leaning back with his eyes closed, sat up. "What's going on?" he asked, instantly alert.

She glanced in her rearview mirror again. "There's a sand-colored pickup quickly closing in on us."

He glanced in the side mirror. "It's one of those hot six-wheelers with the big V-8 engines, but so what? He doesn't know this is a cop car. You can wait until he passes, then pull him over if you want."

"No, it's more than that. The driver is coming *for* us."

"Because he's got a lead foot and driving like a bat out of hell? That just makes him a victim of his own stupidity."

The pickup on steroids was closing, less than fifty yards behind them, and Ella couldn't see the driver because of the tinted glass. Having first sped up a bit, Ella now decided to cut her speed, so she'd be able to maneuver without risking a rollover.

"Okay, now I believe you," he said, as the truck closed in. Blalock unfastened the safety strap on his gun and checked his seat belt and shoulder harness.

Wary of the sound of a weapon being fired inside a vehicle, Ella rolled down her window completely, and Blalock did the same on his side, doubling their options. She looked ahead, noting the oncoming lane was clear. "I'm going to hit the brakes at the same time I move to the shoulder," Ella said. "He'll have to swerve and should zip past me if I time it right. Then we'll take off after him."

"Go for it."

Ella hit the brakes and the tires screamed, but the Jeep tracked properly without fishtailing. The driver of the pickup suddenly pulled up to her left, but instead of racing past them, swung the heavy pickup into the side of the tribal unit.

Ella hadn't expected that move, and the wheel nearly jerked out of her hands. She hit the brakes again, trying to let the pickup by, but the driver sideswiped them again by the left rear fender, and she barely kept her unit on the road.

"Okay, that's it." Blalock pulled out his weapon. "Lean back, Ella."

As the pickup came close and rammed them again, Blalock reached over in front of her and fired off one shot. The round struck the windshield of the truck, but missed the driver.

The shot must have unnerved the driver because he suddenly swerved hard, nearly losing control of the pickup, then roared away.

Ella had to fight to maintain control of the Jeep, her ears still ringing from the blast of the handgun. "We have a flat!" she yelled, steering toward the side of the road and trying to resist the temptation to hit the brakes. The Jeep slowed, weaving slightly, and they eased off onto the shoulder, coming to a stop just before the big curve leading into Shiprock, less than three miles away.

"Did you see the license plate?" Ella asked, her body shaking with anger and from the sudden burst of adrenaline that had shot through her system.

"It had been removed," Blalock said, unfastening his seat belt.

"Too bad." Ella called Dispatch, but had to listen carefully. Her ears were still ringing.

"Are you hurt?" Blalock asked.

"No, but my damned ears are ringing. You?"

"I'm fine—pissed off, but fine." He stepped out of the unit and took a deep breath, then walked around for a moment, taking a look at the front tire, which had lost its tread from one of the collisions with the big truck. "Did you get a look at the driver? He seemed hunkered down, or maybe it was the fact that he was sitting higher up. All I saw clearly was a baseball cap and some kind of jacket."

"Dark hair, too. Sunglasses. Dark-skinned or good tan." She paused, then added, "And there was a pro-NEED bumper sticker stuck to the back bumper."

After they changed the flat and determined that the scratched paint and dented body wouldn't affect the operation of the vehicle, it didn't take long to reach Shiprock. Ella dropped Blalock at his office, then went to her station and made out a full report. The chief wasn't going to like another tribal car needing major bodywork, but it couldn't be helped.

Searching for Big Ed but not finding him, she left the written report on his desk, then drove home.

Though it was dusk, by the time she got there Ella could see her daughter eating her dinner outside, a few feet away from the pony. The animal was not in the corral, but tethered near Dawn's bedroom window, munching on the remnants of a flake of hay.

"What's this?" Ella asked, going directly to the back, where Rose and Dawn were huddled up in their winter coats, standing against the outside wall.

"Your daughter insisted on eating with the pony," Rose said with a sigh. "But when she finishes, she's going right to bed."

Ella looked at her daughter's face. "You know you can't do this every night, right? The pony needs time to be a pony, and that means being by himself."

"But I want to be with him. Ponies need friends, too."

"You wouldn't want to be at school with your friends *all* the time, would you? You like playing by yourself sometimes, too. At night it's time for the pony to eat his dinner and rest. That way the pony can be your friend, but still be true to himself. Then you both will have balance and harmony, and walk in beauty."

Dawn nodded somberly. "Okay."

Out of the corner of her eye, Ella saw Rose looking at her in surprise. Ella smiled, looked at Rose, and, in a soft voice, added, "What? I do accept the old ways, Mom. I just can't live them the way you and my brother do."

Ella saw the spark of hope in Rose's eyes and bit back a sigh. Rose would never stop hoping that she'd embrace the old ways fully. But that hope would always remain unfulfilled. As much as she wanted to believe wholeheartedly in tribal traditions, she'd never be able to do that. Her heart would always be caught in the middle—torn between who she was and who she thought she should be.

After dinner, Ella put Dawn to bed and read her a story about a young mouse and his adventures. Before she'd gotten to the last page, Dawn was fast asleep.

Ella returned to the living room, and found Rose sitting on the sofa, talking to Herman Cloud.

These days it didn't bother Ella that her mother was spending time with Herman. What bothered her was that her mother went out on more dates than she did. Herman nodded when she came in, and started to stand. Ella motioned him to sit, then, with a rueful smile, she plopped down into her mother's favorite chair. If her mother wanted privacy, she'd let her know soon enough.

"Daughter, I was very proud of what you said to my granddaughter about harmony and balance." She smiled. "You may become a traditionalist yet."

"Mom, that'll never happen. But that doesn't mean I don't value the beliefs that have kept our people strong. They're a part of our heritage, beliefs I'd like my daughter to understand and respect. Of course, what she ultimately chooses to do with that knowledge in the future will be up to her."

"Then I will hope that she'll choose to be a traditionalist."

Ella laughed. "We'll see. You never give up, do you?"

Rose just smiled.

"Speaking of that, I need you two to help me with something. I have to find the scientist—the father of the patrolman who was killed," she said, avoiding proper names out of respect for her traditionalist mother and Herman.

Herman nodded. "I know who you mean."

"I think he's in danger, but I'm not sure he knows or cares. I was told he went camping, so he's probably in one of the more remote areas still accessible by vehicle, perhaps the mountains or foothills. I was hoping that you could get word out to the Plant Watchers, and ask them to contact me if they see him or spot signs of a campsite around this part of the Rez."

"We'd be happy to do that for you, daughter," Rose said.

Leaving her mother alone with Herman, Ella went into the kitchen, grabbed a plateful of olives as a snack, then went back to her room. Sitting at her computer, she retrieved e-mail from Harry. Reading on, she smiled at his accounting of one assignment where everything had gone wrong.

Rose came in as Ella finished answering her e-mails. "I worry about you, daughter," she said, and sat down at the edge of her bed.

"Things are dangerous for all our officers now," she answered, thinking she meant the budgetary and equipment problems.

"No, I mean the side of you that's not a cop."

Ella smiled ruefully. "Is that still there?"

"The fact that you have to ask is why I worry," Rose said. "You need to get out more and just have fun."

"I was thinking about that myself," she answered with a chuckle. "How are things between you and *Bizaadii*?" she asked.

"I care for him, and he for me. And he shares my concerns about the land and, in particular, the reclamation efforts that have failed so miserably." Rose took a deep breath, then continued. "It saddens me to see our land lying waste, poisoned, and no one trying hard enough to fix the problem. That's why many my age have died of *ch'ééná*, a sadness for what's gone and can never return. But with *Bizaadii* I can share those feelings and that makes them easier to bear."

"It was never like that between you and Dad, was it?" Ella asked.

Rose shook her head. "I loved him. He had courage, and there was something about him, a presence, that made him stand out in any crowd." She smiled, reminiscing. "Your father could sway people with only a smile. But he believed in the Christian God with all his heart. That made things difficult for us."

"You each remained true to what you felt was right, but I remember the toll it took on you both." She recalled the arguments long into the night. Rose had wanted to bring up her children as traditionalists, but Ella's father wouldn't hear of it.

Eventually, as a teenager Clifford chose to become a traditionalist like Rose. Ella had opted for neither her mother's nor her father's way. That had left her searching for her own identity and desperate to get away from the Rez.

Now she'd returned home for good, but sometimes walking the path she'd chosen was the most difficult of all. Inside, she was as alone as she'd ever been.

"Will you ever marry your marshal friend?" Rose asked her softly. "Do you even want to?"

"A part of me does, but then I stop to think about it, and reality crashes down on me. As a marshal he wouldn't be here half of the time. And when he *was* here, I wouldn't be able to guarantee that I wouldn't be off working on a case. Our lives are too alike in some ways to make them converge."

"Remember that your job is only part of who you are. Don't sacrifice everything for your career. Nothing is worth that price."

"I know. Someday I'll retire, Dawn will be all grown up, and

I'll find myself alone," Ella said, anticipating her mother's objections.

"Yes, that's a possibility. And if all you've ever known and loved is police work, when that's no longer there you may have a more difficult time adjusting to what remains of your life."

"I know," Ella said quietly. "But I have to follow the path that's right for me—whether it's easy or hard makes no difference."

"In that way, we're the same." Rose sighed, then stood up. "I better get some sleep. Tomorrow I'm going to talk to the group that's planning to sue one of the old uranium companies. I'd like them to address the issue of reclamation again and make that part of their suit."

Ella gazed at her mother as she walked out of the room, her back straight and tall. Her mother had changed. Rose was stronger now than she'd ever been. She'd come into her own and walked the new path she'd chosen with the kind of confidence that came from knowing she was in the right. Her mother's courage came from that sure knowledge and, because of it, she'd be unbeatable.

Without news about Kee or the pickup that had collided with her and Blalock, except that the pickup was probably one reported stolen in Farmington, Ella and Justine set out the next morning to find Delbert Shives. They'd been told that he would be in his office at the power plant, where he worked half days.

"We've been around this guy many times, but all we really know about him is that he's a chemist, worked with Kee Franklin at one time, and has been coordinating visits for the police departments and the local power facilities. I wonder what the real Delbert Shives is like away from the job," Ella said.

"He's been on his best behavior around police officers, but I've heard that he's a strange bird. I asked one of my cousins who works at the power plant, and she said that Shives doesn't get along with many people. He does his work, and he's very good at what he does, but he's a pain to deal with."

"What we want from him is information about Kee. Focus on that, and we'll keep hammering him until we get something."

"If what you told me already is correct, he hasn't worked with Kee for a long time," Justine reminded her. "He may not know anything useful."

"If all I get from him is an insight into Kee that'll help me narrow down his whereabouts, I'll be happy."

They arrived at the power plant's administration offices a short time later. After introducing themselves to a receptionist, a young Navajo woman in her early twenties, they waited.

Delbert Shives came out to greet them moments later, smiling and apparently in a good mood. "What can I do for you, ladies?"

"Is there someplace we can speak in private?" Ella asked.

Shives gave her a surprised look, then nodded and took her into his office, which was next to a room labeled Chemistry Lab. "This sounds serious," he commented, shutting the door behind him. "What's going on?"

"We understand that you worked with Dr. Kee Franklin in Los Alamos," Ella said, taking a seat.

His eyebrows went up. "Yes, I did, back when I was a lot younger. But I can't talk about it. My research work remains classified."

"We don't need any details of the work itself. We want to learn more about Dr. Franklin," Ella said.

"May I ask why?"

"It's all part of an ongoing police investigation."

He took a seat behind his desk and gazed at them with a thoughtful, penetrating look. "He didn't get killed, too, did he? Or is he a suspect in his son's death?"

Ella shook her head. "As I said, I can't comment on an ongoing investigation."

"All right. I'll try to answer your questions, just don't ask me about the research itself. I'd have to get special clearance before I could discuss it, even though it was years ago."

"Were you well paid for your work at the labs?" Ella asked.

"Definitely," Shives said without hesitation. "I was working through a subcontractor, though. Dr. Franklin was the one making the big bucks and had a permanent staff position."

"Yet he quit," Justine interjected.

"The problem with Dr. Franklin is that he's an idealist. He should have been in medicine or one of the life sciences. A physicist . . . well that's more like death science," he added with a smile.

"You think Dr. Franklin quit because he couldn't support the more destructive applications of his work?" Ella said.

"That's what I thought. Once he started preaching at the labs about the abuses of the mining industry and at the uranium mills, the handwriting was on the wall. He was becoming antinuke, which made him a security risk and an embarrassment to the labs. He knew he didn't have long before he was given the choice either to quit or be fired, so he did what he had to do."

Ella wondered about this bit of new information. No one at the labs had mentioned it. It sounded logical under the circumstances, and it was the kind of situation that would have been kept from the public. "Have you stayed in touch with Dr. Franklin since he left the labs?"

"Not at all. I haven't seen him for years. All I know is that he ended up teaching at a junior college in Los Alamos."

Delbert's phone rang. "Excuse me a moment," he said, picking up the phone and turning away from them.

Ella studied his office, then her glance fell on the newspaper sticking out from the bottom in-and-out tray on his desk. It was a recent edition of the campus newspaper from the community college in Shiprock. Ella could see that one of the lead stories was about a lecture Kee had given.

Either it was coincidence, or Shives was playing coy with them about Kee Franklin, trying to appear uninformed and uninterested. Ella tuned in to the conversation and heard him call the person at the other end of the line "Margaret."

Ella waited until he hung up, then followed up on her suspicions. "I couldn't help but overhear you mention someone by name. Are you regularly in touch with Margaret Bruno?"

He nodded. "We have a common interest, security at the local power plants and mines. As you know, at her request I've been introducing her to local enforcement groups, and I helped her set up your team's training session at the power plant. Did you need to speak to Ms. Bruno? She left me her cell number."

"I think I have it somewhere. I just wanted her to know how much we got out of her pursuit driving workshop. Will you tell her for me next time you speak?" Ella asked.

"Certainly."

"Our workshops have ended. Is she still giving workshops on the reservation?" Justine added.

"No, but she hasn't left the area. She's staying in Farmington with me right now." His face turned red when he saw Justine's jaw drop. "Margaret is my foster sister, Officer Goodluck. We grew up together."

The news surprised them, but she didn't comment. Justine merely nodded.

"If you have no more questions, ladies, I really should get back to work," Shives said.

"One more thing. Do you recall if Dr. Franklin ever mentioned having a special camping spot on the reservation, or in this area?" Ella tried to sound casual.

He shook his head. "Sorry. Dr. Franklin and I worked together, but we were never close friends. We seldom spoke of anything that didn't pertain to work. When he was at Los Alamos Labs, he was always totally immersed in what he was doing, and he had no patience for chitchat."

"Okay," Ella said, and stood. "Thank you for your time."

As they walked out, Justine glanced at Ella. "What the heck were you looking at on his desk?"

Ella told her. "I think he's lying to us. Now we have to figure out why."

"I'm still working on that background check you wanted."

"Great, but don't waste time on the years he was connected to the labs at Los Alamos. Concentrate on the last, say, five years. I want to know what he's done since he worked with Franklin. And see what kind of evaluation he's getting at the power plant now."

"I'll work on it as soon as we get back."

"I think we should start to consider Shives a suspect," Ella said, "but I can't figure out why he would want to frame NEED businessmen for murder. With his expertise, I'd think he'd have more to gain if a nuclear power plant opened. With his skills and knowledge, it should be relatively easy for him to get a job with the tribe."

She paused, considering her next step. "I'm going to call Blalock. I want Shives's phone records for the past month, and I won't be able to get them without some help from the FBI. With the ongoing war against terrorism, the FBI has more latitude, especially when it concerns nuclear weapons research and employees of government research facilities—past and present."

"Good idea, but what do you expect to find?" Justine asked.

"I have no idea, but what I'm looking for is a recent link between Shives and Franklin. If they've been in touch, I want to know about it. Something smells fishy here. For all we know, he could also be the Anglo that Whitesheep introduced to Billy Red-house."

Justine nodded. "That would tie a lot of unexplained details together, wouldn't it?"

TWENTY-TWO

————— ✕ ✕ ✕ —————

O nce they arrived at the station, Ella phoned Agent Blalock. It took a while to convince him to get the phone records for her. "No matter what he said, Delbert Shives knew that Kee Franklin was back on the Rez, and he may also know where Franklin is now."

"All right," he said at last. "I think I can find a judge that will cut us some slack."

"Thanks. I appreciate the help."

After Ella hung up, she leaned back in her chair and considered her options. If Shives and Franklin were connected, where did Margaret Bruno fit in? Ella remembered the nine-millimeter pistol she carried, but that didn't mean she was guilty of anything. Of course the bottom line was that she didn't have anything incriminating on Shives either, and the only people she knew about who could identify the Anglo who dealt with Redhouse and Whitesheep were dead.

As she continued to weigh things in her mind, George Charley stepped into her office and greeted her. "Can I help you?" she asked.

He took a seat across her desk. "I'm worried about Professor

Franklin," he said. "I've been trying to locate him for a couple of days, but no one's seen him."

"Why are you looking for him?"

"He and I are still on opposite sides of the fence, but I think in the long run he'll be one of NEED's biggest assets. I'm going to try and offer him a compromise he'll accept. There's got to be some way for us to find common ground. But I haven't been able to find him, and that worries me. He's lost his son and has got to be going through a really tough time now."

"So you came because you're personally worried about him?"

"No, not quite. The bottom line is that our tribe needs him, and we can't afford to have anything happen to him. His reputation and area of expertise make him one of a kind."

"You say that with such certainty, yet his work was classified. What haven't you told me?" Ella's eyes narrowed.

He leaned back, his gaze fixed on an indeterminate spot across the room. "All I really have is an informed opinion—nothing either you or I will ever be able to prove one way or another."

"Fair enough."

"When I met him, he was known as Dr. Franklin, and everyone at the labs spoke with great respect about him. As an intern, I was able to meet with him a few times and ask about new applications for lasers. That area of study fascinated me, and I was thinking of specializing in it. He never told me exactly what his own work entailed, but he gave me copies of several scientific papers dealing with enhancing the technology used to purify chemical compounds with the next generation of lasers. He told me that it was a wide-open field I might want to look into. He warned me that the information in the articles wasn't really up-to-date, but that it was the most accurate he'd ever seen outside classified papers."

"So that's what made you think that his research was along those lines," she said, nodding.

"At the time, one of the missions at Los Alamos Labs was to

develop and improve the processes for purifying uranium into weapons-grade quality. I think that's what Kee was doing. He may have even pioneered the technology."

"I see now why you want him so badly."

"I also suspect he made additional breakthroughs that are still classified because the government doesn't want anyone else to know about them. I have a feeling that maybe the reason he dropped out of the program was because he was close to making a discovery that would have made nuclear weapons, or anything requiring enriched uranium, much cheaper. That, in turn, would have increased the demand for uranium, and he knew what it was already doing to the people here."

"I was told he hit a dead end with his research," Ella recalled.

"I don't believe that. He was brilliant, and didn't seem the type ever to give up."

"Thanks for telling me all this. I appreciate it."

"If you happen to find Dr. Franklin, please tell him that I'd like to sit down and talk to him, and that I'm willing to work with him until we find a way to join forces."

"I'll do that."

As George walked out, Ella picked up the phone and called Wilson. With his science background, he might be able to provide her with some extra information.

Wilson answered after a few rings. He didn't need more than a "Hi, Wilson" to know it was her. Good friends seldom did.

"Whatcha need?" Wilson asked. "I know when you call in the mornings it's because you're working a case and need something yesterday."

She laughed. "I've learned some interesting things about Kee Franklin, and I'd like to get your input on the science part. But I don't want to talk about this on the phone. Can I meet you in your office?"

"Sure."

Ella arrived at the campus less than fifteen minutes later. She hurried to Wilson's office and found him sitting behind the desk.

He looked at her and winced. "You're wired, and on a roll, Ella. You make me nervous when you get this way. Sit down and tell me what's up."

"I want to know one thing from you—is it possible that Kee Franklin could have made a breakthrough in his research years ago? Is he as good as people seem to think?"

"Oh, yeah. I've only known him as a physicist who occasionally guest lectures, but his insights on laser technology are incredible."

"Do you think he would have walked away from it all just on principle?"

He considered it for several moments. "Yes. There are some things he feels strongly about, as you know. Even after all these years, he's very cynical about his work at the labs. I just remembered an offhand comment he made to me one day that I think will bring the point home to you. He told me that if the labs ever found a really cheap and efficient way or purifying uranium, they'd make a stack of atomic bombs as high as Shiprock. Then he said that they'd almost had a process that worked once, but they'd hit a human roadblock. I asked him about it, of course, but he shook his head and said that he was an old man who sometimes exaggerated."

"Do you think it's possible Kee found a way of purifying uranium with lasers and kept the details from the labs on purpose?" Ella asked.

"It's possible. He hates the uranium industry for what happened to the *Dineh*."

She told Wilson about Delbert Shives. "If Shives was working with him at the time, shouldn't he have known what was going on?" Ella asked.

"Shives might have guessed that Kee had made a breakthrough, but without specific details and data from Kee, he couldn't have proven anything. I've met Shives, and he's no match for Kee in the brainpower department. I doubt Shives could have been able to duplicate Kee's results on his own."

"But if Shives ever managed to get hold of the data and information he needed, and take it to the right company . . ."

"It might make nuclear power plants very competitive with coal-powered generators. Shives could become a very wealthy man—provided he owned the patents on the process. But that would require him to get it from Kee, either directly, or from his notes. As long as Dr. Franklin hadn't patented the process himself, or published his research, Shives could write it up so it would look like he was the one who'd made the discovery."

"Thanks, Wilson. I owe you one."

"It's all conjecture on my part—and I *hate* conjecture. But it's a reasonable conclusion based on the facts."

"Okay, Professor. I'm heading back to the station. Thanks again."

"Let me know if there's anything else I can do."

By the time Ella got back to her office, Agent Blalock was there waiting.

"Don't tell me you've got phone records for me already!" she said, not really believing it.

He reached into his pocket and brought out an envelope. "The Bureau is capable of cutting some major corners when it needs to, particular in times like these. The fact that nobody seems to know where Dr. Franklin is at the moment makes a lot of my superiors extremely nervous, especially with the death of his son and everything else that's been going on around here."

Ella studied the printouts. "I see you cross-referenced the numbers already."

"I figured it would save us all some time."

"Yeah. And there's the connection I was looking for. Delbert Shives contacted Dr. Franklin no less than five times during the last three weeks. Shives *was* lying to me." She went down the list of numbers. "I recognize this company, Permian Energy Network."

He nodded. "It's a multinational energy conglomerate formerly connected to uranium mining, which owns a big chunk of the power facilities in the West. Their headquarters are in Texas. I looked them up."

Ella looked down at the list, and another name caught her eye. Delbert Shives had called Robert Whitesheep once several days before Billy Redhouse had died. Perhaps Shives *was* the Anglo Whitesheep arranged to meet the councilman.

Justine came to the door just then, and, seeing Blalock, turned and started to walk away when Ella called her back.

"Have you got something for me, partner?"

Justine came back in, nodded at Blalock, then looked at Ella. "I pulled out all the stops and started digging into Delbert Shives's life. The last time Shives made a substantial salary was when he was working with Dr. Franklin years ago. Since then, he's been laid off from two power companies. His last employer sounded vague about the reasons for letting him go, so I pressed harder. It turns out Shives got into some legal trouble. He was accused of trying to patent some proprietary processes that belonged to that company."

"Does he have any patents right now?"

"Yes. Several, in fact—all to do with lasers and chemical extraction processes. I checked with Wilson, and he said it was all basic stuff, nothing extraordinary, but the royalties he gets from his patents help keep him afloat. Despite his degrees and education, Shives has never been able to do more than just barely hang on to his small business. That's why he works part-time at the power company."

"Maybe Shives stole a part of Dr. Franklin's process at the

labs—just not enough of it for him to fill in the gaps and market it as his own. It's possible he's spent all these years trying to duplicate Franklin's genius, and now with the prospect of a nuclear power plant opening here and in other places, he's decided to get it from Franklin—one way or the other. If Shives got the process, he could market it to the highest bidder—not just the tribe or the Permian Energy Network."

"And that's what all the robberies have been targeting? Trying to find Kee Franklin's old research notes?" Justine asked.

"It makes sense," Ella answered. "If Shives came up with a uranium enrichment process that could make the fuel even more powerful, and cheaper than ever, he could undercut the current price of uranium to power plants and become an incredibly wealthy man."

"How did you find out Dr. Franklin worked on this kind of research?" Blalock asked.

She smiled, but didn't answer.

Blalock exhaled softly, then stood. "I've got some of my own contacts on the Rez searching for Franklin, and more, including Agent Payestewa, checking the mountains and campgrounds all around the Four Corners. If I get anything, I'll give you a heads-up."

As Blalock left the office, Justine leaned back in her chair. "Okay, I've got one more tidbit—it's about Margaret Bruno."

"I was wondering if we'd ever figure out how she ties in."

"I don't have that, but like Shives, she's got an interesting record. She was a cop in Amarillo, Texas, and apparently was known for aggressiveness in the field. Bruno never was in a situation where she actually fired her weapon, but she was sued two times for excessive force. In both cases the city settled out of court, but after that she was taken out of the field. They decided to make her a training officer at the police academy there and sent her to classes at the FBI Academy and elsewhere. She resigned as soon as she completed her courses and took a job as a security officer for Permian Energy Network, the big energy company."

"How did she do there?" Ella asked skeptically.

"After several incidents PEN decided she was too competitive and confrontational and gave her the pink slip. She sued, one of the witnesses against her recanted, and she won a settlement. With the nest egg from that she started her own consulting firm, giving workshops to different police departments and private industry security teams. Her business is doing pretty well. That's all mostly a matter of public record."

"But you've got something else off the record?" Ella asked, catching the gleam in her partner's eye.

Justine nodded. "I tracked down an old neighbor of the Shives family. I spoke to her off the record, and I leaned that Bruno was a foster child who was taken in by Delbert's parents. Shives's father was an alcoholic, though few knew about it. He often became abusive, but Delbert, who was quite a bit older, always protected Margaret from him. They became very close but, according to the neighbor, Margaret was basically unstable. She had a dangerous temper, raised hell in the neighborhood, and the only one who could ever control her was Delbert. My contact said that Margaret adored him."

"That's good work, Justine. Do you think Bruno is the one who broke into the garage and killed Jason?"

Justine shook her head. "I don't know. For a former cop, that would be really stretching it, but then again, she apparently has a mean, aggressive streak in her. Did you say she carried a nine-millimeter?"

Ella nodded. "A Smith & Wesson, and not the murder weapon."

"Cops often carry backups of a smaller caliber," Justine pointed out.

"And cops can go bad, especially after being hardened on the job. Sometimes the lure of being in a position of power and control over others attracts people with dangerous tempers—a bad combination. We need to find out more about her. If Margaret or Shives has been involved in any of these crimes, we'll need a lot more to go on than past history. But here's another tidbit. Shives called Robert Whitesheep several days before Billy Redhouse was killed. We now have a connection that supports the possibility that he's the Anglo who dealt with the councilman."

"That's good news. We're on a roll now," Justine said.

"Just keep plugging away at Bruno's background. You're doing a great job, Justine."

"Teamwork, that's all it takes. I'll get back to the terminal and see if I can squeeze any more information from Bruno's and Shives's backgrounds, or from anyone else in their past."

"Go for it, partner." Ella smiled. "I'm going to try and get a little more paperwork done. Let me know if anything new turns up."

Another hour passed, and Ella finally decided she couldn't take another second of red tape. Reports seemed, magically, to multiply on her desk. No matter how hard she worked, the stack never went down.

Her phone rang, and Ella picked it up quickly, hoping for some crisis that would give her an excuse to leave the office.

She recognized Kevin's voice.

"I wanted you to know that by the end of today, the pony will have a stall. I've also had the old corral repaired and a new gate mounted. I hired a high school boy to clean up after the pony every day after school, too. Your mother can use the manure in her garden. Mix in a little alfalfa, let it cure, and you're got a great soil builder, or so I've been told."

"Sounds good."

"One more thing. I've having a load of sand dumped inside

the old corral and leveled so that the area can become a riding arena for Dawn."

"She is *not* taking riding lessons yet, no way. I don't care if you line the corral with feathers."

"I wasn't thinking of anything formal. I figured you could let her sit on the horse and have someone lead it around. She won't be in any danger, and she'll think she's in heaven."

"Kevin, I've got news for you. That's not heaven. That's a nightmare."

"Oh, come on, Ella. You know she loves that pony. You'll make her so happy."

Ella sighed. She was fighting a losing battle. Dawn would hound them all until someone put her on the pony's back. "I'll see if Jennifer Clani will do it."

"She's really an excellent choice, you know. She's got dozens of rodeo ribbons."

Ella's eyes narrowed. "You already spoke to her, didn't you?"

"I refuse to answer that question on the basis that it might incriminate me."

"One of these days, Kevin . . ."

He laughed. "How about meeting me at the Totah Café? I'm treating myself to their stuffed sopaipillas tonight. I want to celebrate."

"What's the occasion?"

"I'll tell you when you get there, and I think you'll be pleased." When she didn't accept his invitation right away, he added, "Aw, come on. You got to eat dinner sometime, and it's news that, as a cop, you're going to find interesting."

"All right. I'll be there."

"Great. Half an hour?"

"Sounds good, order for me if you get there first."

Ella gave the pile of file folders and reports one last glance, then picked up her keys and hurried out of the building.

She arrived at the Totah Café a short time later. Ella could tell, just by looking at Kevin, that he was in a great mood. She approached the table he'd chosen, one in a corner of the room, curious about his news.

As she sat down, she glanced over at Ernest Ration, who stood in the shadows with his back to the wall, like a stone sentinel.

Ella leaned back and sipped the fresh cup of coffee the waitress brought to their table. "So tell me. What's up?"

"George Branch has finally stopped taking on-the-air jabs at me," he said. "Branch finally understands that we're on the same side when it comes to NEED."

"Did you take an official position?"

He nodded. "I gave a statement to the press. But I've got to tell you, it sure feels weird to share common ground with that jerk."

"The fact that he's stopped harassing you may not be NEED-related. He was having his own share of problems, if you remember."

"Actually, I think that it's remarkable that he hasn't had those kinds of problems before. An idiot like him is in the business of making enemies."

The food arrived then, and they both paused their discussion for a moment. Ella took a bite of the sopaipilla, fried bread stuffed with ground beef, beans, salsa, and cheese. No one made them like the Totah Café. "Maybe so, but I think that's the real reason he stopped. George Branch is a bully—he doesn't like it when people fight back. He can dish it out, but he can't take it."

"But even deep in his pea brain, he must have known I had nothing to do with whoever was harassing him. That's just not my style."

Ella nodded then. As Kevin waited for his glass of iced tea to be refilled, she glanced at Ernest Ration. He'd heard what they said, and, as she read the smug expression on his face, she knew with certainty who George Branch's most persistent adversary had been.

"Is it your style, Ernest?" she said softly, as Kevin walked to the counter to get more sugar packets.

"Come on, even if I had been responsible, I'd never admit to something illegal," he said, chuckling. "But the change in Branch's attitude is a definite improvement, don't you think? And I like knowing that my boss can breathe easier now that we don't have a vandal lurking around."

"The vandalism was really starting to get on my nerves," Kevin said, having heard the last part of their conversation as he returned to his chair. "Did you know Ernest finally caught the kid who cut my tires? Nailed him just in the nick of time. The three of us had a real good talk, and I used the terms 'probation violation' and 'state detention facility in Springer' several times. He won't do it again."

"Who was it?" Ella recalled seeing a motorcycle lately, and suddenly knew. "Not Oliver Washburn, by any chance?"

Ernest's eyes gave him away, but this time Kevin was the one with the poker face. "I promised not to give the young man's name to the department, so I can't really say—not unless he tries something else. He's on probation, and all it takes is my word to send him back to Springer."

"Okay. But why were you singled out?"

"I represented the young man on a vandalism charge a year ago. He lied to me and to the court, but the truth came out during trial, and he was convicted. He blamed me, of course. But it'll stop now, I'm sure of it."

"Does that mean Ernest is no longer needed?"

"No way. He and I discussed that right from the start," Kevin replied. "I like having a bodyguard around. The tribal president has one, of course, as do many politicians in the state. Tribal Council members often employ low-profile security while on the campaign trail, so I don't get any comments from my colleagues, especially those who've received threats of their own from time to time. Besides, it's an extra precaution that'll help me feel more confident when my daughter visits me, or when I take her out."

Ella nodded, then smiled. "Right now you're going to be hard-pressed taking her anywhere that's away from the pony."

"Actually, I was thinking of putting her on the pony and going for a short hike around your mother's home. I think she'd love it."

Ella sighed. "Someday, Kevin, you're going to realize that Dawn doesn't need to get everything she wants." She took a sip of coffee, then lowered her voice so Ernest couldn't hear. "How's Emily?" Now that he was no longer worried about having someone after him, she wondered if he'd pursue her.

Something flashed in Kevin's eyes, and it took her a moment to identify it. He was disappointed.

"I like her, Ella, but she's just not the one for me. I prefer someone who'll drive me crazy every once in a while," he added, looking at her with a smile, "just to keep me on my toes."

She searched his eyes and found something that unsettled her—something she hoped Dawn would never see. She had a feeling Kevin wanted to renew their old relationship.

Mercifully, her cell phone rang just then. It was Justine. "I asked my cousin who works at the power plant a few more questions about Shives, and she suggested we talk to a friend of hers, Bertha Finch, who lives next door to him. She arranged for us to meet Bertha this evening. The woman's taking courses at the college, but will meet us after class."

"Great. I'll see you at the station when I've finished dinner, and we'll set out from there."

Ella placed the cell phone back in the case attached to her belt. "I hate to do this, but I'm going to have to eat and run."

"I heard," Kevin said with a nod. "At least I'm glad you could join me for a while."

Ella ate half of her sopaipilla, then got a doggie bag for the rest and excused herself. As she drove to the station, her thoughts shifted back to the case. She was certain they were close to finding critical answers.

After a short meeting with Big Ed to update him on their latest findings, Ella and Justine left the station. "Tell me more about Bertha Finch," Ella asked. "How will we know her?"

"She'll be waiting near the side exit of the campus library. Pat, my cousin, said she'll be easy to recognize because she wears a bright red parka. Pat told me that Bertha's a computer analyst at the power plant and always notices—and remembers—details. I think she may be able to give us the kind of insight that we would never get from personnel reports and evaluation files."

"I'm glad you set this up."

They met Bertha outside a short time later. She was a half-Navajo woman in her early thirties. Her hair was shiny black, thin, and nearly down to her waist. Her large, owlish glasses somehow seemed to fit her style. Since there was a definite chill in the air, they all opted to go to the campus administration building and have something hot to drink.

A few moments later they sat down in a large canteen area filled with vending machines, sipping coffee.

Bertha glanced at Justine. "I have another class in twenty minutes, so we better get down to business."

"We're trying to find out more about Delbert Shives—the kind of stuff I can't get from background files. We'd really appreciate any help you can give us."

"Why are you're so interested in him?" Bertha looked at Justine, then Ella.

Ella shook her head. "It's police business, and we can't discuss any details at the moment. In fact, we'd also like to ask you to keep this meeting between us." Ella was determined to keep Shives from knowing what they were doing for now.

"Okay, but I'm still not sure what kind of information you need," Bertha said.

Justine leaned back in her chair. "What kind of neighbor is he? Does he have lots of parties, or does he keep to himself? Does he come and go a lot at night? Who comes over to his home? Those kinds of things."

"Okay, I'll answer as many of those as I can. He's quiet, I've never heard loud music or even the TV coming from his place, and he's usually home on weekends. He does a little bit of gardening, but not much. Just trimming the roses that are there and mowing his small patch of lawn."

"What kind of people come to visit him?" Ella asked.

"Well, lately he's had a woman living with him. A tall blonde with a deep tan. Athletic-looking, but looks like she got strong working on a farm rather than figure skating, you know? He calls her Meg. If they're romantically involved, you couldn't tell. They act more like old friends. Maybe she's the girlfriend of the dark-haired man I've seen there once in a while lately, though honestly, I've never seen them together."

"The dark-haired man, is he Navajo?" Justine asked.

"I don't know. He's always wearing a long coat and a baseball cap. He's tall."

"Have you ever spoken to either Margaret or the guy with the cap?" Ella said.

"Not really. I said good morning to her a time or two, and she nodded, but the guy, whether he's coming or going, completely ignores me." She stopped then continued. "There's another person, too . . ." she hesitated.

"Go on, please," Justine said.

"I've never seen Delbert with any woman besides Margaret, but on the way home yesterday I stopped at the Jiffy Mart. While I was there, I saw Del with a tall, Anglo woman with dark hair. She wore it short in one of those shaggy styles you just blow-dry and go. She looked vaguely familiar, but I never did get a good look at her."

"What color were her eyes?" Ella asked, hoping she remembered more than she thought.

"I didn't notice. I only had a quick glance as I walked past them. Delbert didn't even say hello. He was completely engrossed in her." Bertha looked at her watch. "I've got to get going. Is there anything else?"

"What kind of car does the guy with the cap drive?" Ella asked on an impulse.

"He may work at a car dealership, because I've seen him come up in an SUV one time, and another in a tan car, maybe a Chevy. If I saw a photo of the model, I'd recognize it. Anything more?"

"Not for now, Bertha. Glad to have met you, and thanks for the information," Ella said. "If you think of anything else, give us a call." She handed Bertha her card.

"No problem. Later, Justine."

As she rushed away, Ella looked at her cousin. "I want to know who these strangers are—the man in the cap and the woman with the short dark hair—and I've got a way to find out, at least with the woman. If I remember right, the Jiffy Mart installed security cameras last year."

"Yeah, they found out that if they have them, their insurance rates go down."

"Yeah, robbers don't like to see their photos on the news. Let's go over there and see if we can still get the videotape."

"Those are usually recycled every twenty-four to forty-eight hours."

"Then let's hope we get lucky. We need a break, and hopefully those tapes will give it to us."

"Are you thinking that this might be the dark-haired intruder who shot at Wilson, and the one who killed Jason? A woman? Or the man in the cap. His vehicles sound like those seen at more than one shooting lately."

Ella shrugged. "One step at a time."

Ella and Justine sat in the back room of the Jiffy Mart. The clerk, a Navajo kid barely out of his teens, had refused to give them the tapes without a court order or his boss's permission. Since neither was possible, they had persuaded him to let them view the tapes at the store.

"I wonder if he's studying to be a lawyer," Justine said with a wry smile.

Ella chuckled. "He'd be a natural."

Justine took the tapes that had been used the day before in the outside security camera and stuck the first one in the machine. They ran it fast-forward, but there was nothing of interest to them there. It wasn't until they got to the third tape that they found what they'd been searching for.

"There's Shives," Ella said, pointing to a figure on the screen. "Stop the tape, run it back and let's see if we can get a better look at the woman."

As the scene unfolded, Ella noticed one thing. "Do you realize that she's deliberately keeping her face away from the camera? Look closely. When she gets out of the SUV, she holds her hand in front of her face as if brushing away a hair, then she positions herself with her back to the camera."

Ella and Justine watched a few more seconds, then ran it back and replayed it again. "That's one cautious lady. Even though she had no reason to believe we'd ever see this tape, she wasn't taking any chances," Ella said.

"You want me to run it through again?" Justine asked.

"No, let's see if we can read the license plate when she pulls out."

The SUV backed out, then for an instant, they could make out three numbers.

"It happens too fast to get the rest," Justine said.

"Yeah, but there's something else there . . . like a rental company sticker." Ella ran it back then froze the screen. "I wish this was in color. There, what's that letter? Is it an *F*?"

"Maybe. I can get equipment that will really clear it up, but I don't think I'll be able to get a court order to take the tape. Maybe we can phone the store owner."

Ella ran it back, then moved closer to the monitor. "I've got it. It's an *E* with a circle around it. There's a new rental place in Farmington. The Circle of Excellence, or the Circle E for short."

Justine checked her watch. "Do you want to pay them a visit tonight?"

Ella sensed her partner's reluctance. "Do you have plans?"

"Yeah, sort of," Justine said. "But I can cancel."

"No, don't," Ella said after a moment. They'd been running themselves ragged on this case. "Let's call it a day."

Justine readily agreed. "Yeah, that's a good idea. It's late. We'll have better results talking to the daytime people—the ones who actually make the decisions."

Ella smiled. "Hot date?"

Justine's face fell. "No. Wilson and I are going to talk, and I have a feeling we'll probably break up tonight. It's just not working out."

"Is he still hinting about marriage?"

She nodded. "And I've come to realize that I'm years away from making a commitment like that."

Ella nodded somberly. "I think Wilson and you have different goals, and that's hard to reconcile. Just make sure you know what you'll be giving up."

Justine dropped her off at the station, and Ella went directly to her vehicle. As she pulled out of the parking lot, she picked up her cell and called home. Jennifer Clani, Dawn's baby-sitter, answered.

"How are things going there?"

"Your daughter's father stopped by after dinner. He took your daughter for a short ride on the pony, and I went with them."

"Good. Where did you all go?"

"Not far, just a few hundred yards away, then back. Mostly I led the pony while he kept her balanced. She had a wonderful time. She's now sound asleep."

Ella felt her heart sink a bit. She'd really hoped that tonight would be one of the times when Dawn would be awake and lively, and they could spend some time playing together.

"Has she come up with a name for the pony yet?"

"Yes. Her father suggested Wind because Wind carries secrets, and that's sort of the way the pony arrived. Your mother approved."

Ella laughed. "Score one for him."

TWENTY-THREE
————— ✖ ✖ ✖ —————

Shortly after sunrise, Ella felt someone bounce up on the bed beside her. "*Shimá*, wake up! Wind wants breakfast."

Ella placed the pillow over her head. "The pony's probably asleep. Go back to bed."

"No, he's awake! I saw him from my window!"

Ella opened her eyes reluctantly and saw her daughter's face less than a foot away from her face.

"Yay! You're up."

Ella sighed. "I didn't have much of a choice." Feeling positively diabolical, she reached for the cell phone on her desk. "Would you like to talk to your daddy and tell him that you're about to go feed Wind?"

"Yes!"

Ella dialed, glad for a chance at payback, then gave her daughter the phone. Dawn's conversation with her father bought her another ten minutes of relaxation and enormous satisfaction.

All too soon, her daughter crawled back in bed beside her, reviving Ella for the second time. "Daddy said that he'll remember today."

Ella laughed. "Okay, daughter, it's time now. Let's go feed Wind."

After the horse had been given a flake of hay, and over Dawn's protests, they went back inside. Ella helped her mother fix breakfast while Dawn rolled the ball for Two, who dutifully fetched it and brought it back for her.

"That one has a way with animals," Rose said softly. "A real gift."

"She's no different from any other kid," Ella said, wishing more than anything that it really were so. The legend concerning their clan would follow them always. It was said that each child received a special gift from the Gods.

Rose shook her head. "She'll inherit a talent . . . maybe intuition, or something else entirely that will mark her as special," Rose said, then grew quiet as Ella's phone rang.

Justine identified herself. "My car broke down. Any way you can come by and pick me up? I was on my way to the station, but now I'm stuck."

"Where?"

"By the highway, at the end of the road leading to my mother's place."

"Okay, I'll be there shortly."

"Before you leave . . . did Rose happen to make some home-made tortillas or fry bread this morning?"

Ella laughed. "Hungry, are you?"

"Starving."

"Okay, hang tight. I'll be there in twenty minutes."

Ella clipped the phone back onto her belt. "I'm going to have to rush off. My cousin's stuck—her car broke down."

"And I heard you say that she's hungry?" Rose asked. "It's so early, I bet she hasn't had breakfast. I'll fix a breakfast burrito for her and you. The eggs are already scrambled."

Ella started to ask for something simpler, but then changed her mind. The truth was that Rose loved mothering people. To deny her that wouldn't help anyone—least of all Justine or her right now, since they were both famished.

By the time Rose had loaded up a grocery sack with a thermos and more food than two people could eat in a week, Ella was ready to go.

"Wow," Ella said, taking the sack. "That smells wonderful!"

"You've each got a breakfast burrito with eggs, potatoes, and a bit of salsa. There's also a thermos of coffee and several pieces of fry bread in a smaller sack inside."

"Thanks, Mom," she said, giving Rose a hug.

Ella went into the living room and found her daughter dancing in front of the TV set. Her favorite cartoon character was singing and dancing, and Dawn was imitating his movements.

"Hey, Pumpkin, I'm off to work. How about a hug?"

Dawn launched herself into Ella's arms enthusiastically, squeezing her as hard as she could. "Bye! Can I ride the pony after day school?"

"Ask Boots," she said, using Jennifer Clani's nickname. Lena had given it to her granddaughter who, as a child, had loved her grandfather's boots and would always wear them around the house.

"Okay." Dawn looked back to the TV set and started dancing again.

Ella watched her a moment longer. Dawn was independent, a trait Ella was sure would cause no end of trouble someday.

About twenty minutes later, she pulled up beside her partner's unit, and Justine jumped out, locked the door, then hurried into Ella's SUV. "It's freezing out here this morning," she said.

"Did the heater in your unit work?" Ella looked over and saw the windshield on Justine's unit had started frosting over.

"Not without heat from the engine. The car ran fine almost up to the turnoff, then it made a strange, coughing sound and stopped cold." Justine took a deep breath, and zeroed in on the sack. "That smells wonderful."

"Help yourself. Mom packed enough for an army, as usual."

Justine unwrapped one of the breakfast burritos, handed it to Ella, then took the other for herself. "Thanks for bringing all this stuff, Ella. I left home this morning before anyone woke up. I'd have to answer too many questions if I'd stayed for breakfast."

"Then I assume you and Wilson did break up?"

She nodded. "I really like him, Ella, but things weren't right between us."

"You want to talk about it?"

Justine shook her head. "I'm all talked out right now."

"I understand."

Both of them remained silent, and Justine finished her breakfast quickly. "Do you want me to drive while you finish yours?"

"You really must have been hungry," Ella said. "Yeah, let me pull over."

Moments later, sitting in the passenger's seat, Ella finished breakfast as they headed into Shiprock. The coffee her mother had made was strong and hot, and the aroma filled the car. She gave Justine the extra mug her mother had packed after pouring coffee into it from the thermos. "Don't stop by the station, let's go directly to the car rental place in Farmington. Those agencies open early."

"Seven o'clock, in their case. I called them this morning to verify their hours."

"Did you also call maintenance and ask them to dispatch a tow truck to go get your unit?"

"Yeah, right before I called you about an hour ago. The really depressing thing is that they told me they had two other calls to get to first."

Ella exhaled softly. "It was cold last night, and things are getting worse. The tribe *has* to allocate more funds to the department."

"I've been really thinking of supporting NEED—actively. Maybe join their organizational meetings, rallies, and so on. A lot of cops are doing that."

Ella nodded. "I can't say I blame them. The tribe has to come up with some long-term income sources to keep things running. Uncle Sam can't be depended upon to help, not with all the cutbacks in federal spending. The tribes, more and more, are on their own."

Ella turned on the small portable radio she carried in her car. The Farmington radio station's morning broadcast with George Branch was on. Ella turned it up and listened, curious to see if Kevin was really out of the woods with the man. Her stomach clenched as she heard Kevin's name mentioned.

"Councilman Tolino has come up with a lot of ideas, but he fails time and time again to implement them. Councilman, if you're listening, put your money where your mouth is. You say you're pro-NEED. Okay, we believe you. Now do something to make things happen. The last time the council took a vote, you were absent. Were you hiding?"

Ella switched it off. Poor Kevin. He'd celebrated too soon. She thought of Ernest Ration, and smiled. Somehow, she had a feeling things would get interesting in the next day or so.

"I wonder what Kevin will have to say about that?" Justine asked.

"I guess we'll find out. For what it's worth, partner, I'm leaning toward a pro-Need stance myself. A nuclear power plant on the Rez entails risk, but this time the tribe has to take the chance. At this point, I'm for anything that will give our people a way to become self-sustaining," Ella said.

When they arrived at the car rental place, Ella hurried inside the small building. Beside it was a large parking lot, half-filled with new, mostly white vehicles of different models. A young Anglo woman in her midtwenties greeted them from behind the desk. Seeing the badge pinned to Ella's belt, she gave them a worried look.

"Is something wrong, Officers?"

"We need to speak to a manager, please," Ella said. She knew she was out of jurisdiction here, but it was a legitimate phase of an ongoing investigation.

She had barely finished her sentence when a man in his late thirties wearing a blue blazer and tie came out of an adjoining office. He glanced at Ella's badge, then back at her. "I'm the owner, Jim Apodaca, Officer. How can I help you?"

"May we speak privately?" Ella asked.

Apodaca waved her inside his office. "Are you from the tribal police?"

Ella nodded, then signaled to Justine to stay in the outer office. She knew Justine would strike up a conversation with the receptionist. One way or another, they'd get the information they needed.

"The tribal police have no jurisdiction here, isn't that right?"

"Yes, but we'd like your cooperation on an investigation that leads off the Navajo Nation. We need some information." Ella described the SUV and the woman, then gave him the three digits they'd gotten from the plates. "We need to know the name and the address of the person who rented this vehicle."

He leaned forward, a worried frown on his face. "Was one of our vehicles used to commit a crime?"

"We just need to locate the driver and talk to her," Ella replied without answering directly. "We're investigating a missing person's case, and we think she may have information that could help us."

The owner leaned back in his seat and regarded her warily. "I don't know about this . . ."

"Your cooperation might end up saving a man's life. We could go through local police agencies for this information, but we wanted to save some time. That's why we came directly to you."

He took a deep breath then let it out again. "All right. But please don't make our involvement public. It might hurt my company, and we're just trying to get off the ground here."

"No problem."

He pulled his chair forward and faced his computer. "Okay, give me what you've got again."

Ella read the numbers on the license plate and gave him a description of the SUV again. Seconds ticked by, then he stopped typing and turned the monitor around so she could see the information.

"That vehicle is rented to a woman by the name of Margaret Bruno. She'd first rented a four-door sedan, but she returned it to us and asked for a four-wheel-drive. She has a Texas operator's license, but gave a local address. Do you need that information?"

"No, it's not necessary. I appreciate your cooperation. Now I need to ask you for another favor. Once the SUV is returned, I want you to call me *before* you clean or detail it. I'd like to go over the vehicle for evidence."

"What kind of evidence?"

"I can't tell you that, but believe me it's very important."

"Can you *guarantee* that you'll keep my name and my company's name out of it?"

"I can't guarantee it, no, but if we tie anyone who rented one of your vehicles to a crime, we'll give your company the highest references, saying that you cooperated and helped us solve a very important case."

"All right, but you can also thank me by recommending my company to all your friends."

"You've got it."

She knew how hard it was for anyone to start a business in this area. Times were tough for people, especially in a poor area of a poor state. Money was scarce, and businesses were taking a substantial hit.

Thanking Apodaca, Ella left his office and met Justine in the lobby. They walked outside and, as soon as they were both in the car, Ella spoke. "How did it go? Did you get anything out of her?"

Justine smiled. "I knew that was what you wanted me to do, so we talked. She remembered the woman who'd rented the SUV because she's first rented a sedan. Apparently she was a pain in the butt all the way around. She didn't know her name, but she said that the woman told her she was an ex-cop, and she wasn't going to be jerked around by anyone."

"I got the name. It was Margaret Bruno."

"Sure sounds like her personality. But that's not who was driving the SUV. The description doesn't fit."

"The hair color doesn't, that's true, but the rest does—more than you realize. Think about it, Justine. Margaret is tall, and not very busty. With a baseball cap and the right wig, she could pass as a guy, particularly to a scared convenience store clerk who's afraid to take a good look at her face. We know she got into the power plant disguised as a male teacher the day of that training fiasco. And think about the woman we saw in the tape—it could have easily been Margaret in a dark-haired wig. Remember that all along I've said that whoever tailed me had special training operating a vehicle."

"But why would Margaret go after Councilman Redhouse?"

"I'm not sure yet, but she's our best suspect, and we think Shives might be the Anglo connected with Whitesheep and Billy. Admittedly, it's easier to tie her into the murder of Officer Franklin and the confrontation Wilson had with the thief. Her connection to Shives and his to Kee Franklin is already established."

Justine thought it over. "They might have also been responsible for the drive-by at Jonas Buck's home and Redhouse's murder as a way to discredit NEED. . . . But why would Shives assume that the tribe wouldn't hire him if that project went through?"

Ella considered it, then spoke. "Maybe he thought that his downgraded security clearance would show up in a background check and raise the kind of questions that would keep him from getting the job. But that's still a slim reason for murder. And what about Whitesheep? How does he fit in, or is that another situation entirely?"

Justine shook her head and shrugged. "Maybe he got killed because he knew about Shives meeting Redhouse."

"Or maybe he knew that Shives had paid the councilman that cash as a bribe, or for information. Whitesheep ended up with some of that money, too." Ella nodded. "Sounds like the pieces are finally coming together."

"So what now?"

"We still need to find and confirm a motive for Delbert Shives and Margaret Bruno. Maybe we can start by asking Permian for more background."

"For that, I'm sure we're going to have to find a back door. I doubt we'll get any official cooperation. They don't want to be connected to any hint of a scandal now that they're trying to convince the tribe that they should be the ones to run the proposed power plant."

"Do you know anyone who works for them?" Ella asked.

Justine shook her head. "Do you?"

"Not that I can think of offhand. Let's head back to the station for now."

It was shortly after eleven by the time they arrived. As they walked inside, Big Ed was out in the hall, and signaled to Ella to come into his office.

Ella followed him there then, as she was seated, their chief closed the door behind them.

"Give me everything you've got."

Ella did, and watched his expression.

"All this time, and we've essentially got nothing we can take to a prosecutor," he said thoughtfully.

"Nothing we can *prove*, but we do have leads."

He nodded. "I've requested a meeting with the committee that's responsible for funding our department. We're in a crisis situation, and I've got to do something to loosen up their wallets. I had hoped to show them some impressive results on our high-profile cases."

"Maybe what they need is a harsh dose of reality. One patrolman's life might have been saved had he had a working radio. If we're not given what we need to do our jobs, they can't expect us to either serve or protect this tribe effectively."

He looked at her for several long moments. "Maybe I should take you with me tonight."

Ella sighed. "You're much better at that kind of thing than I am. I'm not much on diplomacy."

"Yeah, that's true. Any chance of you learning before 7 P.M.?"

"None," Ella answered with a smile.

"Then get to work."

"Yes, sir," Ella said, and quickly left the office. She didn't want to take a chance that Big Ed would change his mind and maybe order her to come with him.

The second Ella returned to her office and sat down, her phone began to ring. She picked it up at the same time Justine came into her office. Ella waved for her to take a seat, then concentrated on the caller.

"This is Jim Apodaca at the Circle E," he said. "Ms. Bruno just returned the SUV she'd rented from us. She wanted to trade it for a larger model with better off-road capability. She and her friend are getting ready to go on a hunting trip. They had their rifles and camping gear already with them."

"Can you describe her friend for me?" Ella asked.

She listened carefully and realized that Jim had just described Delbert Shives. "Don't touch the car. We're on the way."

Justine glanced at her. "What's going on?"

Ella filled her in. "Jim said that they had two rifles with them." She glanced at her partner. "I'm getting a real bad feeling that we're not the only ones looking for Kee Franklin. He's in a world of trouble."

TWENTY-FOUR
——— ✖ ✖ ✖ ———

At the car rental office, while Justine went over the car, Ella called Dispatch and put out a Code Five on the large model SUV rental from the Circle E.

"Did Ms. Bruno give you any idea where she and her companion were headed?" Ella asked Apodaca.

"All she told me was that they were going to go off for a few days to do a little business and maybe get some hunting done. She mentioned they were joining someone else tomorrow morning, then after that, they were planning to rough it for a few days." Jim shrugged. "Wish my wife liked hunting or camping, but she's even afraid of bugs. Ms. Bruno looks like she could handle anything."

Ella nodded. She had sensed from the very beginning that Margaret Bruno could be dangerous. And the more she learned about Bruno, the more worried she became.

Leaving him, Ella went to help Justine go over the vehicle. By the time they were finished, they had several thick, black hairs that Justine was nearly certain had come from a wig. "I've also got two sets of prints. I want to run both through FBI data banks. Let's see if they belong to Shives and Bruno, or another person entirely."

"Good idea."

As they got ready to leave, Sheriff Taylor pulled up in his department vehicle. "Your dispatcher said I'd catch you here."

Ella told Taylor what they'd learned, then asked, "Have you made any further progress on Whitesheep's murder?"

"In addition to the five hundred dollars in cash with Councilman Redhouse's fingerprints on most of them, we found a few medium-length black hairs in the car seat near the body. They came from a wig, according to our lab. But no prints. I wanted to ask you to send the wig hairs you've recovered at your crime scenes over to our lab. Now that we know that the bullet that killed Whitesheep came from the same gun that killed Councilman Redhouse and Officer Franklin, we'd like to compare the other evidence as well."

"You'll have what you need by the end of today," she said, glancing over at Justine, who nodded.

Later, as they drove back to the Rez, Ella lapsed into a long, thoughtful silence.

"Process everything we found in Bruno's car as soon as possible," she said, as they neared the station. "Work every shred of evidence from that vehicle. I want anything and everything you can give me."

As soon as they arrived at the station, Ella went directly to her office. As she walked through the door, she found Kevin and Ernest Ration waiting for her.

"Hey, guys," she said, glancing over at Kevin. "What brings you two here?"

"I got the strangest call from George Branch, promising me that if I called 'my people' off, he'd cease and desist taking shots at me on air for good. Somehow I ended up with the feeling that he was setting me up, so I thought I'd better tell the police department."

"What's happened to him now?" Ella asked.

"I wanted to know that myself, so I asked him. Turns out that after his last broadcast when he bashed me again, someone subscribed him to an Internet porno network. By midafternoon Branch had so many photos of naked men posted to him at his station's computer that his electronic mailbox closed down because it was completely full. The whole thing was an embarrassment to him, and he left work really ticked off. Then he found out that someone had entered his home somehow and rearranged his furniture. There was no forced entry, and nothing was taken, as far as he could see."

"I bet he came unglued and called Sheriff Taylor."

"Yeah, the sheriff and his deputies came out, but there was no evidence that would indicate how the person entered his home and bypassed all of Branch's sophisticated security systems."

"So he offered you a truce?"

"Yeah, but the really weird thing is that I've done nothing to him. I wouldn't have a clue how to disarm his security. Yet, the more I tell him that, the less inclined he is to believe me."

Ella glanced at Ernest, who smiled broadly but didn't speak. Ernest was turning out to be a real asset to Kevin.

"Take it as a win and go with it. You have a guardian angel somewhere," Ella said.

Kevin stood. "Well, I don't know about that, but things are definitely looking up." He glanced at his watch. "I better be going. I've got a meeting tonight. I'm now on the committee funding the police department."

"How did you manage that?"

"By default. No one else wants to be part of it because its a no-win job. We all want to give the police department more money to work with, but to do that, we're going to have to cut other programs. Politically, it's a powder keg. But there's a ray of hope.

We're starting to see some profits from the casino near To'hajiilee. It's doing better than we expected, and maybe we can funnel some of the profits to the department."

"If the tribe wants adequate police protection, they're going to have to fund us somehow."

"I think it's going to happen, Ella. Whether you realize it or not, the police department has the full support of the community. The news of how and why Jason Franklin died has gotten out, and it's made an impact. You have more friends than you think."

"I'm glad to hear that. Morale has been pretty low."

"I expect that'll turn itself around real soon. You're now getting the full support of the anti-NEED factions because they want to prove that we can find ways of funding our emergency services without a project like that one. You're also getting the support of the pro-NEED people because they want investors, and a strong law enforcement presence is a draw." He paused. "It's an odd time for the tribe. For the first time we're not really divided by traditionalist versus modernist. What's at the heart of this new dispute is fear—some are afraid we'll repeat the mistakes of the past. Others fear that if we don't take a risk now, we'll lose what's left of our tribal identity and become no more than a welfare community."

"The ones who appear to carry the most influence now are people like my mother. She's not only a Plant Watcher trying to protect our land, but also a respected tribal rights advocate."

Kevin nodded. "I agree. She's a force to be reckoned with. Right now she has more actual power than most of us on the council."

After Kevin left, Ella sat alone in her office. She thought about her mom and what she was accomplishing. There were no limits to what Rose could do when she made up her mind. But she really worried about her. Even with widespread support, Rose was making enemies—the kind with long memories. If her mother continued down this dangerous path, there wouldn't be much she could do to protect her.

Ella remained at her computer, checking databases, digging into Margaret Bruno's past and that of Shives. But there was nothing there that she didn't already know. Justine made periodic reports on the SUV they'd brought in from the rental agency.

Justine had run two sets of prints and confirmed they belonged to Margaret Bruno and Delbert Shives. The hairs they'd found were synthetic and a match for the wig hairs they'd found before in the science storeroom at the college. While Justine was examining vacuumed-up material from the upholstery and the floor mats to try and determine where the vehicle had been, Ella decided to go home and have a quick dinner.

When Ella arrived she discovered the house was empty. A note stuck to the refrigerator told her that Rose had a meeting of the Plant Watchers, and Dawn had gone shopping with Boots. The pony was in his corral, searching quietly for clumps of grass.

Alone, she sat in the kitchen table and looked around, remembering her teenage years in this house. Her father had usually been away, preaching at a revival somewhere or spreading the gospel to his "flock." Clifford, more often than not, had hung around with his friends at basketball practice or out in Shiprock. Back then, she could come home, run several miles—track had been her sport—finish her homework, then try to find a reason to go back out again before her father got home. She and her brother had never understood the relationship between their mother and father, who'd always seemed to be fighting about something, yet chose to stay together.

The total silence surrounding her here at the house now felt odd and disconcerting. In the all-encompassing quiet, the house could only echo with memories. Ella suddenly wondered how Rose had managed to spend all those years living alone in this place after Clifford had moved out to become a medicine man and she'd joined the FBI.

Ella warmed a bowl of stew in the microwave and sat down to eat. She took a bite, and realized that only the stew at the surface was heated. Stirring it with her spoon, she put it back into the microwave for another minute. Ella stared at the microwave, and the implications of what she'd just experienced jumped to a completely different experience.

If Wilson hadn't found anything so far in his storeroom, maybe it was because he'd never looked past the surface, never stirred up the stew, so to speak. When he recognized what was on the top of a container, he never looked any further.

Ella placed the bowl back into the refrigerator and hurried out to her unit. She knew it was late, but there was nothing she could do about that. This couldn't wait. The layers of hot and cold stew had just given her the answer she'd needed, perhaps, to solve the mystery that lay at the heart of the murder investigations.

By the time she arrived at Wilson's door, it was past eleven. Ella knocked and waited. When no one came to the door, she banged harder on the door. "Wilson, wake up!"

A moment later, a bleary-eyed Wilson came to the door wearing pajama bottoms and no shirt. "What are you doing here? Is something wrong?"

"I need your help. Let's go to the college. I need another look at that storeroom."

He gave her a dark look. "I've spent hours searching already, and haven't found a damn thing. Unless you *know* there's a body in there, I'm going to strangle you for waking me up. I have a seven o'clock class tomorrow."

"I'm looking for papers—important ones. And I need you to help me find them."

"You're crazy. Papers? Go to sleep and let me rest."

He started to slam the door in her face, but she put her foot in the door, and pushed her way inside.

"Have you gone totally off your rocker, Ella?"

"Kee Franklin's life is on the line, and you're going to help me figure out why."

TWENTY-FIVE
———— ✗ ✗ ✗ ————

Sorting through the boxes in the storeroom at the college seemed like an endless job. Finally, after reaching the end of the first aisle, Wilson, red-eyed, and in a foul mood, glanced at Ella. "It's nearly two in the morning. Are you sure there's something here to find?"

"Truthfully, no, but I have a strong hunch."

"You brought me here at this hour for a *hunch*?" His voice rose an octave.

"Wilson, just keep looking down *inside* the boxes below what you expect to be there. I don't care what they're labeled, or what's on top. You were the one who told me that Franklin usually brought boxes of materials whenever he guest lectured here. It's possible he left something behind inside another box. You can't rule it out until you've checked."

"Ella, the boxes marked Test Tubes have test tubes. The ones marked Lab Manuals have lab manuals. There's nothing here," he said wearily.

"So far. But you don't know what we might find if we keep looking. I know you're tired, and so am I. But I believe that the death of his son has sent Kee Franklin over the edge, and now he's involved in something that's going to get him killed."

"Give me a hand with this one," he said, spotting a battered box on the highest shelf. "I have no idea how it ended up over there with those outdated materials. I remember Kee used it to demonstrate alpha particle decay during his lecture. Be careful. It has a working model of a cloud chamber in it, and it's a bit heavy."

Once they'd managed to lower it to the floor, Wilson opened the cardboard flaps and brushed away some of the packing material. "It's essentially just a big black box with a glass front and an asbestos top."

"We know he used what was in the box, so look all the way to the bottom—just in case," Ella said.

Grumbling, Wilson lifted the cloud chamber out and, as he did, he found it had been resting on a large three-ring notebook. "That's not *my* reference material." As he opened the faded-looking notebook, a letter fell out. It was addressed to Kee Franklin, and it had the business letterhead of the Permian Energy Network.

Ella picked up the letter as Wilson went to his desk with the notebook in hand.

She read the letter quickly. "A few months ago Permian offered Kee Franklin a job. They wanted him to come to work for them as a research consultant on their uranium enrichment process using laser technology. It mentions Delbert Shives as the pilot program coordinator and contact person."

"Interesting," Wilson said, looking up from his notebook.

"What I suspected was right," Ella said. "Shives probably stole Kee's process, or at least part of it, then brought it to Permian as his own. He must have thought he could complete the research himself if they funded him. But this letter shows they went to Franklin about it, and let the cat out of the bag, so to speak. There is a 'cc' at the bottom to Shives."

"So Shives was screwed. Franklin knew his work had been appropriated, at least part of it," Wilson said, nodding.

"Right. Shives must have realized he was running out of options. If Franklin got a look at what Shives had used to entice Permian and recognized his own research, he could blow Shives out of the water and sue him and maybe Permian, too. Instead of getting rich, Shives could have been facing jail time."

Wilson, who had been studying the papers in the notebook, looked up. "I can't be one hundred percent sure without a lot of additional reading and confirming with real experts in the field, but these are Kee's notes on his process—and according to his conclusions, Ella, the process worked, quadrupling the efficiency. He says here that the costs of a full-scale operation producing weapons-grade uranium would be cut by two-thirds, and high-grade uranium for fuel rods more than that. These numbers are out-of-date, but even at today's costs that could make nuclear power competitive again."

They didn't have to look any further. By the time they left, it was three-thirty in the morning. Ella took the papers, logged them in as evidence, and went directly home. It was quiet, and only Two woke up to greet her.

Slipping through the house, she made it to her bedroom and closed the door before turning on the light. She reached down for her cell phone, replaced the spent battery with a fresh one, and when she turned it on again saw that she had a voice message waiting.

Punching out the proper codes, she heard the message. It was Clifford. His words were cryptic, saying that he had news about the man she was looking for and should call him whenever she picked up the message, regardless of the hour.

It was nearly 4 A.M. but she dialed his number. After two rings, he picked it up. "Sister?"

"How did you know it was me? Never mind," she whispered. "Who else would be calling at this hour? I just discovered your message. Is it news about the professor?"

"Yes. I heard something earlier today, but couldn't get to a phone until I got home, and by then it was already after midnight. Come over now, and I'll tell you what I heard," Clifford added.

"Why not just tell me now, so we can both go back to sleep?"

"You won't be able to sleep once you hear what I have to say, and I don't want to give out this information over the phone. You'll find out why when you get here," Clifford said.

"I'll be there in ten minutes, okay?" Ella hung up, checked her pistol, then grabbed a flashlight from the nightstand before turning out the bedroom lights. She left the house silently, careful not to wake up her mother or Dawn. Two was in the kitchen, and she patted his head on the way out. "Keep an eye on things, boy," she whispered, locking the door behind her.

She should have been tired, but there was enough adrenaline pumping through her to keep going indefinitely. When her brother was reluctant to tell her something except in person, it usually meant there was a strong element of danger involved.

She arrived at her brother's darkened house, which was farther down the dirt road, in less than ten minutes. Anxious to speak to Clifford, Ella noticed the front door was open, though the screen door was shut. He'd obviously opened the front door since speaking to her, but the lack of a light in the house suggested he was outside somewhere. She naturally looked toward the medicine hogan, but there was no light coming from the interior, nor was there any smoke coming from the metal chimney of the small cast-iron woodstove, which projected from the hole in the center of the hogan roof.

"Brother?" Ella stood by the entrance. When there was no response, she parted the blanket and looked inside, expecting him to be lighting the lantern, or perhaps poking around with a flashlight. Seeing two medicine pouches lying on a sheepskin pelt, her skin began to prickle. The pouches would have never been allowed to remain on the ground, so her brother must have set them here, then left the hogan. Perhaps he'd gone back into the house, and maybe his electricity was out. Even so, she'd have expected to see light from a lantern.

She reached for her weapon and turned around, looking into the darkness. It was pitch-black tonight, and traditionalists like her brother usually didn't wander around outside after sundown. Ella caught a whiff of something in the breeze just then and crinkled her nose. "Skunk. Ugh."

Grabbing the small flashlight she kept in her jacket pocket, Ella went ahead toward the main house, bracing her gun hand with the light. Suddenly hearing twigs snapping, she spun around.

Seeing the pistol aimed at his chest, Clifford froze. "I saw you poking around, and I came over to tell you not to worry. I came outside, intending on waiting for you in the medicine hogan, then discovered a skunk hanging around the henhouse. I had to throw a few rocks in his direction to get him on his way."

"You scared me, you toad. I côuld have shot you. Next time wear a bell." Ella quickly holstered her weapon.

"No, you wouldn't have shot me. You always identify your target," Clifford said calmly.

"I need to know what you've learned about the scientist. It's critical that I find him soon. I've just discovered something that leads me to believe he's in mortal danger. And why couldn't you just tell me over the telephone?"

"I'll get to that in a minute. This afternoon I traveled west into Arizona to perform a healing ceremony for one of my patients. After my work was done we had supper together, and the daughter of the man I was treating said she'd seen the scientist at the old sheepherding camp southwest of Big Water Spring, up in the foothills as far as you can drive a pickup."

"Where is that, over by Narbona Pass?"

"Northwest of there, closer to Crystal."

"That's a pretty isolated area this time of year."

He nodded. "And here's why I didn't want to speak about it on the phone. I have one of those old, wireless units that others might be able to listen in on. We've made some powerful enemies, you and I, and I don't have to name them to get your attention— and I certainly don't want to turn them in my family's direction either."

Ella nodded. Navajo witches, often called skinwalkers because of their custom of sometimes wearing coyote or wolf hides, were evil magic practitioners. Skinwalkers hated and feared medicine men like Clifford, who countered their efforts and knew how to fight against them. And Ella had foiled several of their attempts to harm others in the past.

Clifford continued. "I've been told that the evil ones have taken to gathering in that general area, too. The ground is polluted because uranium tailings were buried there. Navajo witches are the only ones who go there these days, so you should stay away. If they recognize you, and they have the opportunity, they'll kill you, or at least try to harm you with their magic. You've always been a thorn in their side."

"And you as well." Ella noted that her brother always avoided mentioning skinwalkers by that name. Many believed that even saying the word attracted their attention. Although medicine men knew the best defenses against them, Clifford was always very careful. "I'll stay on my guard, but I'm going after them," she added.

Ella glanced at her watch. It was barely five in the morning, and the eastern sky was starting to lighten up a bit. She'd called Justine about thirty minutes after she'd left her brother's house. She'd hated to get her partner out of bed for what could turn out to be a wild-goose chase, but she didn't have a choice. If the tip panned out, they'd have to move quickly, and backup was scarce and slow to arrive.

Although she hadn't slept all night, Ella was very much awake. This lead had to pan out—Kee was as good as dead if it didn't. She thought ahead to what she'd have to do next. She knew the family who owned the trading post over by Crystal, which was in the general vicinity of the sheepherding camp. If luck was with her, one of them would be up offering prayers to the dawn. She wanted to talk to them before proceeding any further.

It was a quarter to six by the time she arrived at the trading post on the western side of the Chuska Mountains and still in the shadow of the tall ridges. These days, Martha Lujan, an old classmate of Ella's, was said to be running the place. Her dad and mother had retired since John Lujan's stroke last year.

As Ella parked, she saw a cadaverously thin Navajo woman with short-cropped hair leading an elderly traditionally dressed lady inside.

Ella waited on the long, narrow wooden porch until someone came to greet her. Several minutes later, the younger woman approached.

Ella took out her ID. "I need to talk to the trader."

"Ella, don't you recognize me? It's me, Martha."

Ella took another look at the woman's face. Martha had never been a large woman, but she'd dropped at least forty pounds since high school. She wondered if her former schoolmate was ill from something like cancer.

"I didn't recognize you," Ella smiled. "Most of your former classmates have *gained* weight, you know," she added with a chuckle.

"You still look about the same."

"I'm only a few pounds heavier, but I really work to stay in shape. In my job, it really helps."

"I've lost a lot of weight since I came back to the Rez. I guess I miss my old life and don't eat as much as I used to. I left the Rez shortly after you did, but I had to come back not long ago when Dad got sick. Mom couldn't handle things alone."

Ella nodded. Family ties were still strong on most areas of the Rez. Sometimes all a person had was their relatives. "I'm sorry to hear about your father."

"Actually, I think they've both gotten better since I took over for them here. They'd always hoped I'd return and run the business someday." She paused. "But that's obviously not why you're here so early. It's police business, isn't it?"

"I need to ask you a few questions," Ella said. "There's an old sheepherding camp up the mountain from here. I was wondering if you knew if anyone's using it right now. Have you noticed any smoke coming from there?"

Martha thought about it. "I haven't seen sheep in this area for a long time. The land's no good around here, so no one comes around with their animals anymore. Several old uranium mine shafts are still uncovered, too, so it's pretty dangerous to wander about."

"So no one's up there at all?" Ella pressed.

"I didn't say that," Martha corrected. "I said I don't see sheep or sheepherders anymore. But I have seen smoke coming from that area after dark."

"Did you ever go take a look?"

"I did about a month ago, but I should have known to avoid a place where you only see smoke at night. I was warned off, and never went back."

"Warned off by whom?" Ella asked.

"I drove about halfway up the old track and a coyote came out of nowhere and just stood in front of the pickup, watching me. I went right back down the hill. I don't need that kind of trouble. Do you know what I mean?"

Ella nodded. As with Clifford, neither of them had mentioned skinwalkers by name.

Ella said good-bye to Martha and, after returning to her unit, contacted Justine on the radio. Fortunately, the reception was good despite the terrain. Maybe there was a relay system up by the radar atop Narbona Pass.

"I'm going up there to take a look," Ella told her partner.

"Let me get down there before you do anything, Ella. I'm only forty-five minutes or so from Crystal."

"I'm afraid to wait any longer. Shives and Bruno have had too much of a lead on us, and there's no telling what they've got planned. They may have an idea where to look, and they are certainly prepared for rough country like this."

Despite her brave words, Ella had no desire to go up there alone. Years ago, she would have said that skinwalkers were just crazy people—delusional and sometimes violent. But these days, she wasn't so willing to dismiss things she didn't understand. The Rez claimed its share of the unexplained and supernatural. The Anglos called it superstition, yet all religions had supernatural events connected to them. Raising the dead from the grave, then joining in prayer to celebrate the event, was about as crazy as it got from the viewpoint of a Navajo.

Ella took out her binoculars and looked off in the distance. Everything looked quiet and, with the sun up, visibility was good except for inside the deeper canyons, where shadows would remain for another few hours.

"It should be safe there now. It's morning. I'm going in. If the professor is there, he's running out of time."

"My ETA is forty minutes. I'll do it in thirty-five if I'm lucky."

Aware that she could end up finding no one except her darkest enemies, Ella called the telephone company office in Farmington and asked for a phone record of all calls made from the pay phone outside the trading post. Many people around this area of the Rez didn't have phone service, so most of them, sooner or later, came to the trading post to make calls. Cell phones still weren't very reliable out here, so if Franklin was in the area, it was possible he'd have used that phone. If he had, she wanted to know who he'd called.

"It may take me some time," Jane Bekis, the manager, said, having dealt with Ella before. "I'll have to go through our Gallup office."

"I don't have time. But I can simplify it for you. Look for calls made to these numbers in particular." Ella thumbed through her notepad and gave her Delbert Shives's office and home numbers.

While Jane checked, Ella used the directions she'd gotten from Martha at the trading post and found the dirt track that led to the camp. Before going uphill, she decided to take a look around for signs of another vehicle.

Ella quickly noticed recent vehicle tracks, a set of three, all of the same tire tread. A study of the pattern told her that someone had gone up the road, back down, then up again. If it was Kee Franklin, he was still there unless he'd left his vehicle behind and walked down.

Walking back to her unit, she noticed a trail of dust farther down the mountain, and heard the engine noise of a vehicle. Reaching into her Jeep, Ella retrieved her binoculars and walked over to a spot where she could see more clearly. About a mile down the mountain was a SUV that matched the description of the one Bruno had rented.

She started to radio Justine when Jane Bekis called her back. Despite the fact that she was on higher ground, the static was suddenly so pronounced she could barely understand her.

"I have the information you requested. Someone called the second number you asked me to check," Jane said reading it off. "The call was made yesterday morning."

It was Delbert Shives's home number. Thanking her, Ella ran

back to her vehicle, picked up the mike, and called Justine on her radio. "I think Kee Franklin called Shives yesterday and arranged to meet him out here. With all that's happened, especially the break-ins connected to him, I'm sure he put things together. Franklin must either want to deal with Shives or, more likely, based on his character, confront the man he figures was responsible for his son's death."

"The bullets recovered at the crime scenes could have come from a backup pistol Bruno carries, a habit she may have kept though she's no longer a cop. If she's our killer, Franklin doesn't have a chance. Between her history of aggression and violence, and her training, Franklin will most likely end up dead."

"I know." Ella felt her mouth go dry. "I have to get there first. If Franklin refuses to let Shives have the rights to his research, he won't have a chance once Bruno cuts loose on him."

"The professor is smart, Ella. He'll play it better than that. I'm sure he has another plan in mind."

Ella exhaled softly. "He may hope to push them into a violent confrontation so he'll have an excuse to kill them. But that's going to be a huge mistake. If Bruno is the killer we're after, she won't hold back."

"I don't think Professor Franklin knows there's a second player in this. And that's exactly what's going to get him killed."

Ella got back into her unit. "I have a visual on Shives and Bruno, but they haven't found the turnoff leading to the camp yet. Or else they're going to check out the area first."

"I'll be there as soon as possible, Ella. I'll turn off the sirens long before I get there, but I'm pushing this loaner unit for all it's got."

"Ten-four."

Ella looked back at the vehicle coming up the mountain. No matter what happened, she had to reach Franklin first. She increased her speed, but the path was rugged, and the ground was soft where Franklin had driven recently, making the going more difficult.

Five minutes later she pulled up behind a dilapidated hogan near the remnants of a split-log corral. She could see smoke coming out the hole in the center of the clay-covered, domed roof, and, oddly, a small dish antenna on the southern edge. That detail convinced her Franklin had to be the one inside. Following the vehicle tracks ahead of her, she saw where he'd parked his SUV in the shade of a small clearing.

Ella drove on, finding a place to park her own unit where it wouldn't be seen by someone approaching, then ran to the hogan. "Kee, it's me, Ella Clah," she said, as she approached the entrance.

Franklin came out immediately, dressed in a warm nylon parka and wool cap. He looked especially old today, and his voice was shaky. "You can't stay, you'll ruin everything. You have to leave right now."

"That's not going to happen. You have no idea what you've started here." Ella slipped into the hogan, pulling him in with her by the sleeve. "They're coming up the mountain right now, so we only have a few minutes. It's not just Shives you're dealing with. His foster sister is an ex-cop with a reputation for violent behavior. Her name is Margaret Bruno, and we think she may have killed at least three people, including your son."

"That's the first I've heard about her, but I do know a lot more than you think I do. Shives has been after me for months, offering me large amounts of money, partnerships, whatever he can think of to get me to give him the details of my laser enrichment process. He needs one crucial piece of information, one more step to make it work, and he knows that without my cooperation it may take him the rest of his life to find the answer. But I've never trusted him. Not twenty years ago at the labs, and certainly not now. He even approached Jason during one of those tours he conducted for law enforcement personnel, asking if he would discuss it with me. Then he found out that Jason was opposed to any nuclear power plant project. Jason later told me what happened, and I wasn't the least bit surprised."

Kee had a haunted look in his eyes, not fear, but something else equally frightening. He continued, his words toneless. "After my son was killed, I had a hunch Shives was somehow involved, so I started my own investigation. I easily hacked into Delbert's computer system, and discovered he had the addresses of the properties my ex-wife, my son, and whatever I owned or rented. Shives knew about the garage, and I had a feeling that Jason's death had been the result of a botched attempt to get my research. But I needed proof, so I came up with a plan."

Kee took a look outside. "Are you sure that they're on the way now? They weren't supposed to be here until this afternoon."

"I'm certain, and it won't be long now before they're here. We have to go," Ella said.

"I'm staying, but you have to get out of here. If they see you, you'll ruin what I set out to do." He walked over to a small folding table he had set up opposite the fire pit. Atop was an expensive-looking laptop computer. A wire lead from the computer and through a gap in the log wall apparently to the small antenna she had seen on the roof.

In a matter of seconds Franklin downloaded information into a CD, then he handed it to her. "You've now got a copy of all the details essential to my uranium enrichment process. It belongs to me, not my former employers, because I didn't perfect the process until well after I resigned. If anyone tries to access my computer and doesn't use the right password, all the files will be erased, and they'll have nothing. Take this and go. I'll see that justice prevails. They won't get a thing from me."

Ella looked at him, placing the disk in her shirt pocket, and understood what he was planning. "You came here to kill them, or to die trying."

"Just go, please?"

Hearing a vehicle coming up the hill, she looked at Kee. "We're out of time, but I can still help you achieve what you have to do. Will you trust me?"

Kee took a deep breath then nodded. "All right. What do you want to do?"

TWENTY-SIX

✖ ✖ ✖

"**W**e're here, Dr. Franklin," Bruno yelled, stepping out of the driver's side of the SUV.

Kee Franklin stepped through the doorway of the hogan, rifle in hand, and walked toward the vehicle as Delbert Shives emerged from the passenger side.

"It's been a long time since we've actually met face-to-face, Doctor," Shives said, smiling affably. "But you can put your rifle down. As you can see, ours are still inside the car." Shives turned and pointed to a rifle and what looked like a shotgun resting between the driver's and passenger's seats, barrels pointing up.

Ella stood silently in the shadows underneath a large pine tree, her body hidden by the large trunk. Justine was less than ten minutes away now. Just in case, her assistant had already requested more backup to be dispatched to their location, but it would take others a minimum of thirty minutes to arrive on the scene.

"Mr. Shives, the uranium enrichment process I created is something that you have no right to claim," Franklin said slowly, keeping his rifle pointed at Bruno's midsection.

Shives smiled. "Doctor, please, fair is fair. I worked with you all those years, then you left me high and dry when you started whining about the plight of the Navajo miners. We could have made a fortune if you'd given me a chance to take it to private industry. Now, as fate would have it, we're being presented with another golden opportunity. Permian Energy Network wants the process and is willing to pay us handsomely for it."

"I know that you or that woman killed my son when he caught you searching for my papers," Kee said. "What guarantee do I have that you won't kill me the second you get the process?"

"Our word?" Shives asked good-naturedly.

"That's not good enough, I'm afraid," Dr. Franklin said. "The rules have changed, Mr. Shives, Ms. Bruno. To put a stop to all the violence I'm willing to give you the rest of the process—but only under certain conditions."

"What exactly do you want?" Bruno asked, her eyes narrowed. She had her hand in her jacket pocket, and Ella knew Bruno was thinking about bringing out her pistol, calculating if she could draw and shoot before Franklin fired the rifle.

"First, foolproof insurance that will keep me alive after you get what you want." Franklin, holding his rifle precariously but still managing to keep it pointed at Bruno, reached into his jacket pocket and brought out a small handheld computer not much larger than a paperback novel. "Our conversation is being relayed via a microphone in this unit to another computer inside the hogan. See the antenna on the roof? A power supply inside provides all the energy needed to send it instantly via satellite to an Internet site only I can access. Later on, if I don't enter a command halting the process, a digital recording of our conversation will automatically be relayed to the police and a dozen media outlets."

In a lightning move, Bruno brought out her weapon and fired at the antennae on the roof. Her third round hit the base squarely, and it shattered. "No more games. That little toy of yours is out of commission now. Give me the process right now, or I'll keep shooting."

Dr. Franklin coolly placed the computer back into his pocket and regained complete control of his rifle. "Putting the antenna out of commission didn't stop the message. Our words are still being relayed, even now. Go ahead and shoot, if you feel it's something you just have to do. But you'll never, ever get what you want if you pull that trigger." Franklin aimed his rifle toward Bruno's head. "Like you, I never intended to make any deal. What I wanted all along were my son's killers." Kee walked toward Bruno, maintaining his aim.

"He's not bluffing, Margaret. He'll shoot you, then me. Kee Franklin doesn't play games. He probably doesn't know how," Shives said calmly, slowly moving to the side, putting some distance between himself and Margaret. Franklin ignored the man and kept his rifle aimed at Margaret. "You are the one who murdered my son, aren't you? Delbert has been using you like an attack dog."

"Oh, I'm a bitch all right, old man. But you'll have a better chance of staying alive if you lower the rifle. We have a standoff, and I might just shoot first," Bruno replied. She was starting to get nervous now, her gun hand shaking slightly and her voice raising a pitch. Margaret took a step back and glanced over at Shives.

Taking advantage of the diversion Franklin was creating, Ella moved in silently behind Bruno. She was only ten feet away when Shives saw her out of the corner of his eye. "Meg!" he yelled, looking right at Ella. "Look out!"

Bruno instantly whirled, cursing and firing frantically, her inexperience in a firefight now evident as she pumped out round after round into the ground around her target. But Ella, who'd come in at a crouch, was battle-hardened and ready, and offered a smaller target as she flattened, then squeezed off two shots.

The woman clutched her chest, staggered back, and dropped her pistol before dropping to the earth.

Ella stood to full height, swinging the smoking barrel of her pistol around to Shives, who was reaching for the pistol Bruno had dropped. "Don't try it. You won't win," she said.

Shives looked up. "Okay," he said, raising his hands. "Just calm down," he added, leaving the pistol exactly where it had fallen.

Never taking her eyes off the man, Ella picked up the weapon, noting it was the nine-millimeter Smith & Wesson she'd seen before, then placed it in her jacket pocket.

Ella holstered her own weapon and reached for her handcuffs.

"She's still alive!" Franklin shouted, pointing.

Ella turned her head. Bruno was scrambling to her feet, groping for something strapped to her ankle. As Ella drew her own weapon again, Bruno sprinted for the SUV. Ella shot out the front tire. Bruno swerved at the sound and leaped downhill instead.

Ella turned to Franklin, at the same time forcing Shives down on the ground. "Shoot him if he moves. I have to go after Bruno."

"Be careful!" Franklin shouted, as Ella hurried away. "There are several open mine shafts around here."

Ella knew now that Bruno had been wearing a bullet resistant vest. It was the only way she could have survived. But after taking two point-blank shots, she was undoubtedly in great pain, and despite her murderous nature, had obviously never been in a real firefight where her opponent was in a position to defend herself. By now she was rattled and unpredictable.

Ella slowed down slightly, recalling Franklin's warning about the old uranium mines. She'd have to move carefully, but Bruno was a cop killer, and she was going down.

Ella was a good tracker, but after the first fifty yards downslope, Bruno's footprints became difficult to spot. Careful examination showed she'd stepped to the right, gone back, then jumped onto a rock to her left, scuffing off a little sandstone. From there she stepped onto a clump of grass before leaping away downhill at least fifteen feet before landing.

Picking up Bruno's tracks, she continued downhill, listening for movement. Within a few seconds she heard the faint crackle of pine needles underfoot just ahead and caught glimpses of Margaret moving through the underbrush, ducked down almost on her knees.

Ella waited, pistol ready. Soon Margaret stepped out from behind cover less than ten feet in front of her, holding a small automatic pistol.

"Drop it, Margaret," Ella ordered.

Bruno cursed and dived to her left, snapping off a wild shot that had no chance of hitting anything but sky as she disappeared into some brush.

Ella waited, knowing that when Bruno came out into the open this time, she'd have to shoot her without warning before the woman finally got lucky. It would be the only way to stop Margaret now.

Bruno sprang out of the brush like a deer, firing blindly as she dodged from left to right. Ella drew a bead on her legs. Just as she was about to fire, Bruno zigged to her right. There was a loud snap and crackle, like boards splintering, and in an instant, Bruno tumbled from sight. Dust flew up in the air, then slowly began to settle.

Wary of the mine shaft that Bruno had inadvertently found, Ella proceeded slowly. Bruno could be dead, incapacitated, or lying in wait, ready to shoot her in the head at point-blank range once Ella peered inside.

As she got close, Ella could see a few gray, decaying wooden planks on either side of the jagged opening Bruno had fallen through. The woman was cursing and moaning intermittently, but the sound had an echo, so she wasn't very close to the surface.

"Are you injured, Margaret?" Ella called out, keeping far enough back so she wouldn't cave off the edge, either falling through herself or knocking debris onto the fugitive.

"Yeah. My luck finally ran out. I think I broke my leg."

"Toss out your backup pistol, then I'll consider helping you."

"I can't. I dropped it when I fell. Look, I wouldn't shoot you now even if I could."

"Yes, you would. You're facing three murder charges, and that's just at the top of a long list."

"Crap. Okay, I would shoot you. But I can't do it without my damn pistol, can I?"

Ella looked around and saw the automatic sitting on the ground three feet away. It was a .380. She reached over and grabbed it by the trigger guard to avoid smearing any prints, then stuck it into her pocket with Bruno's other handgun.

"You're right about your luck having run out. I just found your .380. Don't move. I'll call for help." Ella reached Justine on the handheld radio and gave her partner a situation report.

"I'm up here with Dr. Franklin and Shives, who's now handcuffed to the SUV. Where are you from the hogan?"

Ella looked around, and could see Bruno's SUV farther up the mountain. She quickly gave her position.

"I'll be down there in a few minutes," Justine replied.

"Ten-four."

Ella reached for the small penlight she kept in her jacket pocket, then moved closer to the opening, getting down on her hands and knees. From what she could determine, the eight-foot-wide shaft went straight down for about fifteen feet, then angled off perpendicular to the shaft into a side tunnel. One of Bruno's legs was visible and, from its odd angle, it was clear the woman wasn't lying about the injury.

Ella removed her jacket and set it clear of the opening, then placed her own pistol and twenty-two-caliber backup derringer on top of it. The only way to get to Bruno was to climb down, but she didn't want to risk her making a grab for a weapon in the confined space.

"I'm over here," Ella waved to Justine, who was picking her way down the slope. Once Justine waved back, Ella lowered herself into the shaft, sliding down to the dusty bottom and managing to miss the rotten lumber that had given way. She then crawled over to where Bruno was lying flat on her back. Her leg was twisted at an unnatural angle, and a check with the penlight showed Bruno's face was covered with small cuts.

"You look like hell," Ella said.

"Yeah? Good. Maybe I can tell my lawyer you beat me with a piece of lumber. Could get me a few years off."

"Or better yet, I can do as you suggested and beat the hell out of you, climb out of here, walk away, and tell everyone I just couldn't find you."

"You're too worried what other people might think. It'll never happen. Just get me out of here."

Trying to get her bearings so she could find the best way to move Bruno out of that side tunnel, Ella aimed her flashlight around. As she saw what lay just beyond the tunnel she shuddered. On the ground, in the widened chamber just ahead, were the remnants of a sandpainting made with ashes. Human skull fragments were scattered over it. Hanging from a peg driven into the rocky wall was what looked like the skin of a coyote. "We have to get out of here quickly. Let's go."

"Afraid of the dark?" Margaret asked, laughing nervously.

"No, but this place . . . isn't safe. It's been used by skinwalkers for their rituals. Trust me, we don't want to be here."

Bruno turned her head. "What the hell are skinwalkers? You superstitious?"

Ella gave her a cold look. "Navajo witches can use magic and poisons, but they also carry knives and guns to kill their enemies—which is what we've become just by being here in their den. Dead is dead. Do you want to stick around? If so, I'll be glad to leave you here."

Bruno looked behind her. "Oh crap, that's a skull. Let's go." Bruno tried to sit up, then groaned loudly.

"Lie back, and I'll try to immobilize your leg first."

Ella used pieces of old lumber and their belts to fashion a quick splint for Bruno's injured leg. Margaret never cried out, but she passed out once. Five minutes later, Bruno was awake again, cursing softly.

Justine was above them now and had cleared away some of the rotten wood, then lowered a rope anchored to a tree.

"We'll have to do some of the work," Ella warned Bruno. "I'll tie a bowline around your waist, then I'll stay below and help push you up. I'll try to be careful, but with your leg the way it is, it's going to hurt. Pull yourself up as much as possible with your arms. My partner will grab hold of you once you get close enough to the surface."

"The leg won't kill me, but these crazies might, so let's get going." Bruno looked toward the side tunnel again. "I heard something in there. Are you sure we're alone?"

"Hell if I know."

They struggled together, making progress slowly, but the woman had strong arms and was able to pull herself up hand over hand a foot at a time. When Bruno got within reach, Officer Michael Cloud was there with Justine to pull her, then Ella, out of the shaft. Officer Philip Cloud, Michael's twin brother, hand-cuffed the prisoner and guarded her beside the opening as they waited for the paramedics to arrive from Shiprock.

"I want this mine shaft covered up again as quickly as possible," Ella told Justine, and explained what she'd found below.

"We'll take care of it."

"How did Franklin do with Shives?" Ella asked.

"Just fine. When I arrived, Shives was spread-eagled on the ground, facedown. Dr. Franklin had the barrel of his rifle at the back of Shives's head. Sergeant Neskahi is there now, but Shives didn't have much to say, except worrying about 'Meg,' as he calls Bruno."

"Shives knows that he'll be facing the death penalty for all three murders, either as the killer or coconspirator, if the .380 pistol Bruno was carrying as backup turns out to be the murder weapon. I'm sure he'll want an attorney present before he says anything. My guess is he'll fight it out in court every step of the way."

"Did you notice the rifle in Bruno's vehicle?" Justine asked.

"No. Don't tell me it's Wilson's lever action Savage?"

"Sure looks like it. Bruno must have thought she was above suspicion, carrying it around like that in the open." Justine shook her head.

As they approached the campsite, Dr. Franklin came to meet Ella. "I'm glad you're okay," he said.

"Things worked out," she said quietly. Seeing his rifle on the ground, she pointed to it. "You can unload that now."

He smiled, picked it up, and opened the bolt action, exposing the chamber. "It was never loaded. I knew I couldn't shoot another human being—not even the one who killed my son." Seeing the surprise on Ella's face, he smiled sadly. "You were right about me. I came here to die. I had a feeling that Bruno would never confess, so I hoped to push her into killing me. Then I could join my son."

"I'm glad that didn't happen. My plan *was* better," she said with a gentle smile, "though it didn't go exactly as we'd hoped. Our work is far from done—mine and yours. Your expertise is needed more than ever to keep the tribe from repeating past mistakes. *Dineh* like you will be our first line of defense if the nuclear power plant does open here."

"Yes, I suppose you're right."

"By the way, we finally found your research papers in the storeroom," Ella said with a smile.

"I didn't have the courage to destroy all that work, but I had to hide it. I didn't want it to be misused to make more bombs.

Shives was always my biggest threat. He'd guessed that I'd made a breakthrough in my research years ago and was covering it up. When nuclear power plants began to be discussed again as viable alternatives to fossil fuels, he apparently promised to deliver the process to Permian Energy Network. But Shives knew he had to discredit NEED—at least enough to make sure that the tribe would deal with Permian instead."

"That explains the NEED bumper stickers on the vehicles at the crime scenes." Ella nodded. "Unless Permian got involved in the project, Shives was out in the cold. He certainly couldn't deal with NEED—you'd find out as soon as his name came up."

"Delbert was running out of time, too. He started to panic about a week ago. I read his e-mail. Permian was pressuring him for details of the process so they could undercut whatever cost estimates NEED came up with. Redhouse was e-mailing him, too, asking for more payoff money or he'd also support NEED. But Delbert was running out of money and just couldn't deliver on his own." Professor Franklin shook his head.

"We knew that the motive for all the break-ins was related to you in some way," Ella said.

Franklin nodded. "I'm sorry I deceived you from the beginning. I was trying to sort out things in my mind, and once I realized why my son and others were dying, I knew that I had to end this."

"It's been a long, hard road since the killings began that night at the garage. Bruno shot your son because he'd recognized her," Ella said thoughtfully. "But it's over, and you've done what was needed. So what now? What will you do with the process?" Ella asked.

"I thought about it while I was guarding Shives. I've made up my mind to patent the enrichment process and turn the rights over to the tribe. If nuclear power plants and uranium production in the US begins again, on the Rez or elsewhere, the tribe can license the process and make millions in royalties." He gazed off in the distance for a moment before continuing. "I've come to realize that sooner or later, another scientist is bound to duplicate my findings. But if I do something now ahead of everyone else, I can at least make sure it'll benefit the tribe." He met her gaze. "It's the best way I have of restoring harmony and walking in beauty. And maybe now it won't be so hard to sleep at night."

Ella was the last to leave the crime scene. It was a little past noon, and the sheepherding camp, now deserted, was quiet as she walked back to her unit.

Today had gone well—better than the disaster it might have turned into. Kee Franklin was a valuable asset to the tribe, and his process had the potential to open all sorts of doors to their people. Remembering the disk that he'd given her, she reached into her jacket pocket. Ella inhaled sharply as she felt the long tear and the piece of cloth that dangled where her pocket had been. She'd ripped up her jacket, probably when she'd been trying to pull Bruno out of the mine shaft, and the disk was gone.

Ella grabbed her flashlight, and the rope that had been left in the sheepherder's hogan, then hurried back downhill to the mine shaft. The last thing she wanted to do was climb down again, but there was no other choice. It was imperative that the disk not fall into the wrong hands.

Ella removed the boards that had been replaced, tied one end of the rope around the same stout tree they'd used before, then lowered herself inside. She searched thoroughly, even running her fingers through the soft earth to see if it had been accidentally buried, but had no luck. Swallowing back the fear that spiraled through her as she went into the skinwalker's den, she lowered herself even deeper, well past where the skull still sat among a frightening stack of human bones.

She remained in the cave, searching, but thirty minutes later she still hadn't found it. As much as she wanted to continue looking, Ella knew it was too risky to go into some of the adjoining tunnels beyond that central chamber, obviously a ceremonial center for the evil ones, without a ladder and special equipment.

The badger fetish on her throat felt warm, indicating she was in danger, but she heard nothing, though the air seemed thicker and foul-smelling now. If the disk had fallen down into the depths of the mine, no one else would be able to retrieve it either. The thought gave her some comfort. And, by tomorrow, explosives experts would come by and seal off the entrance, caving in the tunnels.

Ella returned to the police station, knowing that hours of paperwork remained before she could call it a day. Finally, as she made her way back to her office, she saw Dr. Franklin, who was getting ready to leave.

Ella took the physicist aside and explained what had happened to the disk.

"Don't worry. I mailed a complete, updated version of my process to you here at this station before I met with Shives. It was my way of protecting the process in case things went wrong."

As he left, Ella went to her office. Her desk was covered with paperwork. She sighed wearily, and was trying to motivate herself to tackle the job, when Big Ed walked into her office.

"I thought you'd want to know," he said. "Margaret Bruno wanted to cut a deal for her and Delbert Shives. They're hoping to get life instead of the death penalty, but in this state that was pretty much guaranteed already. She told us that Shives knew Whitesheep because they'd both worked at the power plant, so they used him to introduce Shives to Billy Redhouse. Shives needed to find a way to get inside influence with the tribe, and that's why they decided to bribe Redhouse."

"So why did they kill them?"

"Redhouse got greedy and asked for a lot more money or he'd blow the whistle about their connection to Permian."

Ella nodded. "And once Redhouse was killed, they had to silence Whitesheep because he knew about their connection to Redhouse."

"Precisely," he said with a nod. "One more thing. The Tribal Council has voted to meet with the NEED project leaders. If all the big questions concerning a nuclear power plant, such as funding, safety, waste disposal, and the environment can be answered, the council is ready to seal the deal with NEED."

"Can they do that?"

Big Ed laughed, then shrugged. "The legal team told them that as an independent entity within the United States, they don't have to be overly concerned with federal approval. I think they're drawing battle lines. At least the lawyers will get rich."

"This could be a huge win for the New Traditionalists," Ella said. "The tribe seems to be moving forward—even with the legacy of the past hanging on."

Big Ed headed for the door, then, without turning his head, added, "Oh and, by the way, good job."

Ella smiled, then picked up her cell phone and called Harry to share the news, but he wasn't available. Disappointed, she left a voice mail.

Too exhausted to do much else at the office, she decided to go home and get some well-earned rest. Ella walked outside, opened the door to her unit, then froze. On her seat was a human bone. Attached to it with a bright red ribbon looped through a hole in the corner, was a polaroid snapshot of the CD she'd lost in the mine. On the bottom of the photo was the word "Thanks."

Ella stared at it in horror. Her old enemies, the skinwalkers, had gone high-tech.

Look for

WIND
SPIRIT

by AIMÉE AND DAVID THURLO

—— ✖ ✖ ✖ ✖ ——

Available from
Tom Doherty Associates